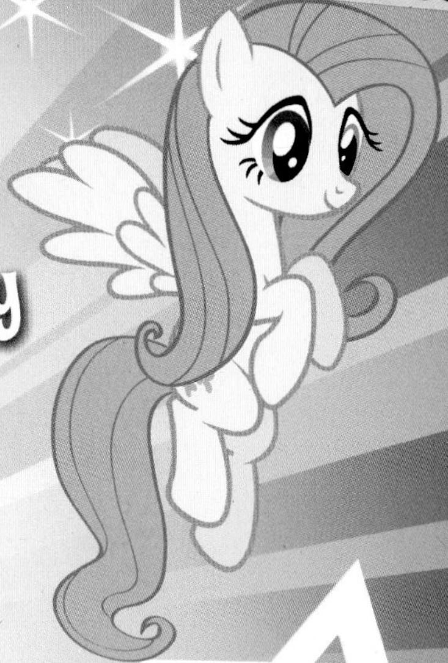

Fluttershy

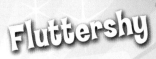

FLUTTERSHY IS A KIND AND GENTLE PONY WITH A BIG HEART. SHE LIKES TO TAKE CARE OF OTHERS, ESPECIALLY HER LITTLE ANIMAL FRIENDS.

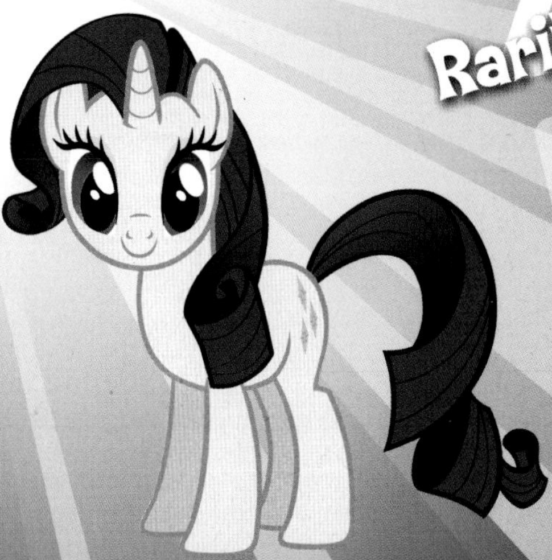

Rarity

RARITY KNOWS HOW TO ADD SPARKLE TO ANY OUTFIT! SHE LOVES TO GIVE HER PONY FRIENDS ADVICE ON THE LATEST PONY FASHIONS AND HAIRSTYLES.

Pinkie Pie

PINKIE PIE KEEPS HER PONY FRIENDS LAUGHING AND SMILING ALL DAY! CHEERFUL AND PLAYFUL, SHE ALWAYS LOOKS ON THE BRIGHT SIDE.

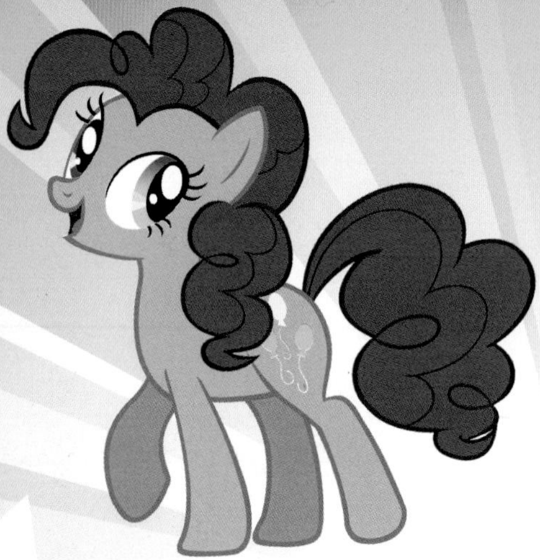

Rainbow Dash

RAINBOW DASH LOVES TO FLY AS FAST AS SHE CAN! SHE IS ALWAYS READY TO PLAY A GAME, GO ON AN ADVENTURE, OR HELP OUT ONE OF HER PONY FRIENDS.

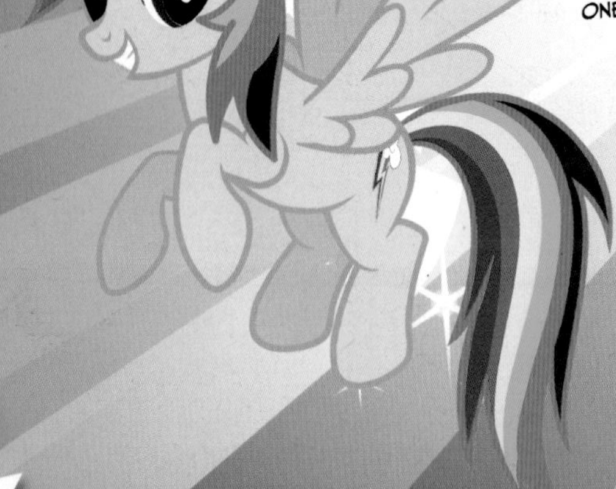

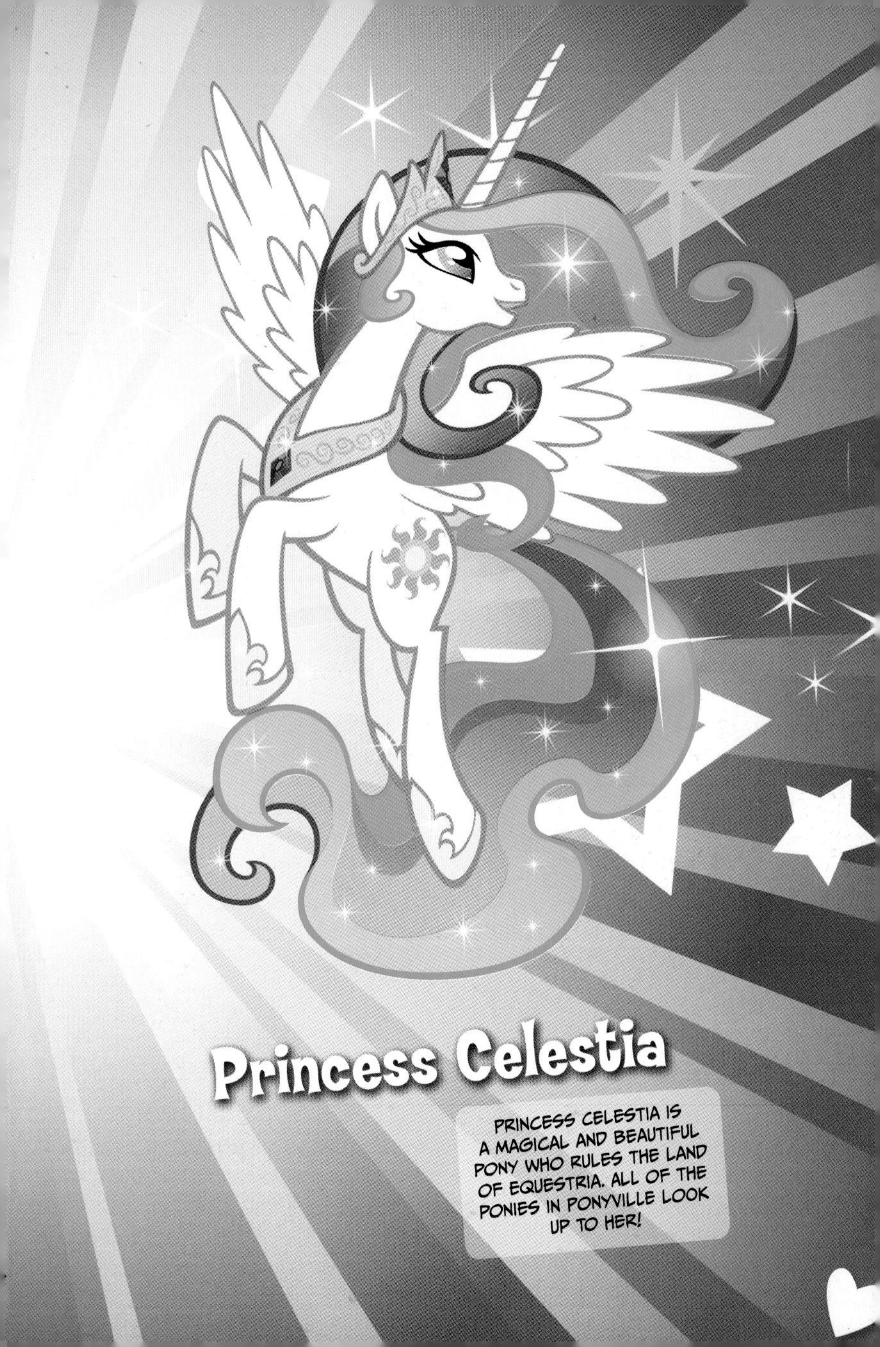

Princess Celestia

PRINCESS CELESTIA IS A MAGICAL AND BEAUTIFUL PONY WHO RULES THE LAND OF EQUESTRIA. ALL OF THE PONIES IN PONYVILLE LOOK UP TO HER!

Princess Twilight Sparkle

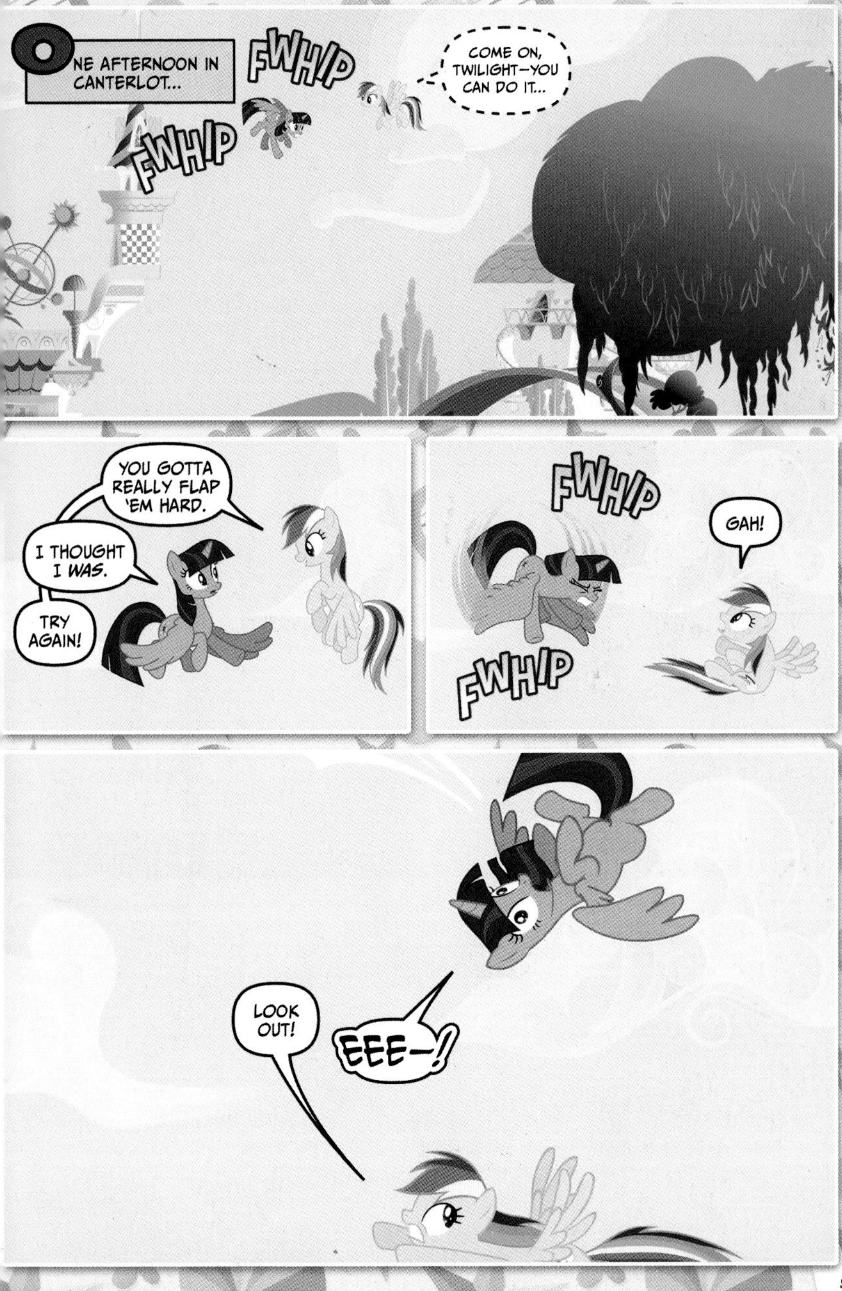
ONE AFTERNOON IN CANTERLOT...
FWHIP
FWHIP
COME ON, TWILIGHT—YOU CAN DO IT...
YOU GOTTA REALLY FLAP 'EM HARD.
I THOUGHT I WAS.
TRY AGAIN!
FWHIP
GAH!
FWHIP
LOOK OUT!
EEE—!

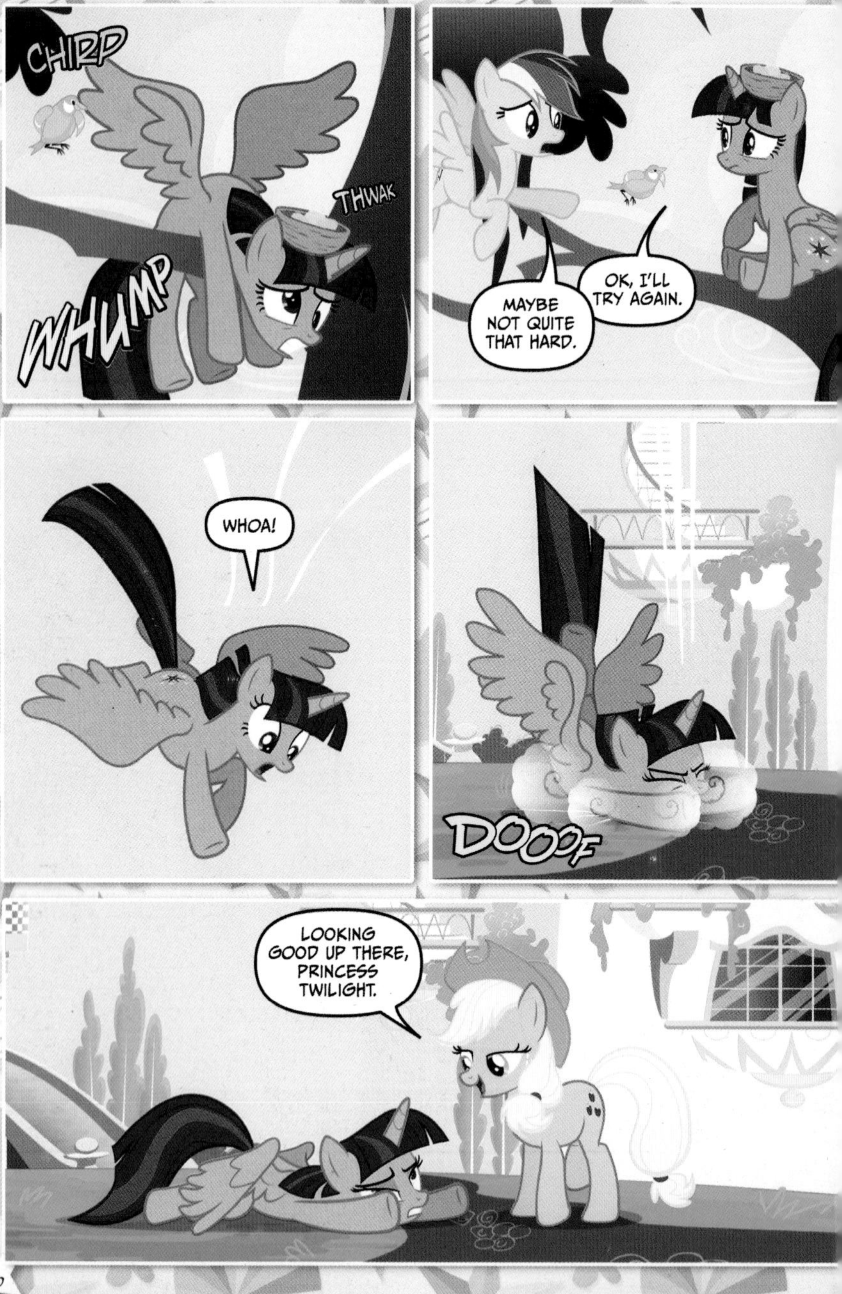
CHIRP
THWAK
WHUMP
MAYBE NOT QUITE THAT HARD.
OK, I'LL TRY AGAIN.
WHOA!
DOOOF
LOOKING GOOD UP THERE, PRINCESS TWILIGHT.

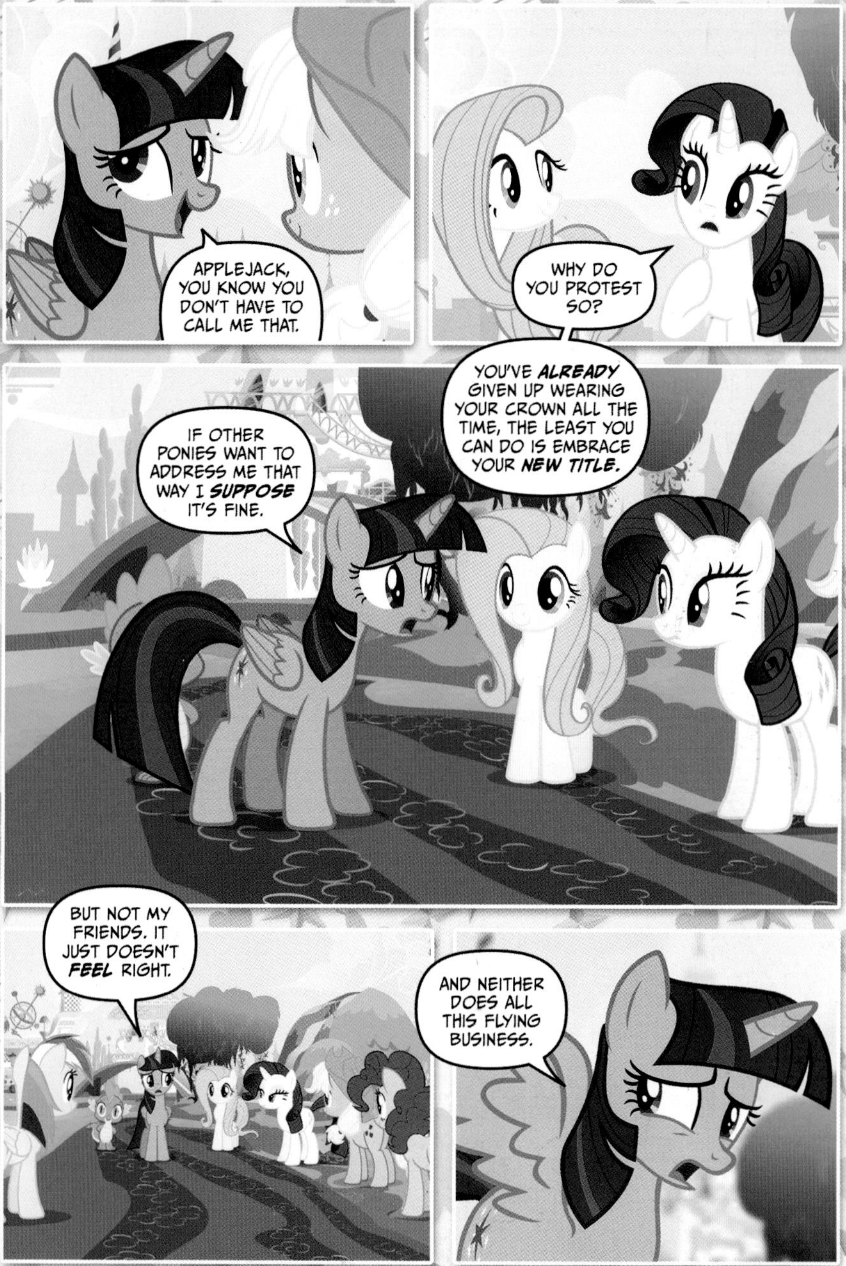
APPLEJACK, YOU KNOW YOU DON'T HAVE TO CALL ME THAT.
WHY DO YOU PROTEST SO?
YOU'VE ALREADY GIVEN UP WEARING YOUR CROWN ALL THE TIME, THE LEAST YOU CAN DO IS EMBRACE YOUR NEW TITLE.
IF OTHER PONIES WANT TO ADDRESS ME THAT WAY I SUPPOSE IT'S FINE.
BUT NOT MY FRIENDS. IT JUST DOESN'T FEEL RIGHT.
AND NEITHER DOES ALL THIS FLYING BUSINESS.

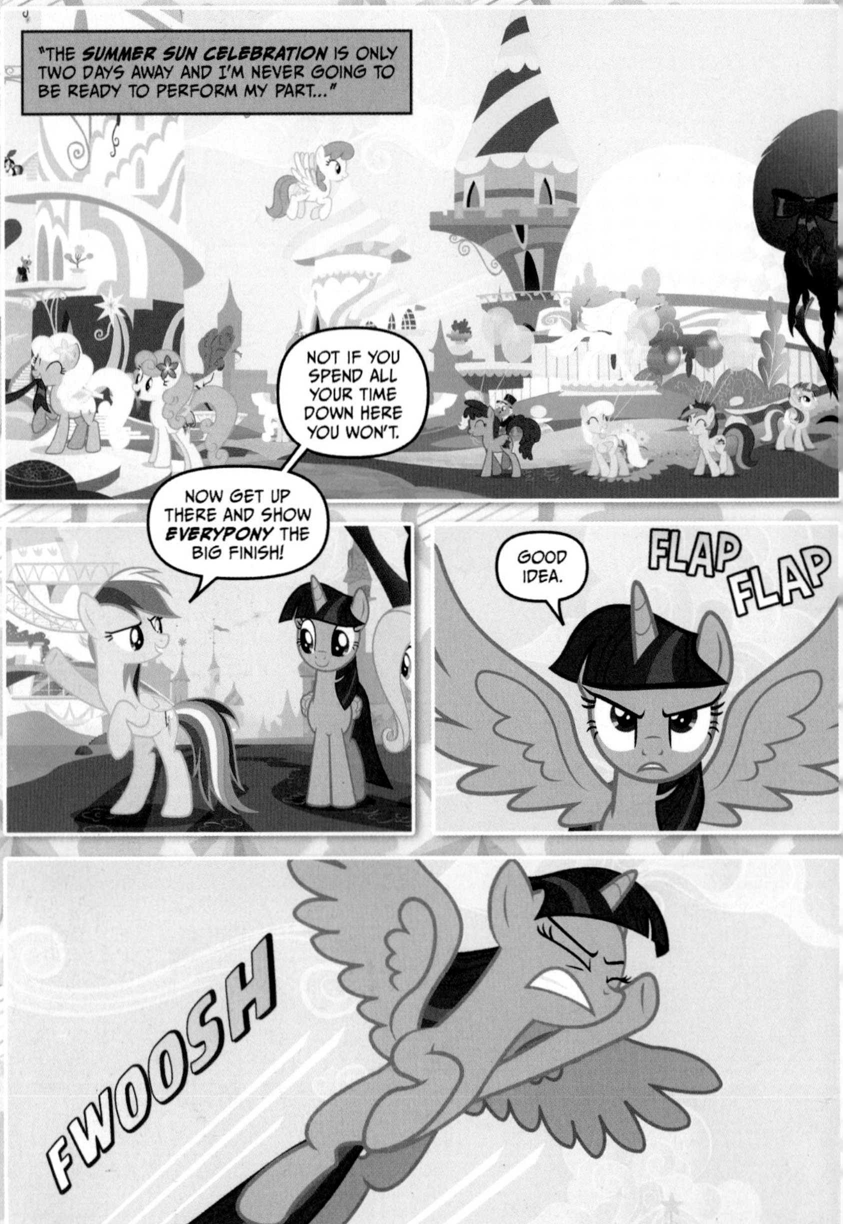
"THE SUMMER SUN CELEBRATION IS ONLY TWO DAYS AWAY AND I'M NEVER GOING TO BE READY TO PERFORM MY PART..."
NOT IF YOU SPEND ALL YOUR TIME DOWN HERE YOU WON'T.
NOW GET UP THERE AND SHOW EVERYPONY THE BIG FINISH!
GOOD IDEA.
FLAP FLAP
FWOOSH

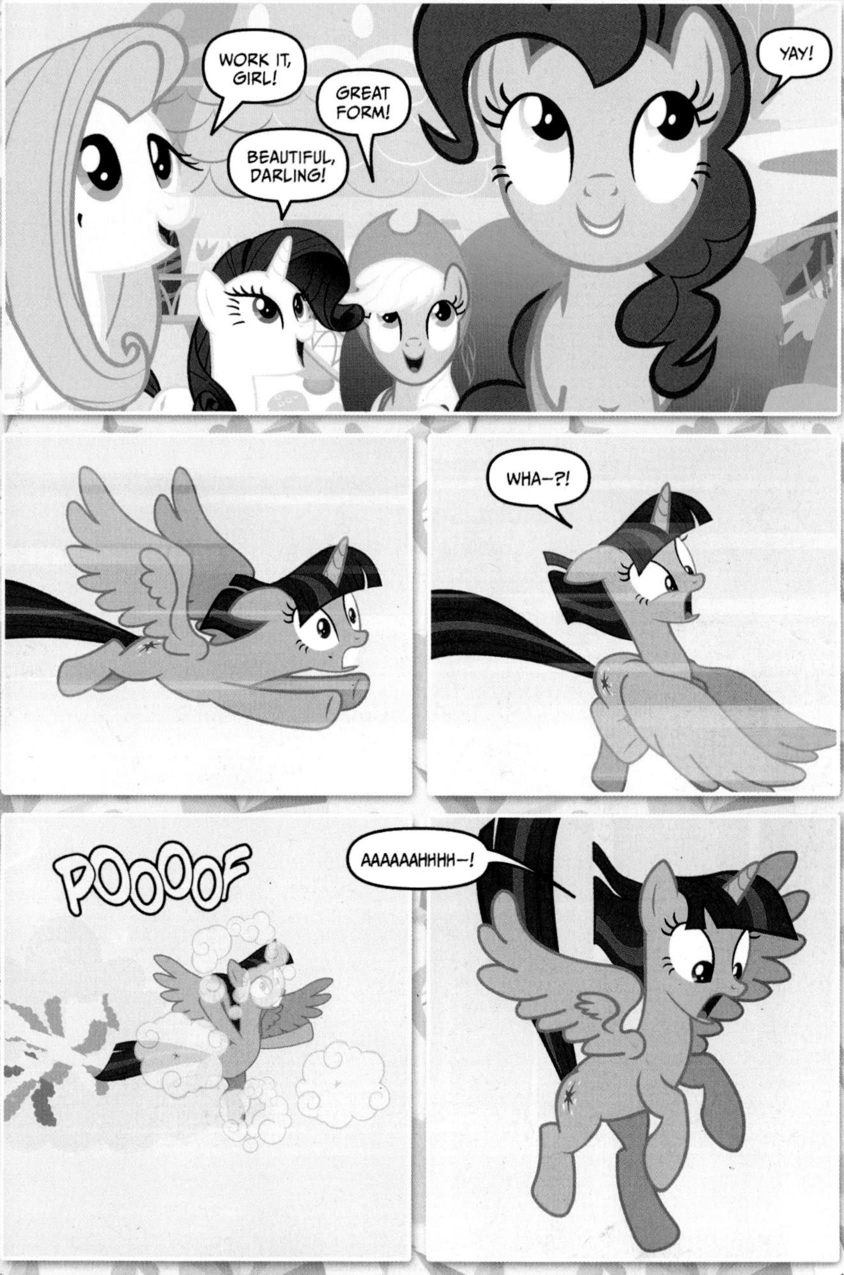
WORK IT, GIRL!
BEAUTIFUL, DARLING!
GREAT FORM!
YAY!
WHA-?!
POOOOF
AAAAAAHHHH-!

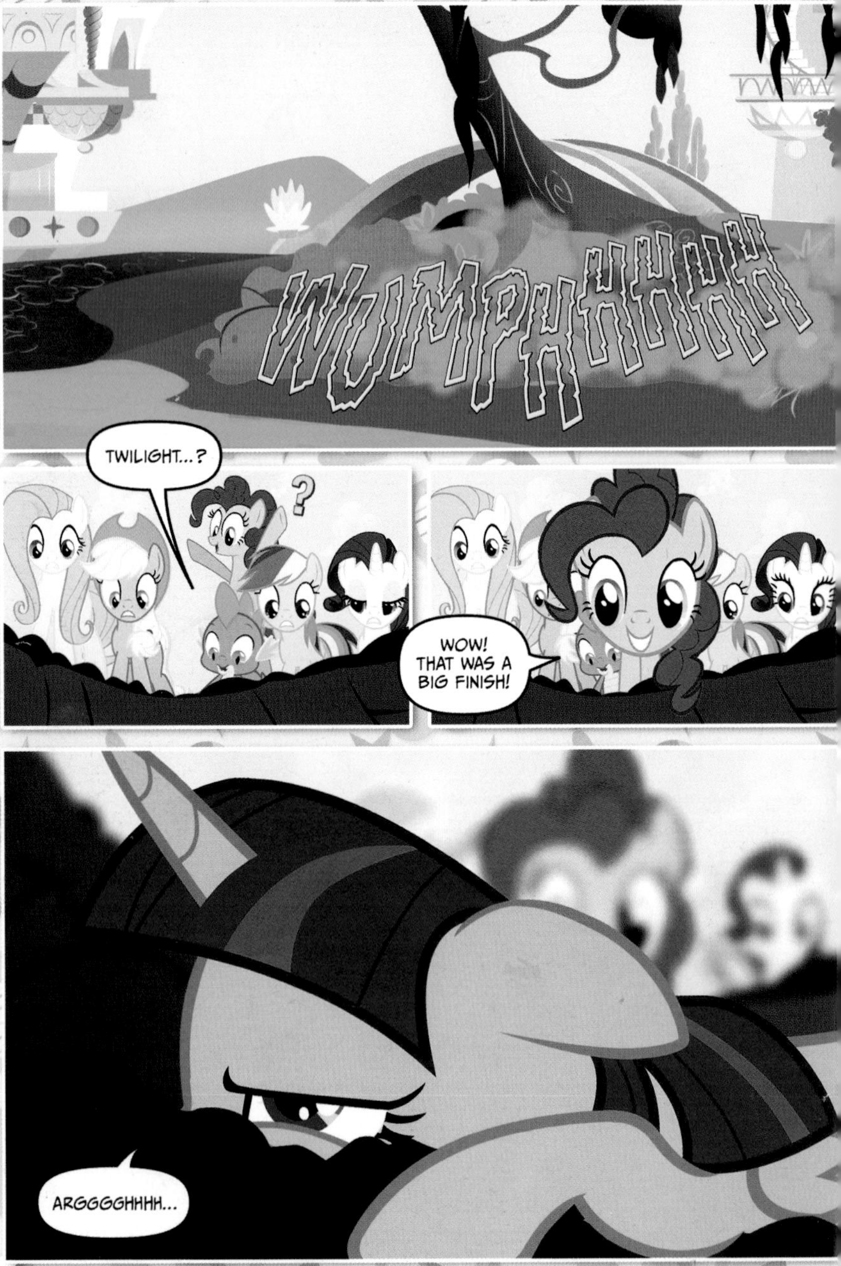
WUMPHHHHH
TWILIGHT...?
?
WOW! THAT WAS A BIG FINISH!
ARGGGGHHHH...

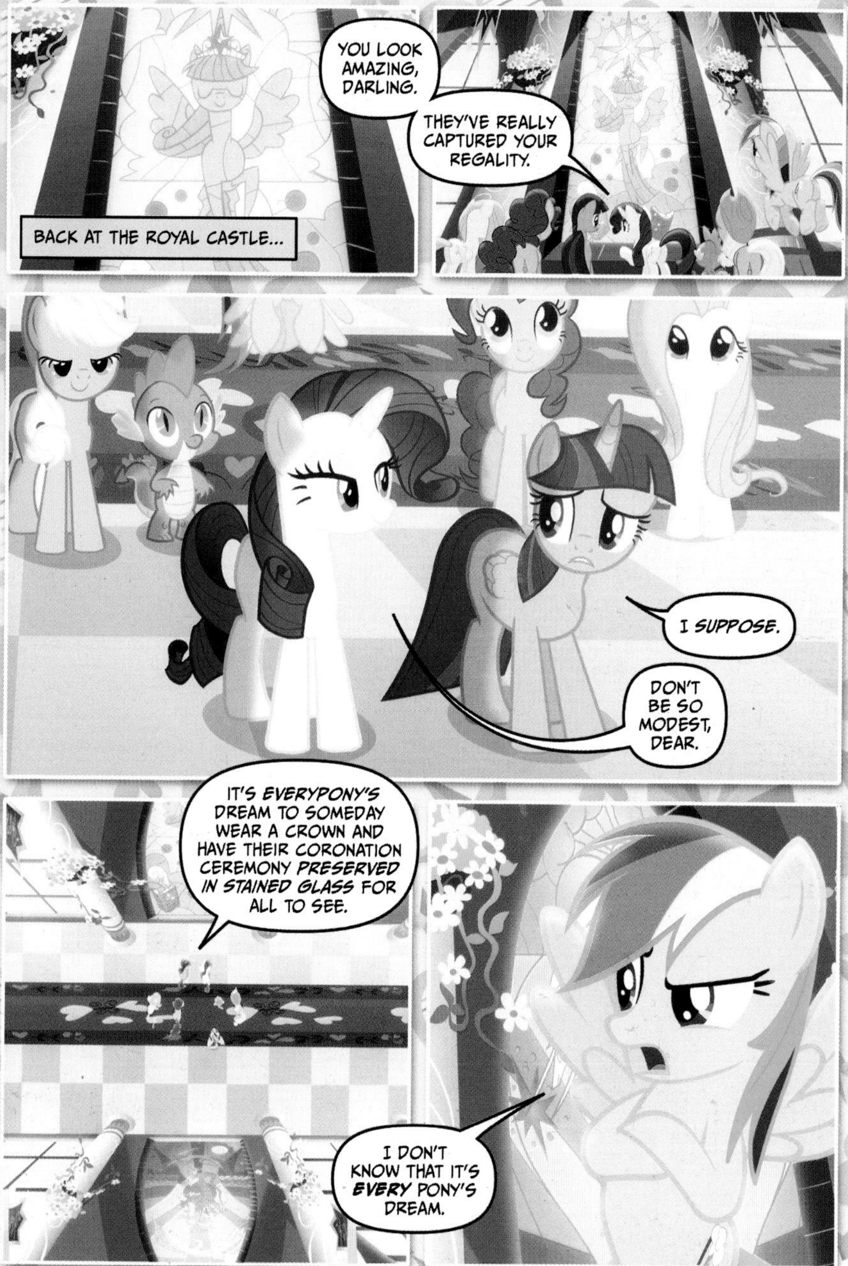

BACK AT THE ROYAL CASTLE...
YOU LOOK AMAZING, DARLING.
THEY'VE REALLY CAPTURED YOUR REGALITY.
I *SUPPOSE.*
DON'T BE SO MODEST, DEAR.
IT'S *EVERYPONY'S* DREAM TO SOMEDAY WEAR A CROWN AND HAVE THEIR CORONATION CEREMONY *PRESERVED IN STAINED GLASS* FOR ALL TO SEE.
I DON'T KNOW THAT IT'S ***EVERY*** PONY'S DREAM.

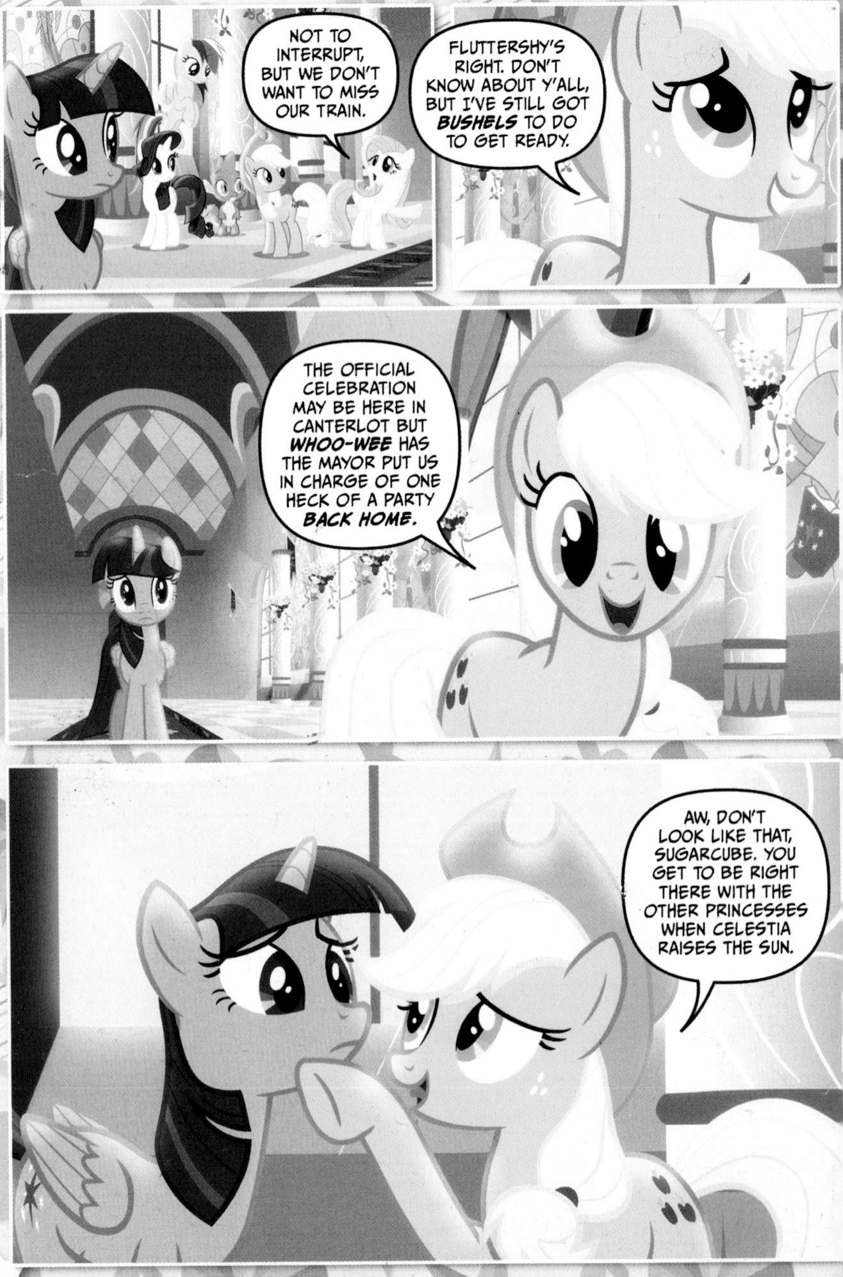
NOT TO INTERRUPT, BUT WE DON'T WANT TO MISS OUR TRAIN.
FLUTTERSHY'S RIGHT. DON'T KNOW ABOUT Y'ALL, BUT I'VE STILL GOT BUSHELS TO DO TO GET READY.
THE OFFICIAL CELEBRATION MAY BE HERE IN CANTERLOT BUT WHOO-WEE HAS THE MAYOR PUT US IN CHARGE OF ONE HECK OF A PARTY BACK HOME.
AW, DON'T LOOK LIKE THAT, SUGARCUBE. YOU GET TO BE RIGHT THERE WITH THE OTHER PRINCESSES WHEN CELESTIA RAISES THE SUN.

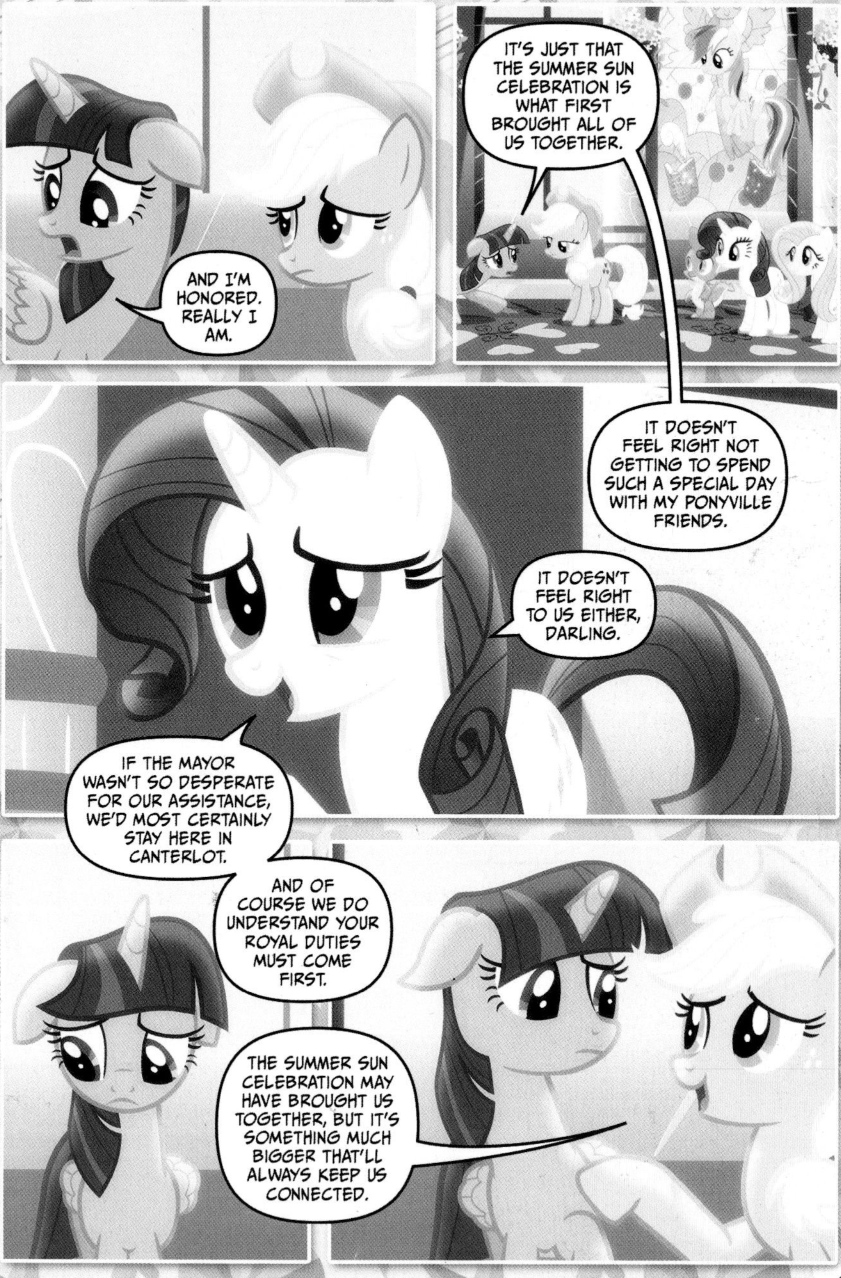
AND I'M HONORED. REALLY I AM.
IT'S JUST THAT THE SUMMER SUN CELEBRATION IS WHAT FIRST BROUGHT ALL OF US TOGETHER.
IT DOESN'T FEEL RIGHT NOT GETTING TO SPEND SUCH A SPECIAL DAY WITH MY PONYVILLE FRIENDS.
IT DOESN'T FEEL RIGHT TO US EITHER, DARLING.
IF THE MAYOR WASN'T SO DESPERATE FOR OUR ASSISTANCE, WE'D MOST CERTAINLY STAY HERE IN CANTERLOT.
AND OF COURSE WE DO UNDERSTAND YOUR ROYAL DUTIES MUST COME FIRST.
THE SUMMER SUN CELEBRATION MAY HAVE BROUGHT US TOGETHER, BUT IT'S SOMETHING MUCH BIGGER THAT'LL ALWAYS KEEP US CONNECTED.

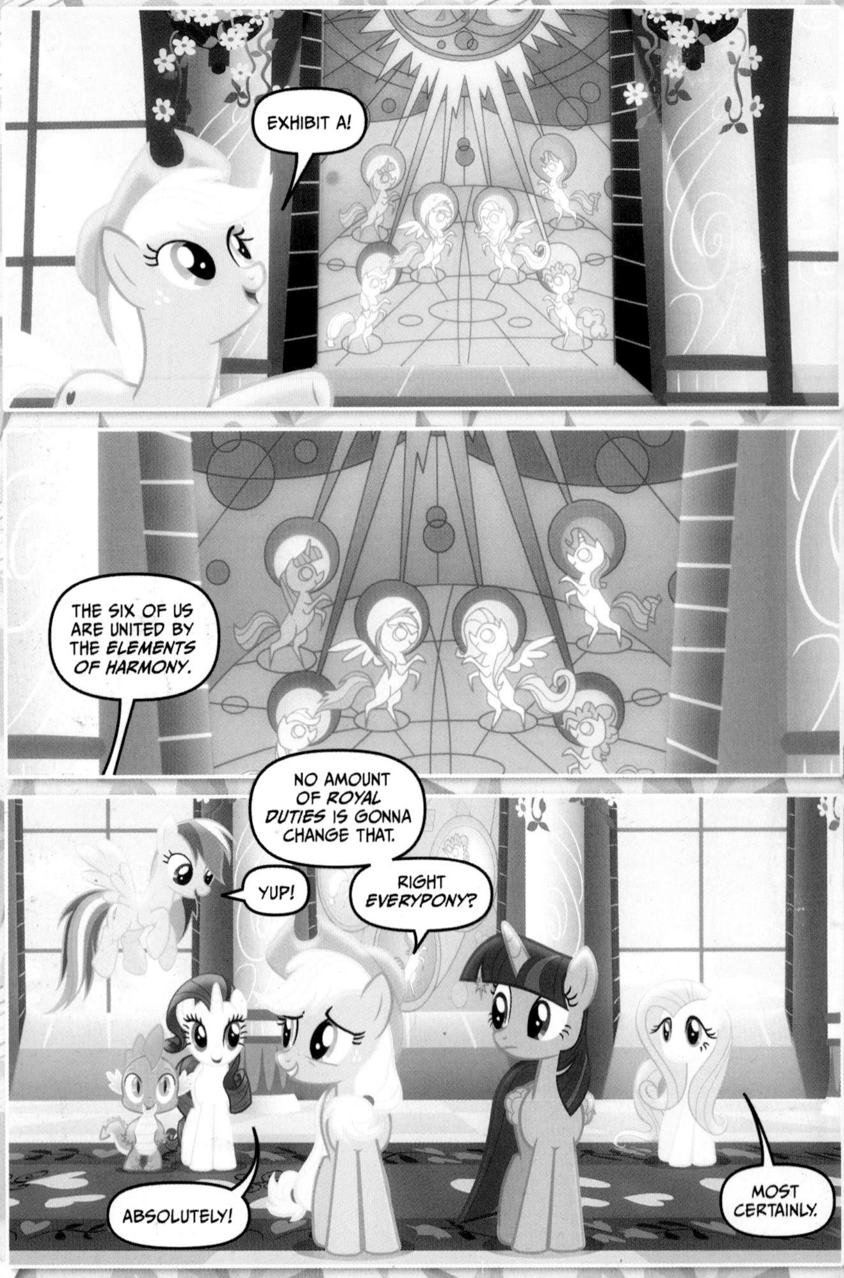
EXHIBIT A!
THE SIX OF US ARE UNITED BY THE *ELEMENTS OF HARMONY*.
NO AMOUNT OF *ROYAL DUTIES* IS GONNA CHANGE THAT.
RIGHT *EVERYPONY?*
YUP!
ABSOLUTELY!
MOST CERTAINLY.

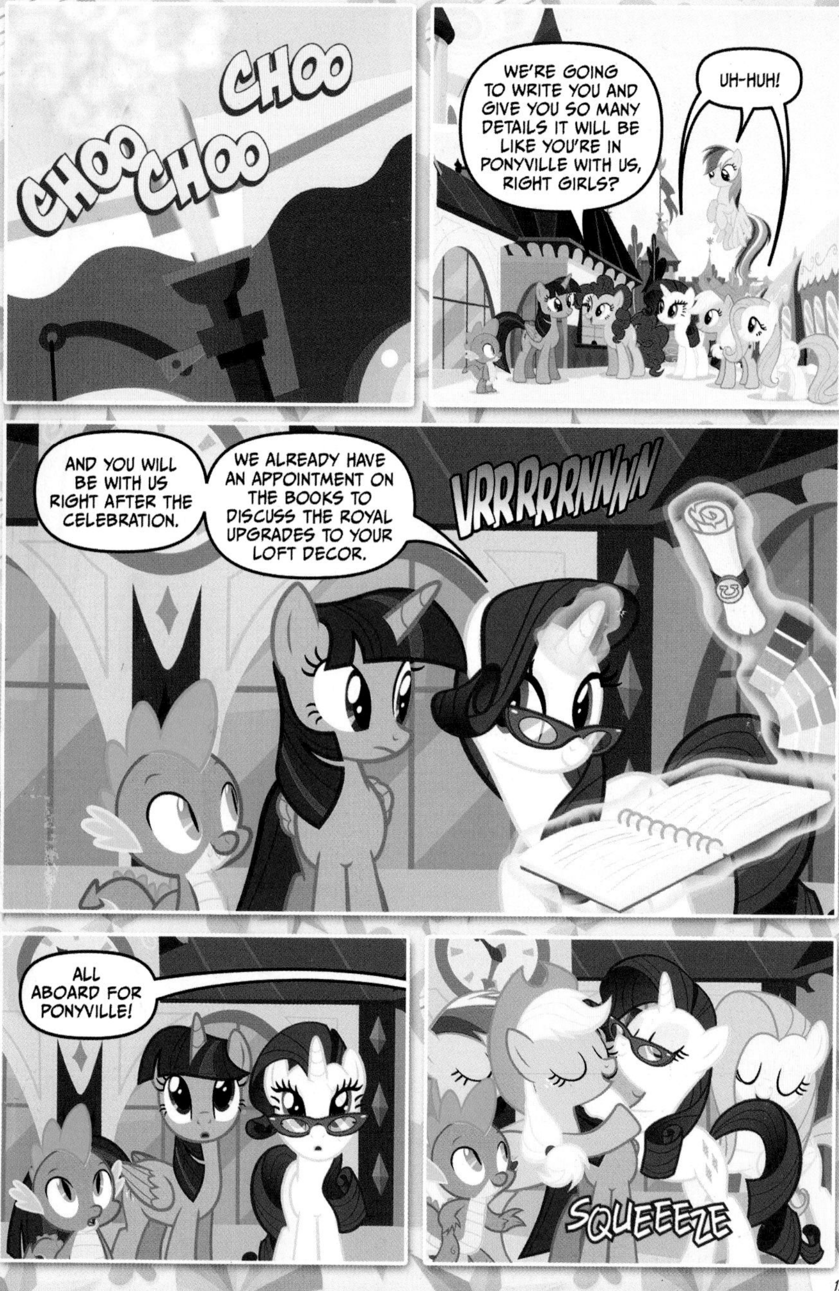
CHOO CHOO
CHOO
WE'RE GOING TO WRITE YOU AND GIVE YOU SO MANY DETAILS IT WILL BE LIKE YOU'RE IN PONYVILLE WITH US, RIGHT GIRLS?
UH-HUH!
AND YOU WILL BE WITH US RIGHT AFTER THE CELEBRATION.
WE ALREADY HAVE AN APPOINTMENT ON THE BOOKS TO DISCUSS THE ROYAL UPGRADES TO YOUR LOFT DECOR.
VRRRRRNNNN
ALL ABOARD FOR PONYVILLE!
SQUEEEEZE

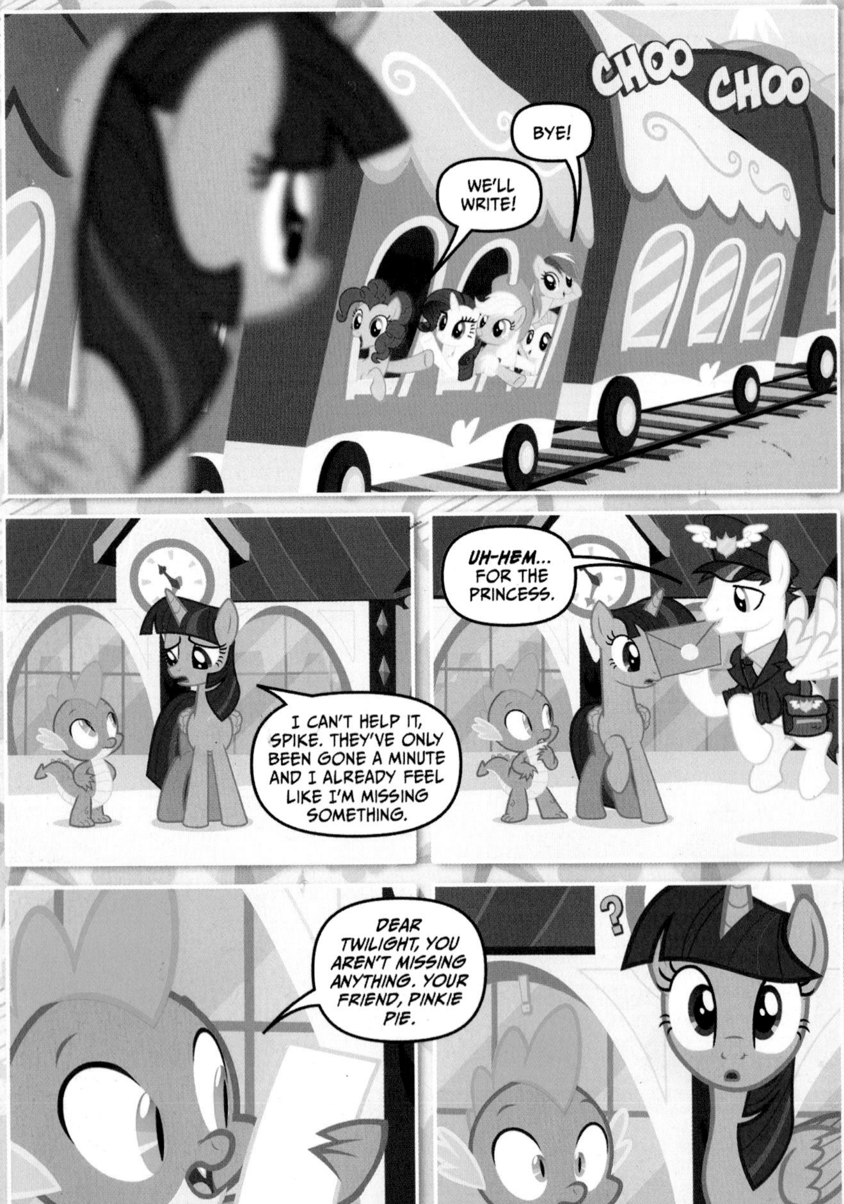
CHOO CHOO
WE'LL WRITE!
BYE!
I CAN'T HELP IT, SPIKE. THEY'VE ONLY BEEN GONE A MINUTE AND I ALREADY FEEL LIKE I'M MISSING SOMETHING.
UH-HEM... FOR THE PRINCESS.
DEAR TWILIGHT, YOU AREN'T MISSING ANYTHING. YOUR FRIEND, PINKIE PIE.
?
!

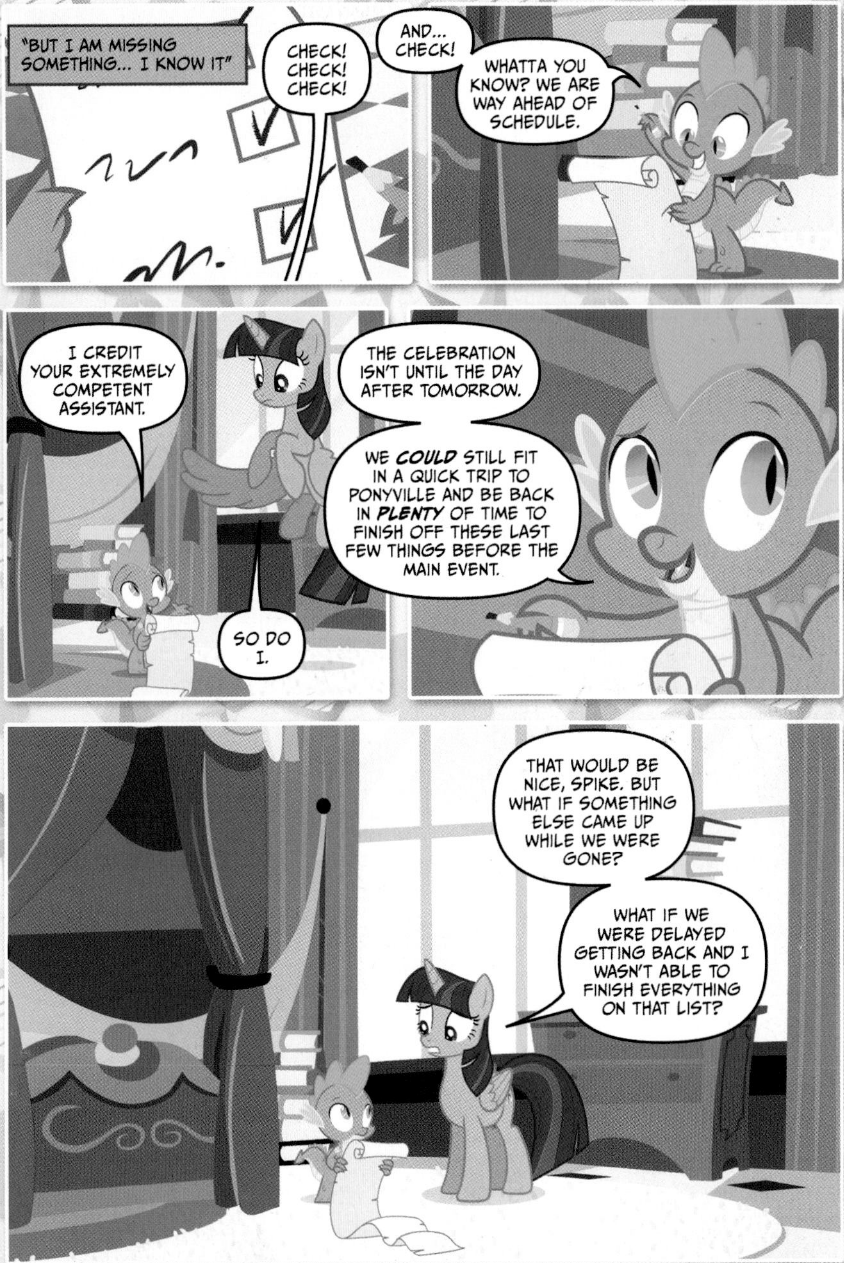
"BUT I AM MISSING SOMETHING... I KNOW IT"
CHECK! CHECK! CHECK!
AND... CHECK!
WHATTA YOU KNOW? WE ARE WAY AHEAD OF SCHEDULE.
I CREDIT YOUR EXTREMELY COMPETENT ASSISTANT.
SO DO I.
THE CELEBRATION ISN'T UNTIL THE DAY AFTER TOMORROW.
WE *COULD* STILL FIT IN A QUICK TRIP TO PONYVILLE AND BE BACK IN *PLENTY* OF TIME TO FINISH OFF THESE LAST FEW THINGS BEFORE THE MAIN EVENT.
THAT WOULD BE NICE, SPIKE. BUT WHAT IF SOMETHING ELSE CAME UP WHILE WE WERE GONE?
WHAT IF WE WERE DELAYED GETTING BACK AND I WASN'T ABLE TO FINISH EVERYTHING ON THAT LIST?

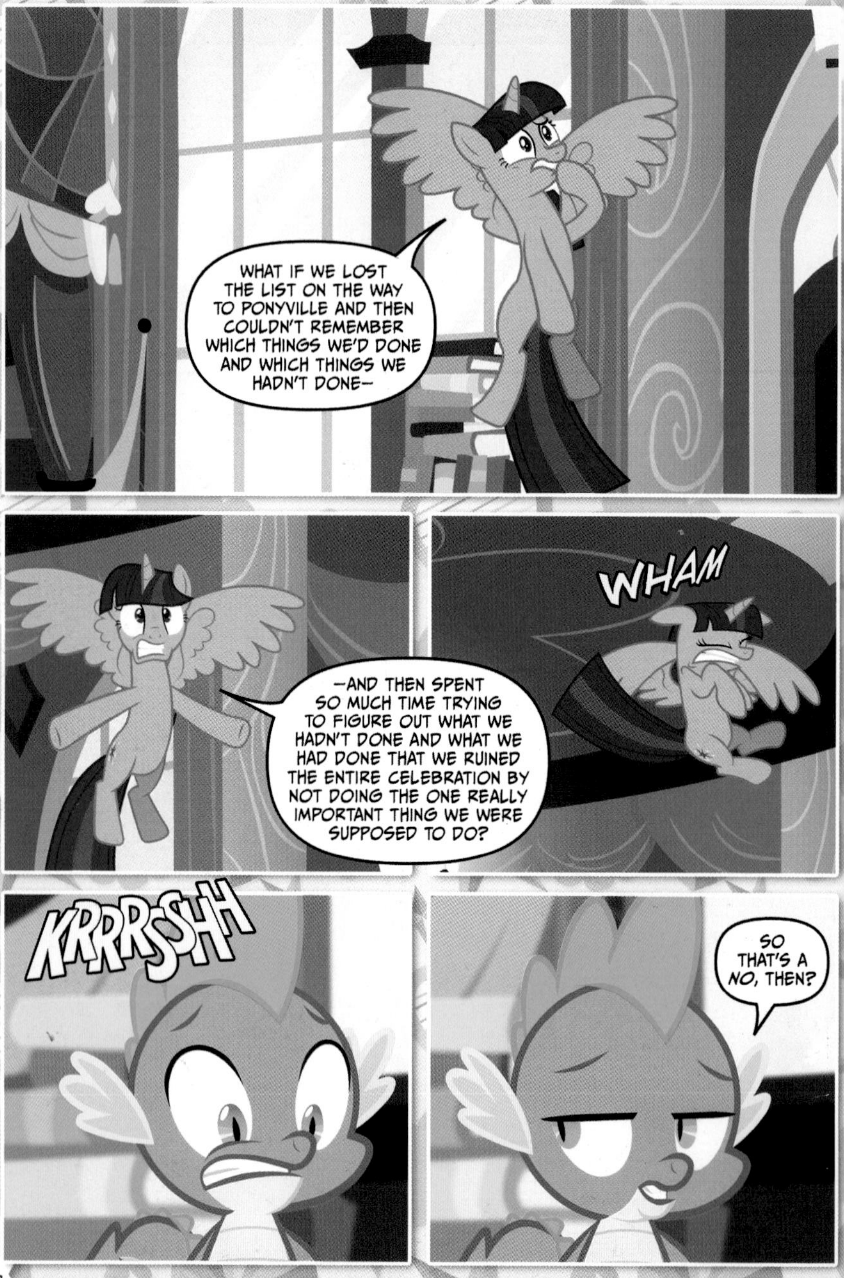
WHAT IF WE LOST THE LIST ON THE WAY TO PONYVILLE AND THEN COULDN'T REMEMBER WHICH THINGS WE'D DONE AND WHICH THINGS WE HADN'T DONE—
—AND THEN SPENT SO MUCH TIME TRYING TO FIGURE OUT WHAT WE HADN'T DONE AND WHAT WE HAD DONE THAT WE RUINED THE ENTIRE CELEBRATION BY NOT DOING THE ONE REALLY IMPORTANT THING WE WERE SUPPOSED TO DO?
WHAM
KRRRSHH
SO THAT'S A *NO*, THEN?

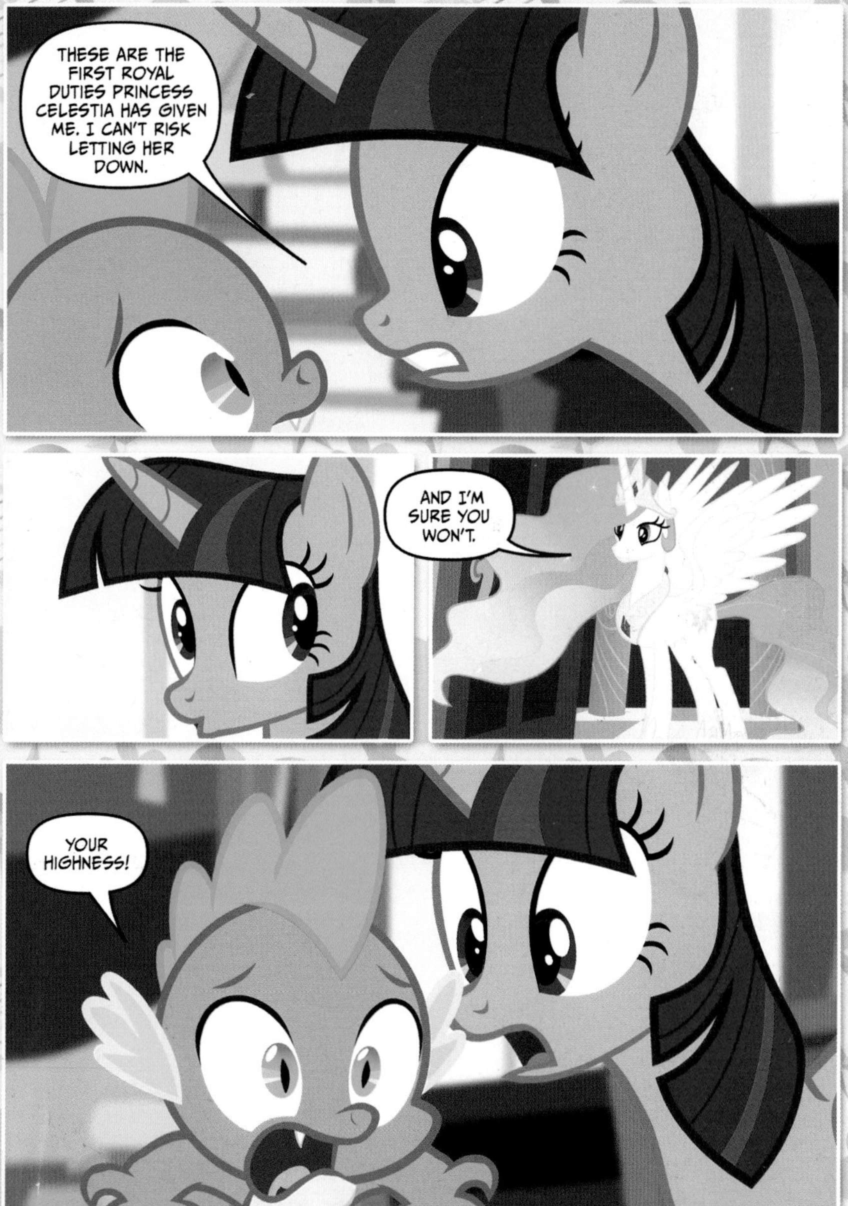
THESE ARE THE FIRST ROYAL DUTIES PRINCESS CELESTIA HAS GIVEN ME. I CAN'T RISK LETTING HER DOWN.
AND I'M SURE YOU WON'T.
YOUR HIGHNESS!

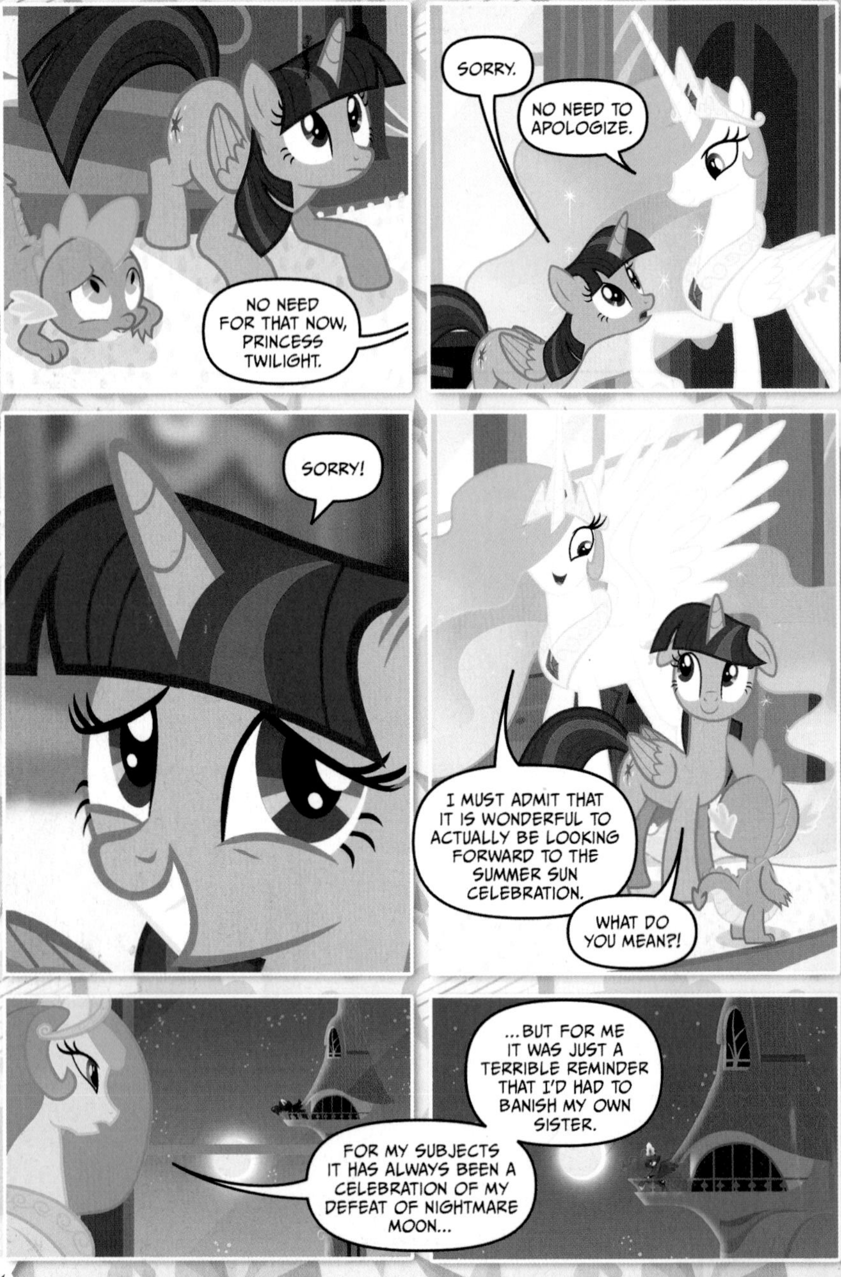
NO NEED FOR THAT NOW, PRINCESS TWILIGHT.
SORRY.
NO NEED TO APOLOGIZE.
SORRY!
I MUST ADMIT THAT IT IS WONDERFUL TO ACTUALLY BE LOOKING FORWARD TO THE SUMMER SUN CELEBRATION.
WHAT DO YOU MEAN?!
FOR MY SUBJECTS IT HAS ALWAYS BEEN A CELEBRATION OF MY DEFEAT OF NIGHTMARE MOON...
...BUT FOR ME IT WAS JUST A TERRIBLE REMINDER THAT I'D HAD TO BANISH MY OWN SISTER.

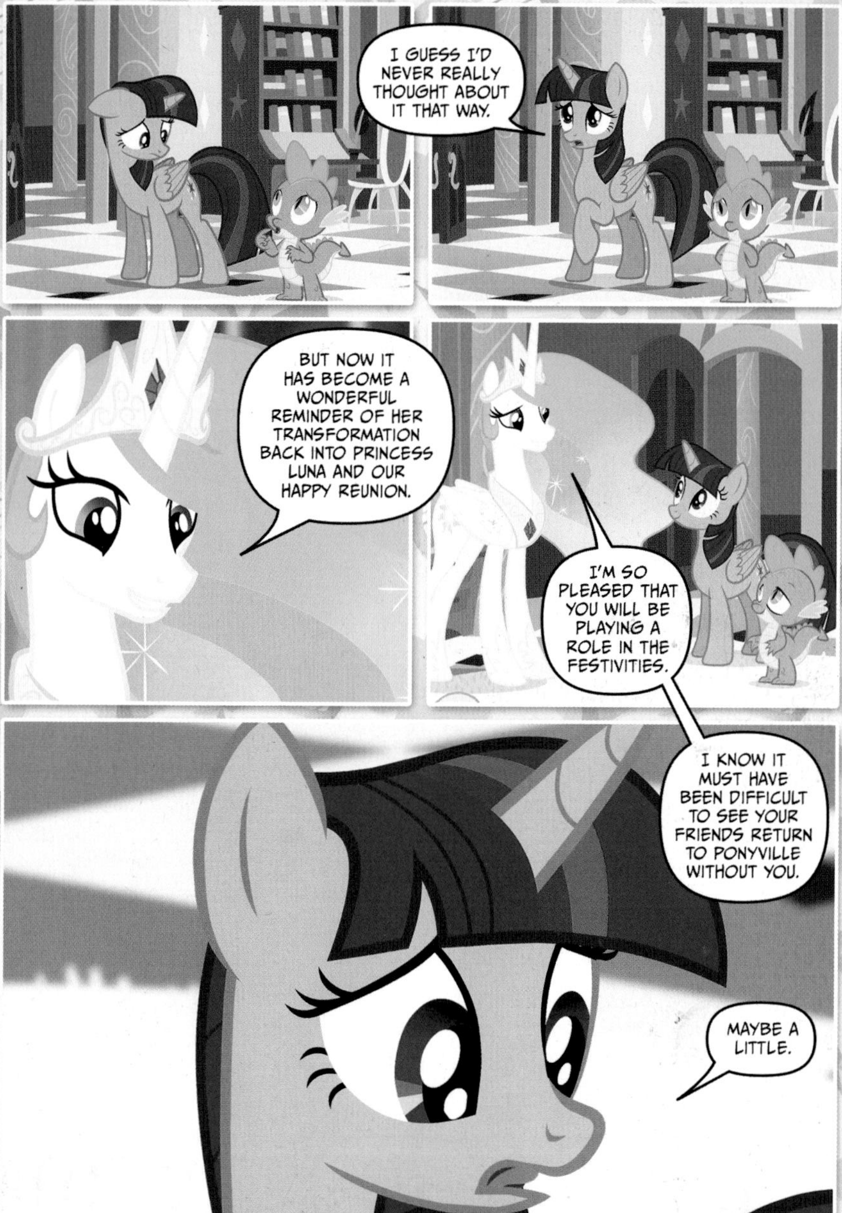
I GUESS I'D NEVER REALLY THOUGHT ABOUT IT THAT WAY.
BUT NOW IT HAS BECOME A WONDERFUL REMINDER OF HER TRANSFORMATION BACK INTO PRINCESS LUNA AND OUR HAPPY REUNION.
I'M SO PLEASED THAT YOU WILL BE PLAYING A ROLE IN THE FESTIVITIES.
I KNOW IT MUST HAVE BEEN DIFFICULT TO SEE YOUR FRIENDS RETURN TO PONYVILLE WITHOUT YOU.
MAYBE A LITTLE.

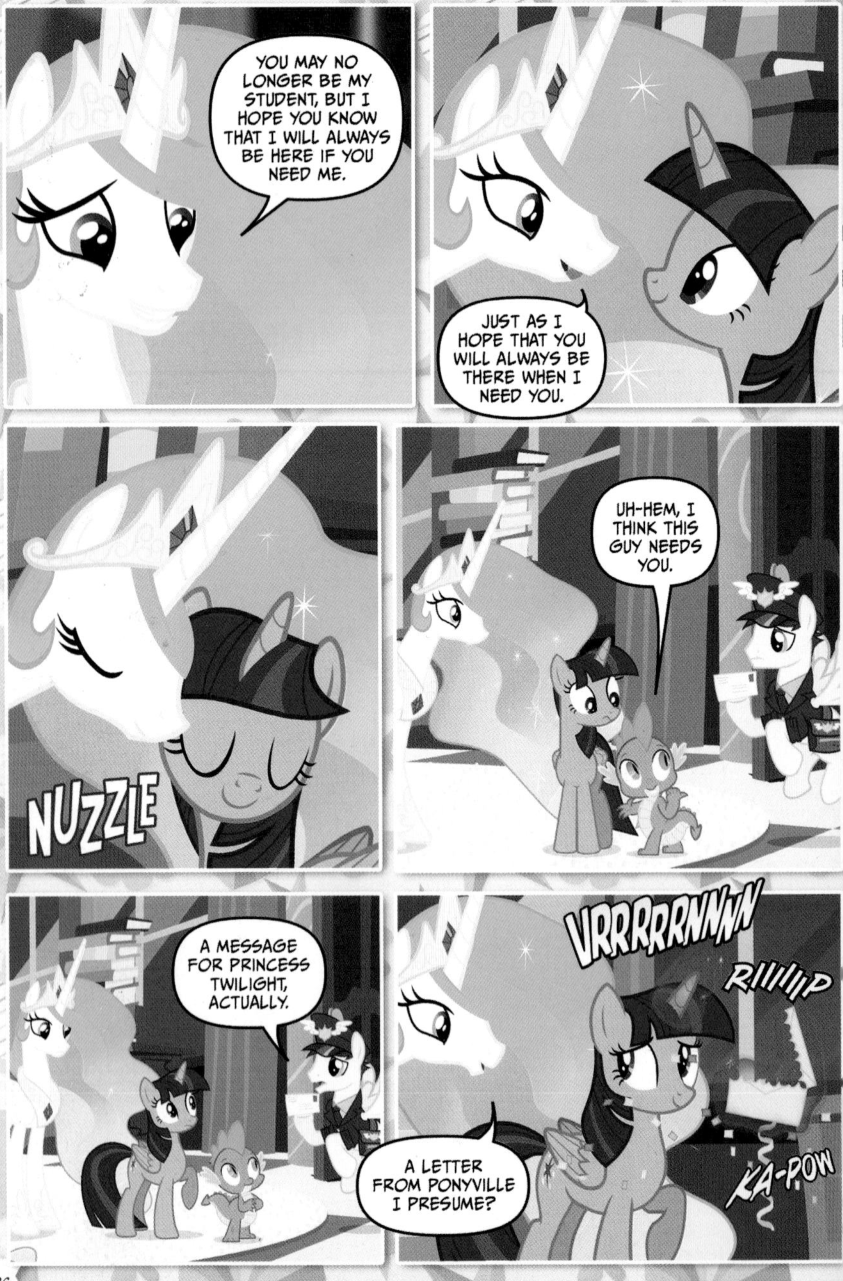
YOU MAY NO LONGER BE MY STUDENT, BUT I HOPE YOU KNOW THAT I WILL ALWAYS BE HERE IF YOU NEED ME.
JUST AS I HOPE THAT YOU WILL ALWAYS BE THERE WHEN I NEED YOU.
NUZZLE
UH-HEM, I THINK THIS GUY NEEDS YOU.
A MESSAGE FOR PRINCESS TWILIGHT, ACTUALLY.
VRRRRRNNNN
RIIIIIP
A LETTER FROM PONYVILLE I PRESUME?
KA-POW

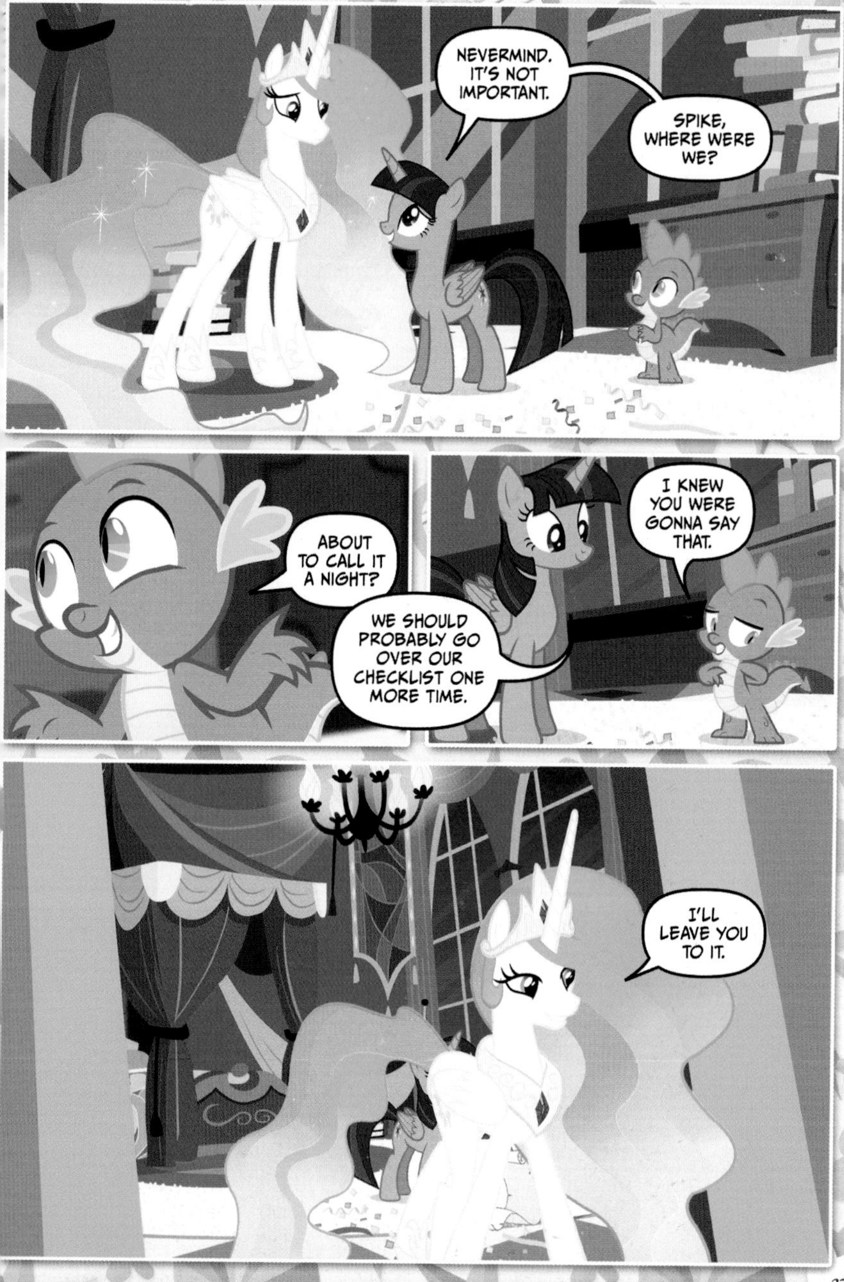
NEVERMIND. IT'S NOT IMPORTANT.
SPIKE, WHERE WERE WE?
ABOUT TO CALL IT A NIGHT?
WE SHOULD PROBABLY GO OVER OUR CHECKLIST ONE MORE TIME.
I KNEW YOU WERE GONNA SAY THAT.
I'LL LEAVE YOU TO IT.

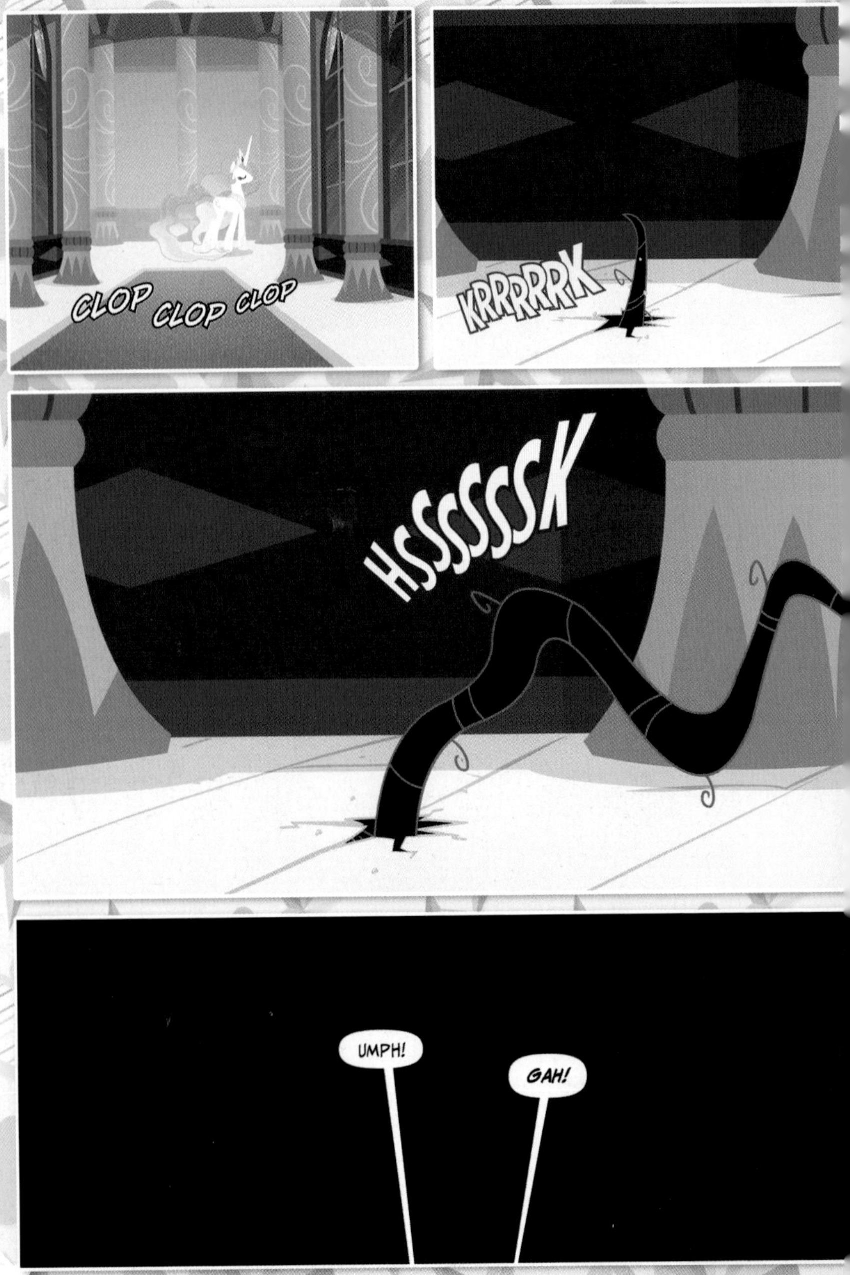
CLOP CLOP CLOP
KRRRRRK
HSSSSSSK
UMPH!
GAH!

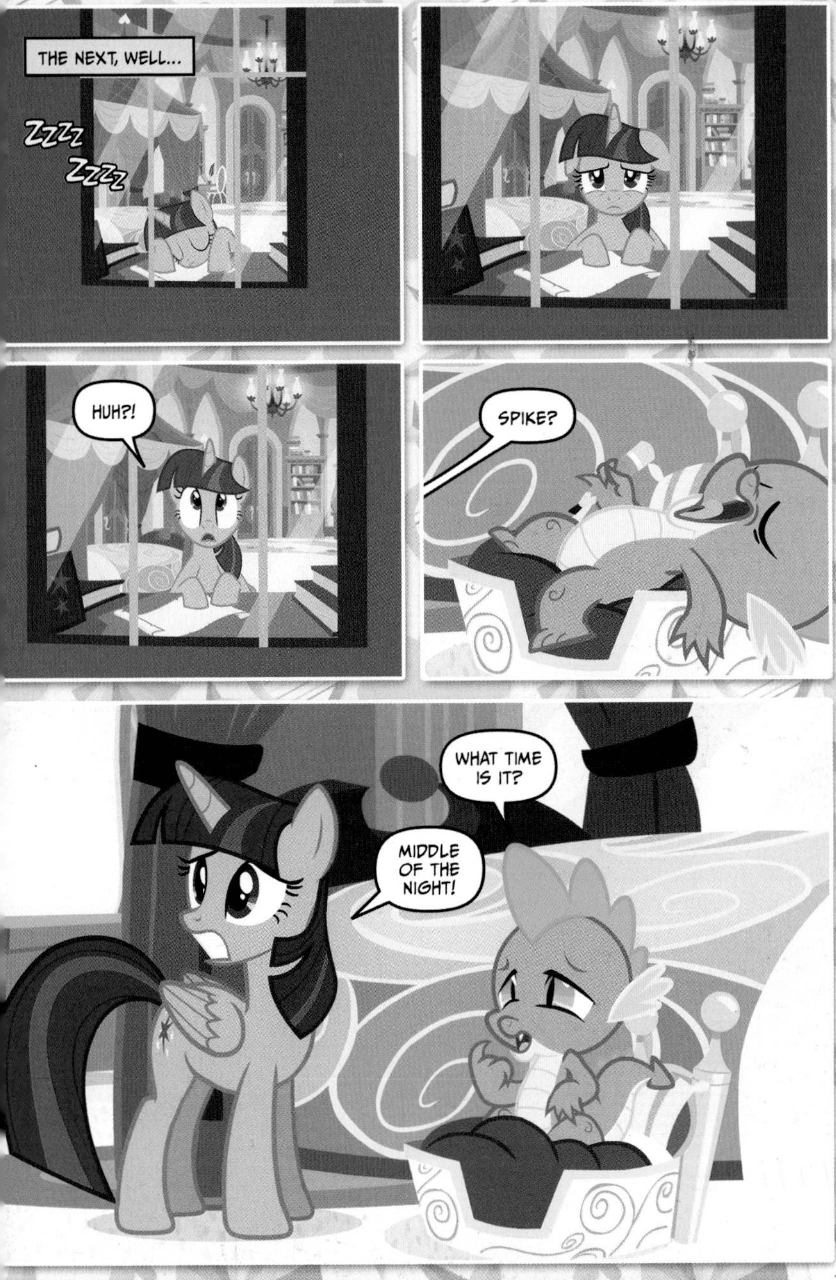
THE NEXT, WELL...
ZZZZ
ZZZZ
HUH?!
SPIKE?
WHAT TIME IS IT?
MIDDLE OF THE NIGHT!

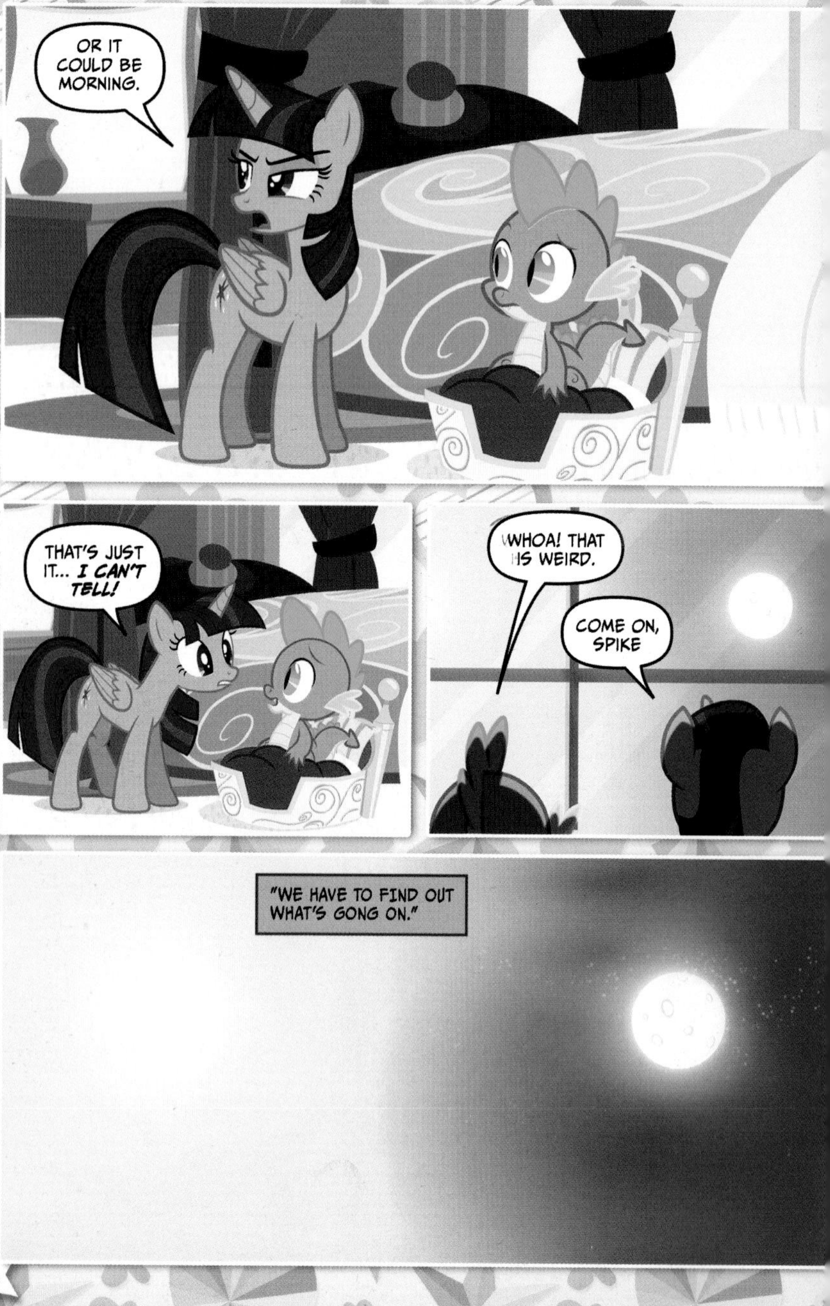
OR IT COULD BE MORNING.
THAT'S JUST IT... I CAN'T TELL!
WHOA! THAT IS WEIRD.
COME ON, SPIKE
"WE HAVE TO FIND OUT WHAT'S GONG ON."

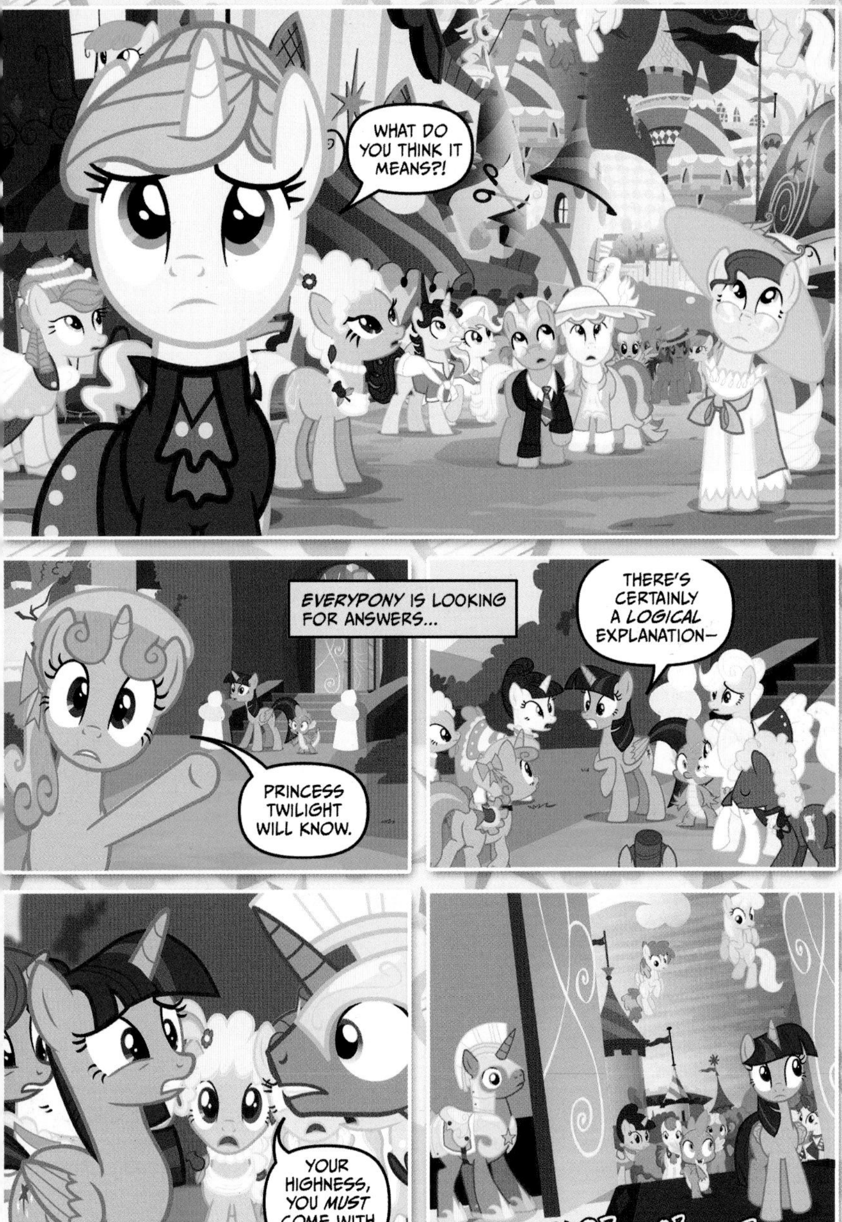
WHAT DO YOU THINK IT MEANS?!
EVERYPONY IS LOOKING FOR ANSWERS...
PRINCESS TWILIGHT WILL KNOW.
THERE'S CERTAINLY A LOGICAL EXPLANATION—
YOUR HIGHNESS, YOU MUST COME WITH US.
CLOP CLOP CLOP

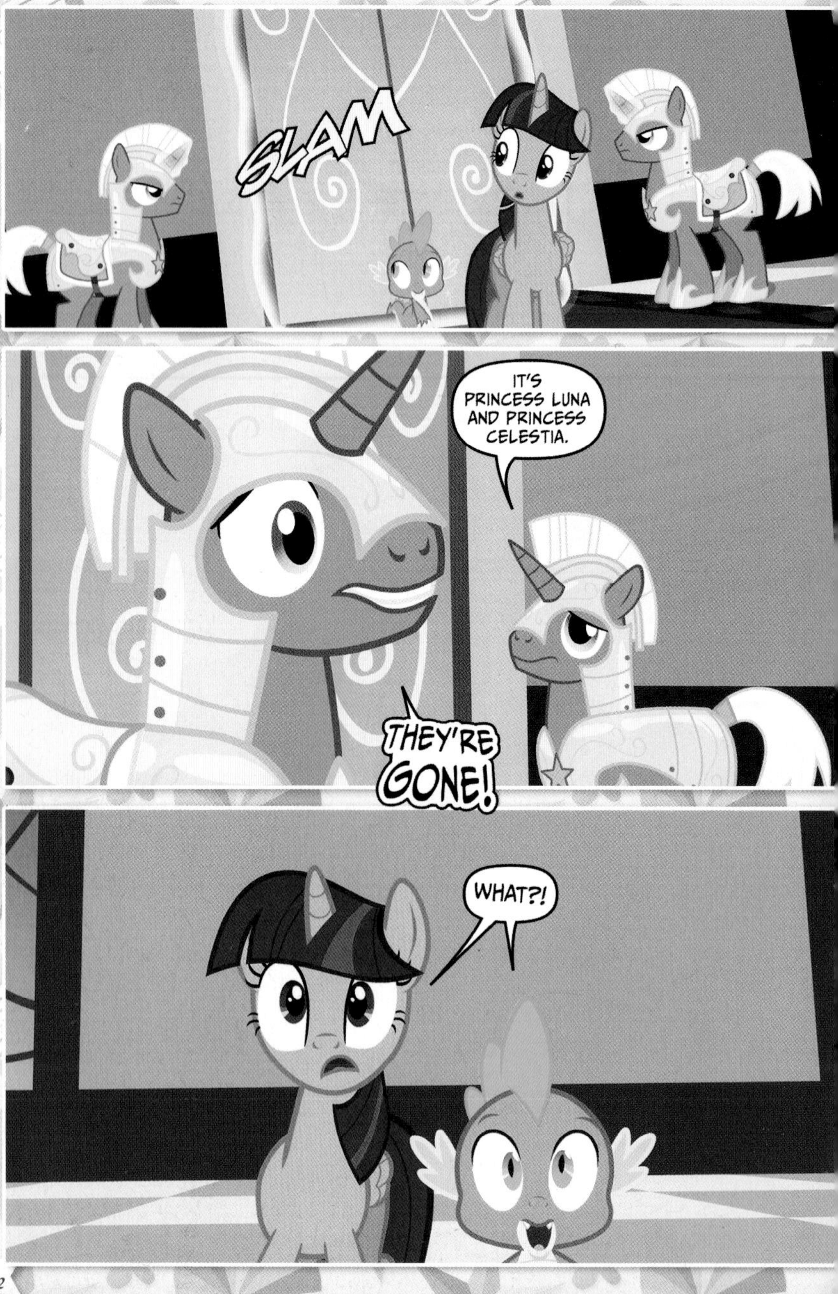
SLAM
IT'S PRINCESS LUNA AND PRINCESS CELESTIA.
THEY'RE GONE!
WHAT?!

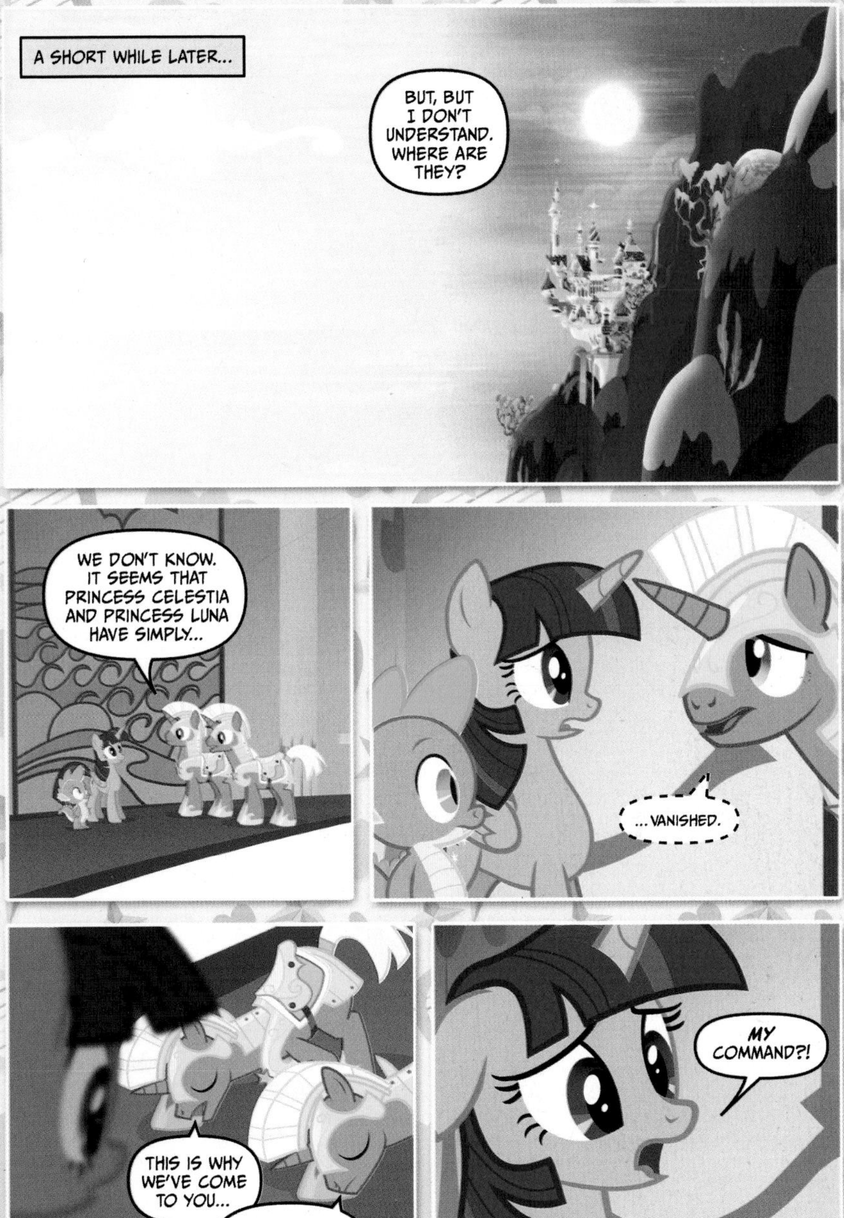
A SHORT WHILE LATER...
BUT, BUT I DON'T UNDERSTAND. WHERE ARE THEY?
WE DON'T KNOW. IT SEEMS THAT PRINCESS CELESTIA AND PRINCESS LUNA HAVE SIMPLY...
...VANISHED.
THIS IS WHY WE'VE COME TO YOU...
WE AWAIT YOUR COMMAND.
MY COMMAND?!

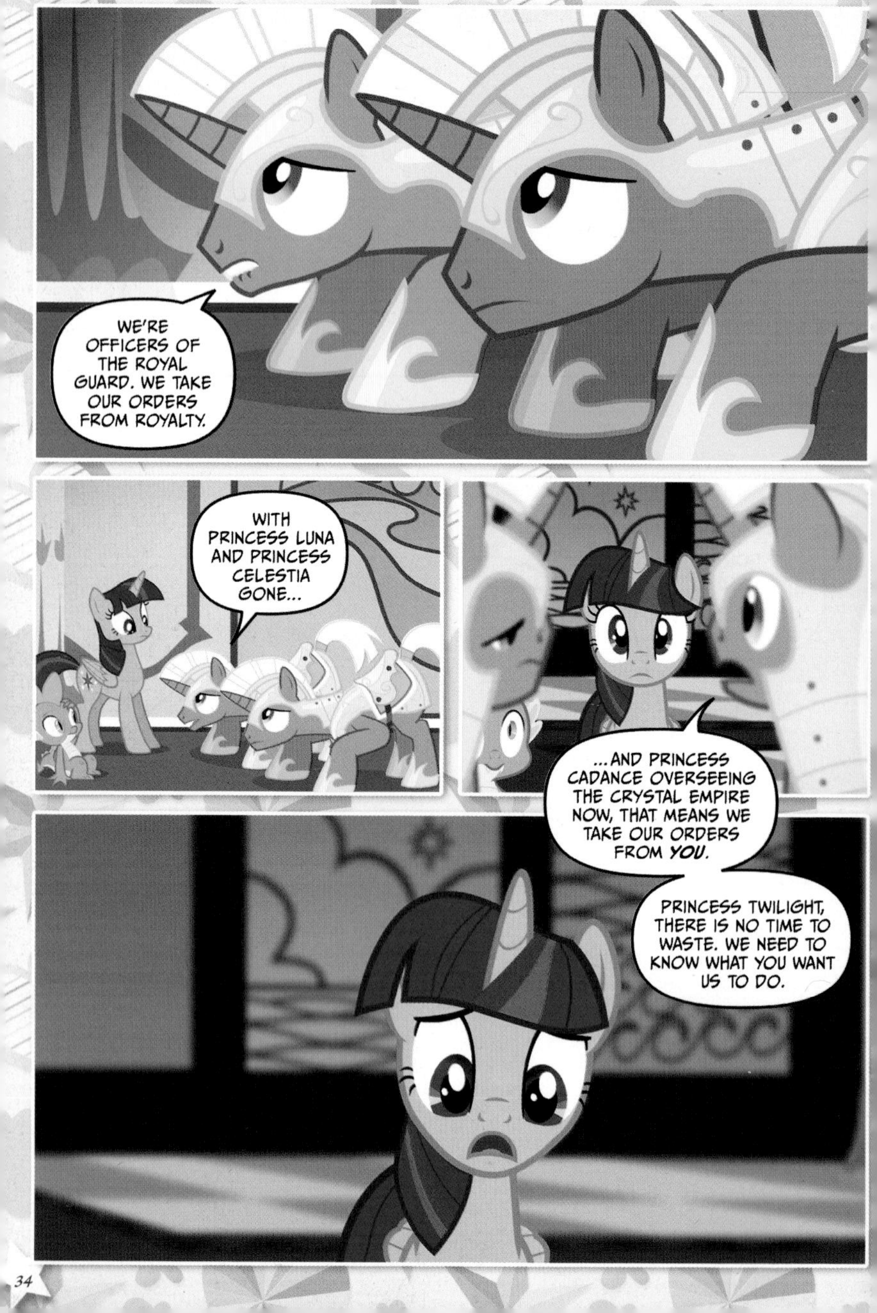
WE'RE OFFICERS OF THE ROYAL GUARD. WE TAKE OUR ORDERS FROM ROYALTY.
WITH PRINCESS LUNA AND PRINCESS CELESTIA GONE...
...AND PRINCESS CADANCE OVERSEEING THE CRYSTAL EMPIRE NOW, THAT MEANS WE TAKE OUR ORDERS FROM *YOU*.
PRINCESS TWILIGHT, THERE IS NO TIME TO WASTE. WE NEED TO KNOW WHAT YOU WANT US TO DO.

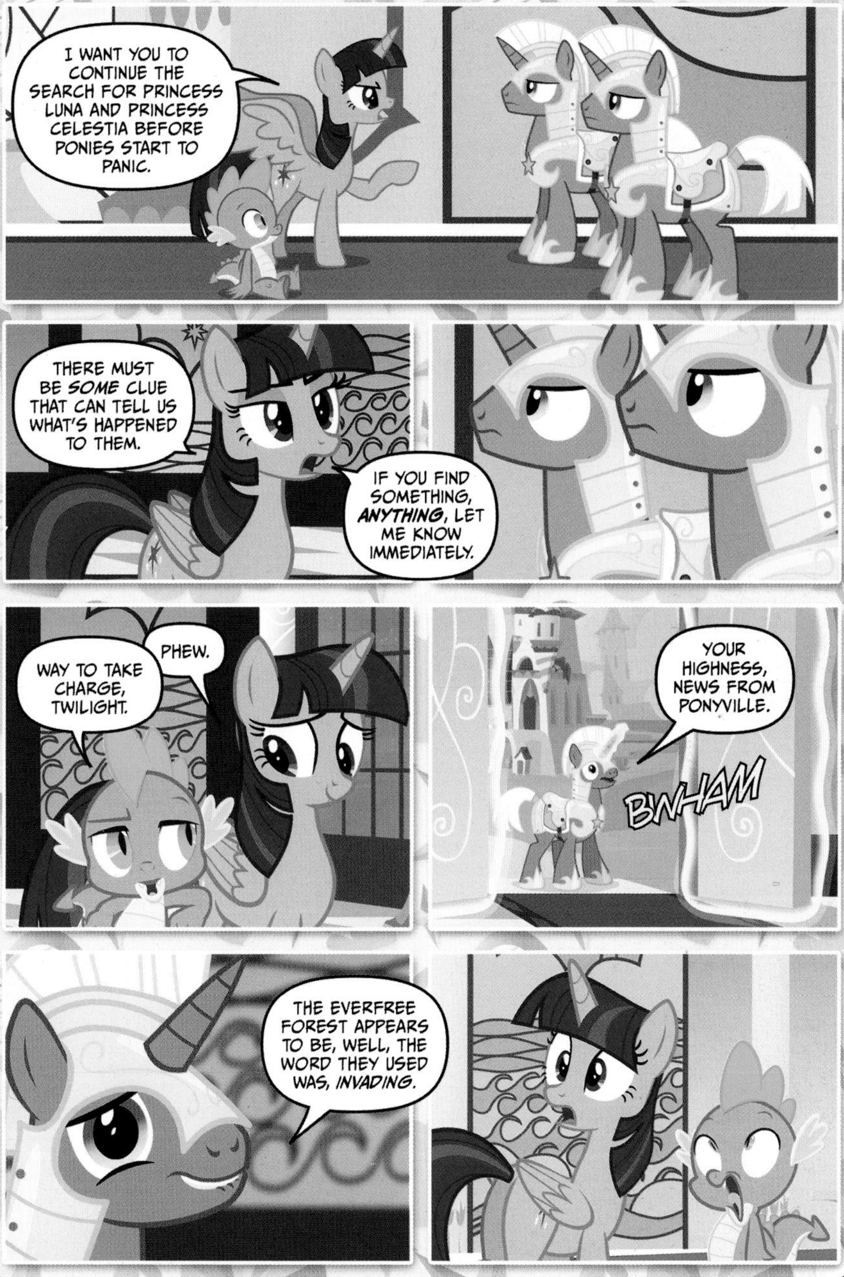

I WANT YOU TO CONTINUE THE SEARCH FOR PRINCESS LUNA AND PRINCESS CELESTIA BEFORE PONIES START TO PANIC.
THERE MUST BE *SOME* CLUE THAT CAN TELL US WHAT'S HAPPENED TO THEM.
IF YOU FIND SOMETHING, ***ANYTHING***, LET ME KNOW IMMEDIATELY.
PHEW.
WAY TO TAKE CHARGE, TWILIGHT.
YOUR HIGHNESS, NEWS FROM PONYVILLE.
BWHAM
THE EVERFREE FOREST APPEARS TO BE, WELL, THE WORD THEY USED WAS, *INVADING*.

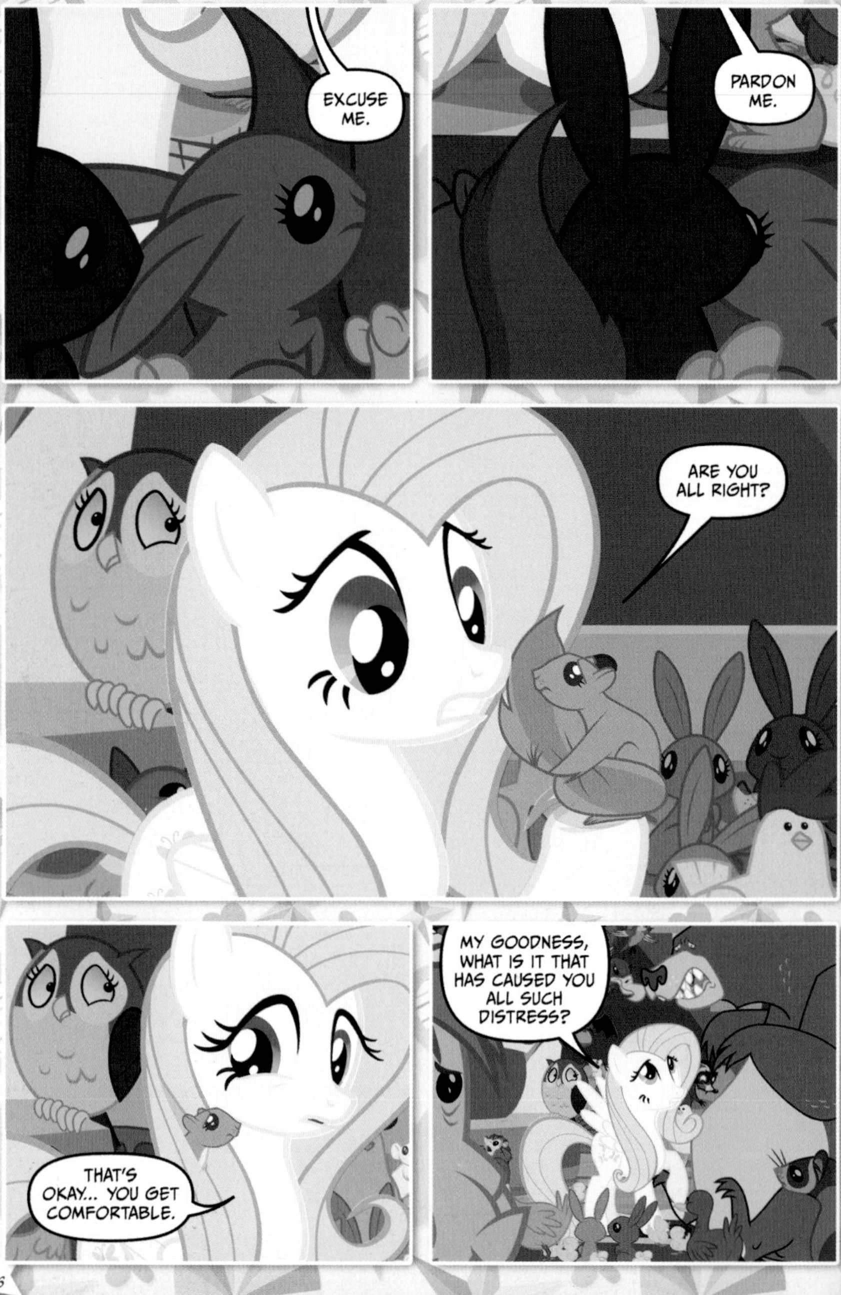

EXCUSE ME.
PARDON ME.
ARE YOU ALL RIGHT?
THAT'S OKAY... YOU GET COMFORTABLE.
MY GOODNESS, WHAT IS IT THAT HAS CAUSED YOU ALL SUCH DISTRESS?

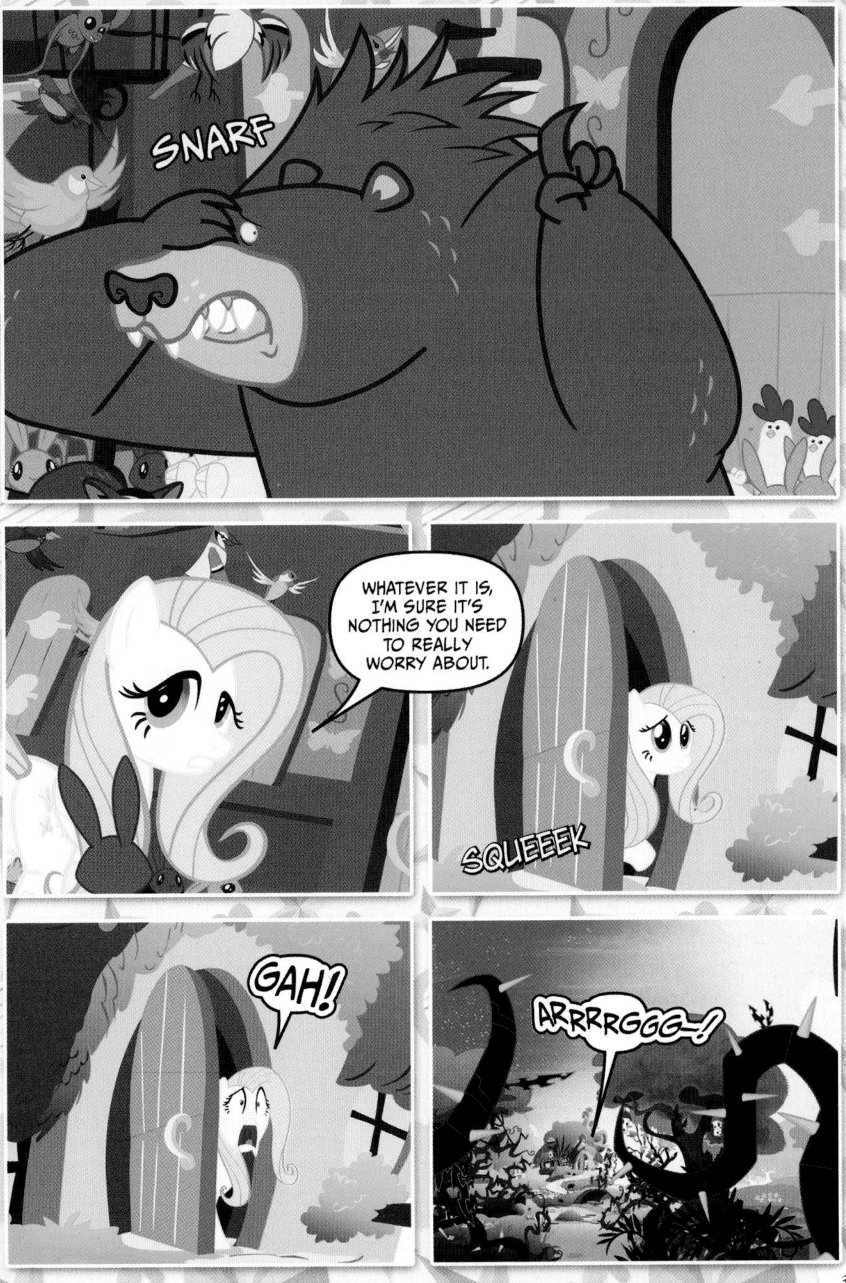
SNARF
WHATEVER IT IS, I'M SURE IT'S NOTHING YOU NEED TO REALLY WORRY ABOUT.
SQUEEEK
GAH!
ARRRRGGG--!

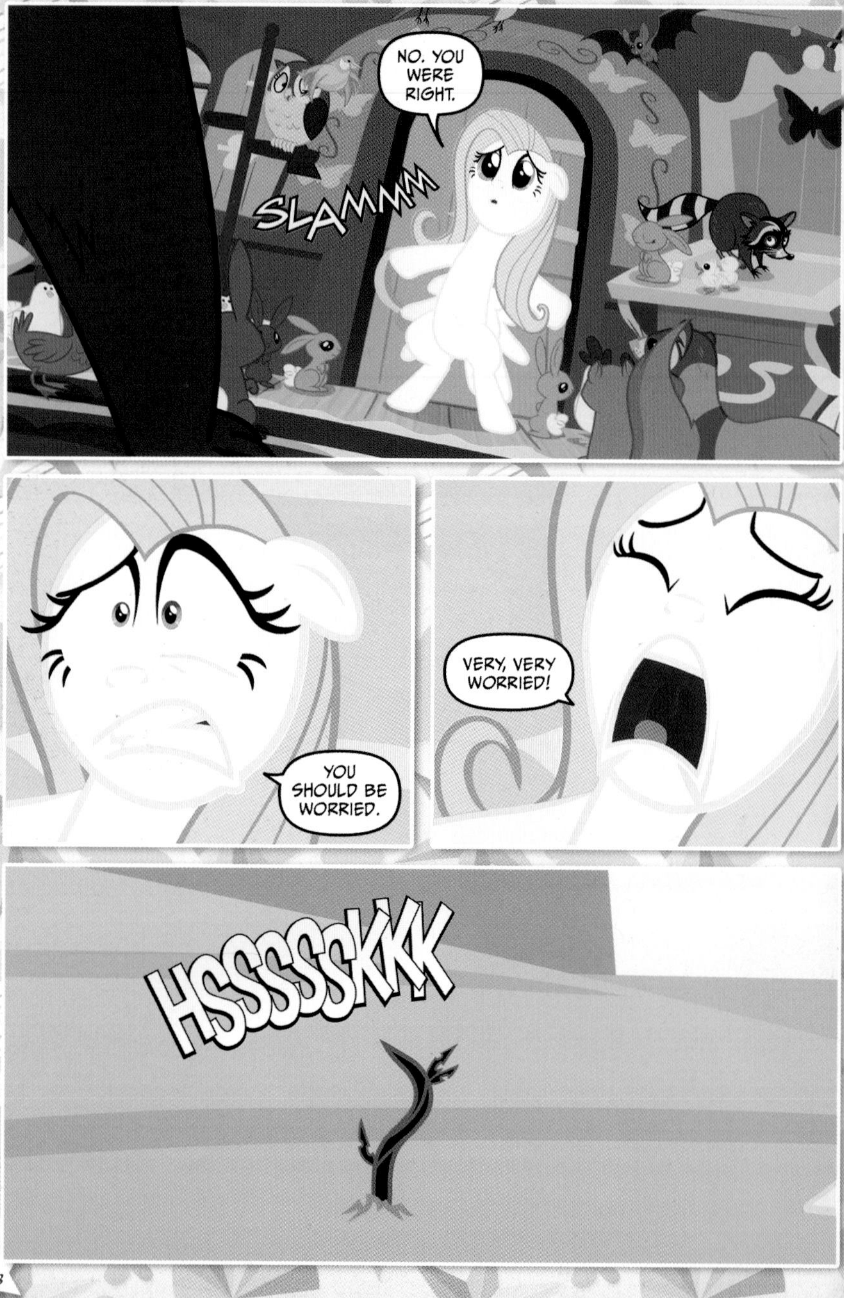
NO. YOU WERE RIGHT.
SLAMMM
YOU SHOULD BE WORRIED.
VERY, VERY WORRIED!
HSSSSSKKK

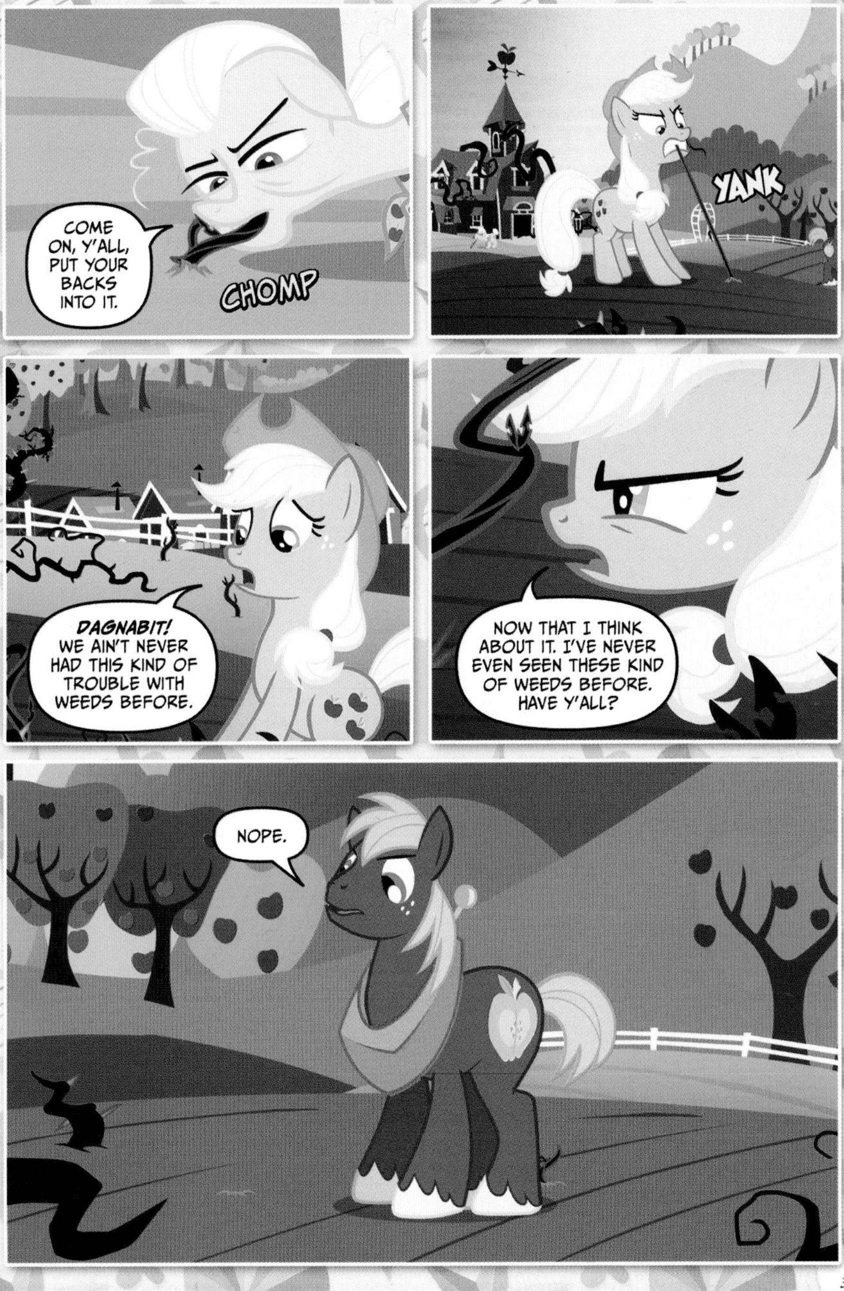
COME ON, Y'ALL, PUT YOUR BACKS INTO IT.
CHOMP
YANK
DAGNABIT! WE AIN'T NEVER HAD THIS KIND OF TROUBLE WITH WEEDS BEFORE.
NOW THAT I THINK ABOUT IT. I'VE NEVER EVEN SEEN THESE KIND OF WEEDS BEFORE. HAVE Y'ALL?
NOPE.

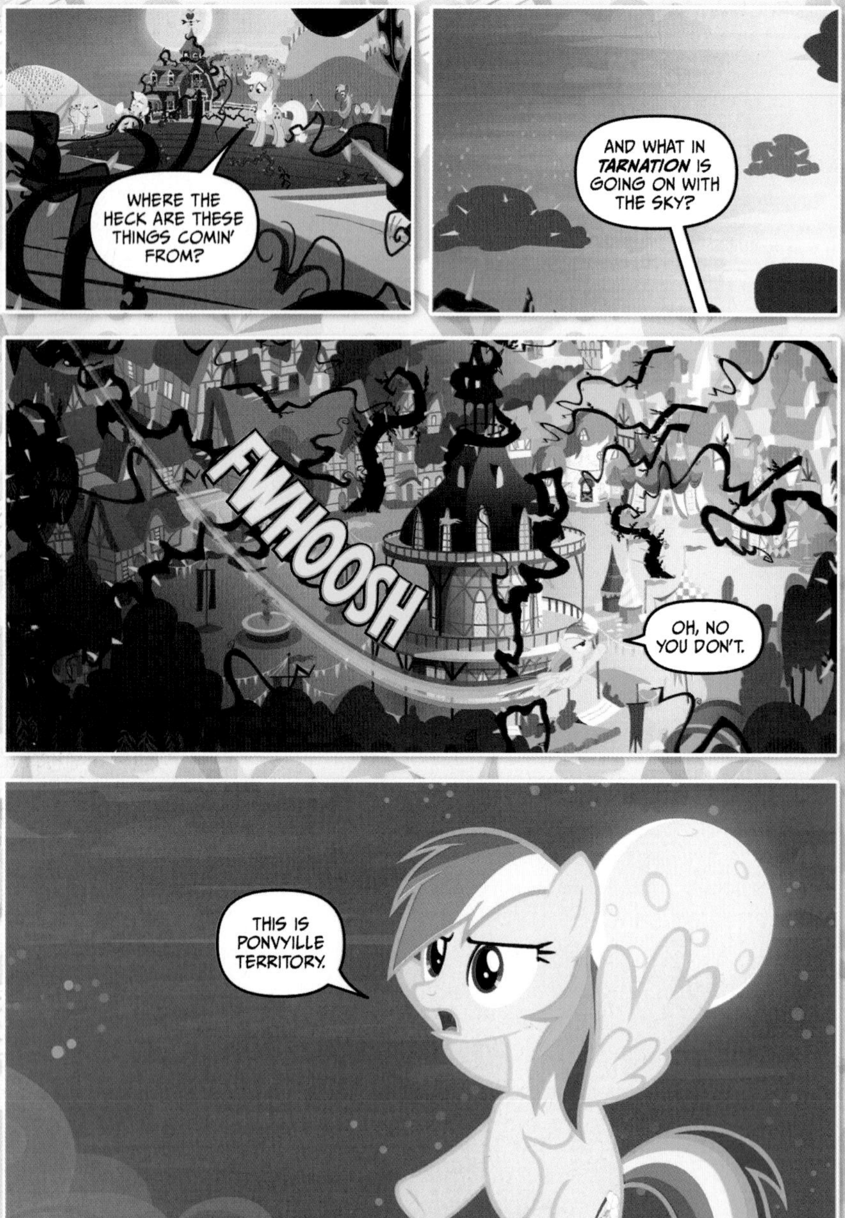
WHERE THE HECK ARE THESE THINGS COMIN' FROM?
AND WHAT IN TARNATION IS GOING ON WITH THE SKY?
FWHOOSH
OH, NO YOU DON'T.
THIS IS PONVYILLE TERRITORY.

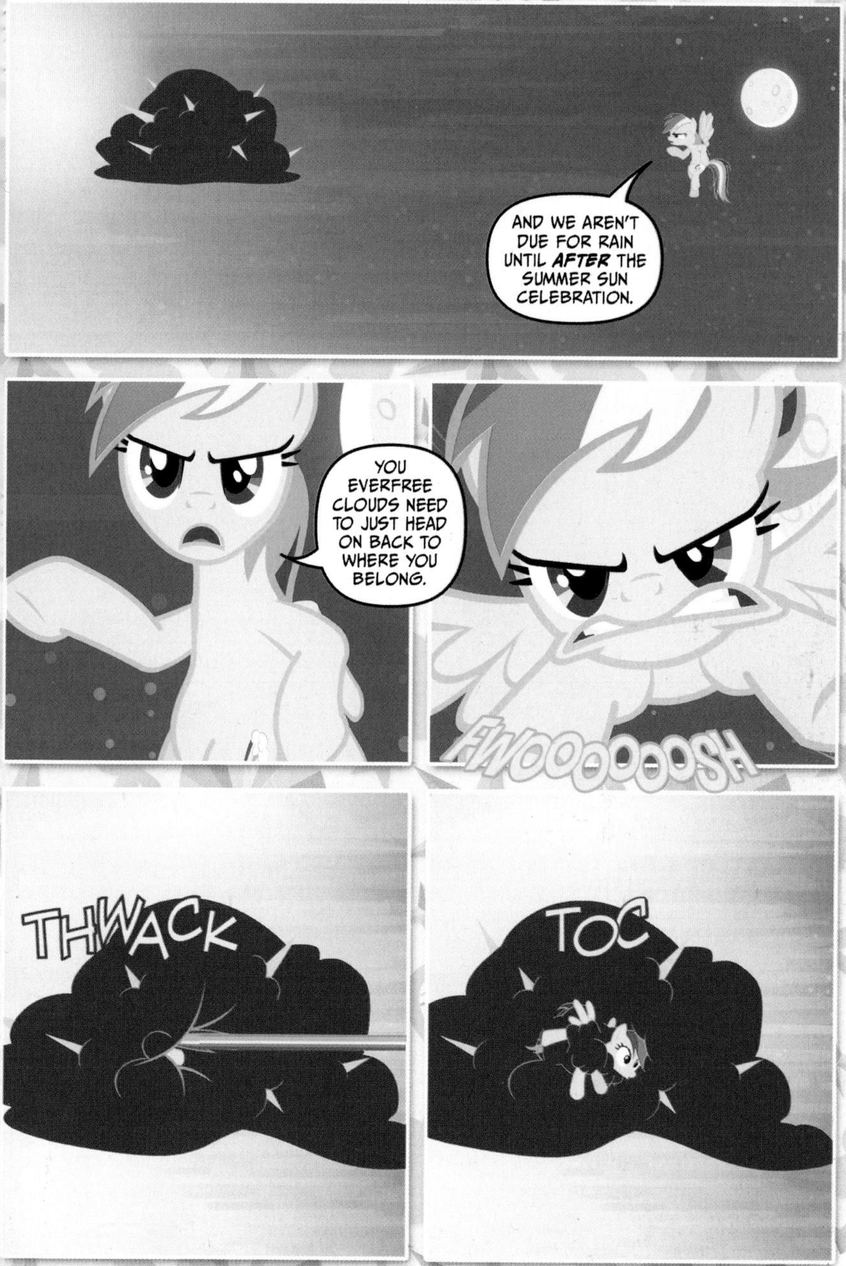
AND WE AREN'T DUE FOR RAIN UNTIL AFTER THE SUMMER SUN CELEBRATION.
YOU EVERFREE CLOUDS NEED TO JUST HEAD ON BACK TO WHERE YOU BELONG.
FWOOOOOOOSH
THWACK
TOC

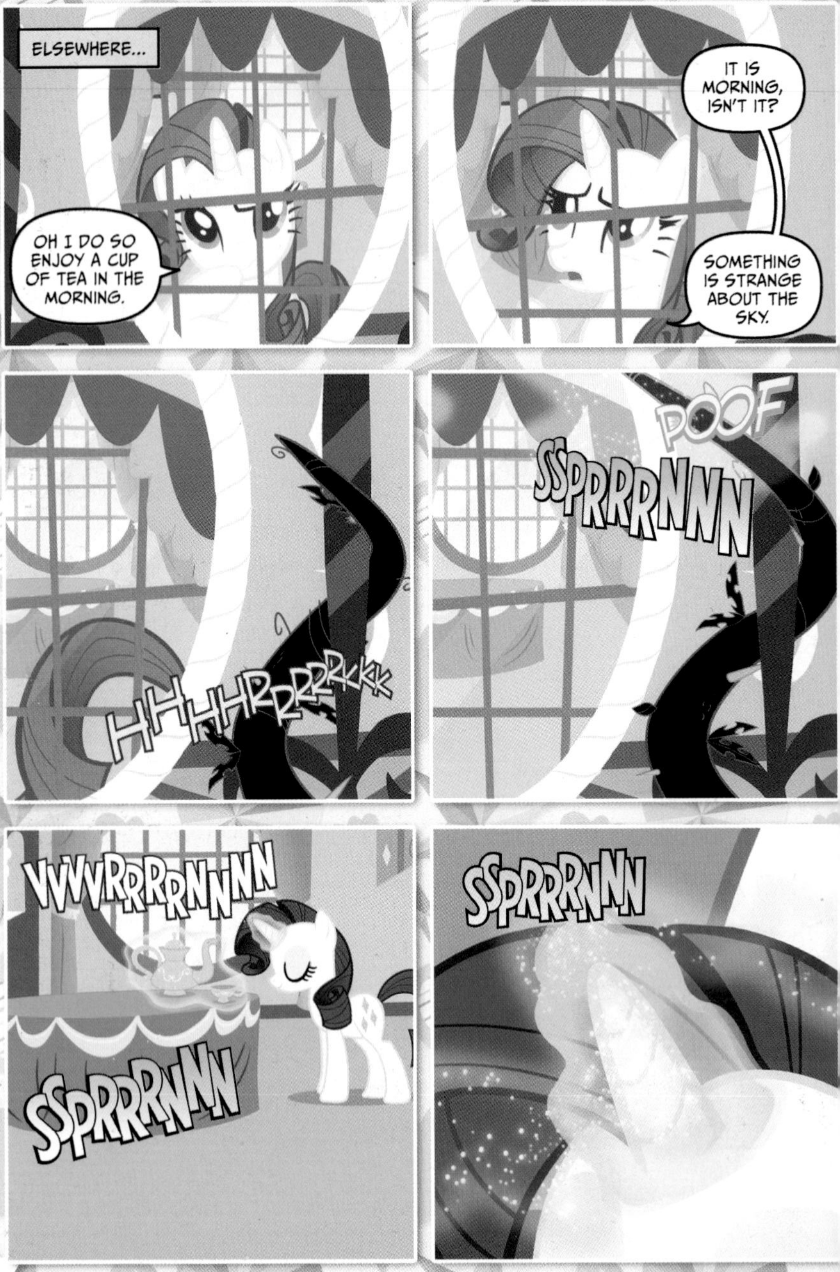
ELSEWHERE...
OH I DO SO ENJOY A CUP OF TEA IN THE MORNING.
IT IS MORNING, ISN'T IT?
SOMETHING IS STRANGE ABOUT THE SKY.
HHHHRRRRKKK
POOF
SSPRRRNNN
VVVVRRRRNNNN
SSPRRRNNN
SSPRRRNNN

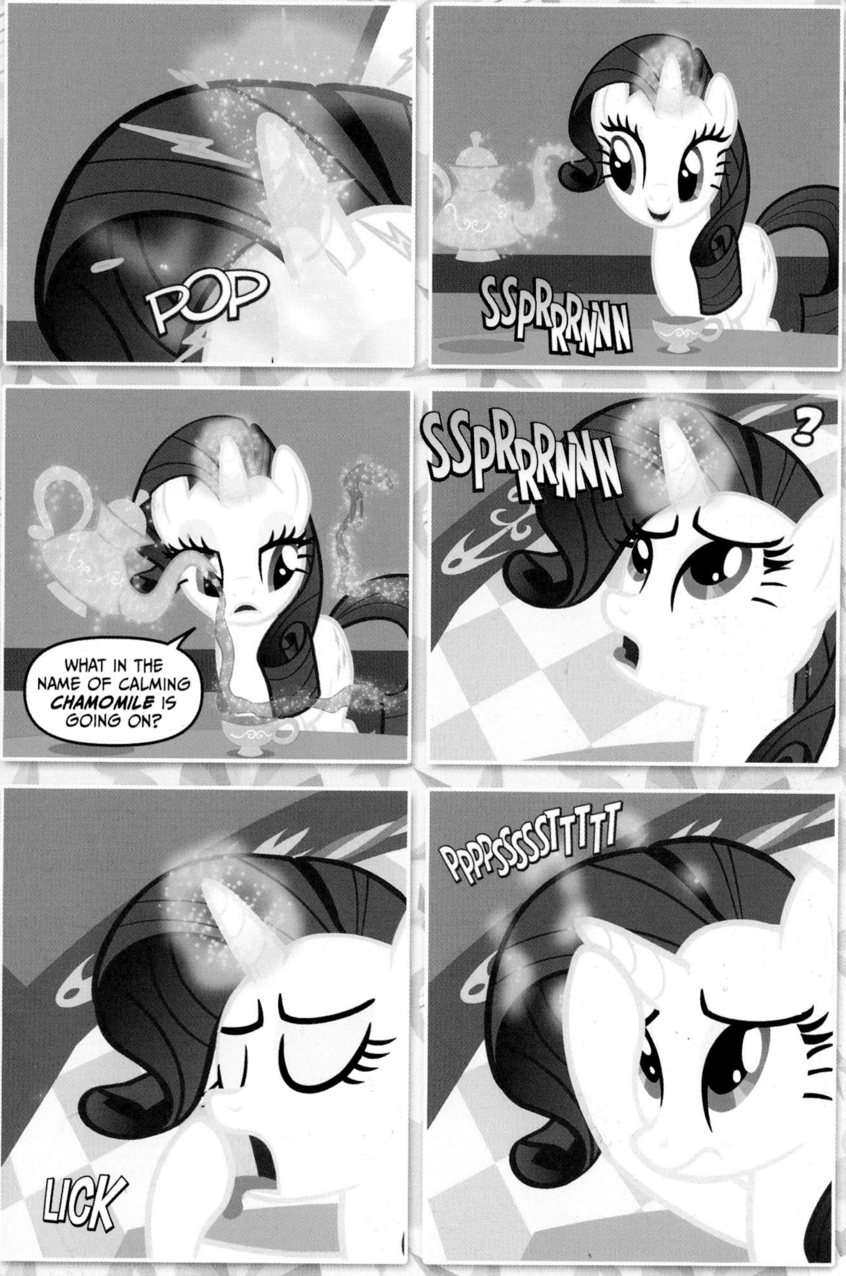
POP
SSPRRRNNN
WHAT IN THE NAME OF CALMING ***CHAMOMILE*** IS GOING ON?
SSPRRRNNN
?
LICK
PPPPSSSSSTTTTT

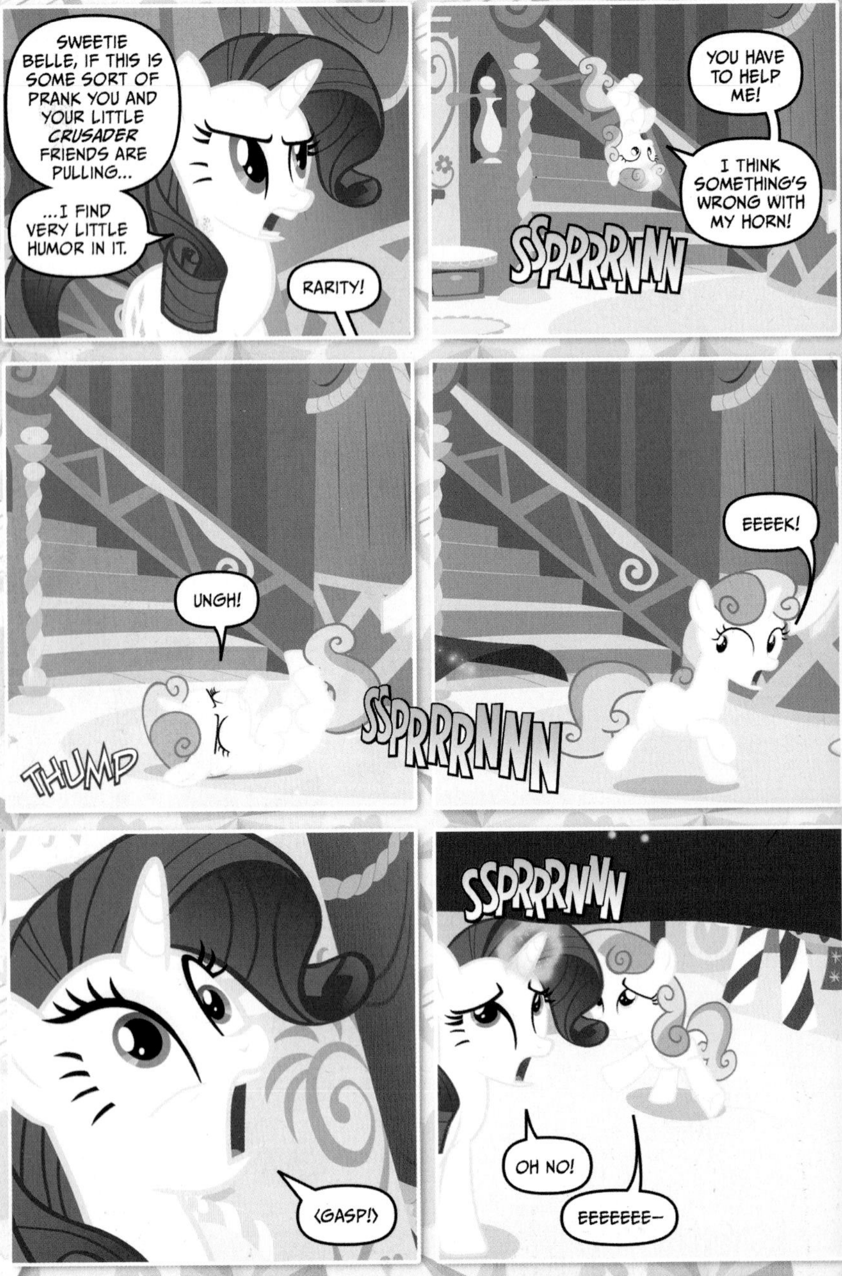
SWEETIE BELLE, IF THIS IS SOME SORT OF PRANK YOU AND YOUR LITTLE *CRUSADER* FRIENDS ARE PULLING...
...I FIND VERY LITTLE HUMOR IN IT.
RARITY!
YOU HAVE TO HELP ME!
I THINK SOMETHING'S WRONG WITH MY HORN!
SSPRRRNNN
UNGH!
THUMP
SSPRRRNNN
EEEEK!
<GASP!>
SSPRRRNNN
OH NO!
EEEEEEE–

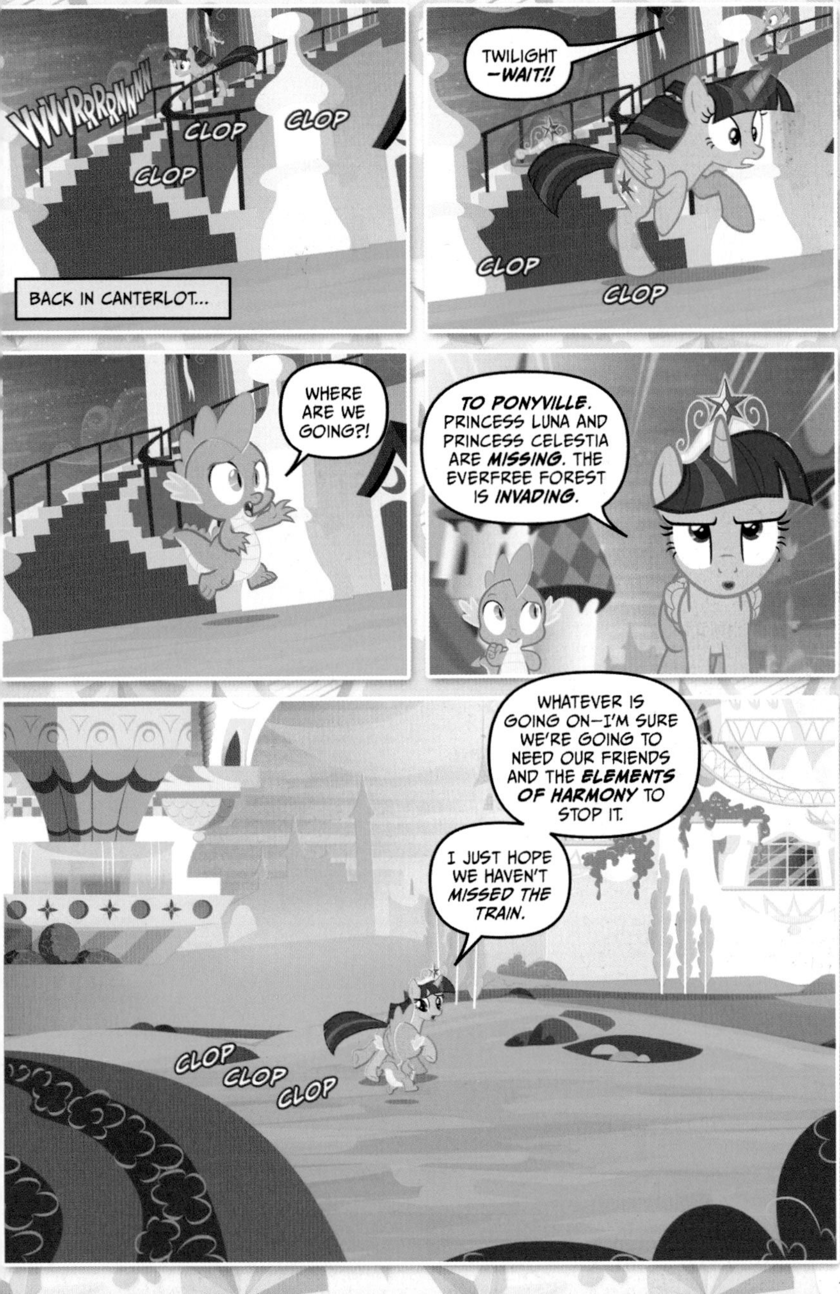
BACK IN CANTERLOT...
VVVVRRRRNNNN
CLOP
CLOP
CLOP
TWILIGHT —WAIT!!
CLOP
CLOP
WHERE ARE WE GOING?!
TO PONYVILLE. PRINCESS LUNA AND PRINCESS CELESTIA ARE MISSING. THE EVERFREE FOREST IS INVADING.
WHATEVER IS GOING ON—I'M SURE WE'RE GOING TO NEED OUR FRIENDS AND THE ELEMENTS OF HARMONY TO STOP IT.
I JUST HOPE WE HAVEN'T MISSED THE TRAIN.
CLOP
CLOP
CLOP

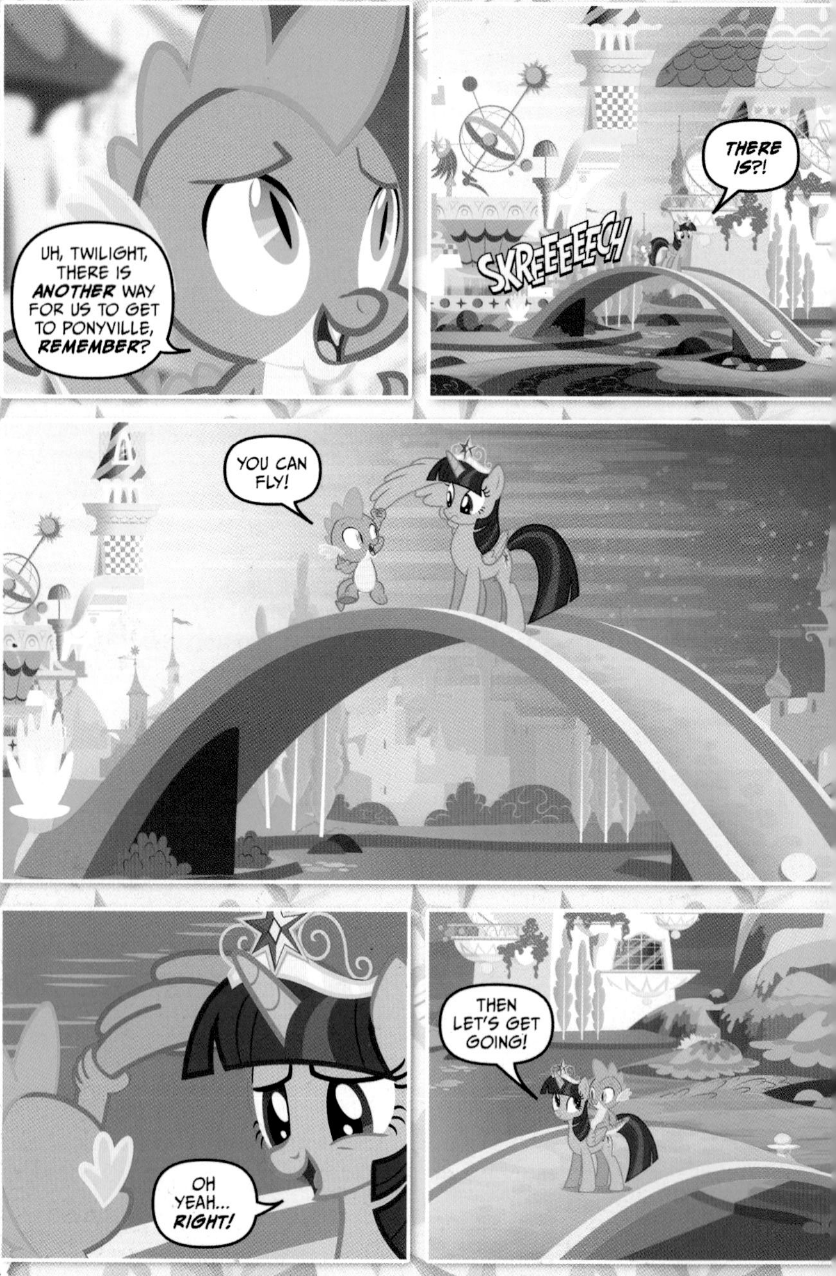

UH, TWILIGHT, THERE IS ANOTHER WAY FOR US TO GET TO PONYVILLE, REMEMBER?
SKREEEEEECH
THERE IS?!
YOU CAN FLY!
OH YEAH... RIGHT!
THEN LET'S GET GOING!

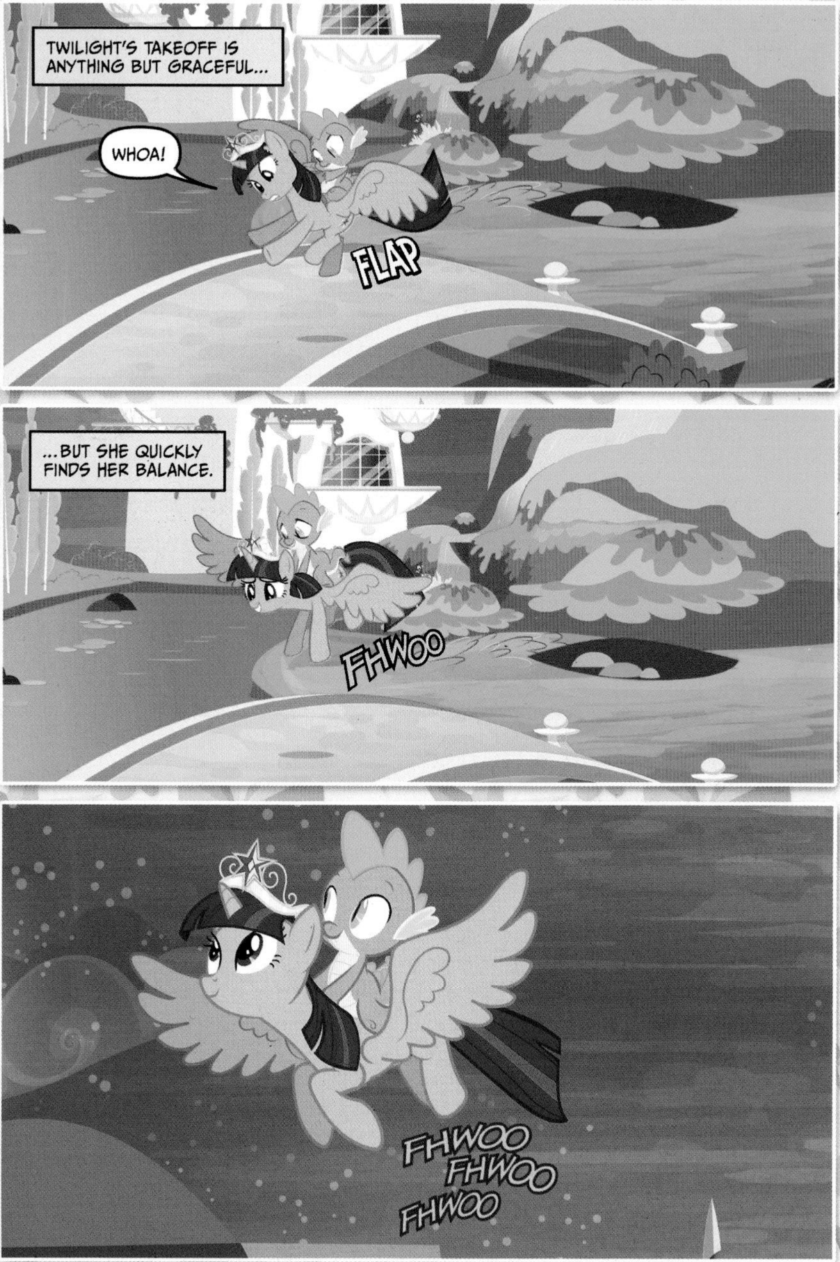
TWILIGHT'S TAKEOFF IS ANYTHING BUT GRACEFUL...
WHOA!
FLAP
...BUT SHE QUICKLY FINDS HER BALANCE.
FHWOO
FHWOO
FHWOO
FHWOO

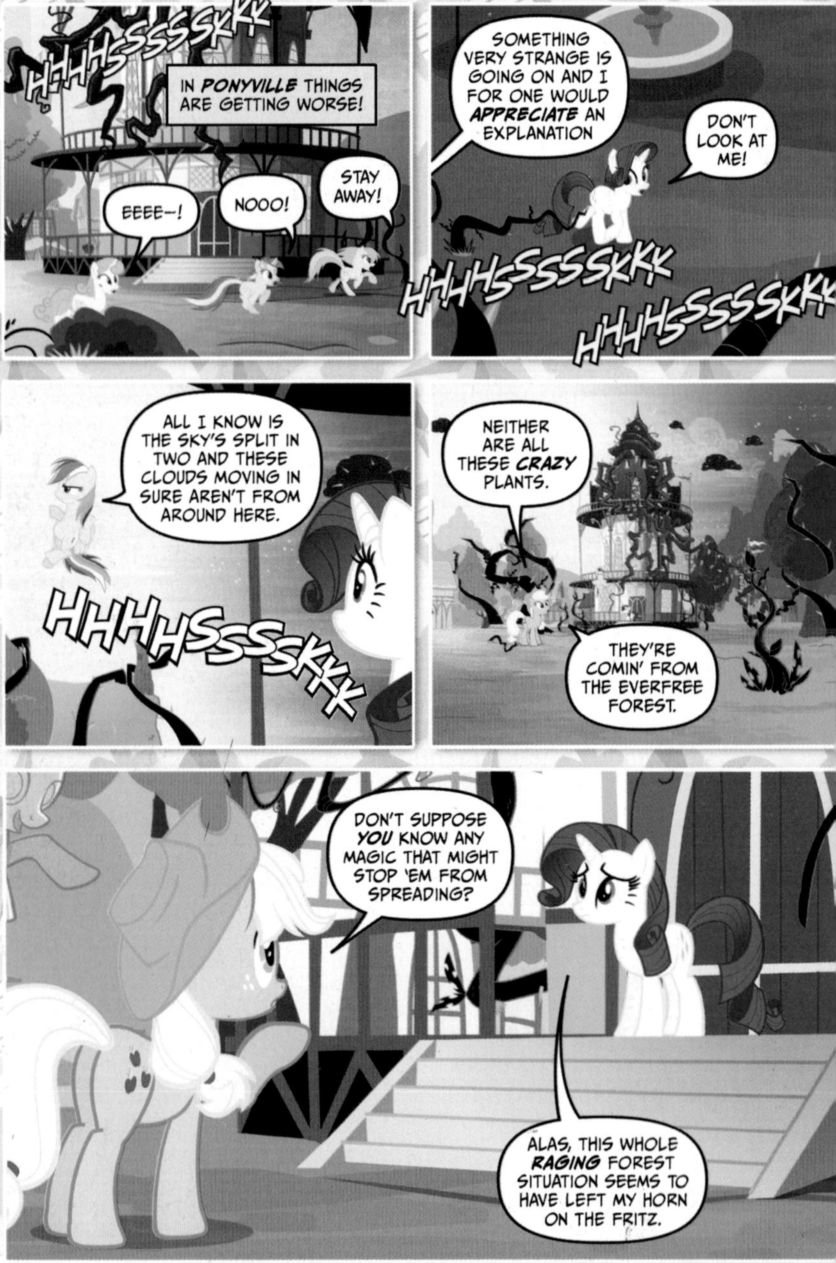
HHHHSSSSSKKK
IN PONYVILLE THINGS ARE GETTING WORSE!
EEEE--!
NOOO!
STAY AWAY!
SOMETHING VERY STRANGE IS GOING ON AND I FOR ONE WOULD APPRECIATE AN EXPLANATION
DON'T LOOK AT ME!
HHHHSSSSSKKK
HHHHSSSSSKKK
ALL I KNOW IS THE SKY'S SPLIT IN TWO AND THESE CLOUDS MOVING IN SURE AREN'T FROM AROUND HERE.
HHHHSSSSSKKK
NEITHER ARE ALL THESE CRAZY PLANTS.
THEY'RE COMIN' FROM THE EVERFREE FOREST.
DON'T SUPPOSE YOU KNOW ANY MAGIC THAT MIGHT STOP 'EM FROM SPREADING?
ALAS, THIS WHOLE RAGING FOREST SITUATION SEEMS TO HAVE LEFT MY HORN ON THE FRITZ.

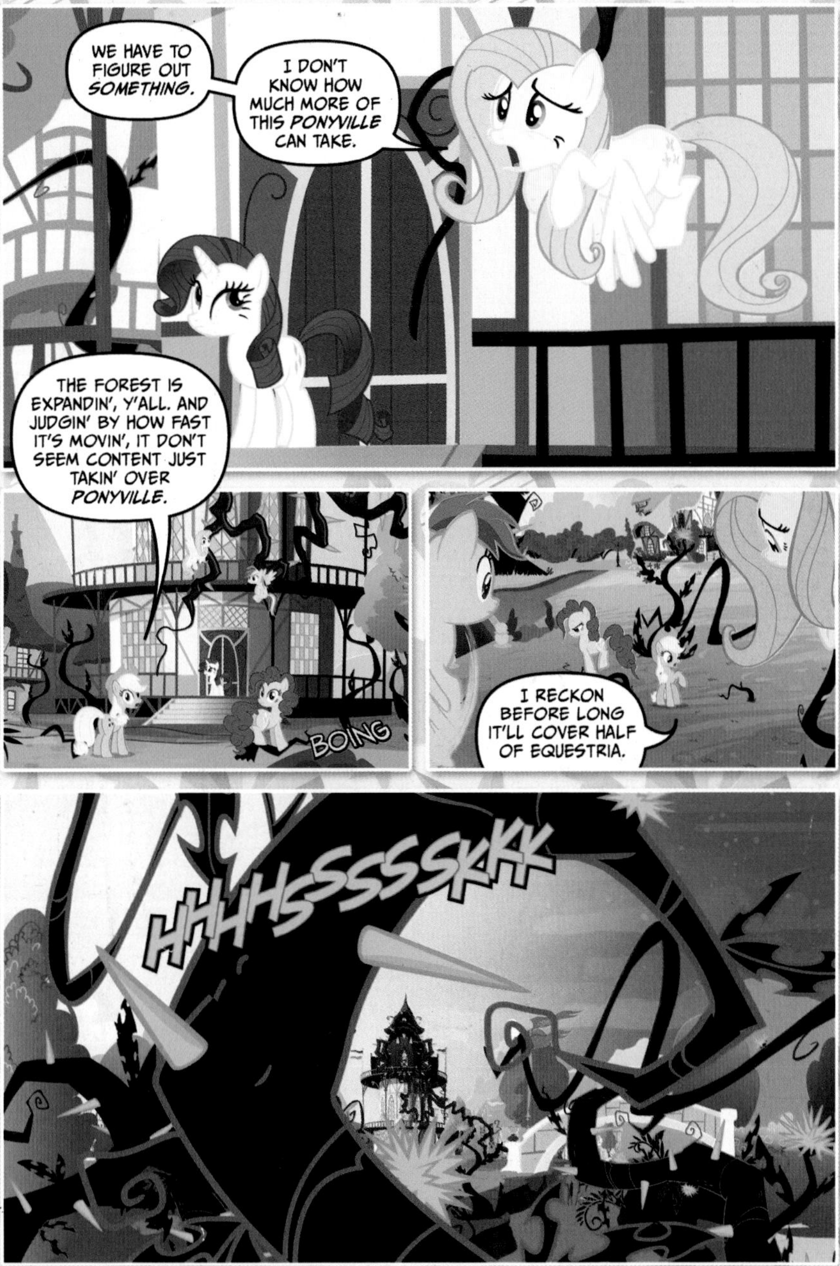
WE HAVE TO FIGURE OUT *SOMETHING.*
I DON'T KNOW HOW MUCH MORE OF THIS *PONYVILLE* CAN TAKE.
THE FOREST IS EXPANDIN', Y'ALL. AND JUDGIN' BY HOW FAST IT'S MOVIN', IT DON'T SEEM CONTENT JUST TAKIN' OVER *PONYVILLE.*
BOING
I RECKON BEFORE LONG IT'LL COVER HALF OF EQUESTRIA.
HHHHSSSSSKKK

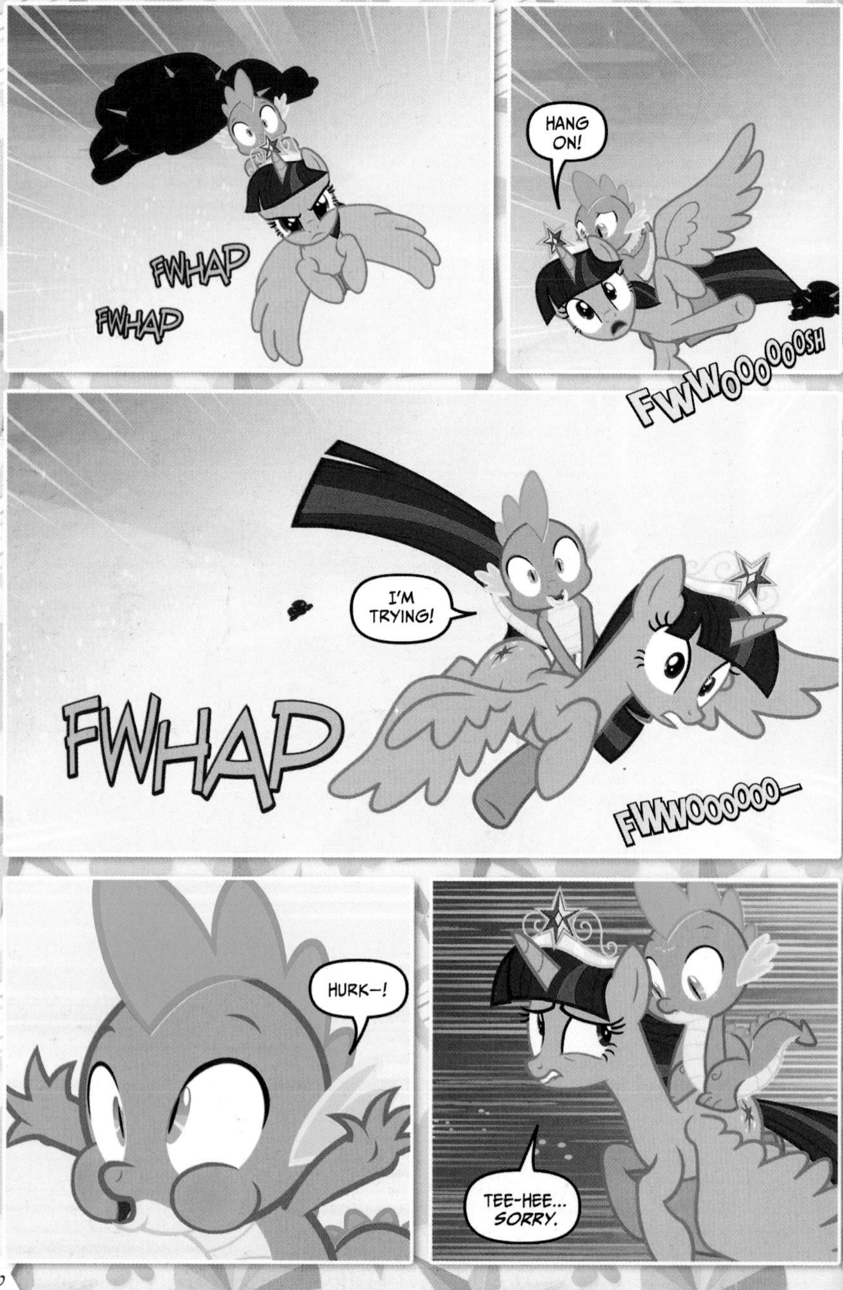
FWHAP
FWHAP
HANG ON!
FWWOOOOOOSH
I'M TRYING!
FWHAP
FWWOOOOOO—
HURK—!
TEE-HEE... SORRY.

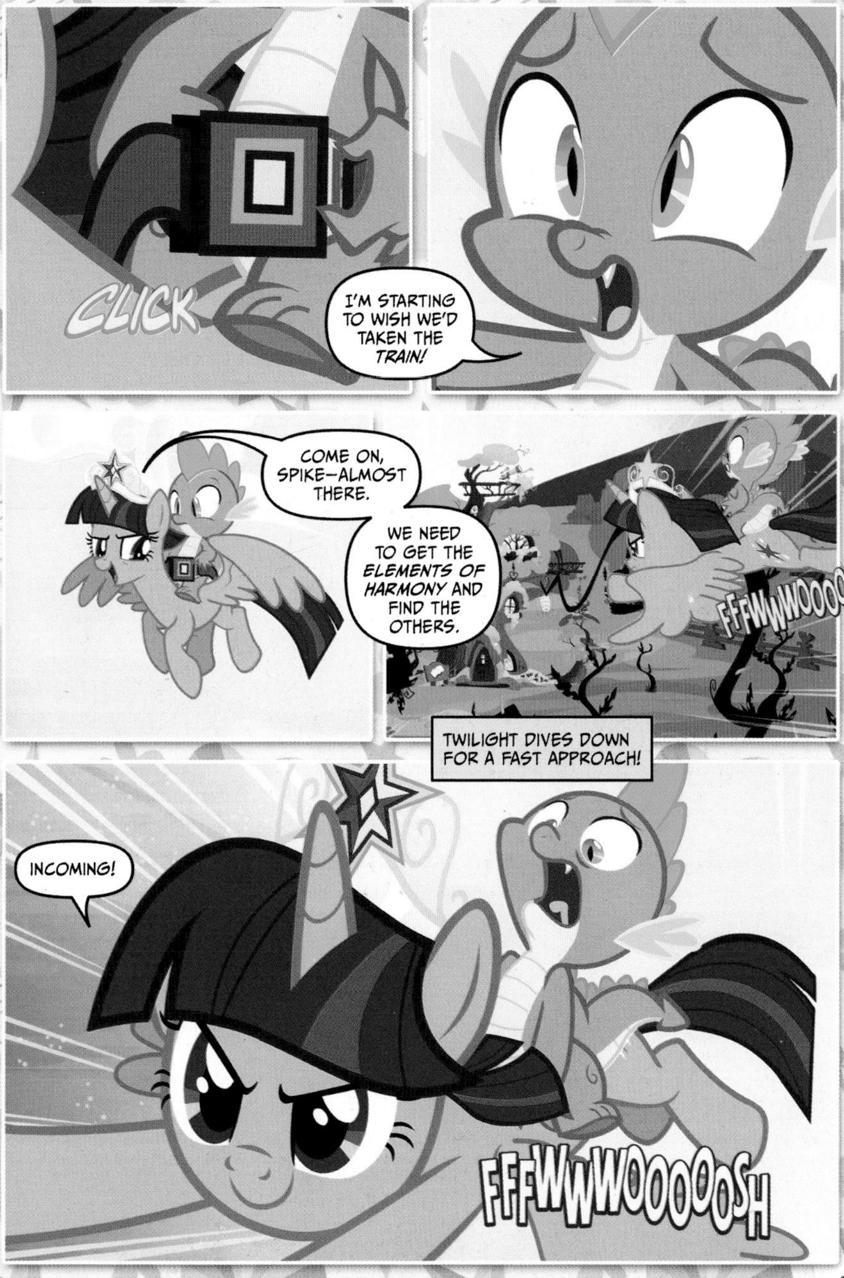
CLICK
I'M STARTING TO WISH WE'D TAKEN THE *TRAIN!*
COME ON, SPIKE—ALMOST THERE.
WE NEED TO GET THE *ELEMENTS OF HARMONY* AND FIND THE OTHERS.
FFFWWWOOOOO
TWILIGHT DIVES DOWN FOR A FAST APPROACH!
INCOMING!
FFFWWWOOOOOSH

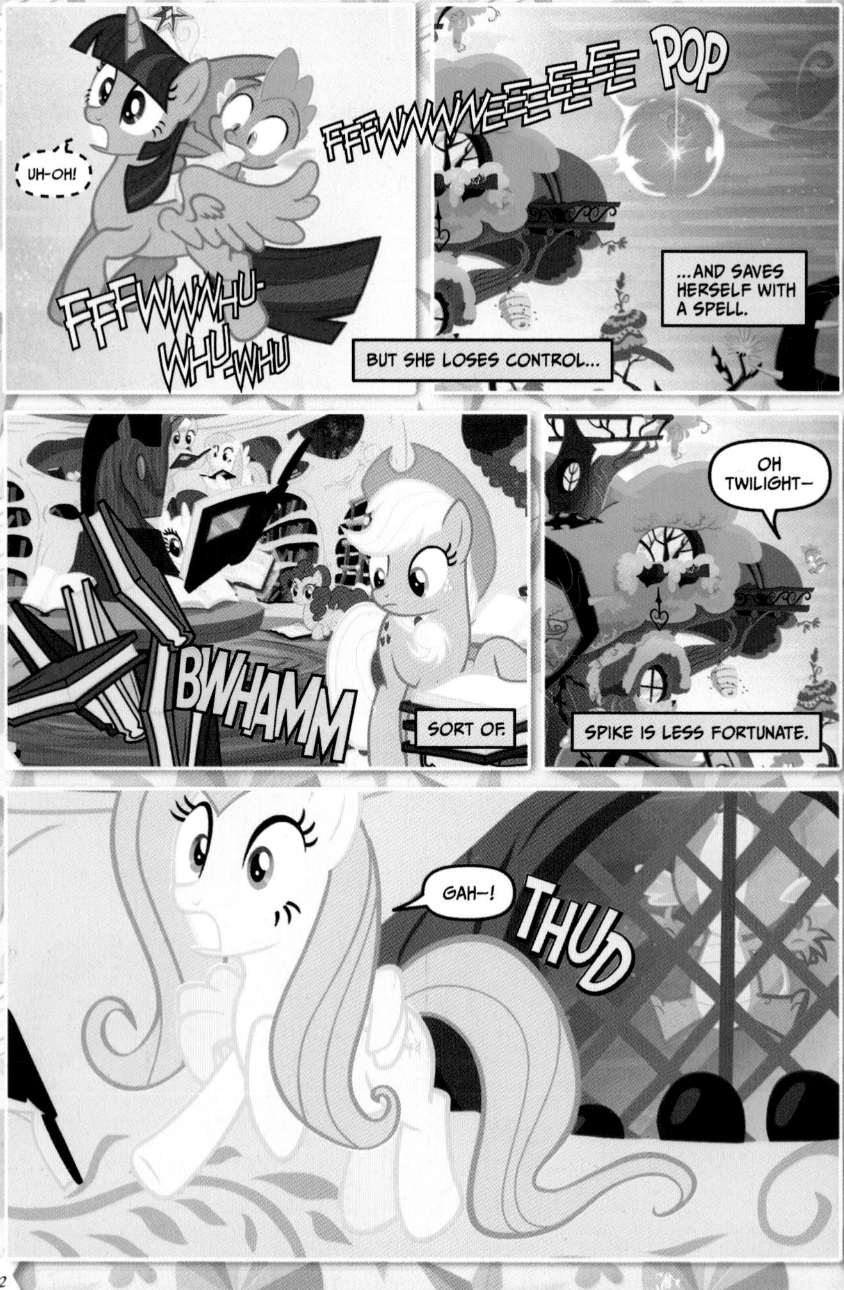
UH-OH!
FFFWWWHU-WHU-WHU
FFFWWWWEEEEEEEE POP
BUT SHE LOSES CONTROL...
...AND SAVES HERSELF WITH A SPELL.
BWHAMM
SORT OF.
OH TWILIGHT—
SPIKE IS LESS FORTUNATE.
GAH—!
THUD

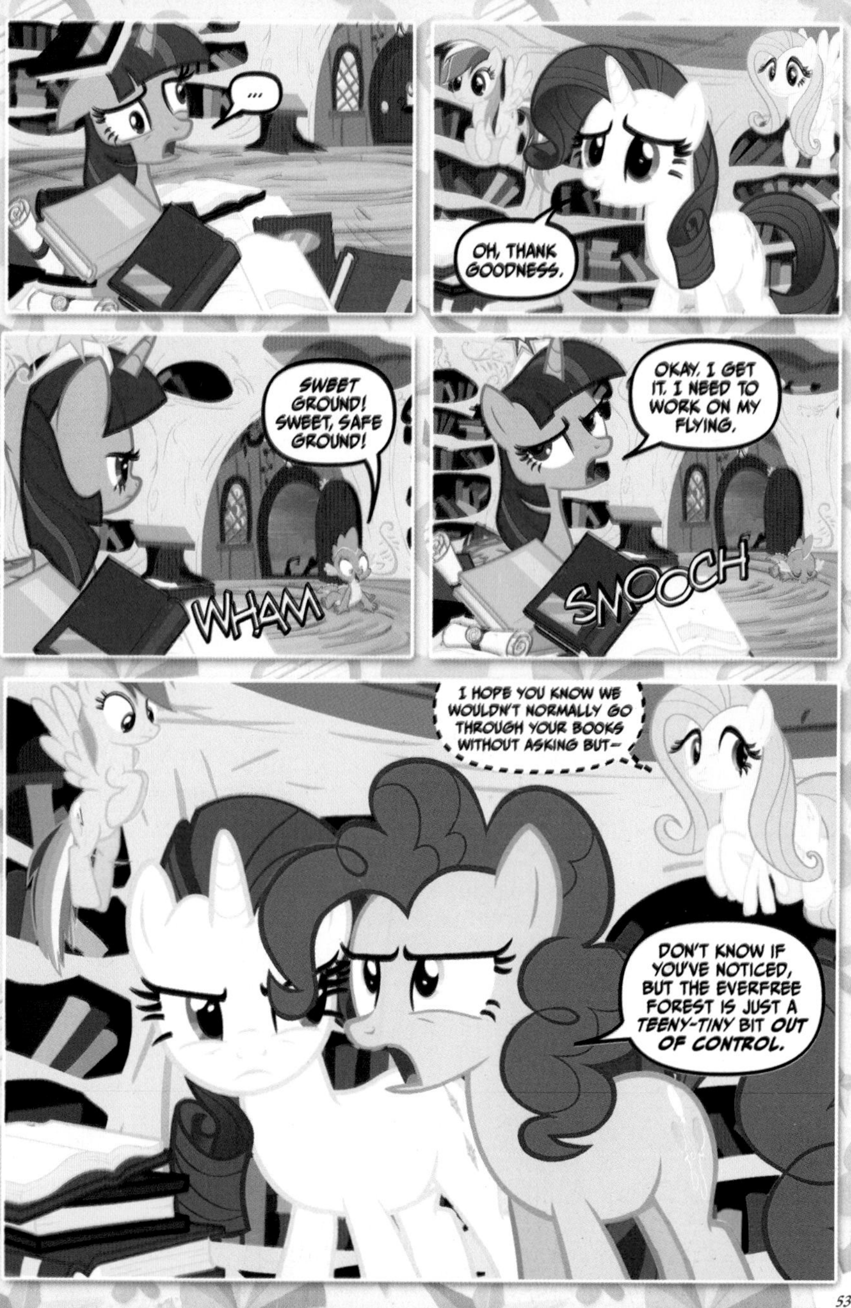
...
OH, THANK GOODNESS.
SWEET GROUND! SWEET, SAFE GROUND!
WHAM
OKAY. I GET IT. I NEED TO WORK ON MY FLYING.
SMOOCH
I HOPE YOU KNOW WE WOULDN'T NORMALLY GO THROUGH YOUR BOOKS WITHOUT ASKING BUT—
DON'T KNOW IF YOU'VE NOTICED, BUT THE EVERFREE FOREST IS JUST A *TEENY-TINY* BIT **OUT OF CONTROL.**

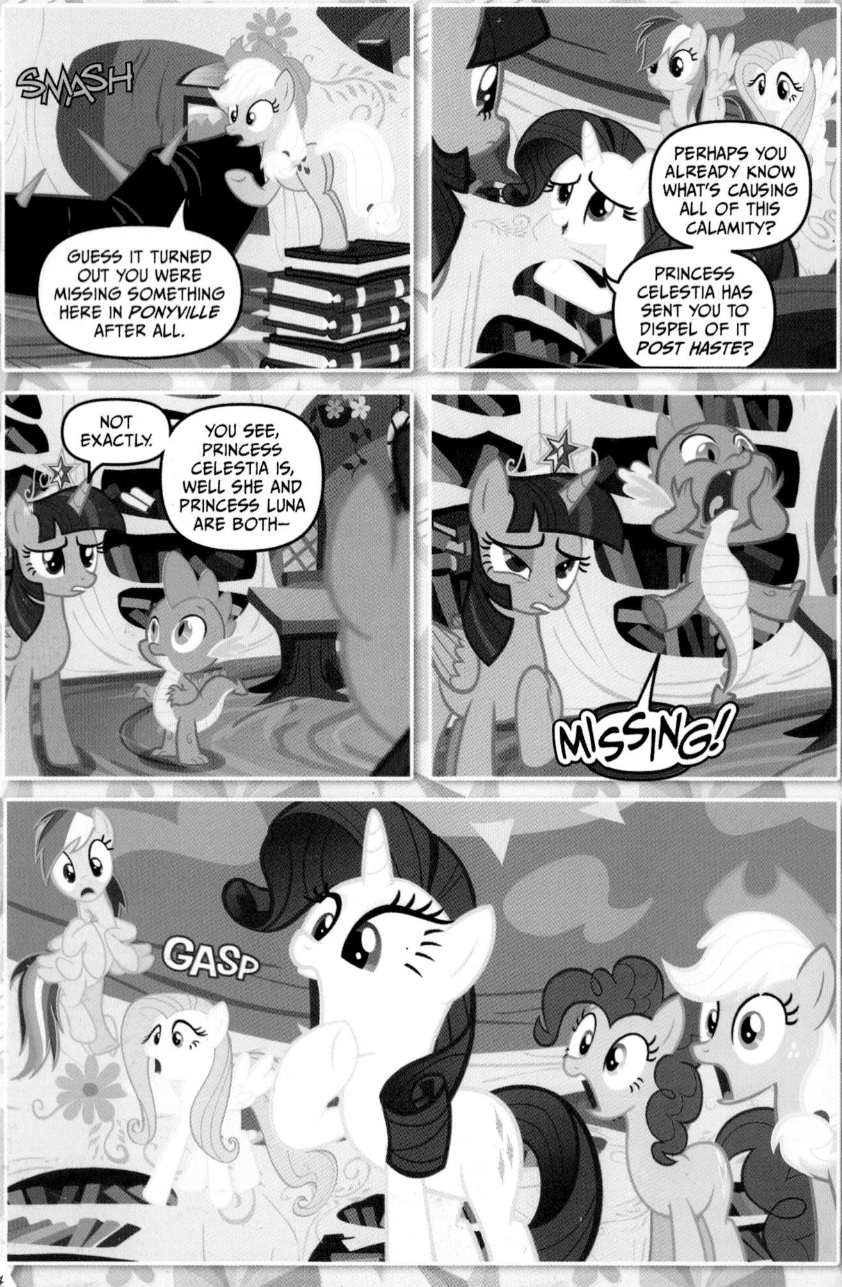
SMASH
GUESS IT TURNED OUT YOU WERE MISSING SOMETHING HERE IN *PONYVILLE* AFTER ALL.
PERHAPS YOU ALREADY KNOW WHAT'S CAUSING ALL OF THIS CALAMITY?
PRINCESS CELESTIA HAS SENT YOU TO DISPEL OF IT *POST HASTE*?
NOT EXACTLY.
YOU SEE, PRINCESS CELESTIA IS, WELL SHE AND PRINCESS LUNA ARE BOTH—
MISSING!
GASP

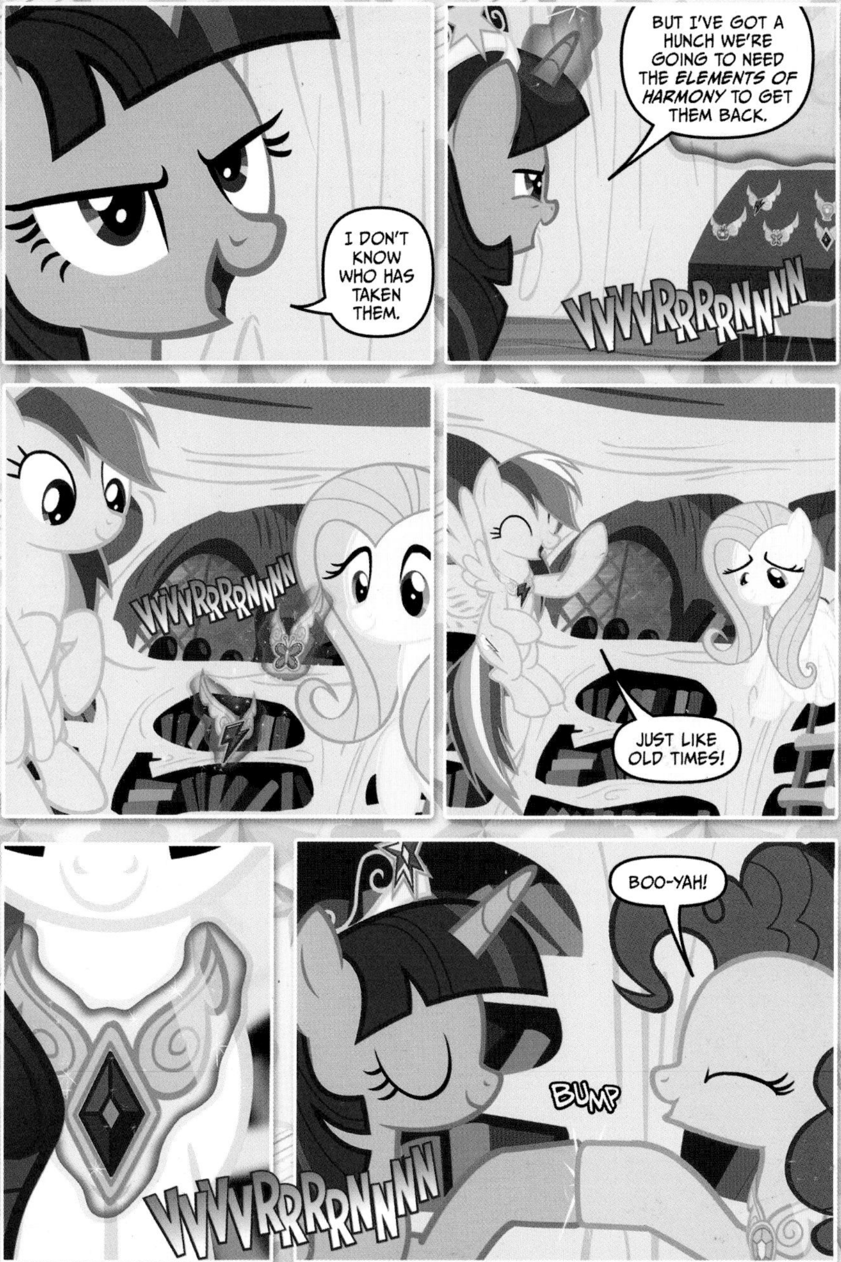

I DON'T KNOW WHO HAS TAKEN THEM.
BUT I'VE GOT A HUNCH WE'RE GOING TO NEED THE *ELEMENTS OF HARMONY* TO GET THEM BACK.
VVVVRRRRNNNN
VVVVRRRRNNNN
JUST LIKE OLD TIMES!
VVVVRRRRNNNN
BOO-YAH!
BUMP

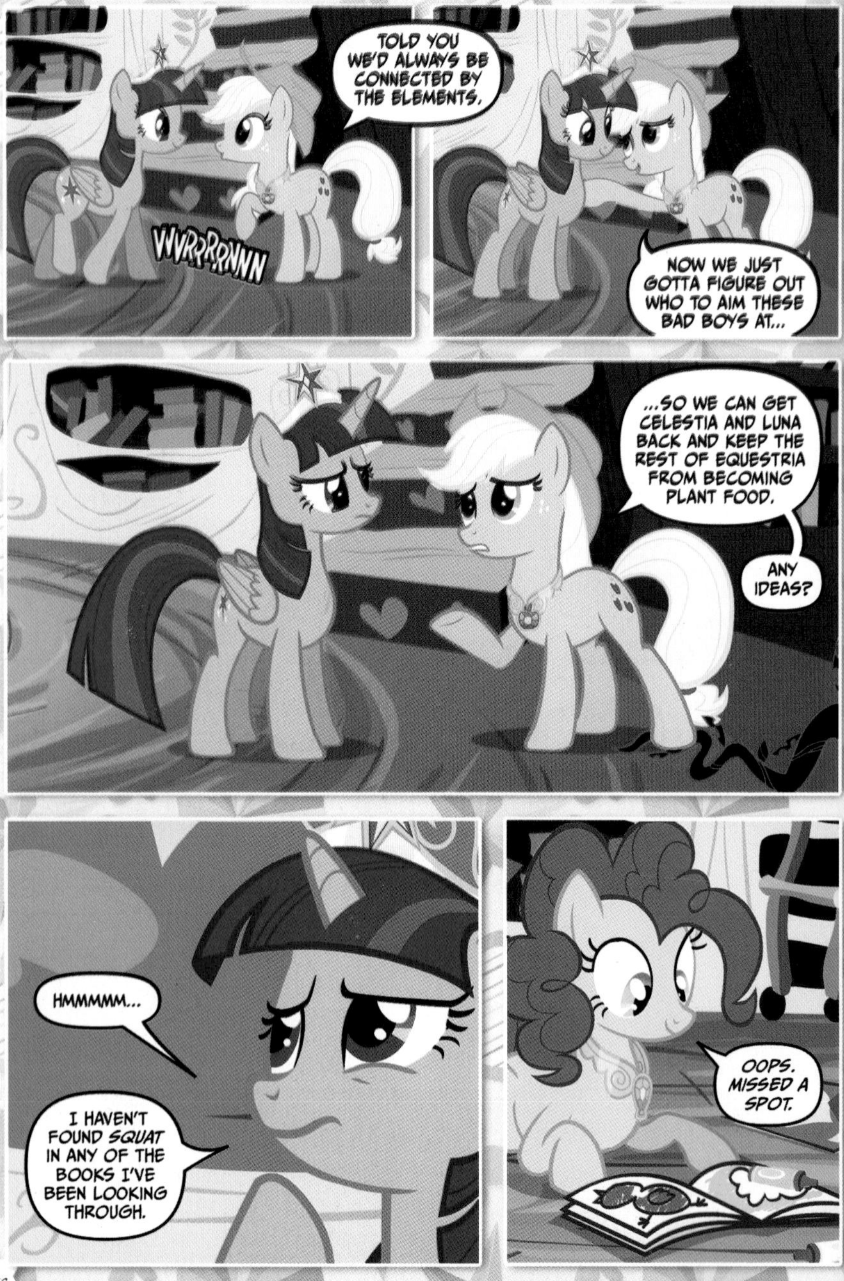
TOLD YOU WE'D ALWAYS BE CONNECTED BY THE ELEMENTS.
VVVRRRRNNN
NOW WE JUST GOTTA FIGURE OUT WHO TO AIM THESE BAD BOYS AT...
...SO WE CAN GET CELESTIA AND LUNA BACK AND KEEP THE REST OF EQUESTRIA FROM BECOMING PLANT FOOD.
ANY IDEAS?
HMMMMM...
I HAVEN'T FOUND *SQUAT* IN ANY OF THE BOOKS I'VE BEEN LOOKING THROUGH.
OOPS. MISSED A SPOT.

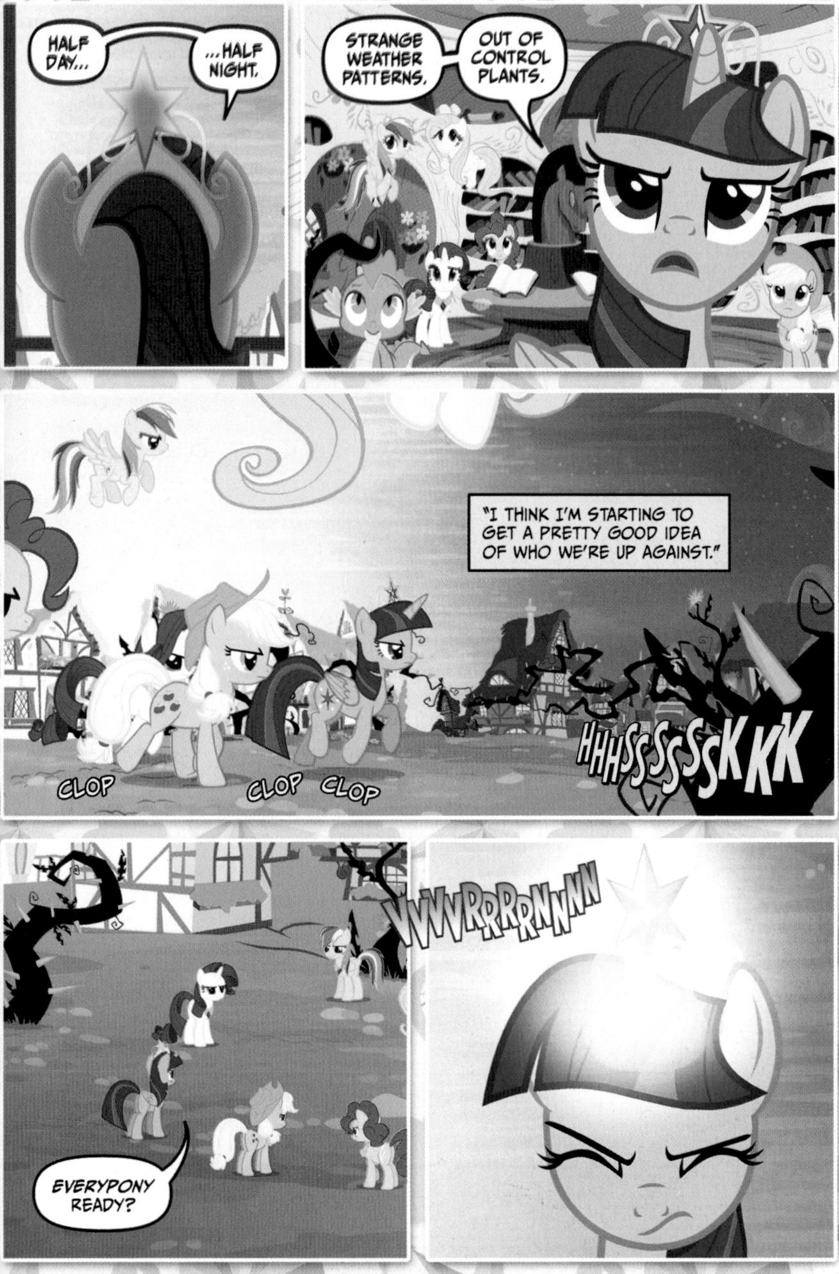
HALF DAY...
...HALF NIGHT.
STRANGE WEATHER PATTERNS.
OUT OF CONTROL PLANTS.
"I THINK I'M STARTING TO GET A PRETTY GOOD IDEA OF WHO WE'RE UP AGAINST."
CLOP
CLOP CLOP
HHHSSSSSSKKK
EVERYPONY READY?
VVVVRRRRNNNN

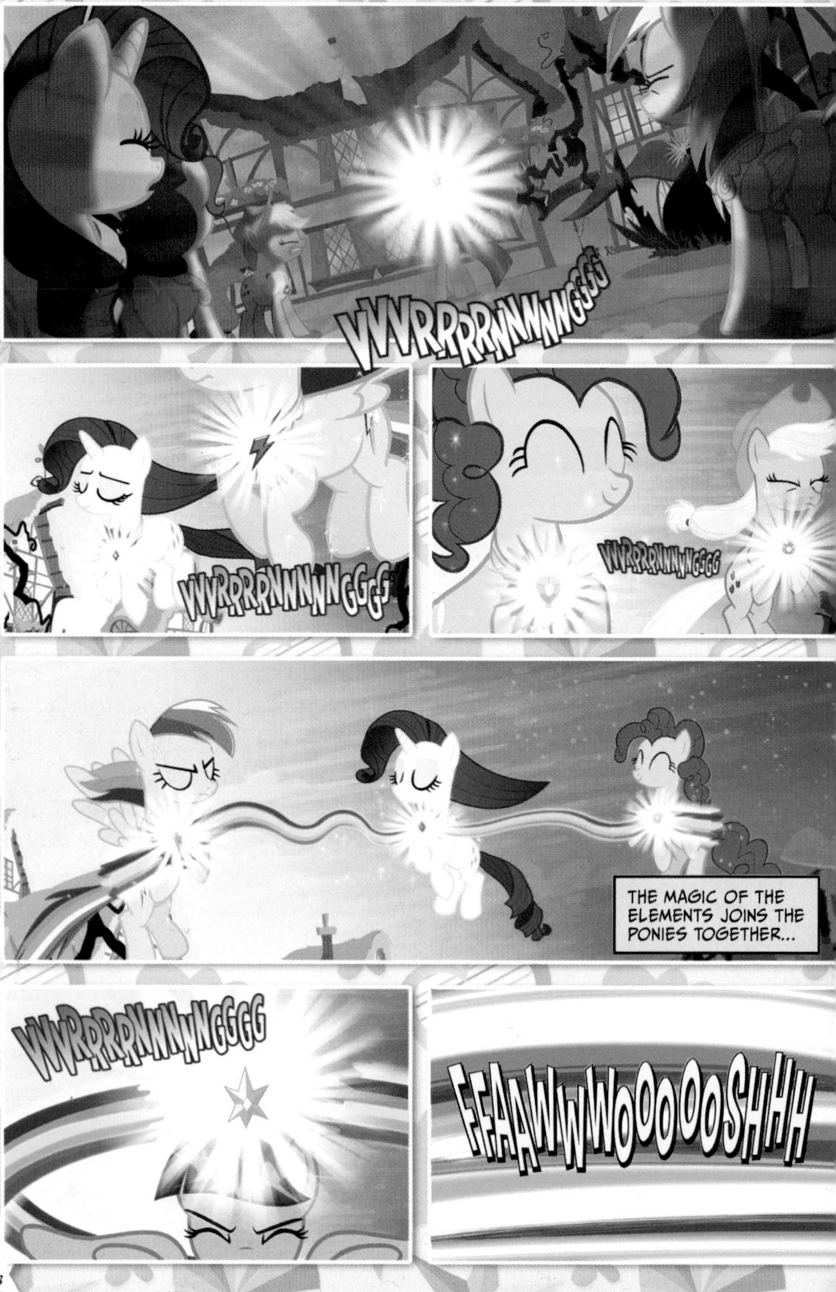
VVVRRRRNNNNNGGGG
VVVRRRRNNNNNGGGG
VVVRRRRNNNNNGGGG
THE MAGIC OF THE ELEMENTS JOINS THE PONIES TOGETHER...
VVVRRRRNNNNNGGGG
FFAAWWWOOOOOSHHH

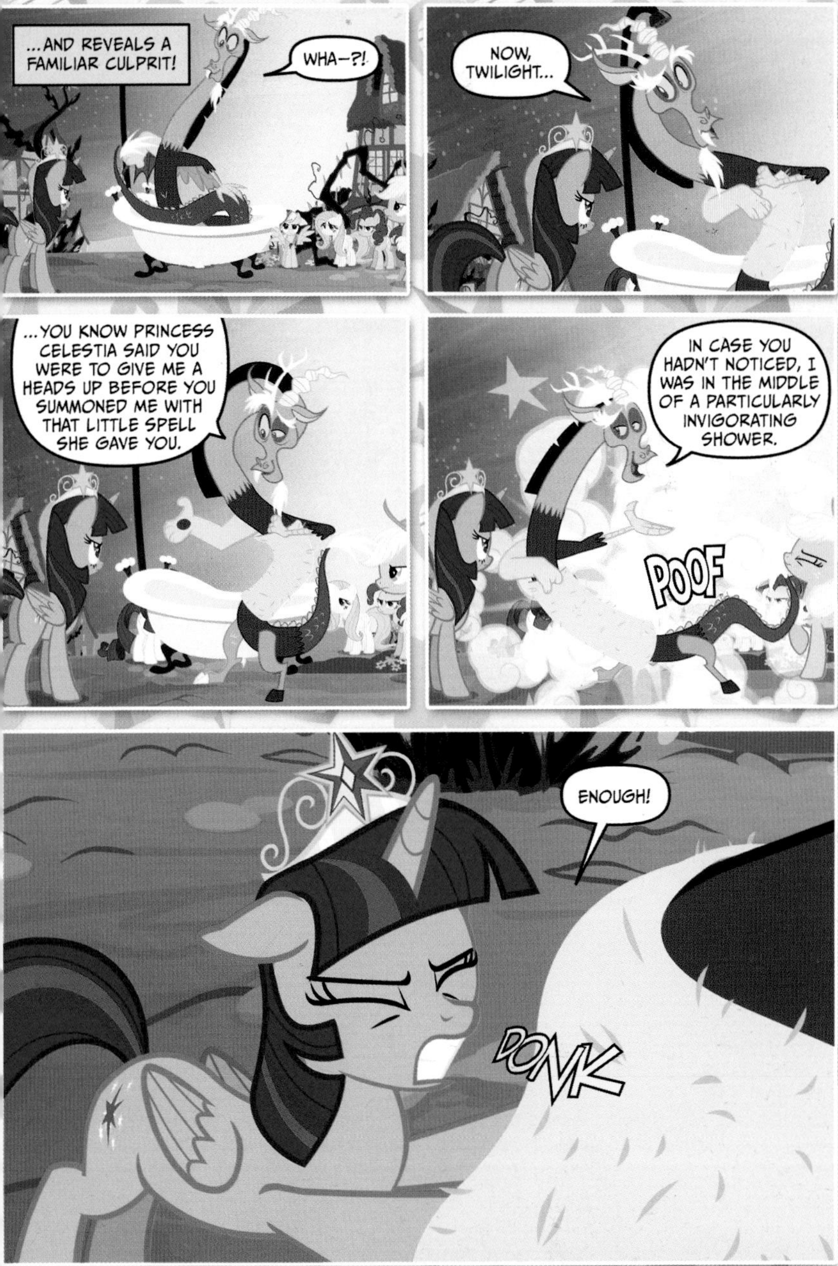
...AND REVEALS A FAMILIAR CULPRIT!
WHA–?!
NOW, TWILIGHT...
...YOU KNOW PRINCESS CELESTIA SAID YOU WERE TO GIVE ME A HEADS UP BEFORE YOU SUMMONED ME WITH THAT LITTLE SPELL SHE GAVE YOU.
IN CASE YOU HADN'T NOTICED, I WAS IN THE MIDDLE OF A PARTICULARLY INVIGORATING SHOWER.
POOF
ENOUGH!
DONK

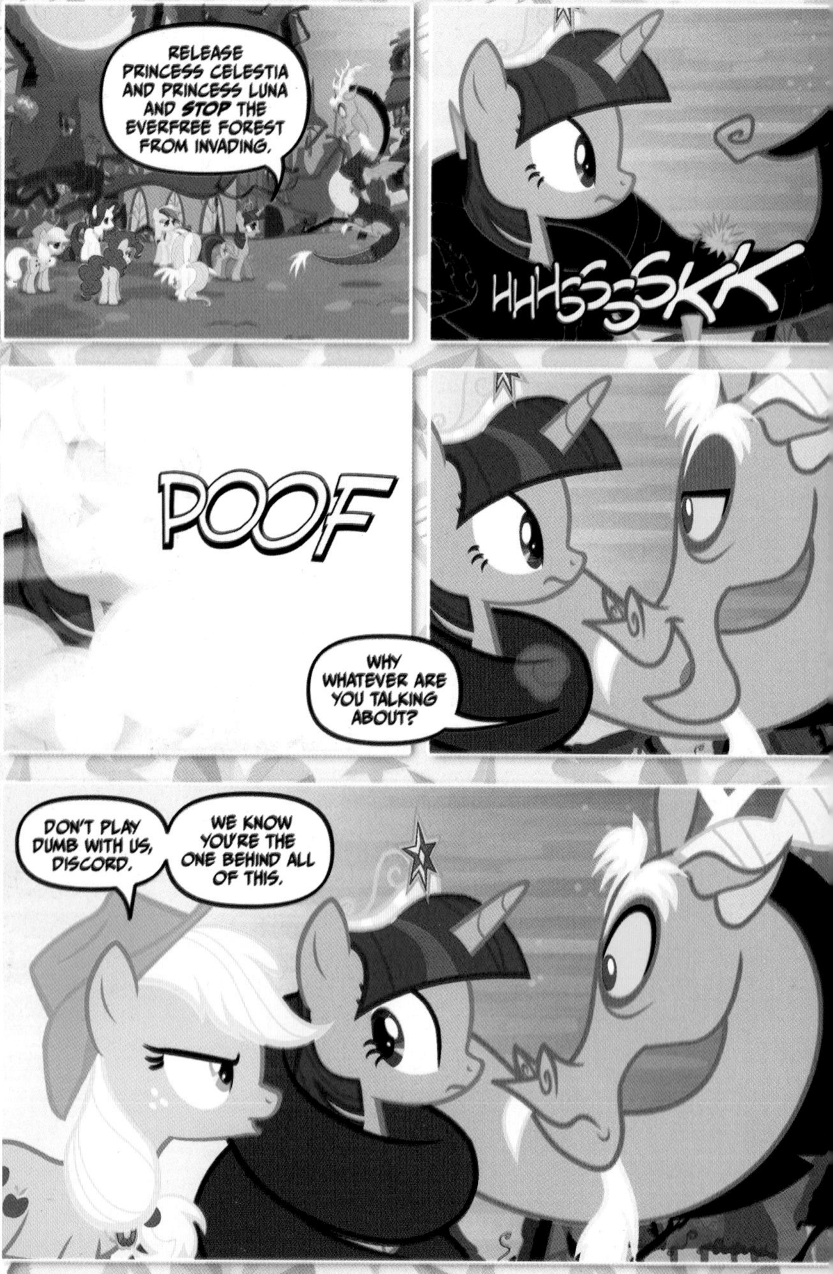
RELEASE PRINCESS CELESTIA AND PRINCESS LUNA AND STOP THE EVERFREE FOREST FROM INVADING.
HHHSSSSKK
POOF
WHY WHATEVER ARE YOU TALKING ABOUT?
DON'T PLAY DUMB WITH US, DISCORD.
WE KNOW YOU'RE THE ONE BEHIND ALL OF THIS.

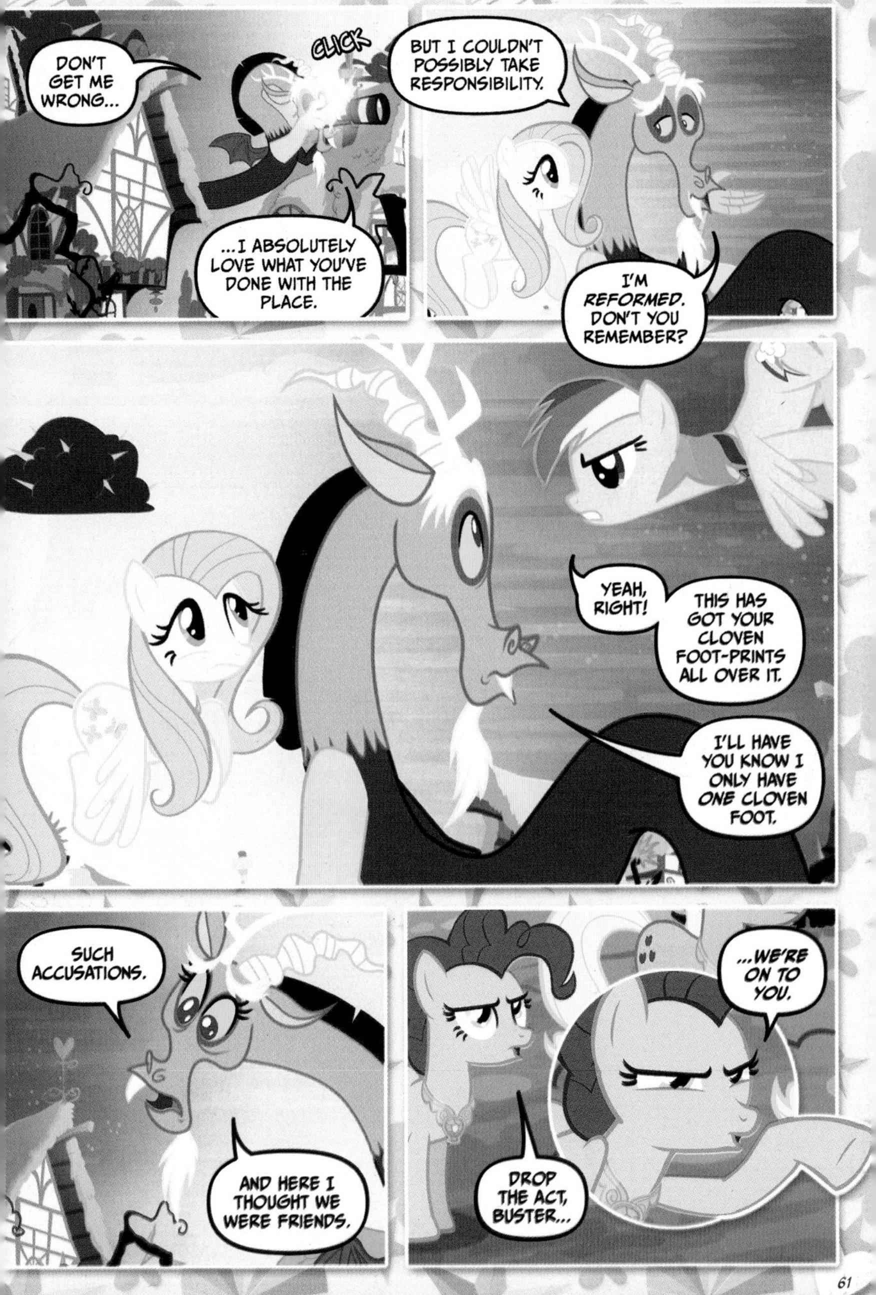
DON'T GET ME WRONG...
CLICK
...I ABSOLUTELY LOVE WHAT YOU'VE DONE WITH THE PLACE.
BUT I COULDN'T POSSIBLY TAKE RESPONSIBILITY.
I'M *REFORMED.* DON'T YOU REMEMBER?
YEAH, RIGHT!
THIS HAS GOT YOUR CLOVEN FOOT-PRINTS ALL OVER IT.
I'LL HAVE YOU KNOW I ONLY HAVE *ONE* CLOVEN FOOT.
SUCH ACCUSATIONS.
AND HERE I THOUGHT WE WERE FRIENDS.
DROP THE ACT, BUSTER...
...WE'RE ON TO YOU.

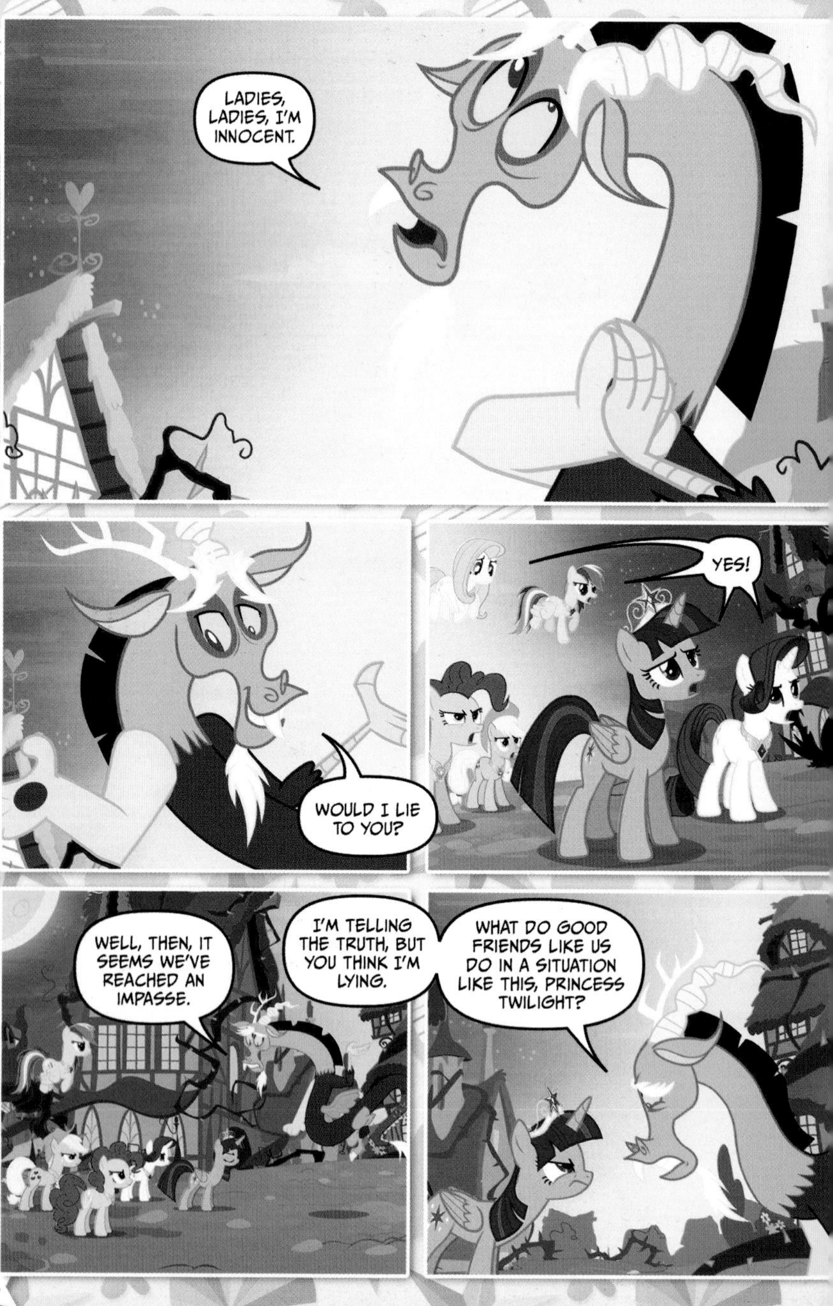
LADIES, LADIES, I'M INNOCENT.
WOULD I LIE TO YOU?
YES!
WELL, THEN, IT SEEMS WE'VE REACHED AN IMPASSE.
I'M TELLING THE TRUTH, BUT YOU THINK I'M LYING.
WHAT DO GOOD FRIENDS LIKE US DO IN A SITUATION LIKE THIS, PRINCESS TWILIGHT?

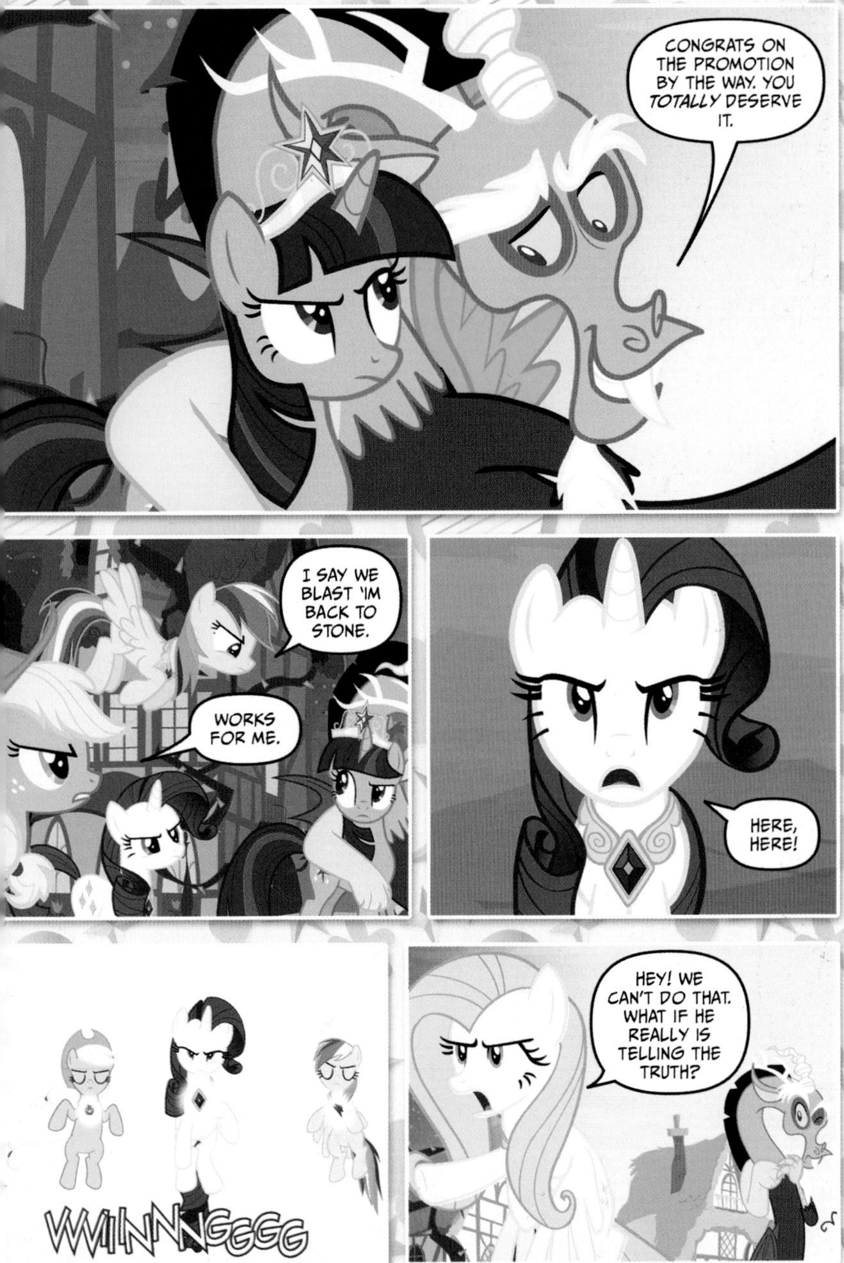
CONGRATS ON THE PROMOTION BY THE WAY. YOU *TOTALLY* DESERVE IT.
I SAY WE BLAST 'IM BACK TO STONE.
WORKS FOR ME.
HERE, HERE!
VVIINNNGGGG
HEY! WE CAN'T DO THAT. WHAT IF HE REALLY IS TELLING THE TRUTH?

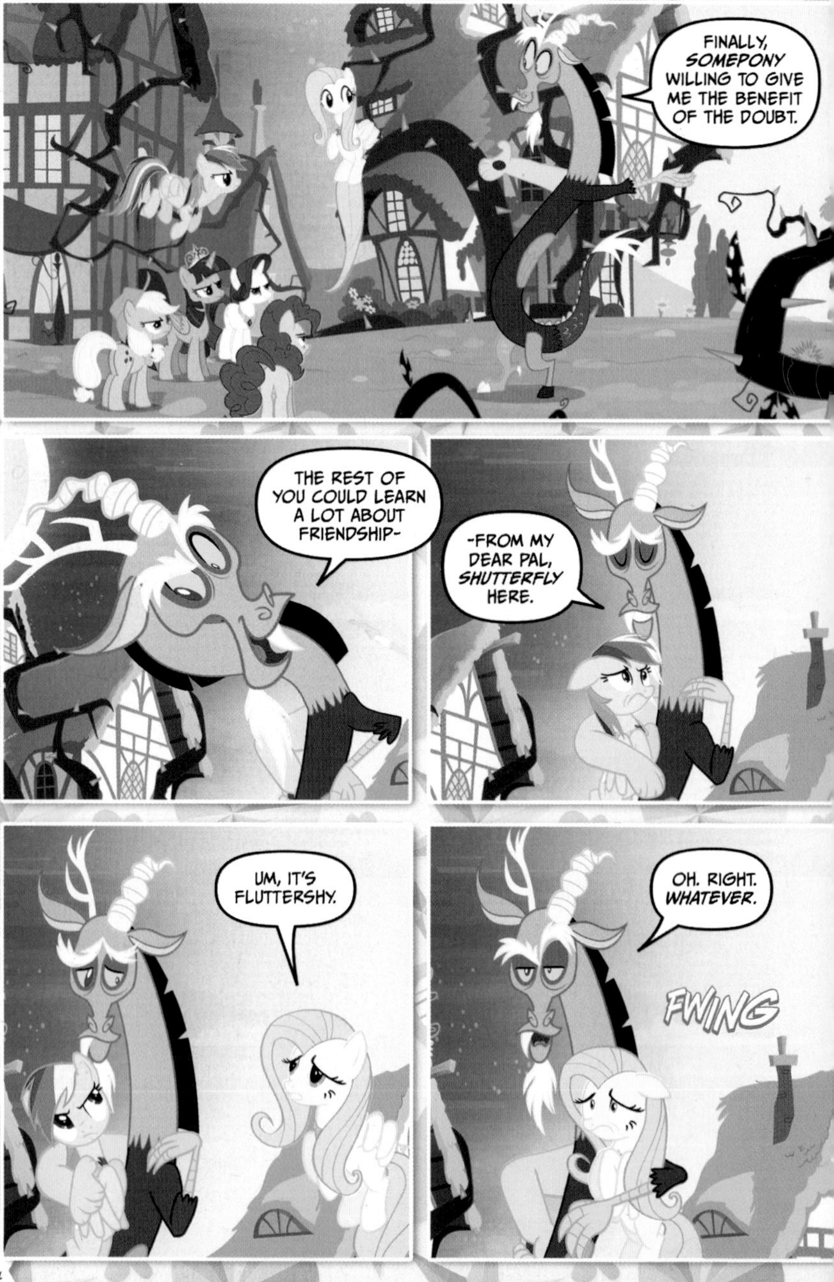

FINALLY, *SOMEPONY* WILLING TO GIVE ME THE BENEFIT OF THE DOUBT.
THE REST OF YOU COULD LEARN A LOT ABOUT FRIENDSHIP-
-FROM MY DEAR PAL, *SHUTTERFLY* HERE.
UM, IT'S FLUTTERSHY.
OH. RIGHT. *WHATEVER.*
FWING

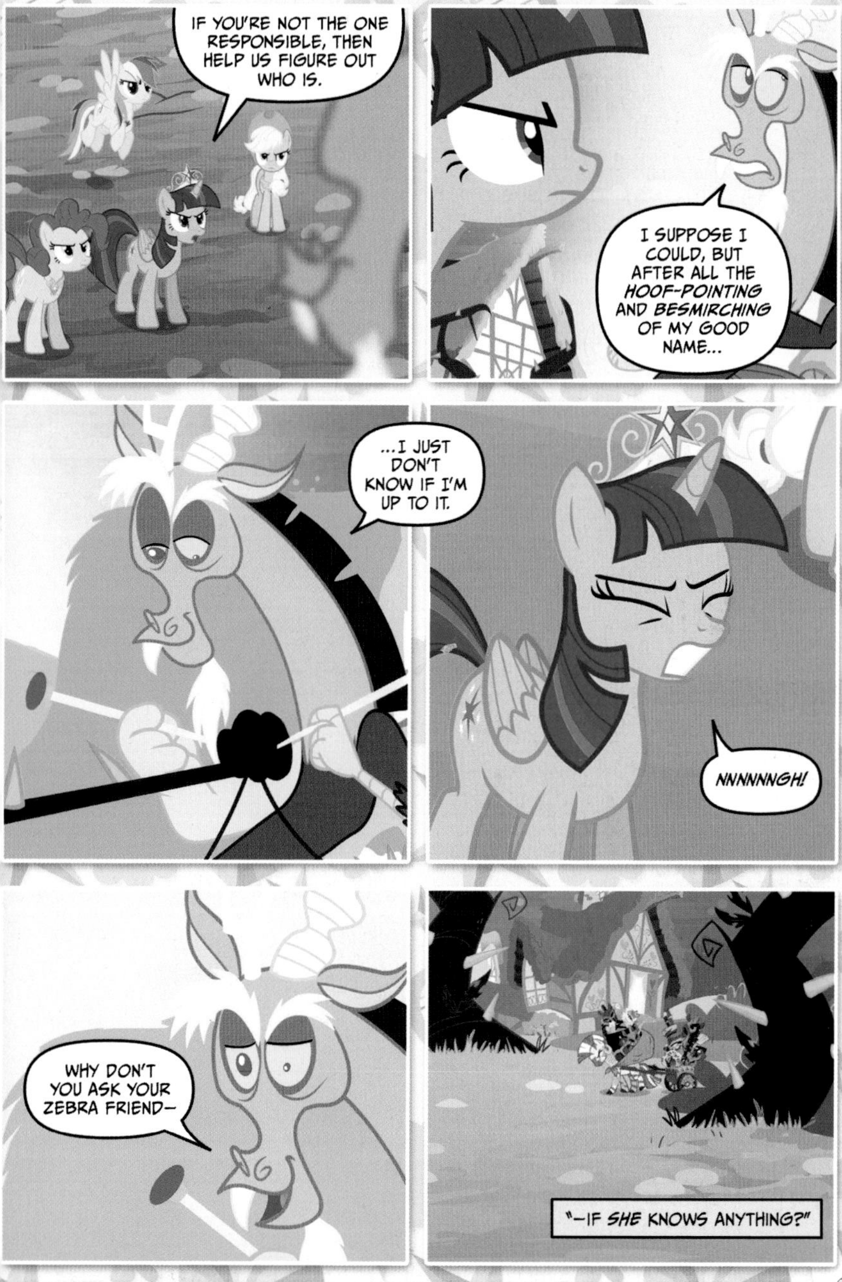
IF YOU'RE NOT THE ONE RESPONSIBLE, THEN HELP US FIGURE OUT WHO IS.
I SUPPOSE I COULD, BUT AFTER ALL THE *HOOF-POINTING* AND *BESMIRCHING* OF MY GOOD NAME...
...I JUST DON'T KNOW IF I'M UP TO IT.
NNNNNNGH!
WHY DON'T YOU ASK YOUR ZEBRA FRIEND—
"—IF *SHE* KNOWS ANYTHING?"

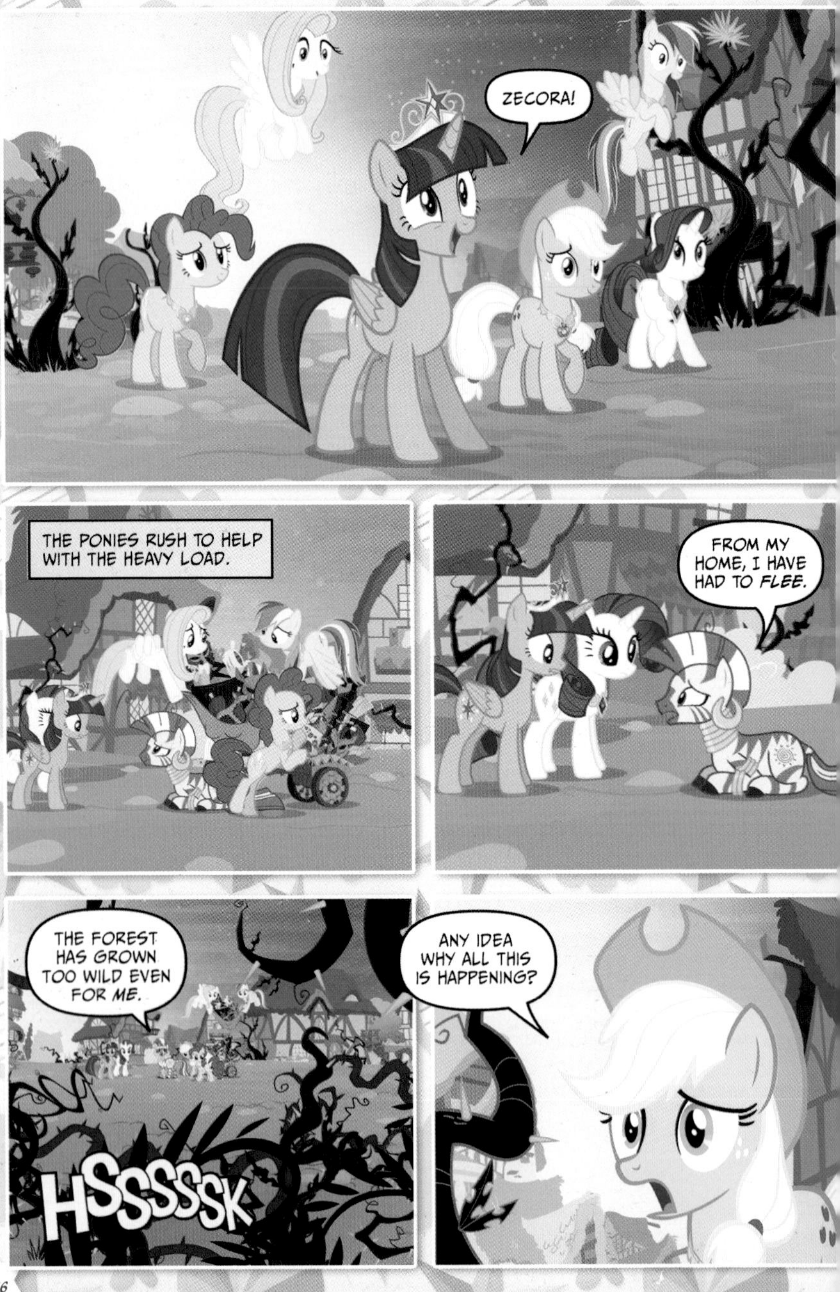

ZECORA!
THE PONIES RUSH TO HELP WITH THE HEAVY LOAD.
FROM MY HOME, I HAVE HAD TO *FLEE*.
THE FOREST HAS GROWN TOO WILD EVEN FOR *ME*.
HSSSSSK
ANY IDEA WHY ALL THIS IS HAPPENING?

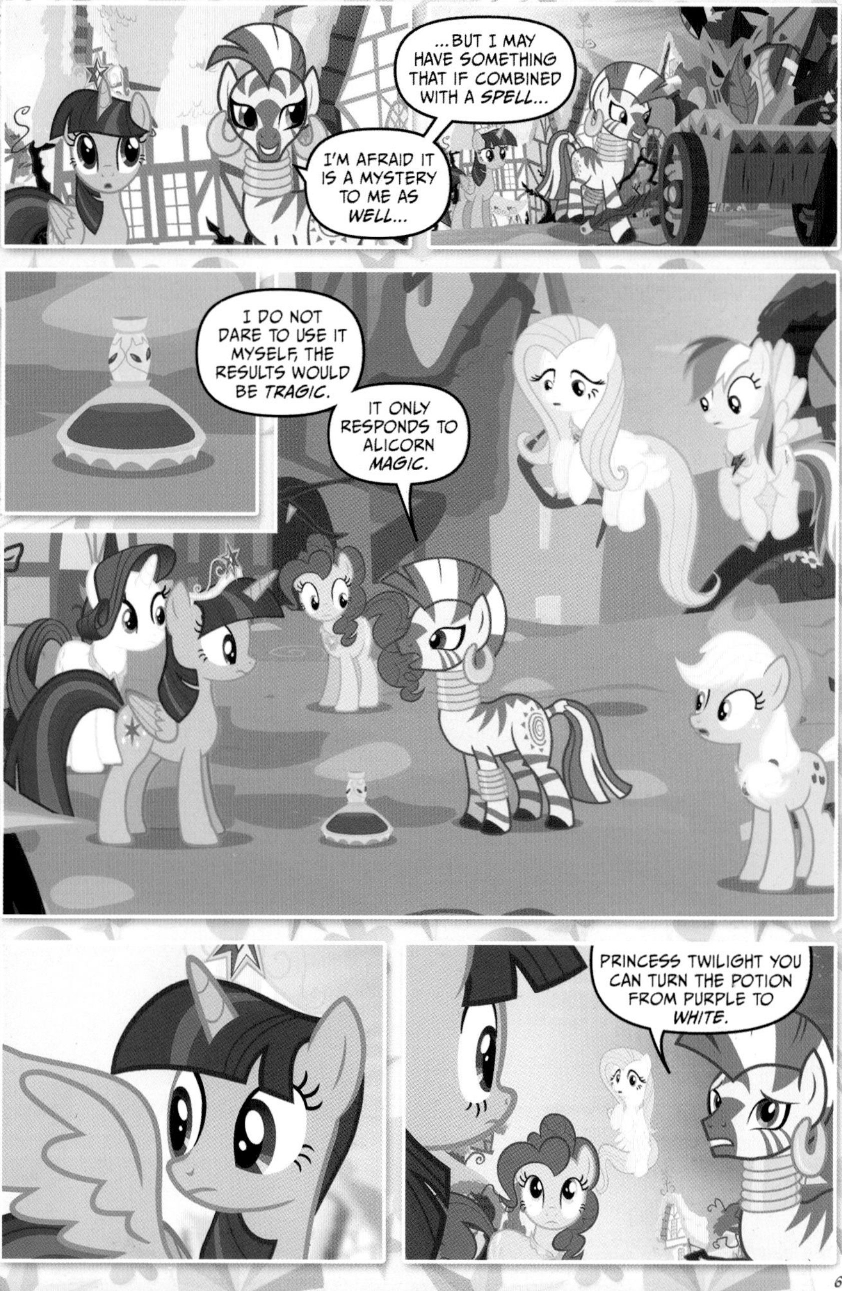
I'M AFRAID IT IS A MYSTERY TO ME AS *WELL*...
...BUT I MAY HAVE SOMETHING THAT IF COMBINED WITH A *SPELL*...
I DO NOT DARE TO USE IT MYSELF, THE RESULTS WOULD BE *TRAGIC*.
IT ONLY RESPONDS TO ALICORN *MAGIC*.
PRINCESS TWILIGHT YOU CAN TURN THE POTION FROM PURPLE TO *WHITE*.

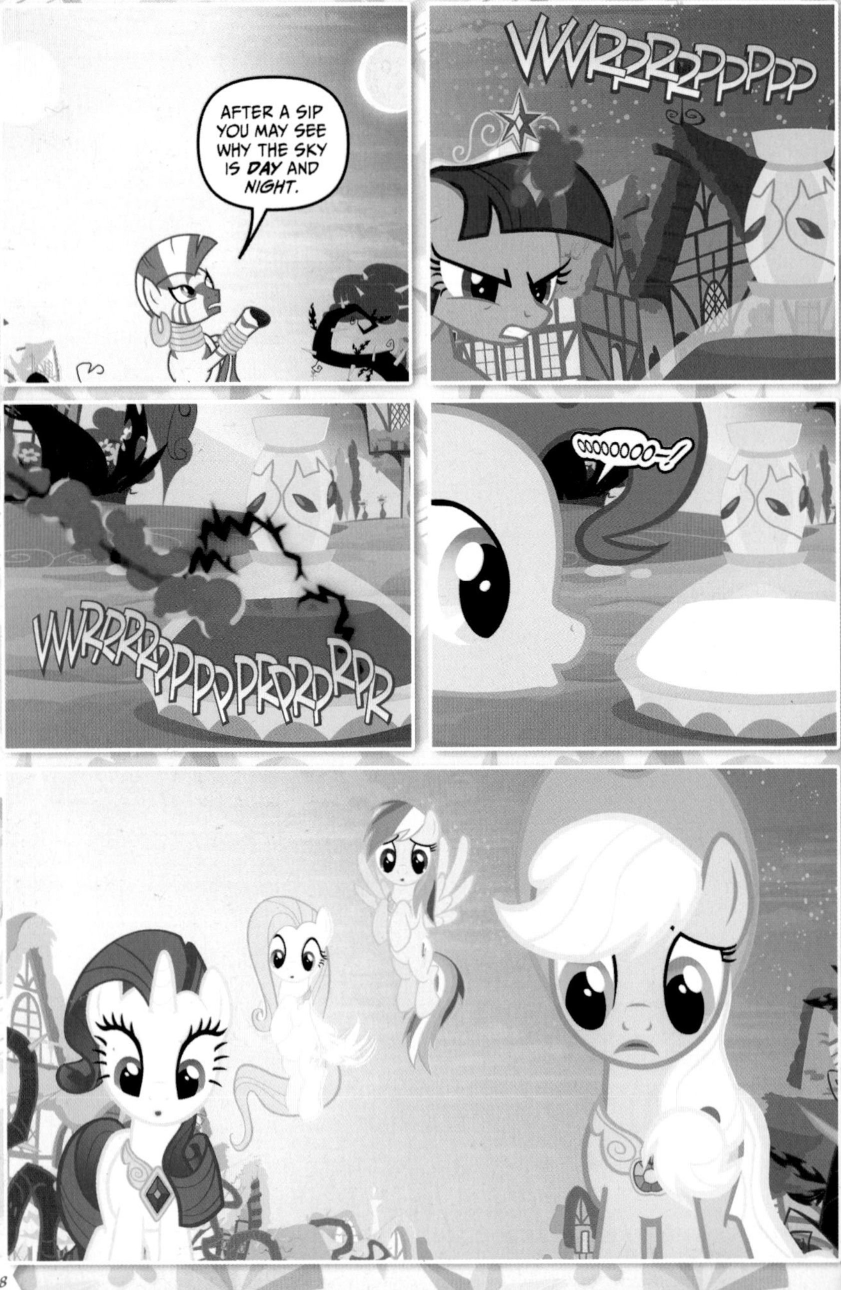
AFTER A SIP YOU MAY SEE WHY THE SKY IS *DAY* AND *NIGHT*.
VVVRZRRZPPPPPP
VVVRRRRPPPPPRPRPRPR
OOOOOOOO—!

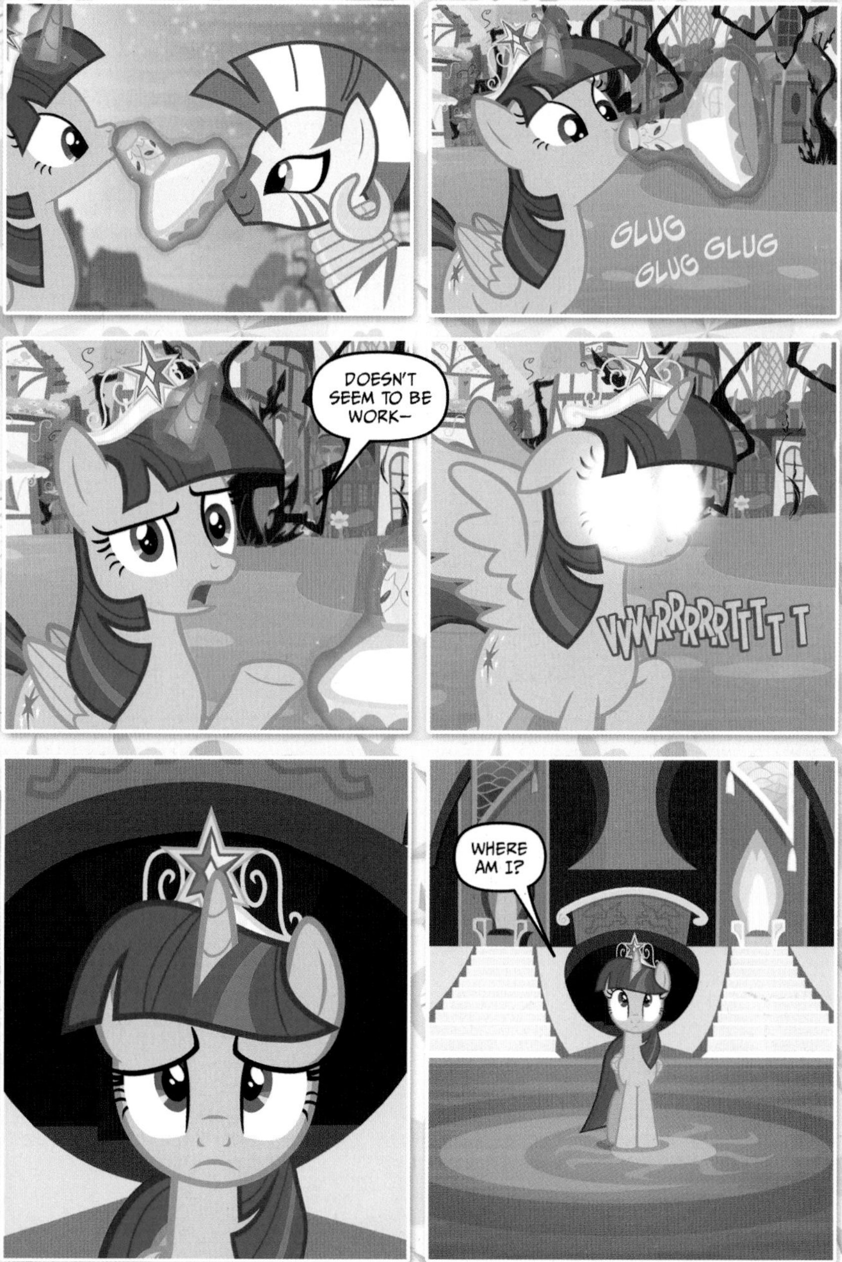
GLUG
GLUG GLUG
DOESN'T SEEM TO BE WORK–
VVVVRRRRRTTTT T
WHERE AM I?

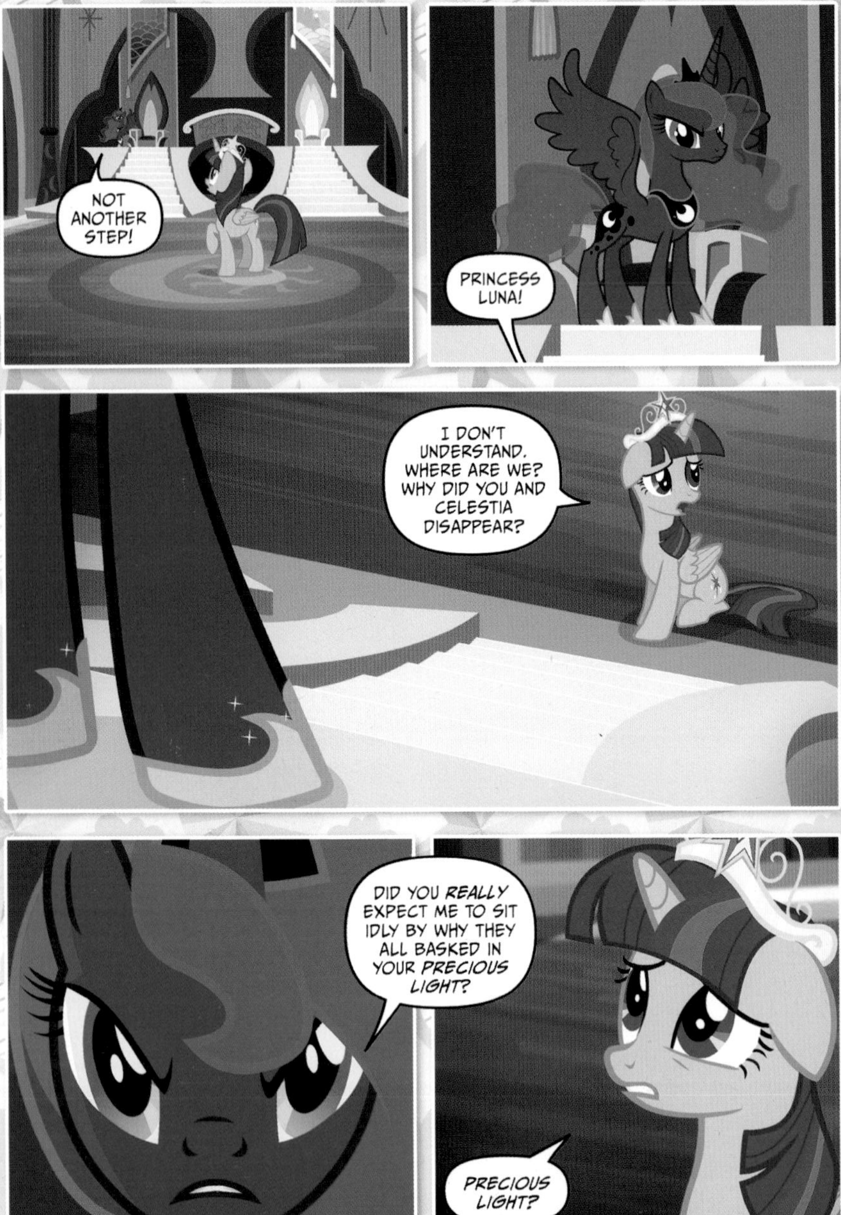
NOT ANOTHER STEP!
PRINCESS LUNA!
I DON'T UNDERSTAND. WHERE ARE WE? WHY DID YOU AND CELESTIA DISAPPEAR?
DID YOU *REALLY* EXPECT ME TO SIT IDLY BY WHY THEY ALL BASKED IN YOUR *PRECIOUS LIGHT*?
PRECIOUS LIGHT?

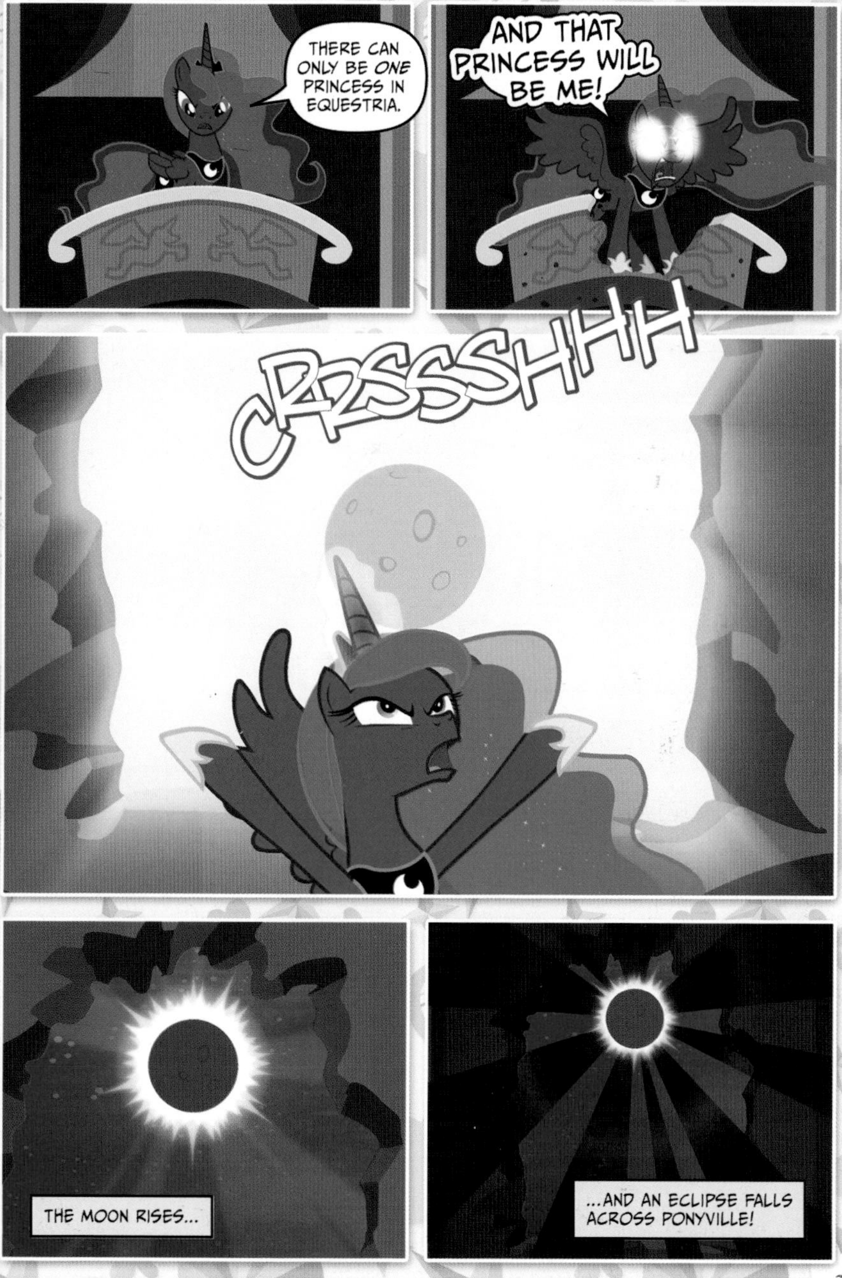
THERE CAN ONLY BE ONE PRINCESS IN EQUESTRIA.
AND THAT PRINCESS WILL BE ME!
CRRSSSHHH
THE MOON RISES...
...AND AN ECLIPSE FALLS ACROSS PONYVILLE!

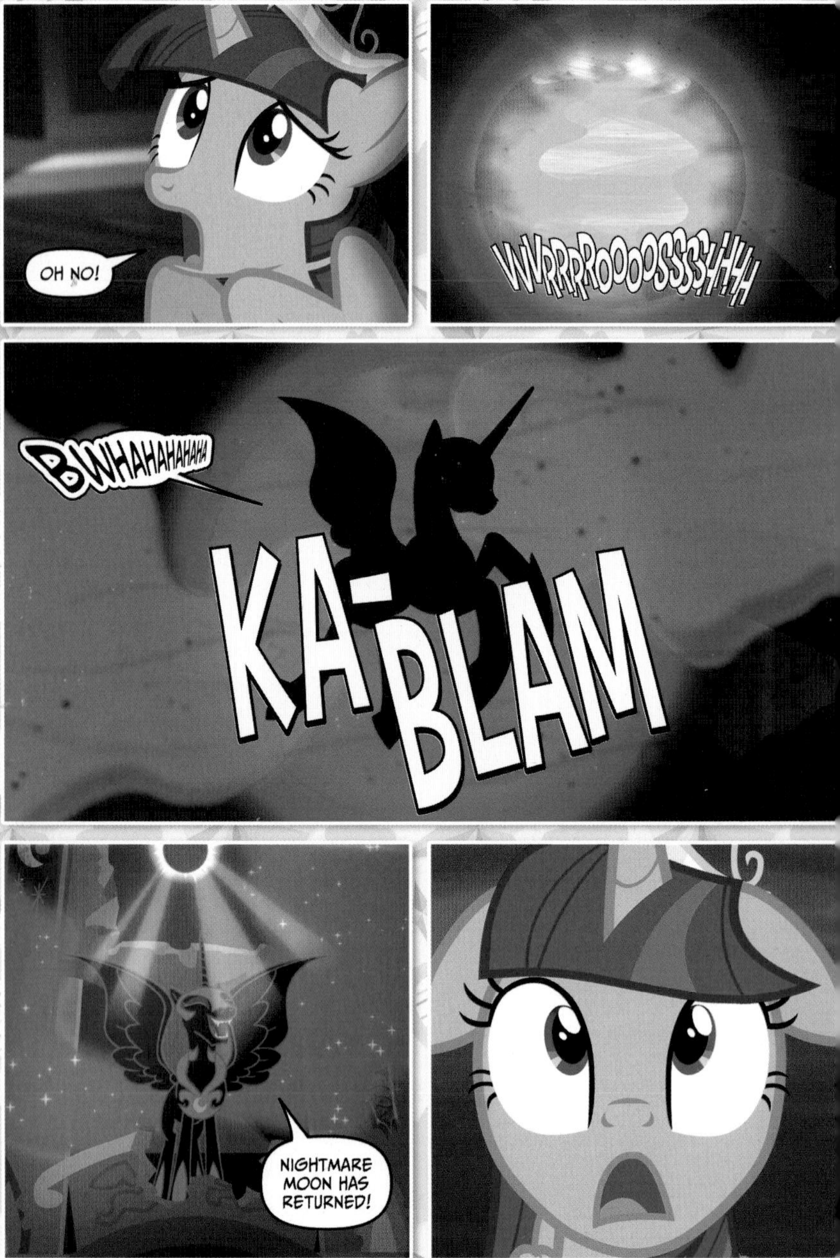
OH NO!
WVRRRROOOOSSSSHHHH
BWHAHAHAHAHA
KA-BLAM
NIGHTMARE MOON HAS RETURNED!

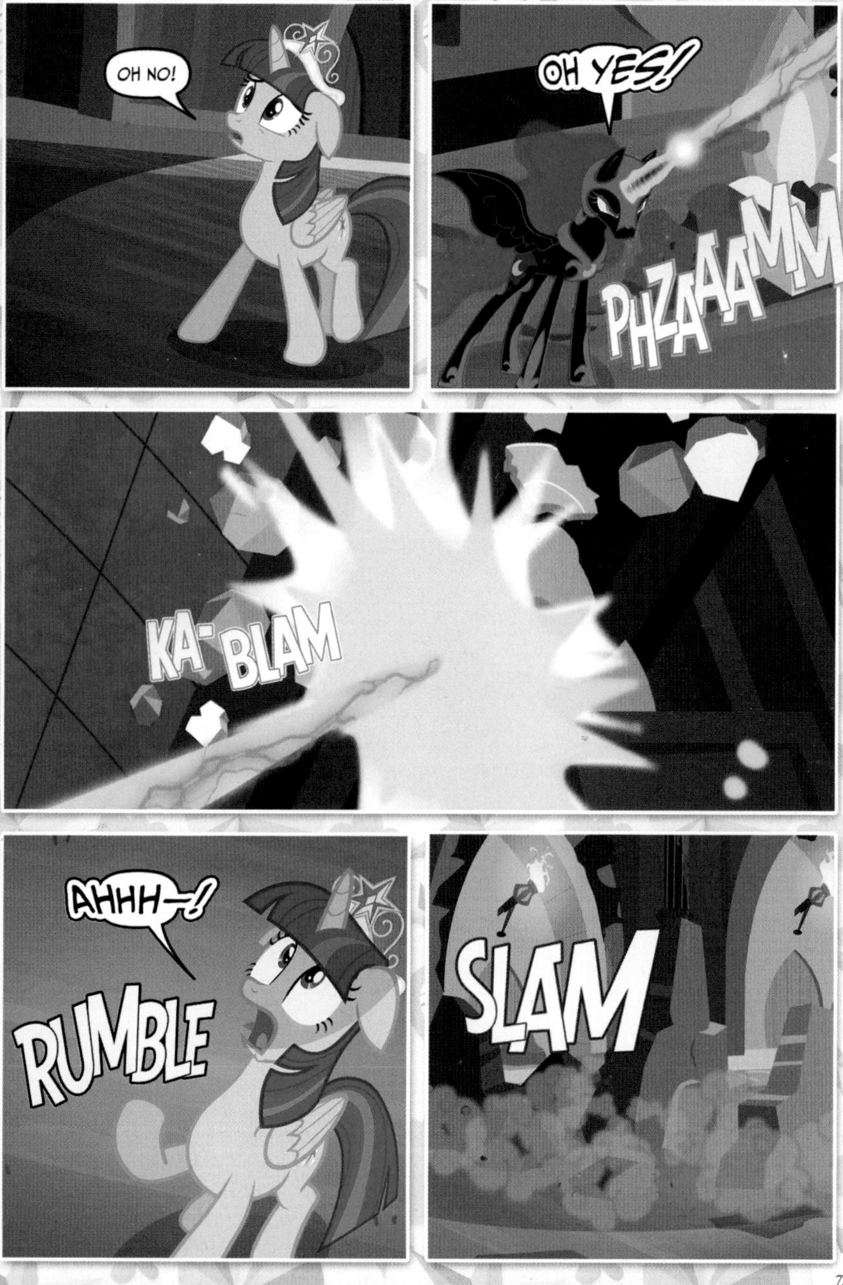
OH NO!
OH YES!
PHZAAAMMM
KA-BLAM
AHHH—!
RUMBLE
SLAM

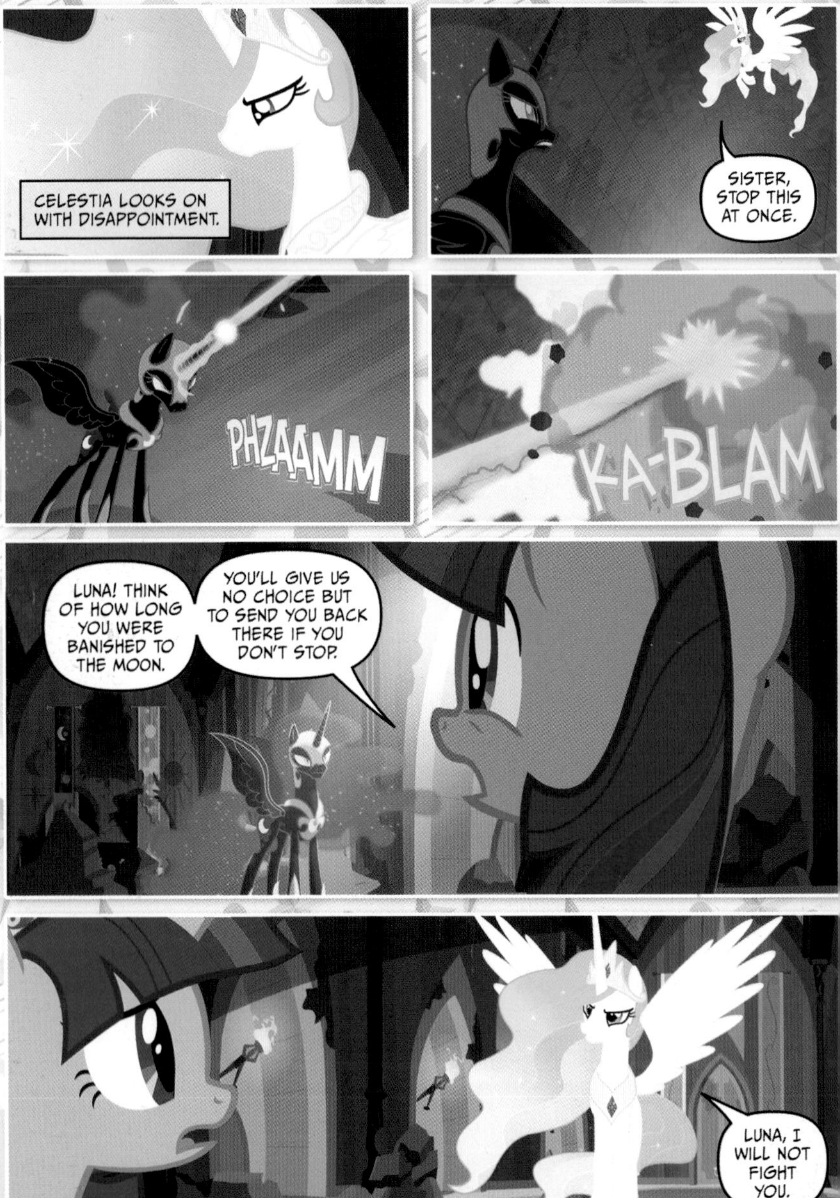
CELESTIA LOOKS ON WITH DISAPPOINTMENT.
SISTER, STOP THIS AT ONCE.
PHZAAMM
KA-BLAM
LUNA! THINK OF HOW LONG YOU WERE BANISHED TO THE MOON.
YOU'LL GIVE US NO CHOICE BUT TO SEND YOU BACK THERE IF YOU DON'T STOP.
LUNA, I WILL NOT FIGHT YOU.

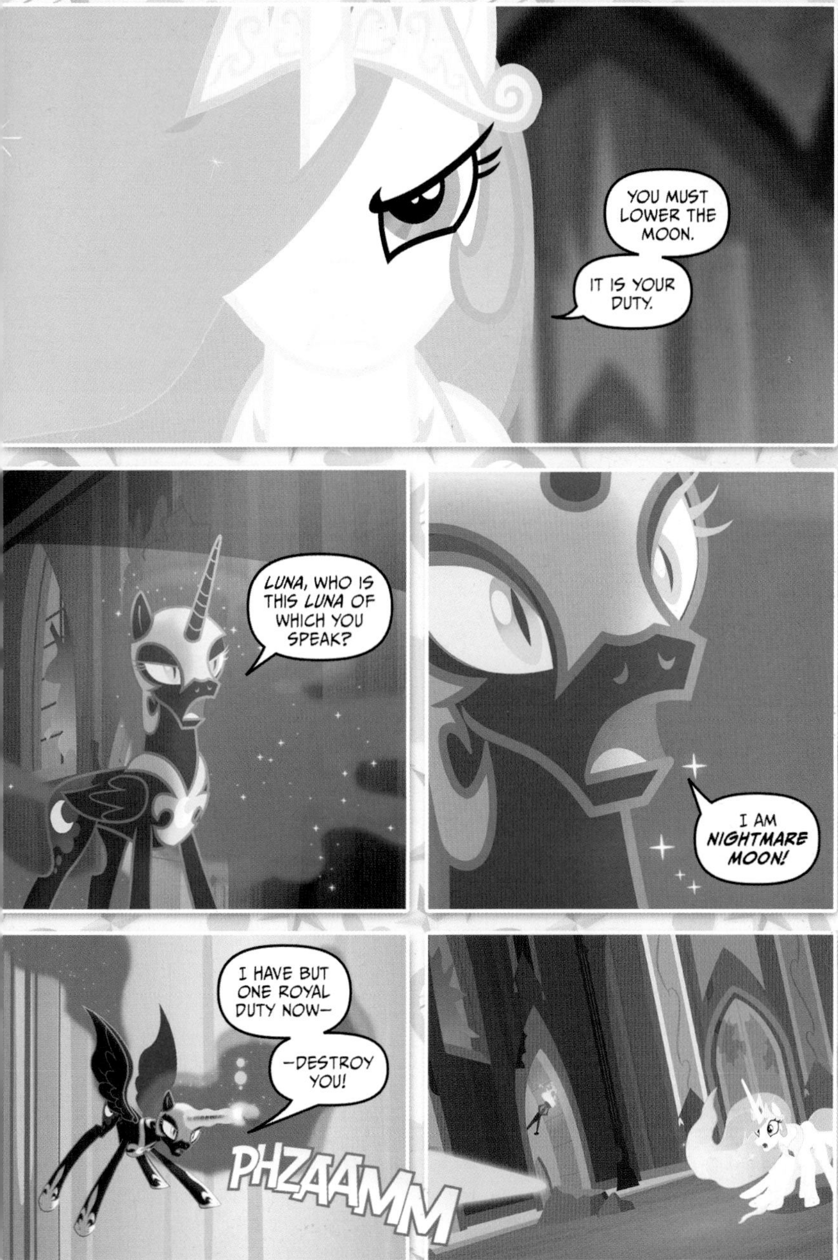
YOU MUST LOWER THE MOON.
IT IS YOUR DUTY.
LUNA, WHO IS THIS *LUNA* OF WHICH YOU SPEAK?
I AM ***NIGHTMARE MOON!***
I HAVE BUT ONE ROYAL DUTY NOW–
–DESTROY YOU!
PHZAAMM

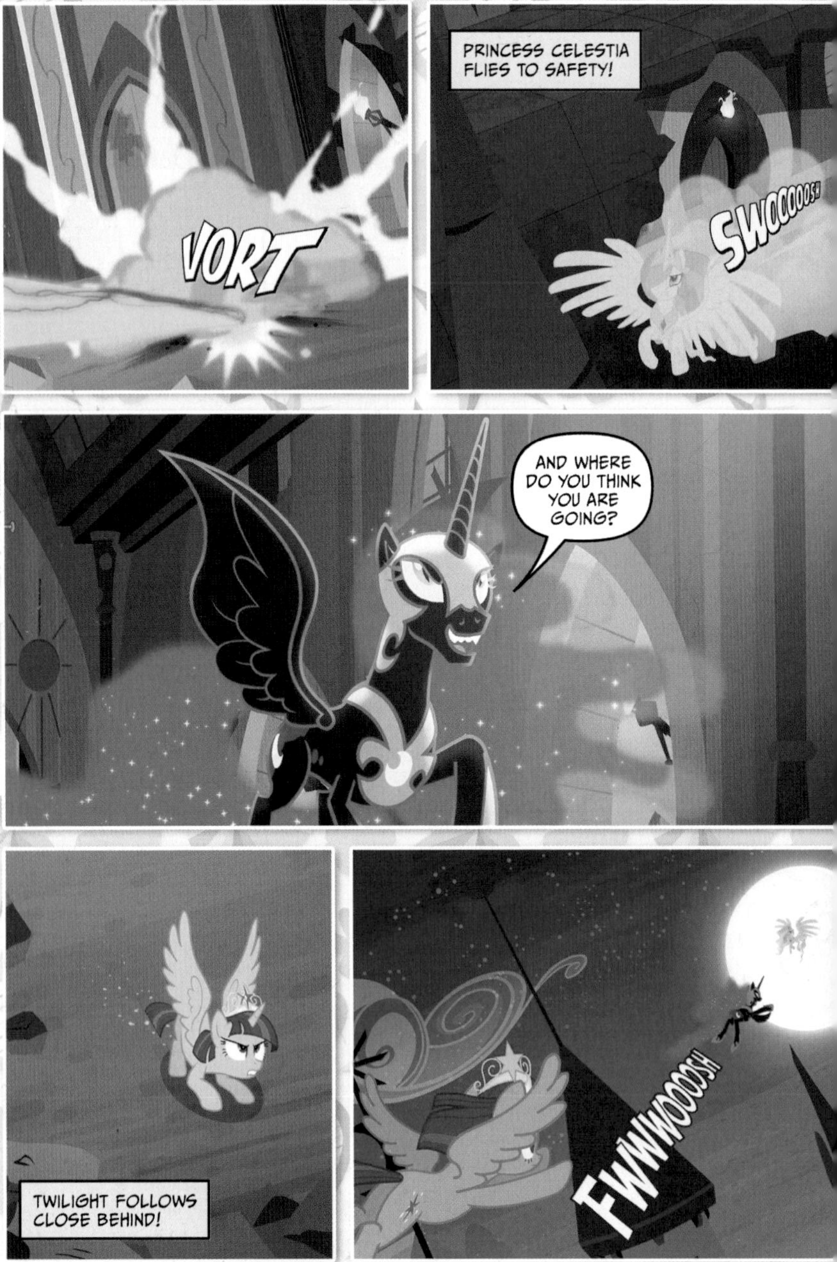
VORT
PRINCESS CELESTIA FLIES TO SAFETY!
SWOOOOOSH
AND WHERE DO YOU THINK YOU ARE GOING?
TWILIGHT FOLLOWS CLOSE BEHIND!
FWWWOOOSH

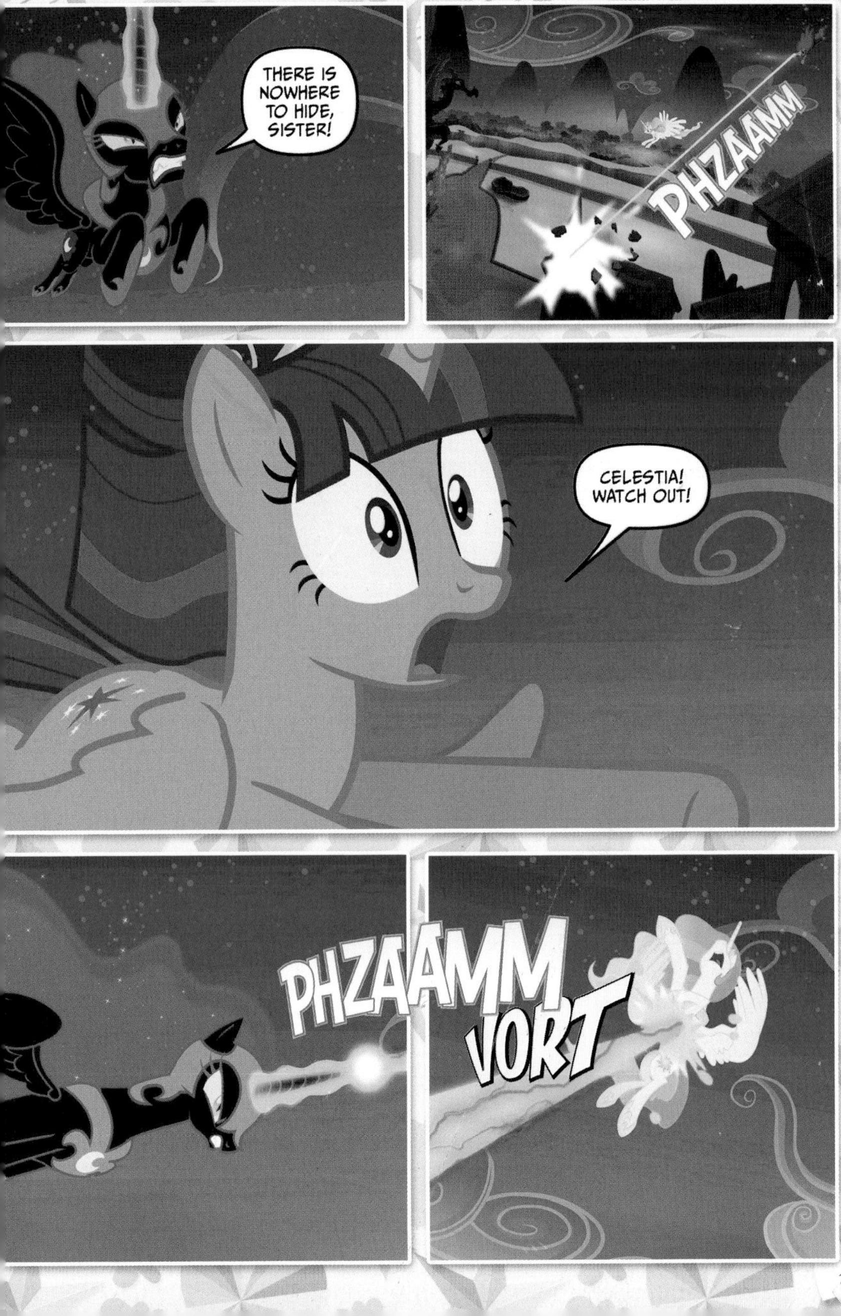
THERE IS NOWHERE TO HIDE, SISTER!
PHZAAMM
CELESTIA! WATCH OUT!
PHZAAMM
VORT

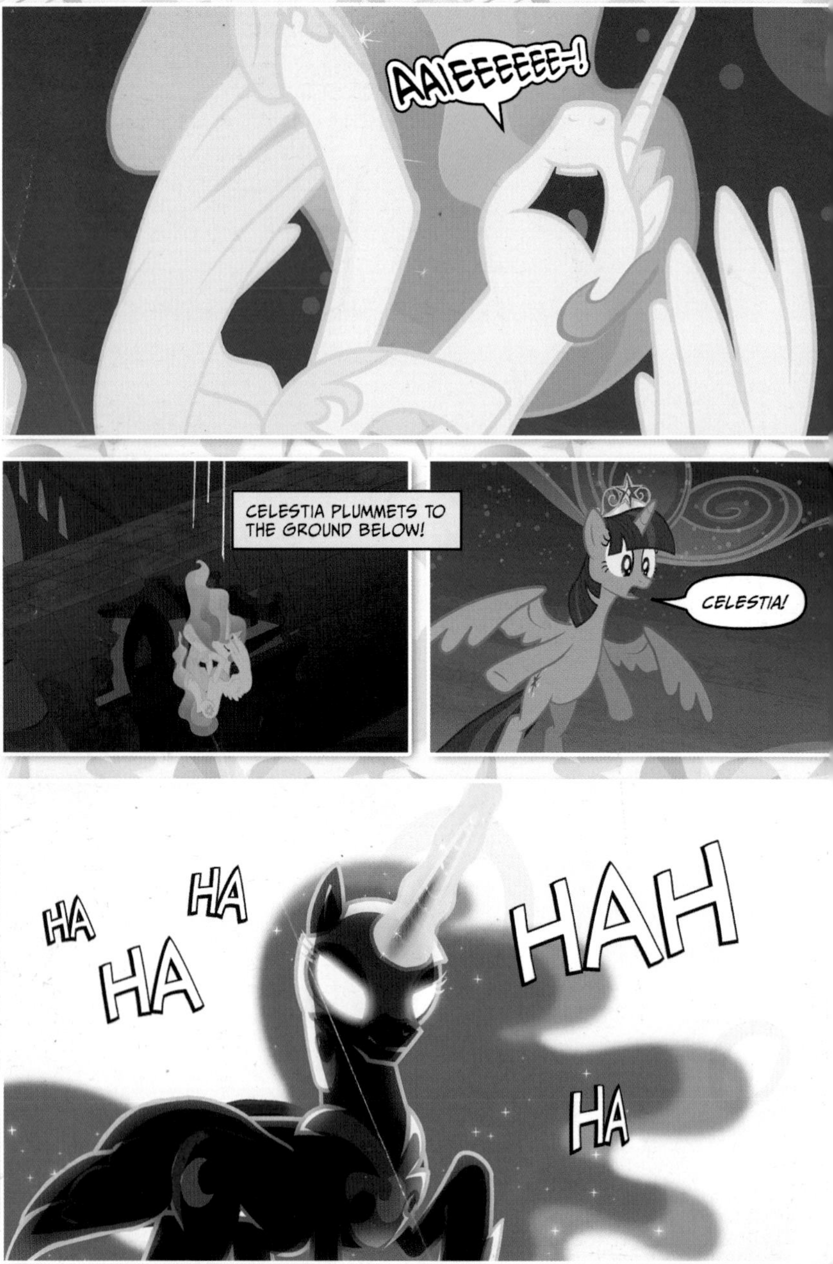
AAIEEEEEEE-!
CELESTIA PLUMMETS TO THE GROUND BELOW!
CELESTIA!
HA
HA
HA
HAH
HA

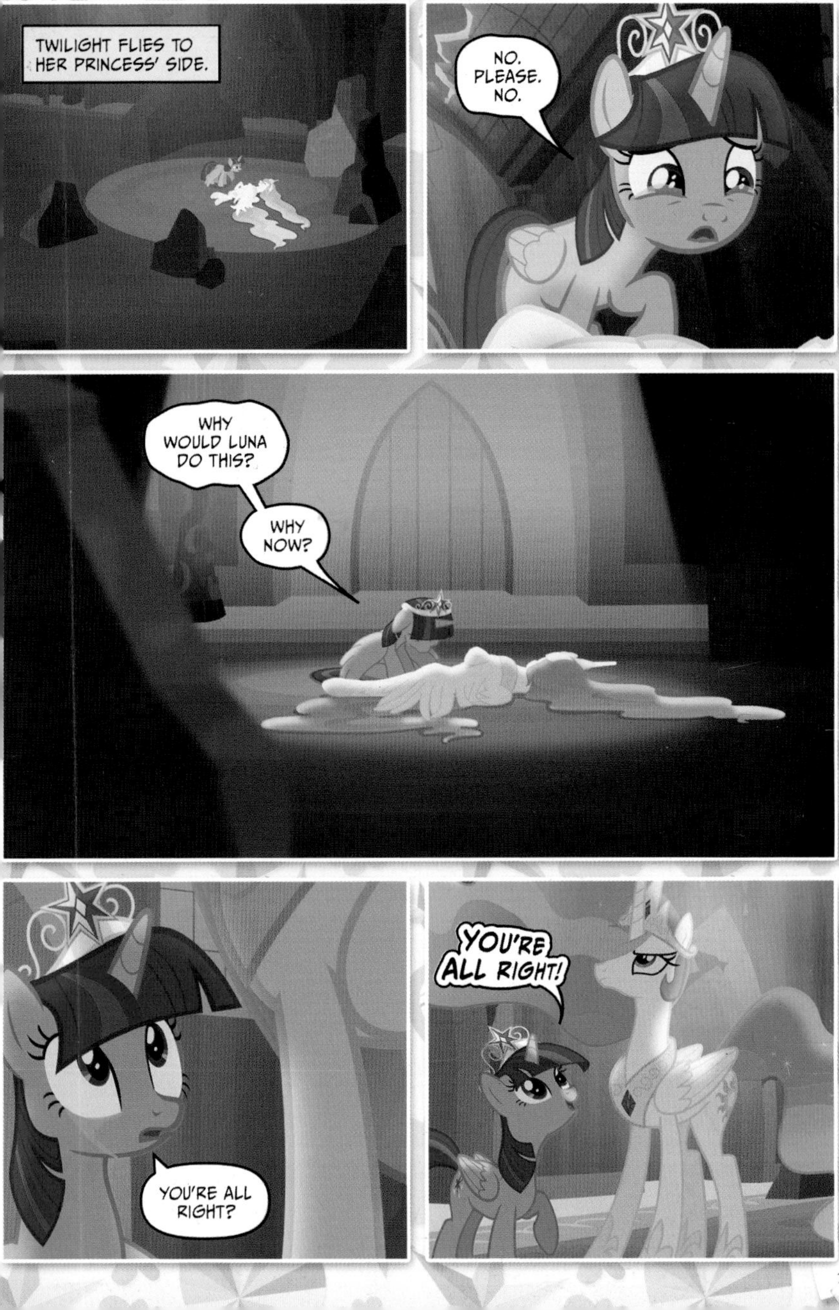
TWILIGHT FLIES TO HER PRINCESS' SIDE.
NO. PLEASE. NO.
WHY WOULD LUNA DO THIS?
WHY NOW?
YOU'RE ALL RIGHT?
YOU'RE ALL RIGHT!

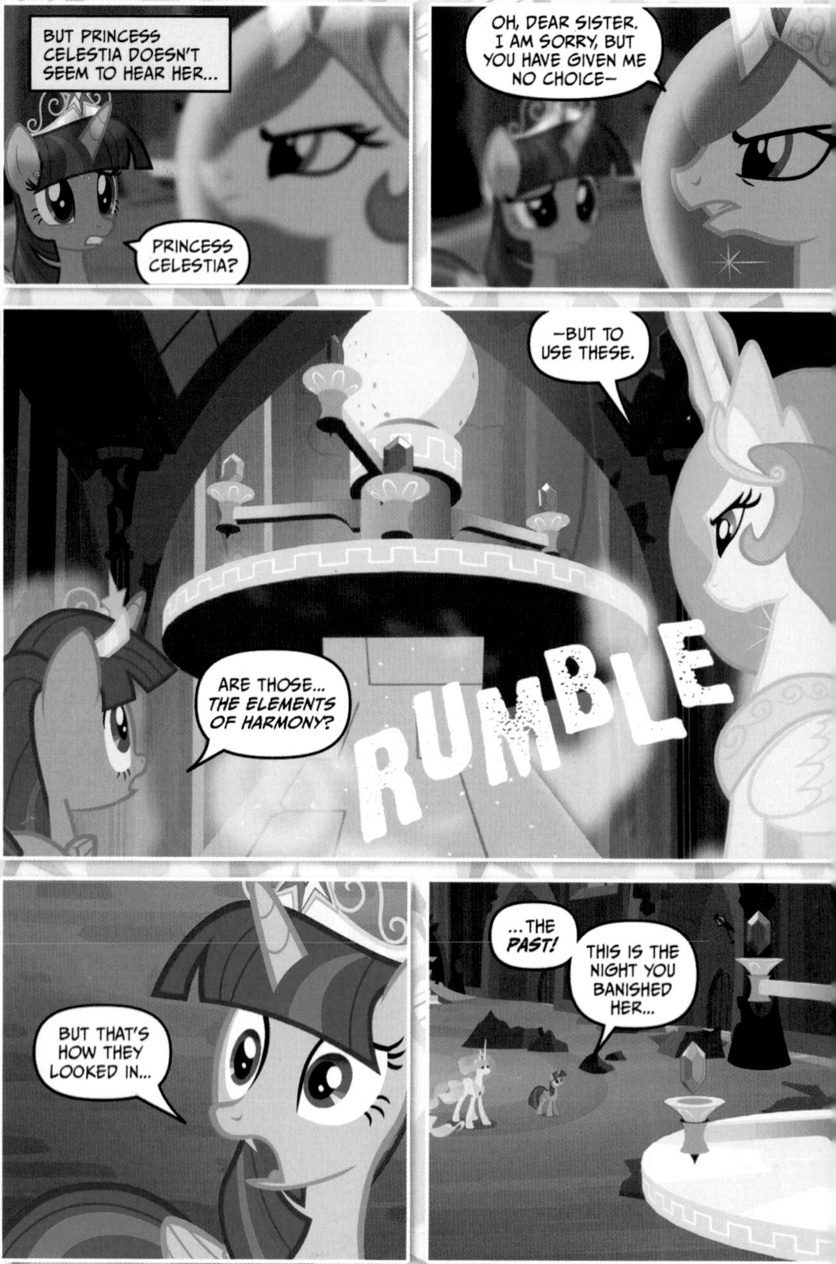
BUT PRINCESS CELESTIA DOESN'T SEEM TO HEAR HER...
PRINCESS CELESTIA?
OH, DEAR SISTER. I AM SORRY, BUT YOU HAVE GIVEN ME NO CHOICE—
—BUT TO USE THESE.
ARE THOSE... THE ELEMENTS OF HARMONY?
RUMBLE
BUT THAT'S HOW THEY LOOKED IN...
...THE PAST!
THIS IS THE NIGHT YOU BANISHED HER...

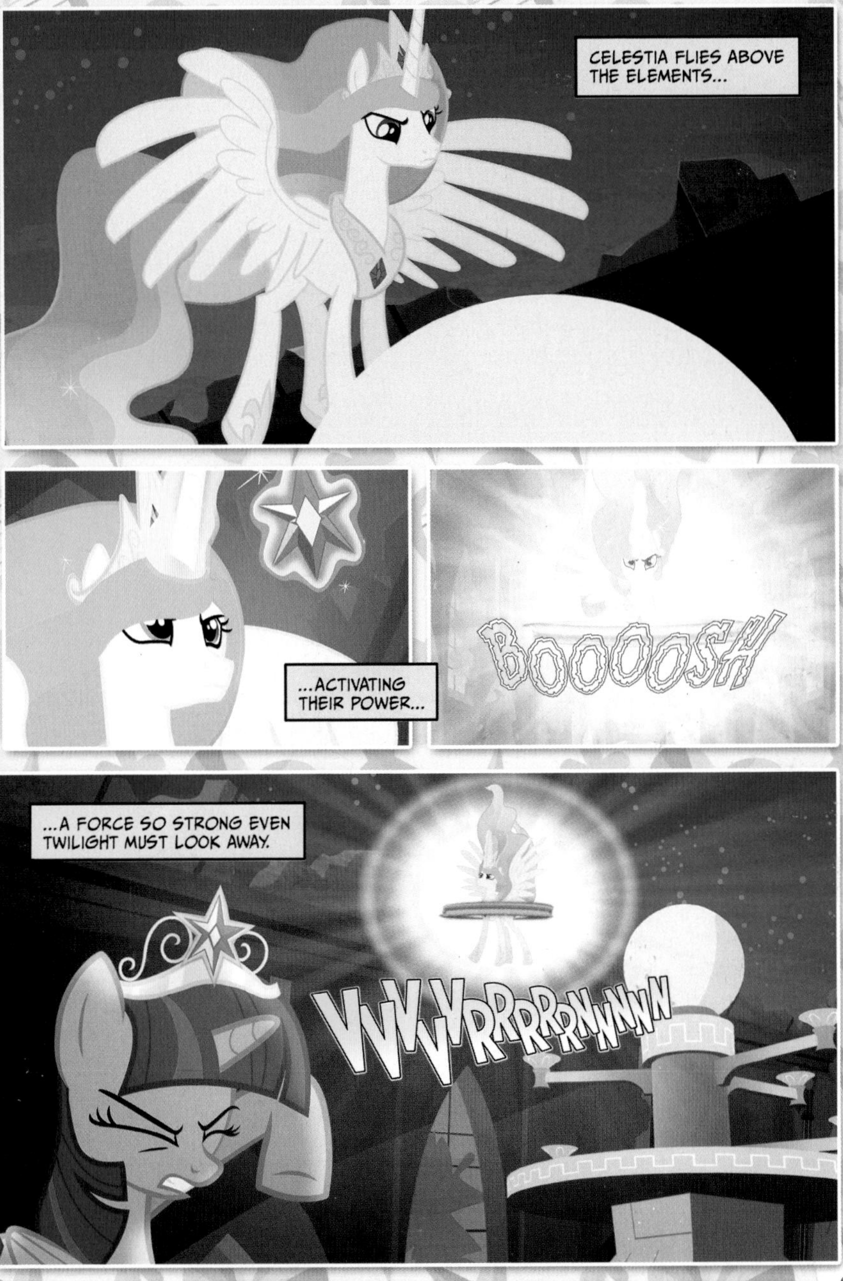
CELESTIA FLIES ABOVE THE ELEMENTS...
...ACTIVATING THEIR POWER...
BOOOOOSH
...A FORCE SO STRONG EVEN TWILIGHT MUST LOOK AWAY.
VVVVVRRRRRNNNNN

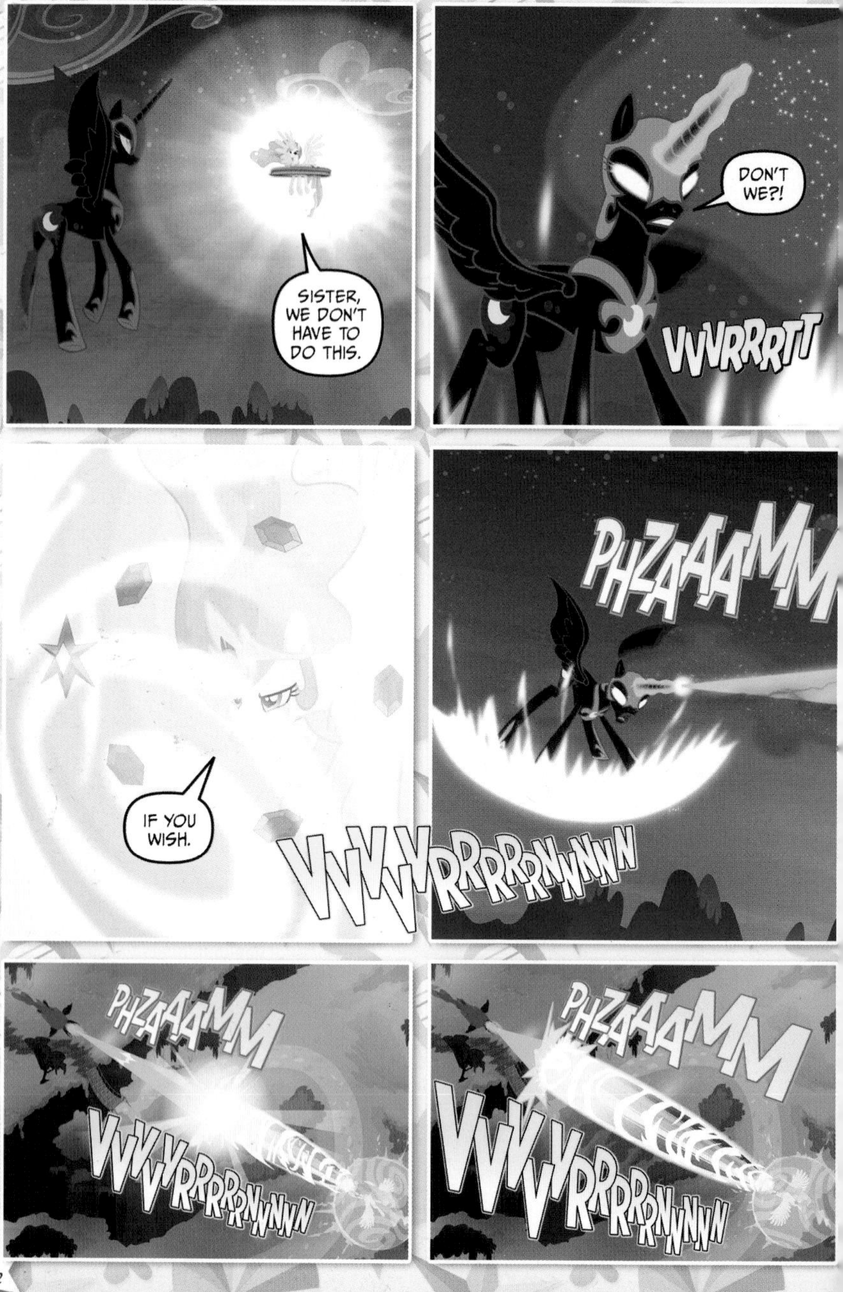
SISTER, WE DON'T HAVE TO DO THIS.
DON'T WE?!
VVVRRRTT
IF YOU WISH.
PHZAAAMM
VVVVYRRRRRNNNNN
PHZAAAMM
VVVVYRRRRRNNNNN
PHZAAAMM
VVVVYRRRRRNNNNN

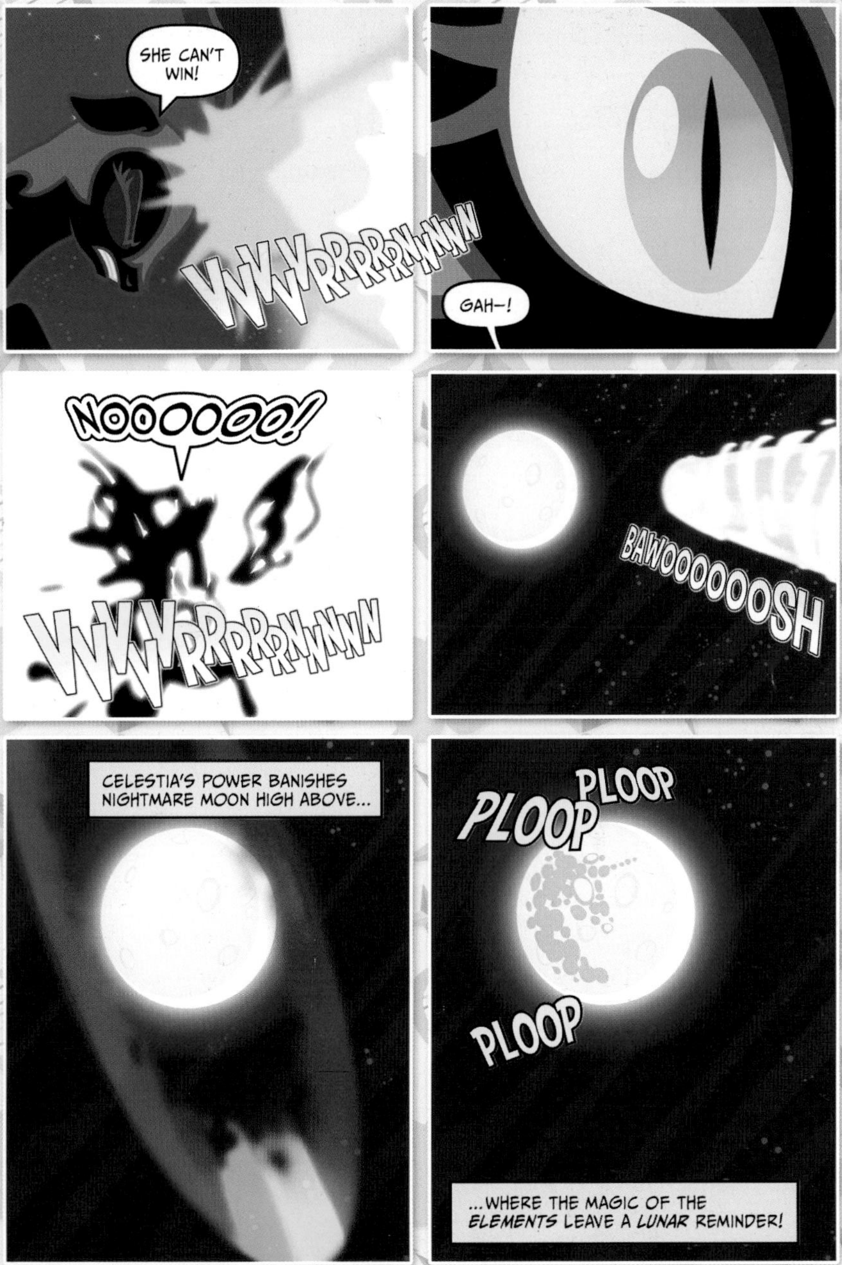
SHE CAN'T WIN!
VVVVVRRRRNNNNN
GAH–!
NOOOOOO!
VVVVVRRRRNNNNN
BAWOOOOOOOSH
CELESTIA'S POWER BANISHES NIGHTMARE MOON HIGH ABOVE...
PLOOP
PLOOP
PLOOP
...WHERE THE MAGIC OF THE *ELEMENTS* LEAVE A *LUNAR* REMINDER!

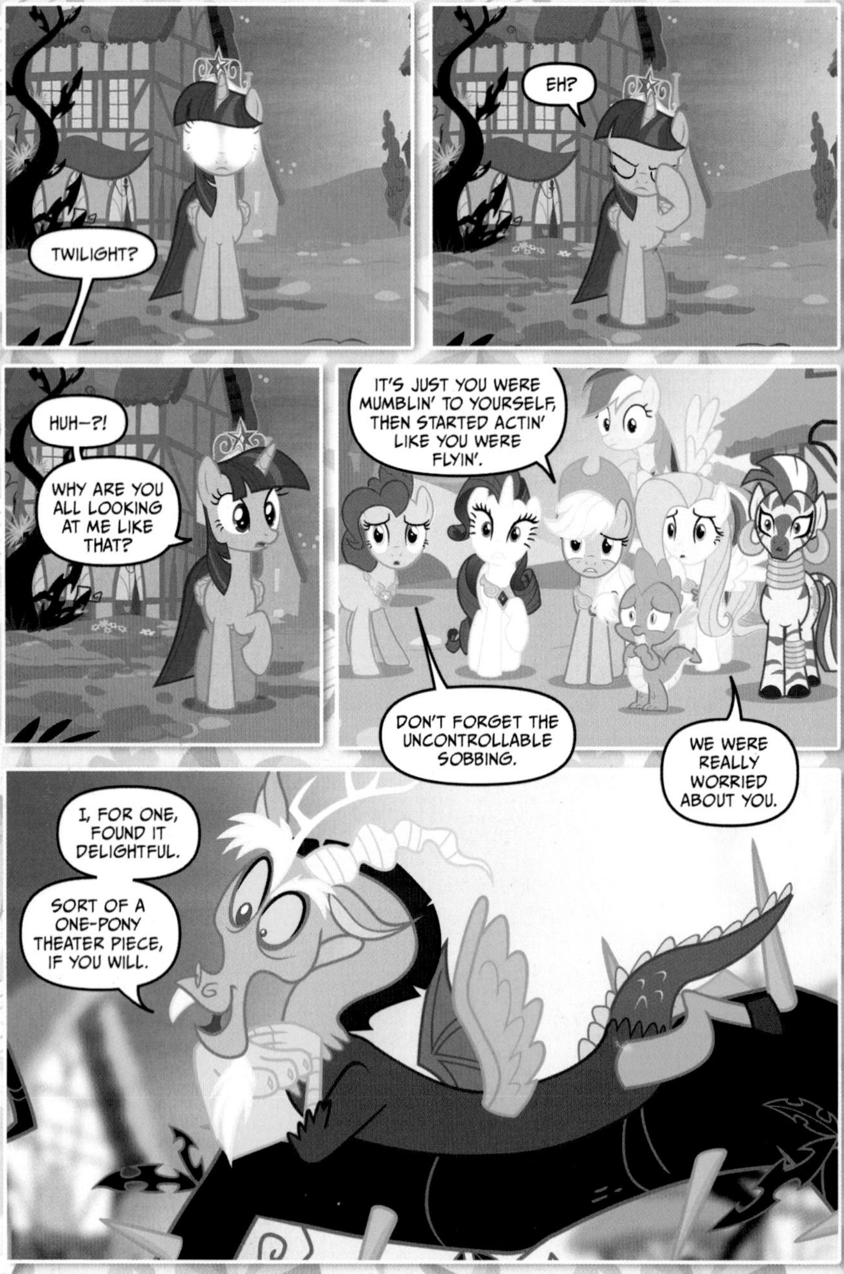
TWILIGHT?
EH?
HUH—?!
WHY ARE YOU ALL LOOKING AT ME LIKE THAT?
IT'S JUST YOU WERE MUMBLIN' TO YOURSELF, THEN STARTED ACTIN' LIKE YOU WERE FLYIN'.
DON'T FORGET THE UNCONTROLLABLE SOBBING.
WE WERE REALLY WORRIED ABOUT YOU.
I, FOR ONE, FOUND IT DELIGHTFUL.
SORT OF A ONE-PONY THEATER PIECE, IF YOU WILL.

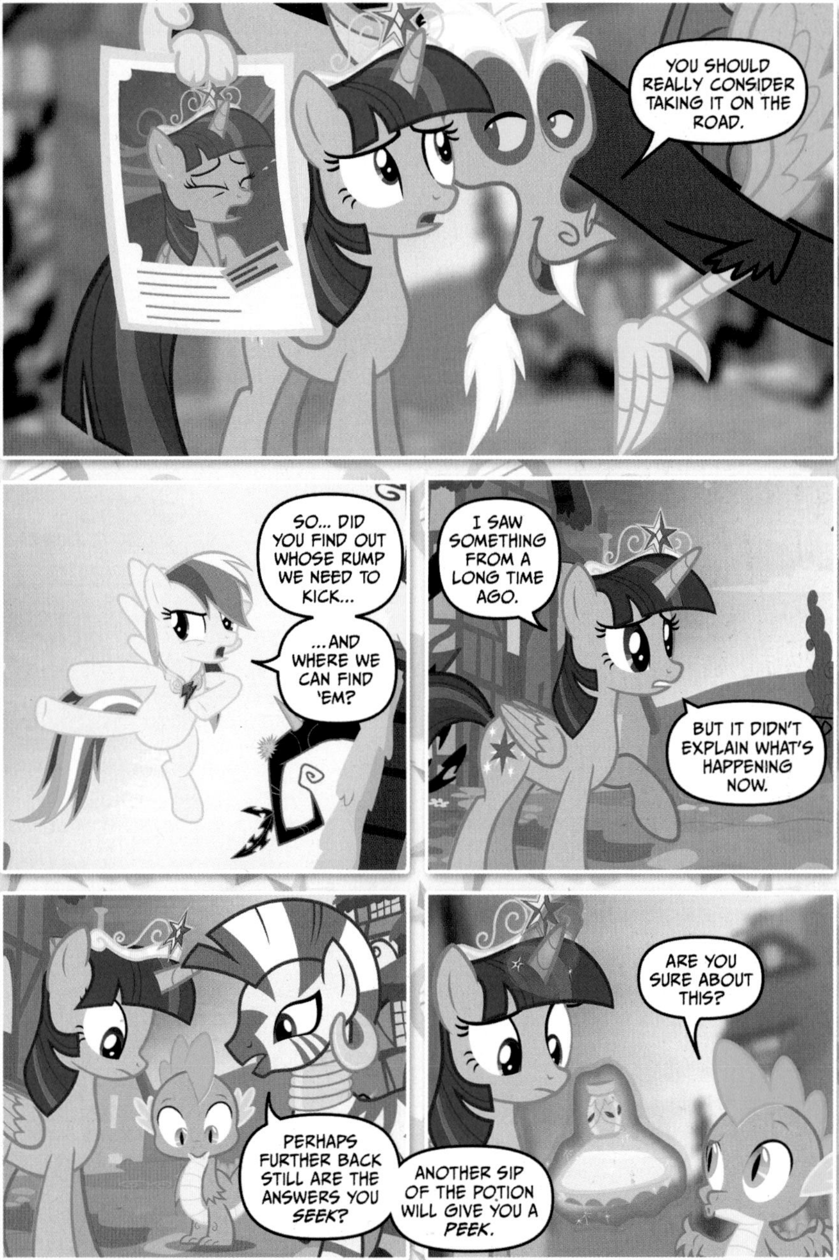
YOU SHOULD REALLY CONSIDER TAKING IT ON THE ROAD.
SO... DID YOU FIND OUT WHOSE RUMP WE NEED TO KICK...
...AND WHERE WE CAN FIND 'EM?
I SAW SOMETHING FROM A LONG TIME AGO.
BUT IT DIDN'T EXPLAIN WHAT'S HAPPENING NOW.
PERHAPS FURTHER BACK STILL ARE THE ANSWERS YOU SEEK?
ANOTHER SIP OF THE POTION WILL GIVE YOU A PEEK.
ARE YOU SURE ABOUT THIS?

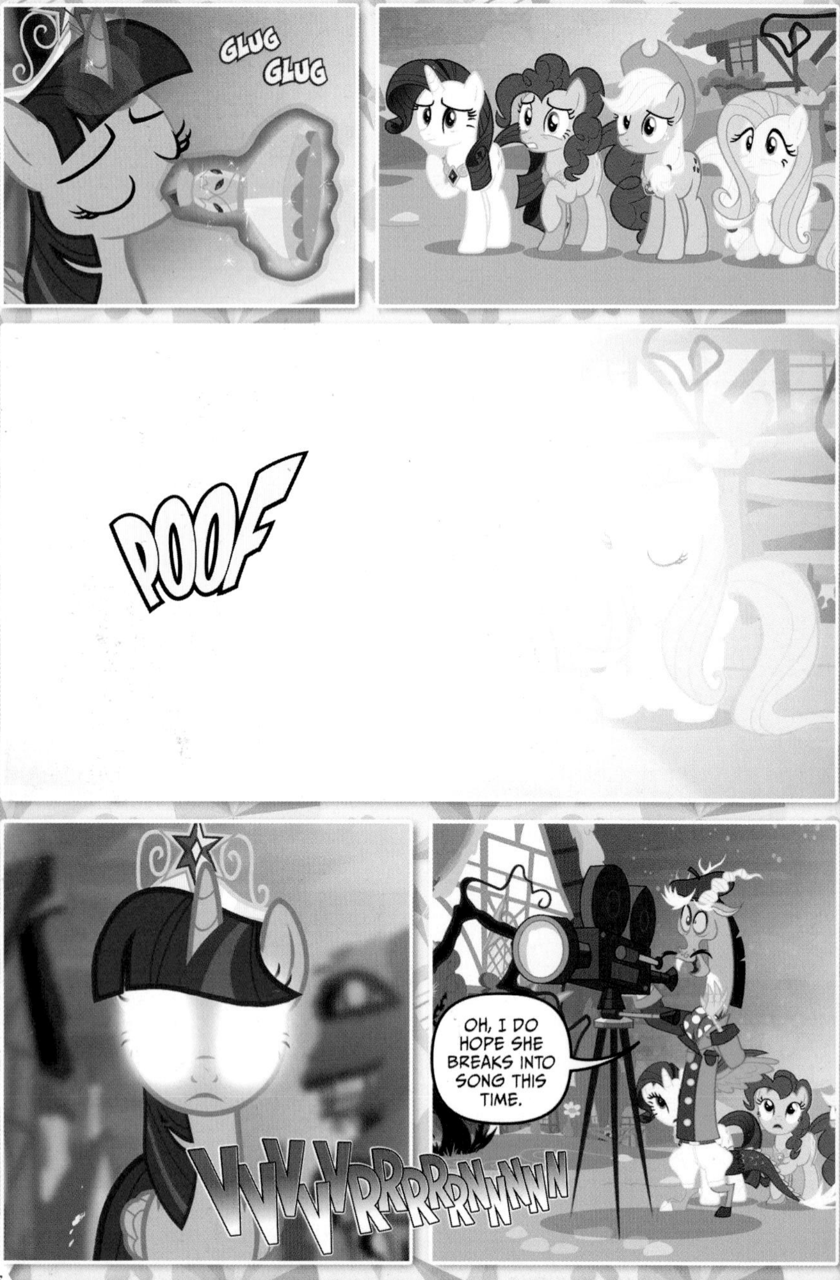

GLUG
GLUG
POOF
VVVVVVRRRRRNNNNN
OH, I DO HOPE SHE BREAKS INTO SONG THIS TIME.

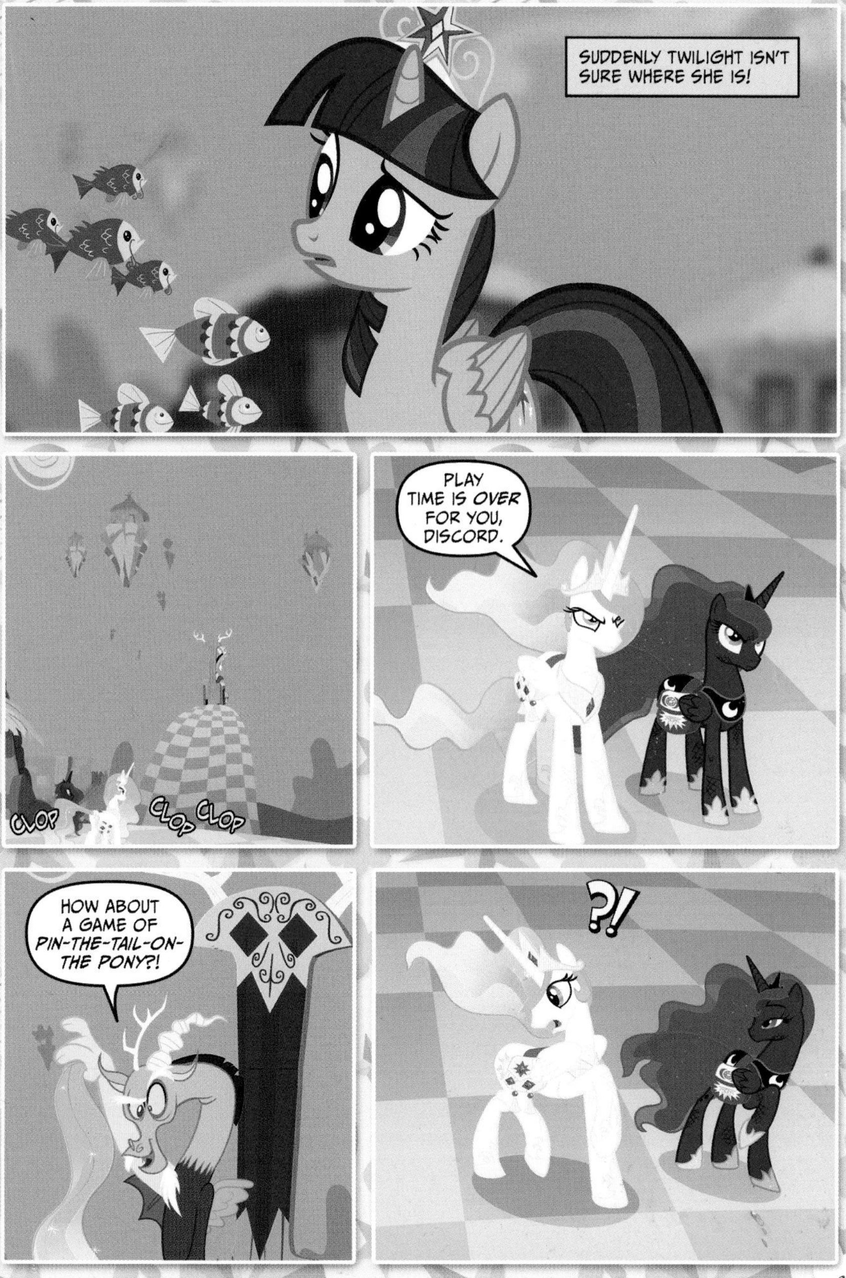
SUDDENLY TWILIGHT ISN'T SURE WHERE SHE IS!
CLOP
CLOP CLOP
PLAY TIME IS *OVER* FOR YOU, DISCORD.
HOW ABOUT A GAME OF *PIN-THE-TAIL-ON-THE PONY?!*
?!

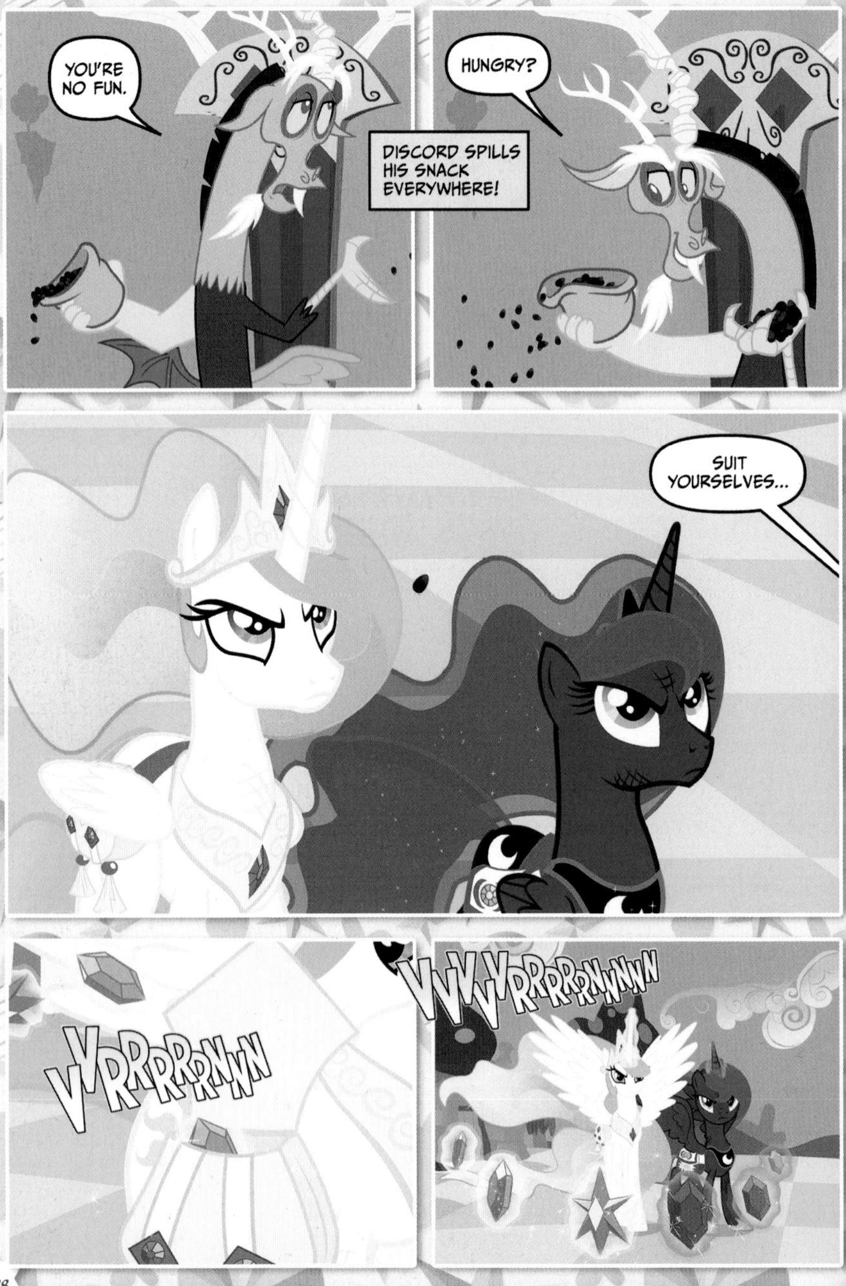
YOU'RE NO FUN.
HUNGRY?
DISCORD SPILLS HIS SNACK EVERYWHERE!
SUIT YOURSELVES...
VYRRRRRNNNN
VVVVYRRRRRNNNNN

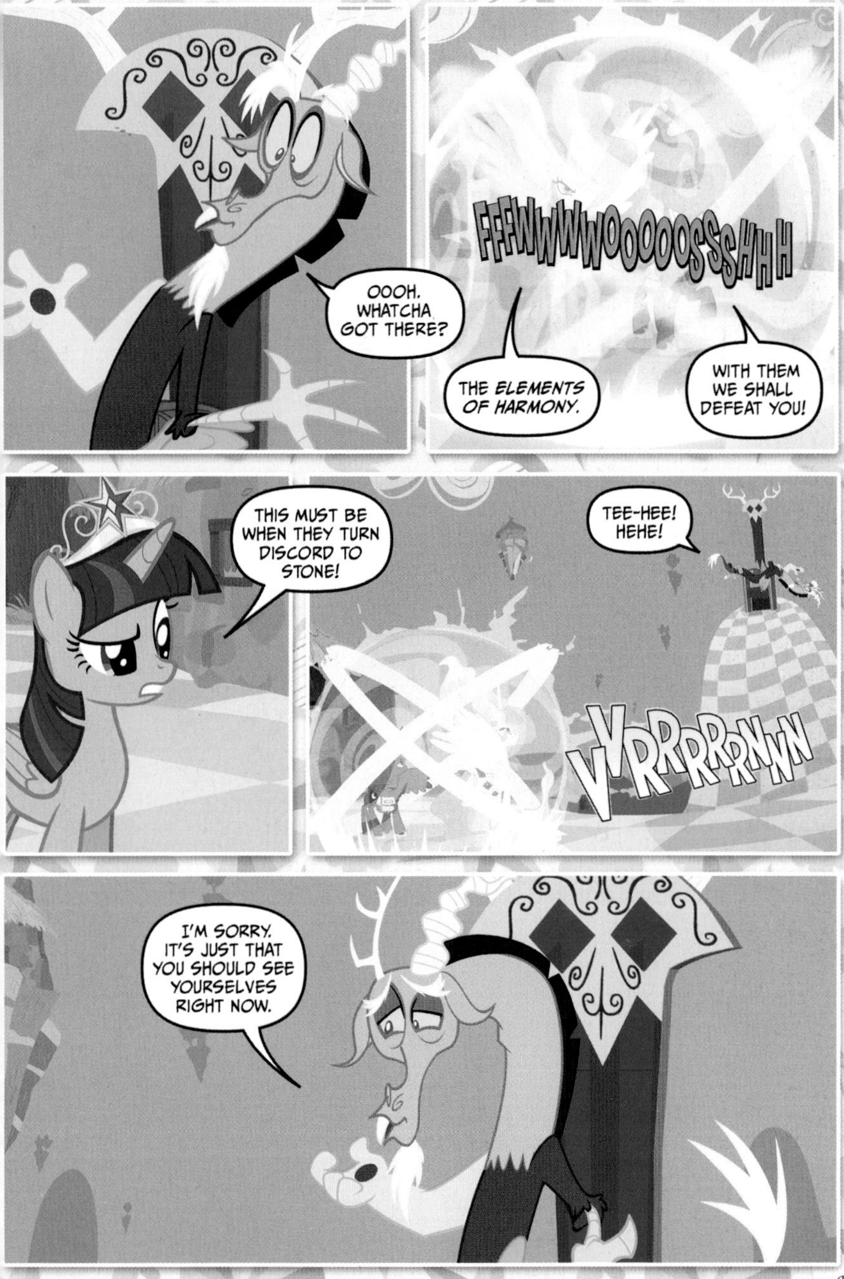

OOOH. WHATCHA GOT THERE?
FFFWWWWOOOOOOSSSHHH
THE *ELEMENTS OF HARMONY.*
WITH THEM WE SHALL DEFEAT YOU!
THIS MUST BE WHEN THEY TURN DISCORD TO STONE!
TEE-HEE! HEHE!
VVRRRRRNNN
I'M SORRY. IT'S JUST THAT YOU SHOULD SEE YOURSELVES RIGHT NOW.

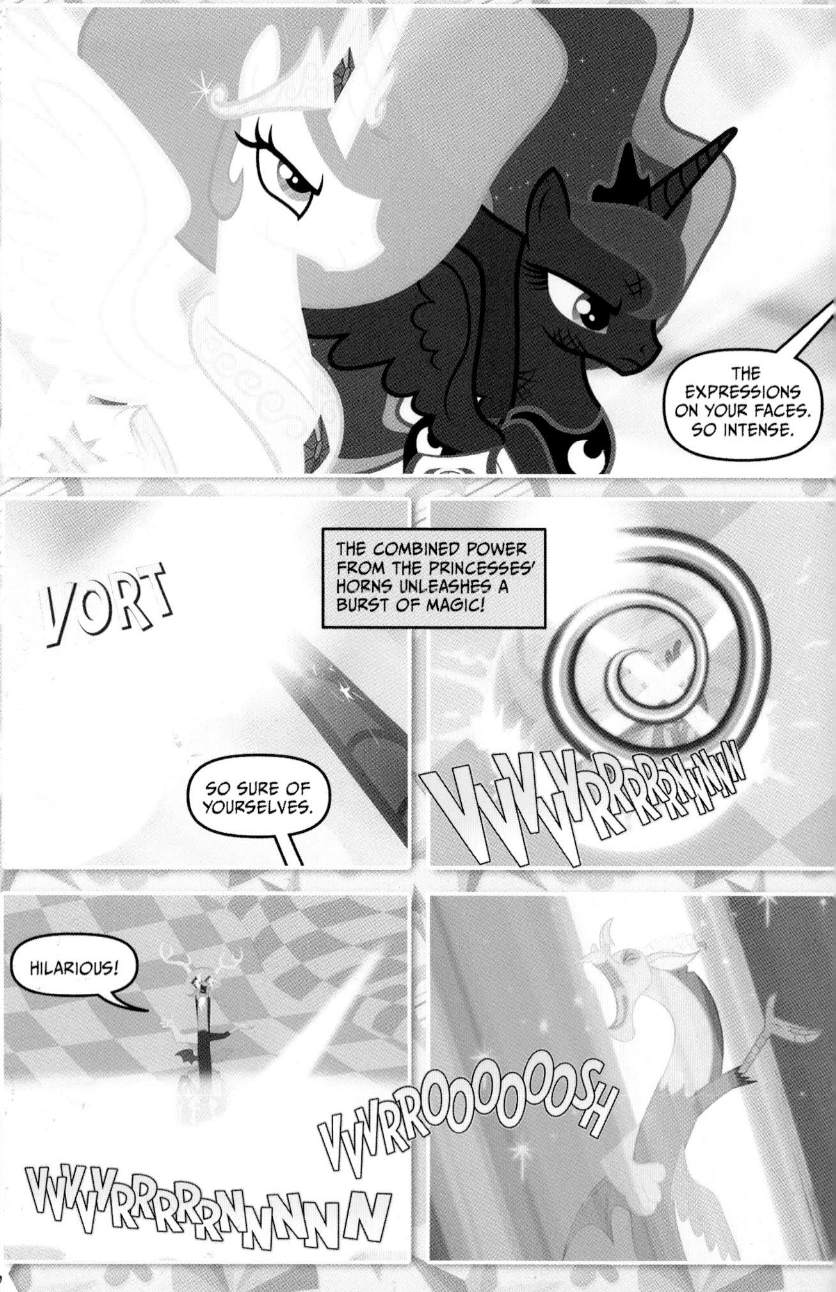
THE EXPRESSIONS ON YOUR FACES. SO INTENSE.
VORT
THE COMBINED POWER FROM THE PRINCESSES' HORNS UNLEASHES A BURST OF MAGIC!
SO SURE OF YOURSELVES.
VVVVYRRRRRNNNNN
HILARIOUS!
VVVVYRRRRRNNNNNN
VVVRROOOOOOOSH

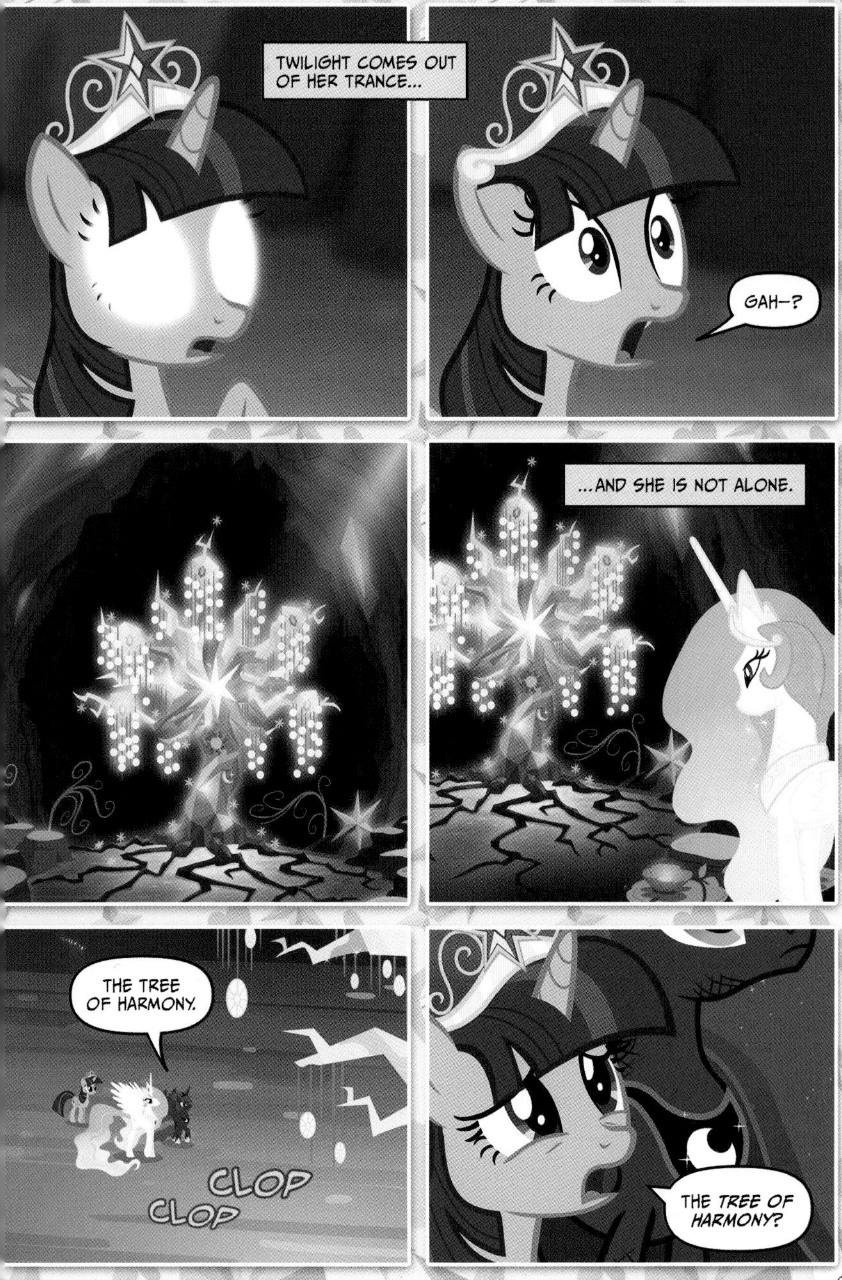

TWILIGHT COMES OUT OF HER TRANCE...
GAH–?
...AND SHE IS NOT ALONE.
THE TREE OF HARMONY.
CLOP
CLOP
THE TREE OF HARMONY?

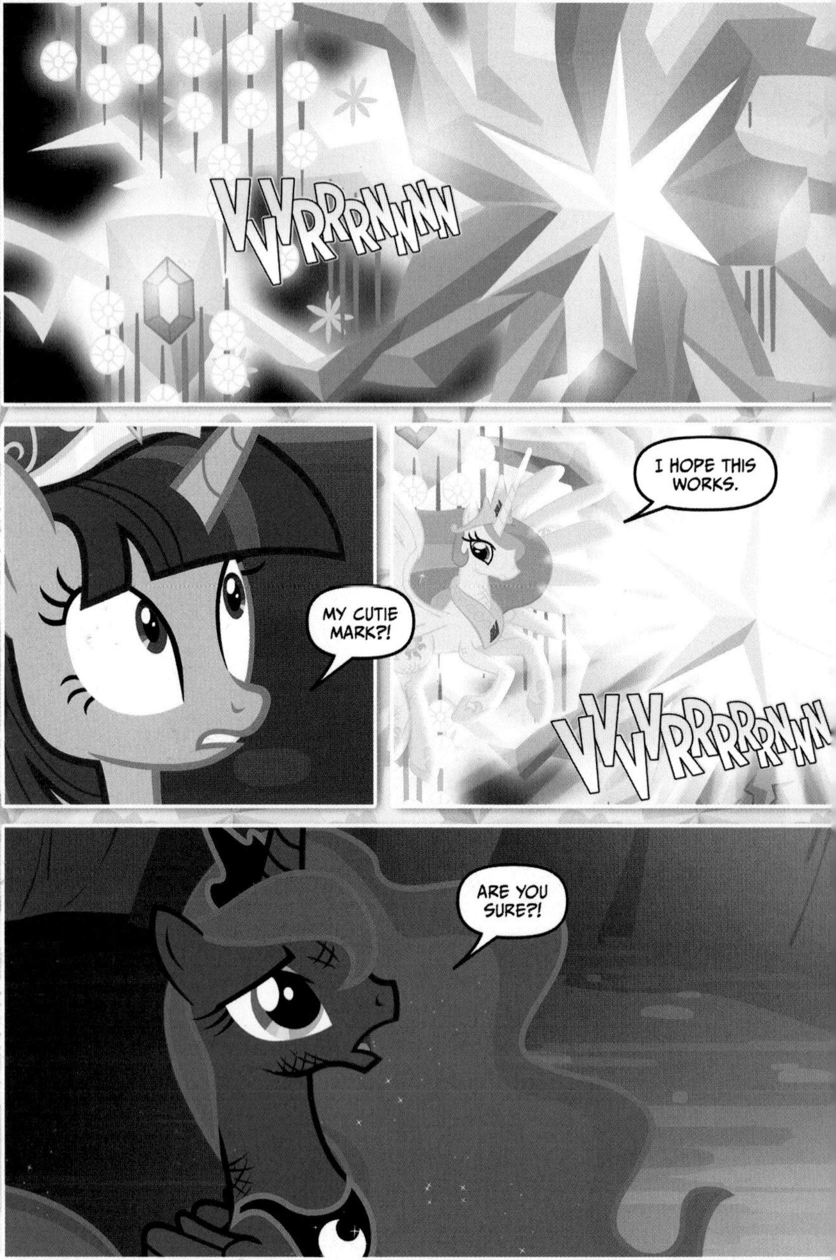
VVVRRRNNNN
MY CUTIE MARK?!
I HOPE THIS WORKS.
VVVVRRRRNNN
ARE YOU SURE?!

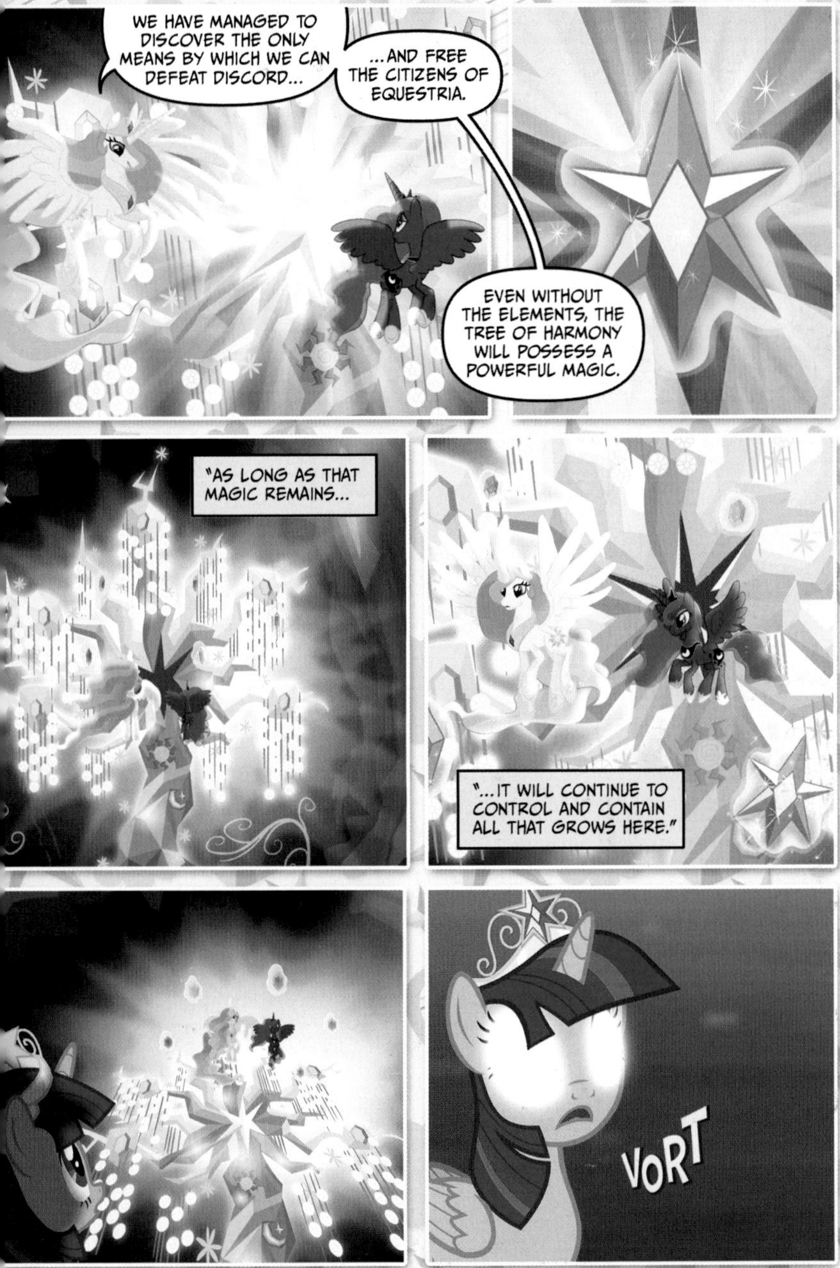
WE HAVE MANAGED TO DISCOVER THE ONLY MEANS BY WHICH WE CAN DEFEAT DISCORD...
...AND FREE THE CITIZENS OF EQUESTRIA.
EVEN WITHOUT THE ELEMENTS, THE TREE OF HARMONY WILL POSSESS A POWERFUL MAGIC.
"AS LONG AS THAT MAGIC REMAINS...
"...IT WILL CONTINUE TO CONTROL AND CONTAIN ALL THAT GROWS HERE."
VORT

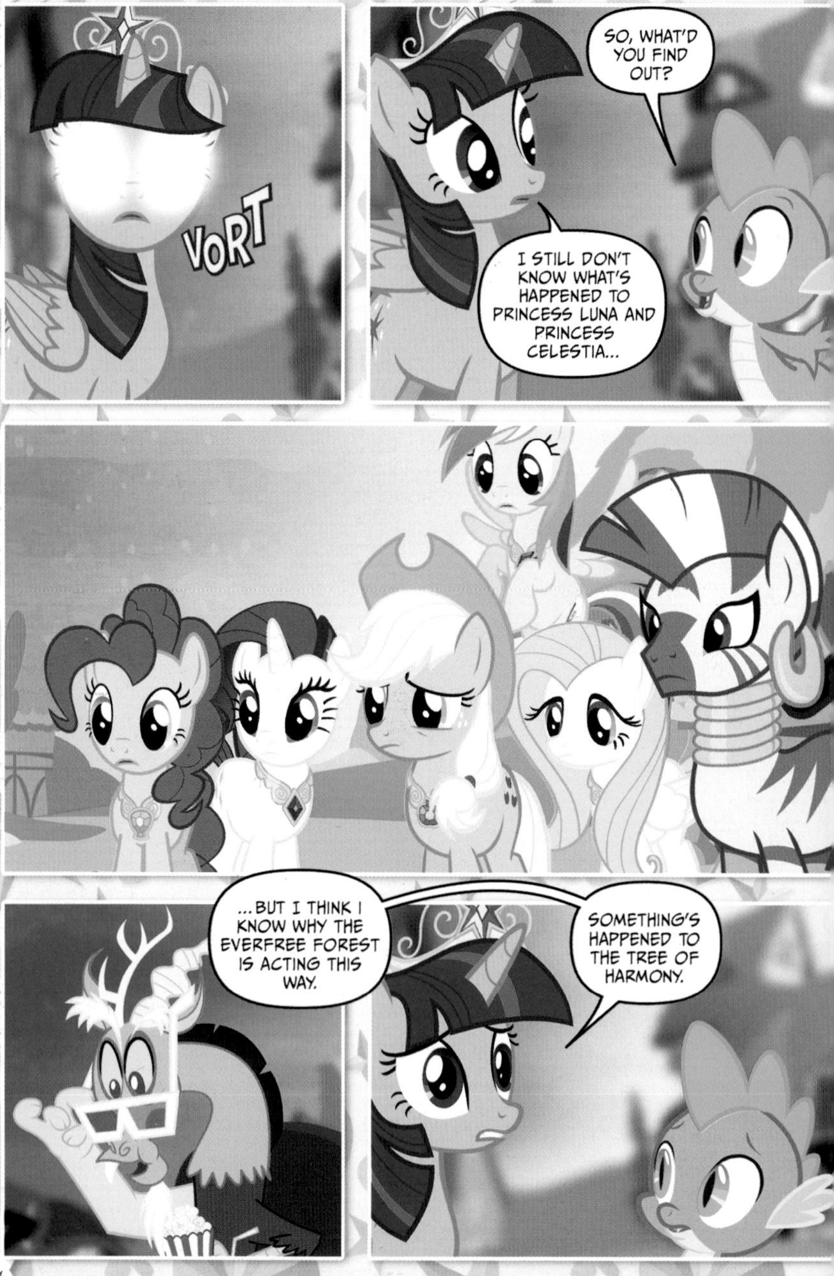
VORT
SO, WHAT'D YOU FIND OUT?
I STILL DON'T KNOW WHAT'S HAPPENED TO PRINCESS LUNA AND PRINCESS CELESTIA...
...BUT I THINK I KNOW WHY THE EVERFREE FOREST IS ACTING THIS WAY.
SOMETHING'S HAPPENED TO THE TREE OF HARMONY.

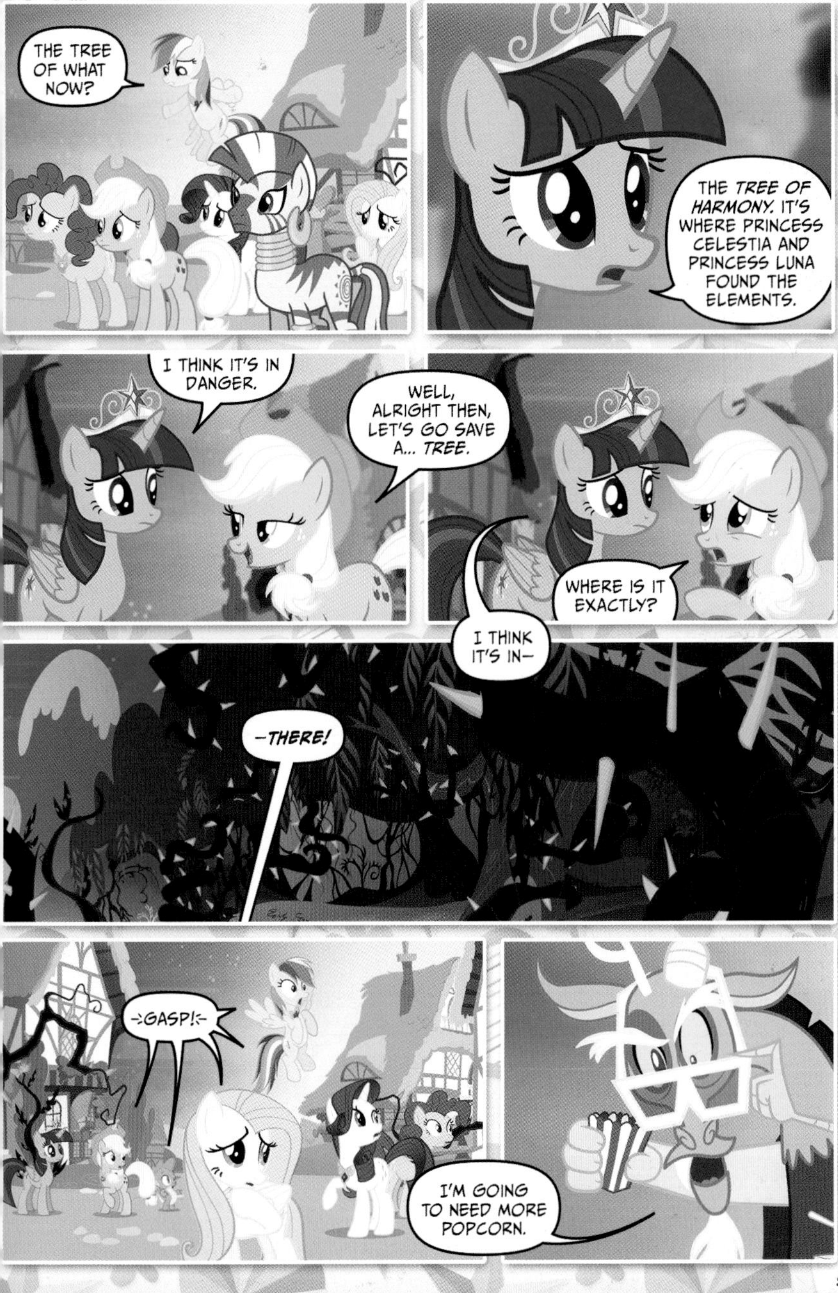
THE TREE OF WHAT NOW?
THE *TREE OF HARMONY.* IT'S WHERE PRINCESS CELESTIA AND PRINCESS LUNA FOUND THE ELEMENTS.
I THINK IT'S IN DANGER.
WELL, ALRIGHT THEN, LET'S GO SAVE A... *TREE.*
WHERE IS IT EXACTLY?
I THINK IT'S IN—
—*THERE!*
-GASP!-
I'M GOING TO NEED MORE POPCORN.

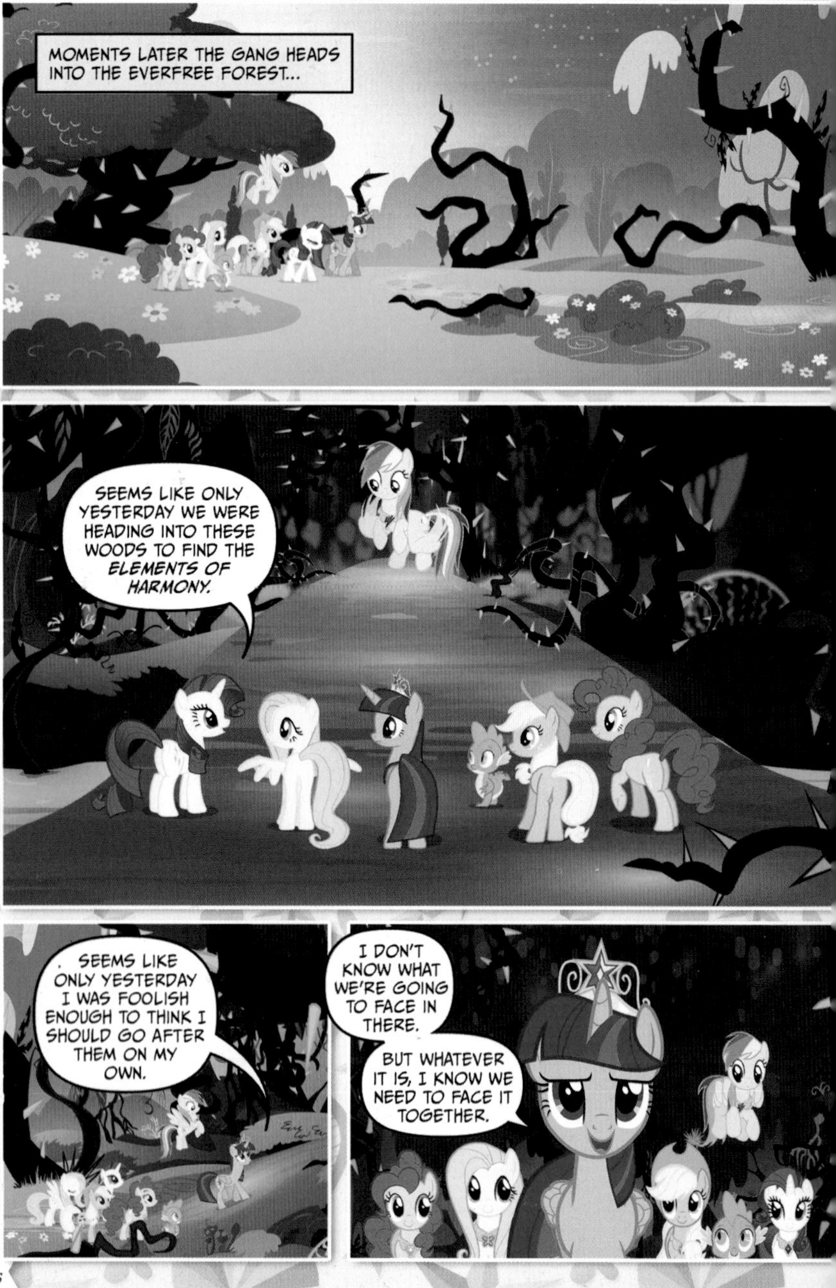
MOMENTS LATER THE GANG HEADS INTO THE EVERFREE FOREST...
SEEMS LIKE ONLY YESTERDAY WE WERE HEADING INTO THESE WOODS TO FIND THE *ELEMENTS OF HARMONY.*
SEEMS LIKE ONLY YESTERDAY I WAS FOOLISH ENOUGH TO THINK I SHOULD GO AFTER THEM ON MY OWN.
I DON'T KNOW WHAT WE'RE GOING TO FACE IN THERE.
BUT WHATEVER IT IS, I KNOW WE NEED TO FACE IT TOGETHER.

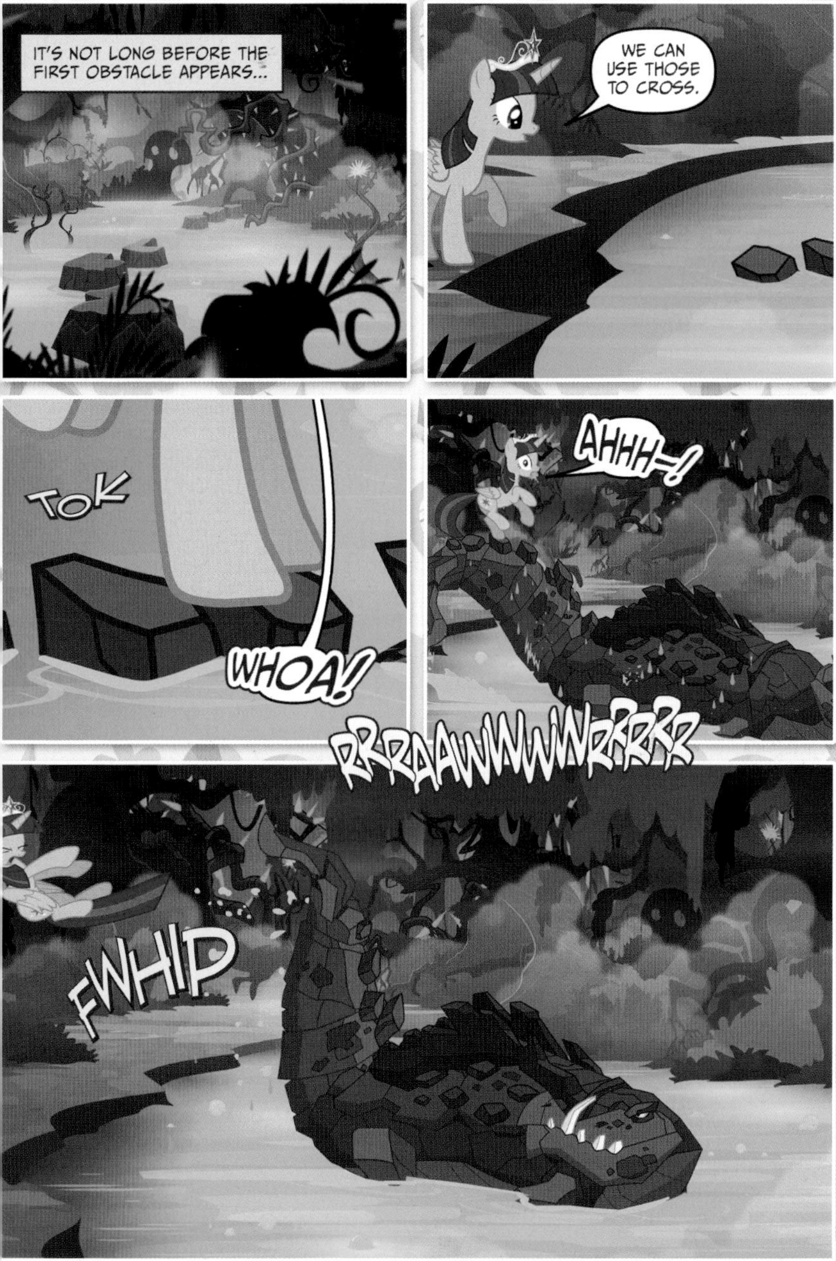
IT'S NOT LONG BEFORE THE FIRST OBSTACLE APPEARS...
WE CAN USE THOSE TO CROSS.
TOK
WHOA!
AHHH--!
RRRAAWWWWRRRRR
FWHIP

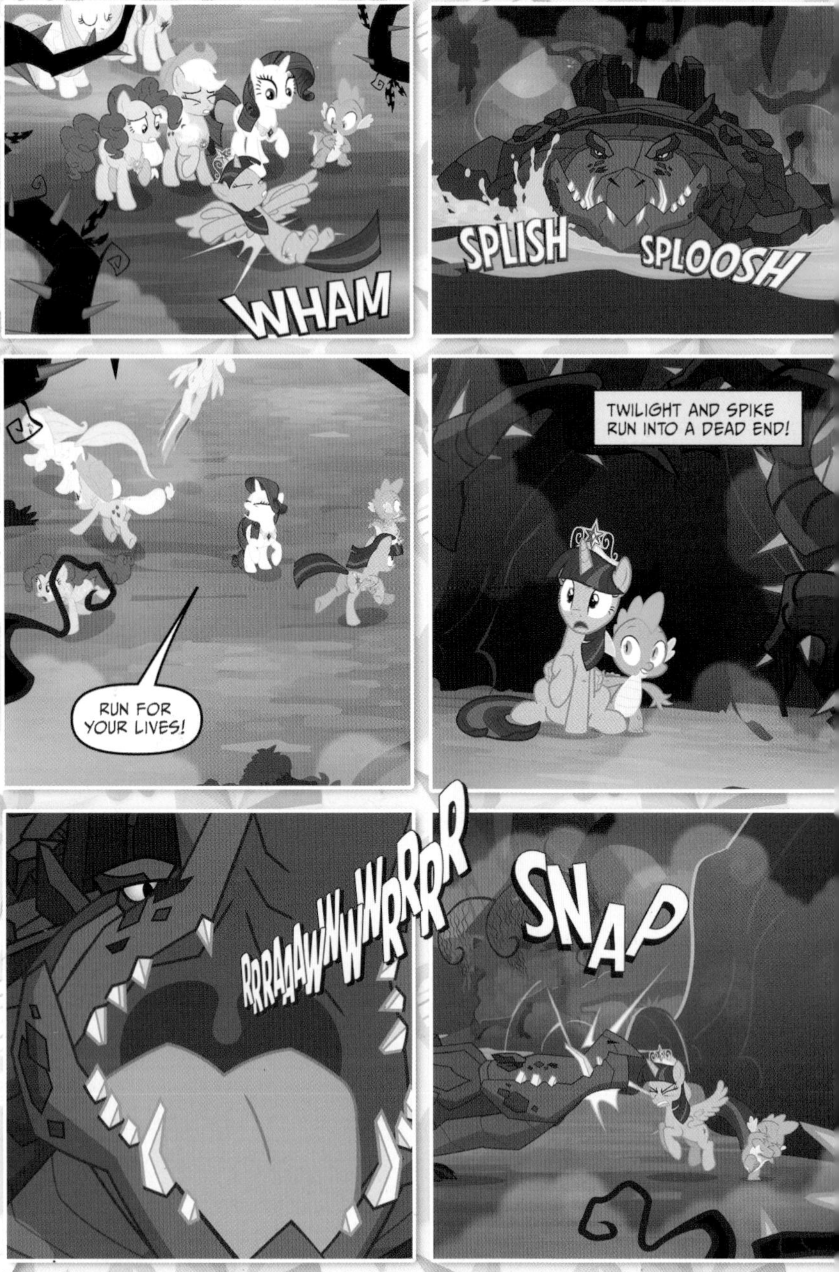
WHAM
SPLISH
SPLOOSH
RUN FOR YOUR LIVES!
TWILIGHT AND SPIKE RUN INTO A DEAD END!
RRRAAAWWWRRRR
SNAP

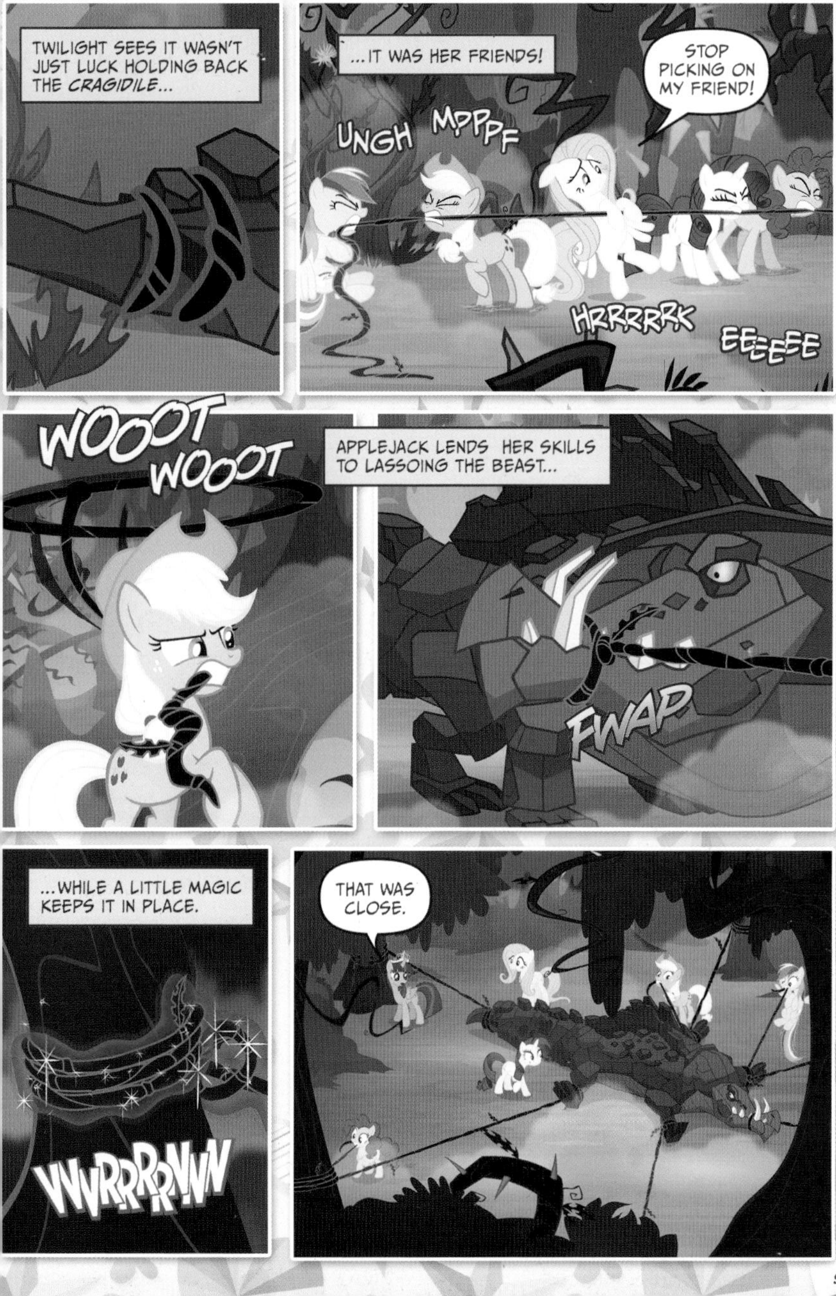

TWILIGHT SEES IT WASN'T JUST LUCK HOLDING BACK THE CRAGIDILE...
...IT WAS HER FRIENDS!
STOP PICKING ON MY FRIEND!
UNGH
MPPPF
HRRRRRK
EEEEEE
WOOOT WOOOT
APPLEJACK LENDS HER SKILLS TO LASSOING THE BEAST...
FWAP
...WHILE A LITTLE MAGIC KEEPS IT IN PLACE.
VVVRRRRRNNN
THAT WAS CLOSE.

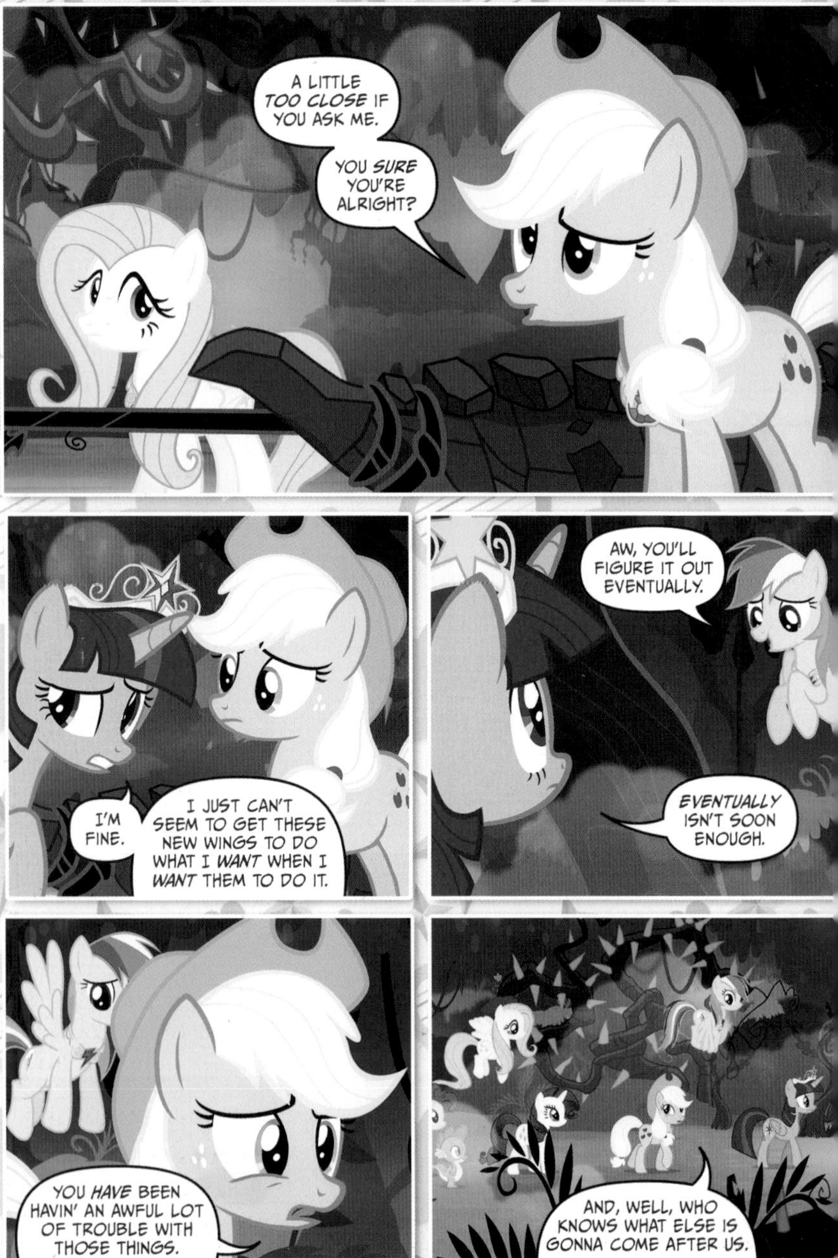
A LITTLE *TOO CLOSE* IF YOU ASK ME.
YOU *SURE* YOU'RE ALRIGHT?
I'M FINE.
I JUST CAN'T SEEM TO GET THESE NEW WINGS TO DO WHAT I *WANT* WHEN I *WANT* THEM TO DO IT.
AW, YOU'LL FIGURE IT OUT EVENTUALLY.
EVENTUALLY ISN'T SOON ENOUGH.
YOU *HAVE* BEEN HAVIN' AN AWFUL LOT OF TROUBLE WITH THOSE THINGS.
AND, WELL, WHO KNOWS WHAT ELSE IS GONNA COME AFTER US.

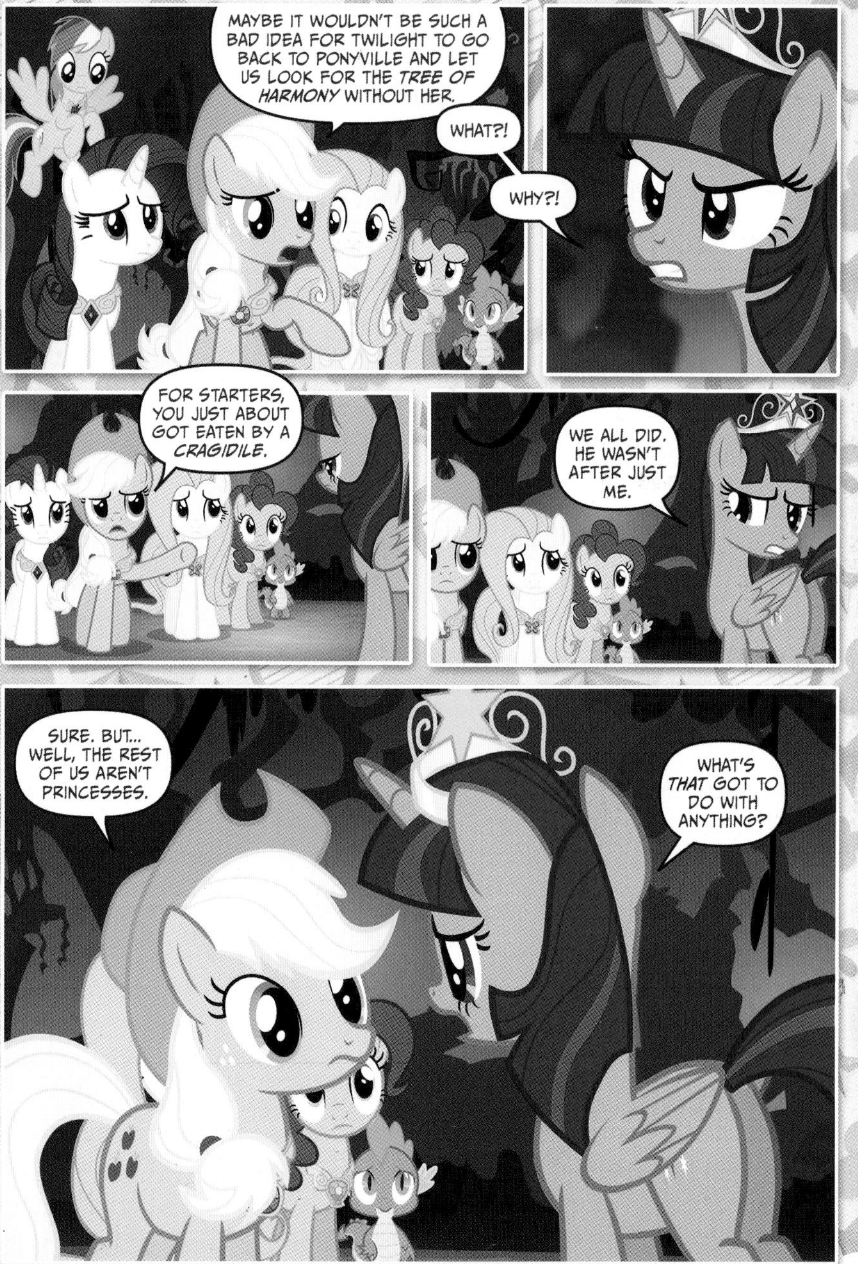
MAYBE IT WOULDN'T BE SUCH A BAD IDEA FOR TWILIGHT TO GO BACK TO PONYVILLE AND LET US LOOK FOR THE *TREE OF HARMONY* WITHOUT HER.
WHAT?!
WHY?!
FOR STARTERS, YOU JUST ABOUT GOT EATEN BY A *CRAGIDILE*.
WE ALL DID. HE WASN'T AFTER JUST ME.
SURE. BUT... WELL, THE REST OF US AREN'T PRINCESSES.
WHAT'S *THAT* GOT TO DO WITH ANYTHING?

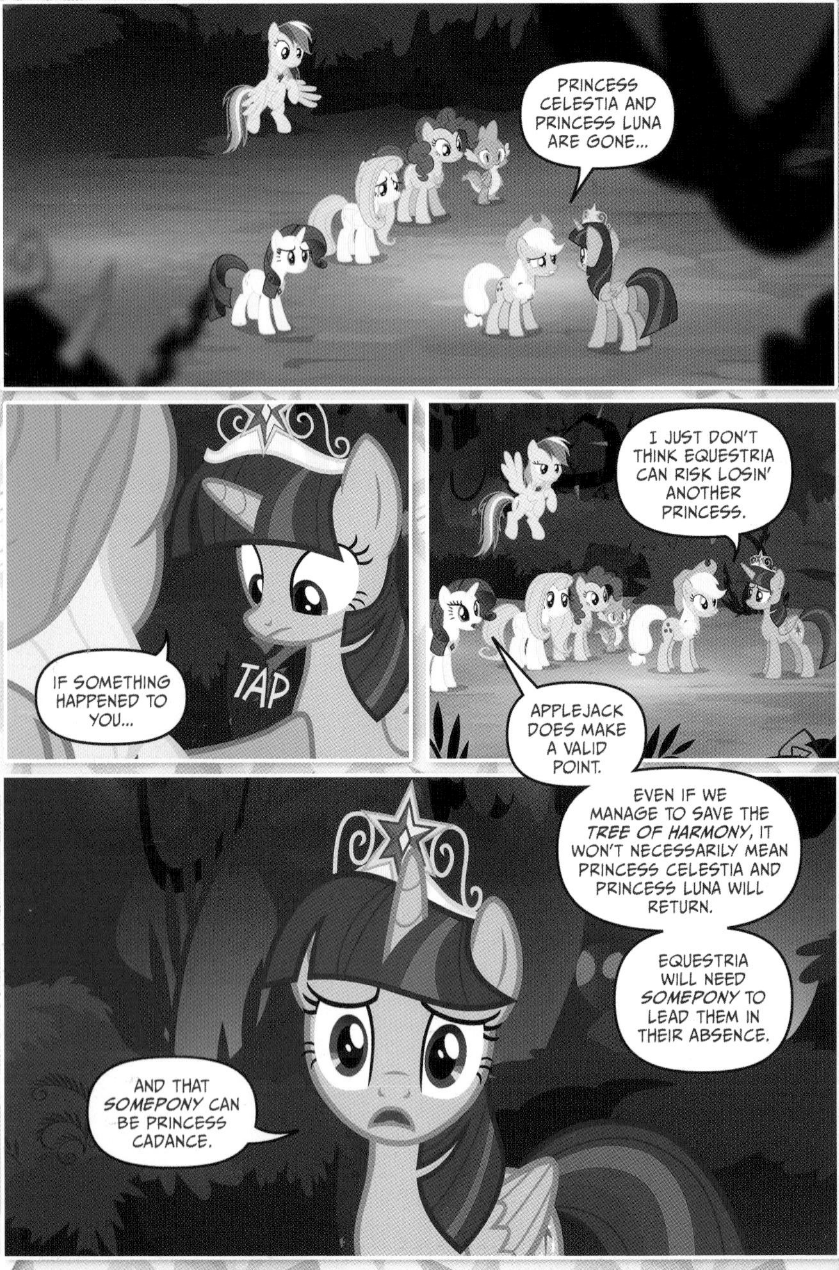
PRINCESS CELESTIA AND PRINCESS LUNA ARE GONE...
IF SOMETHING HAPPENED TO YOU...
TAP
I JUST DON'T THINK EQUESTRIA CAN RISK LOSIN' ANOTHER PRINCESS.
APPLEJACK DOES MAKE A VALID POINT.
EVEN IF WE MANAGE TO SAVE THE *TREE OF HARMONY*, IT WON'T NECESSARILY MEAN PRINCESS CELESTIA AND PRINCESS LUNA WILL RETURN.
EQUESTRIA WILL NEED *SOMEPONY* TO LEAD THEM IN THEIR ABSENCE.
AND THAT *SOMEPONY* CAN BE PRINCESS CADANCE.

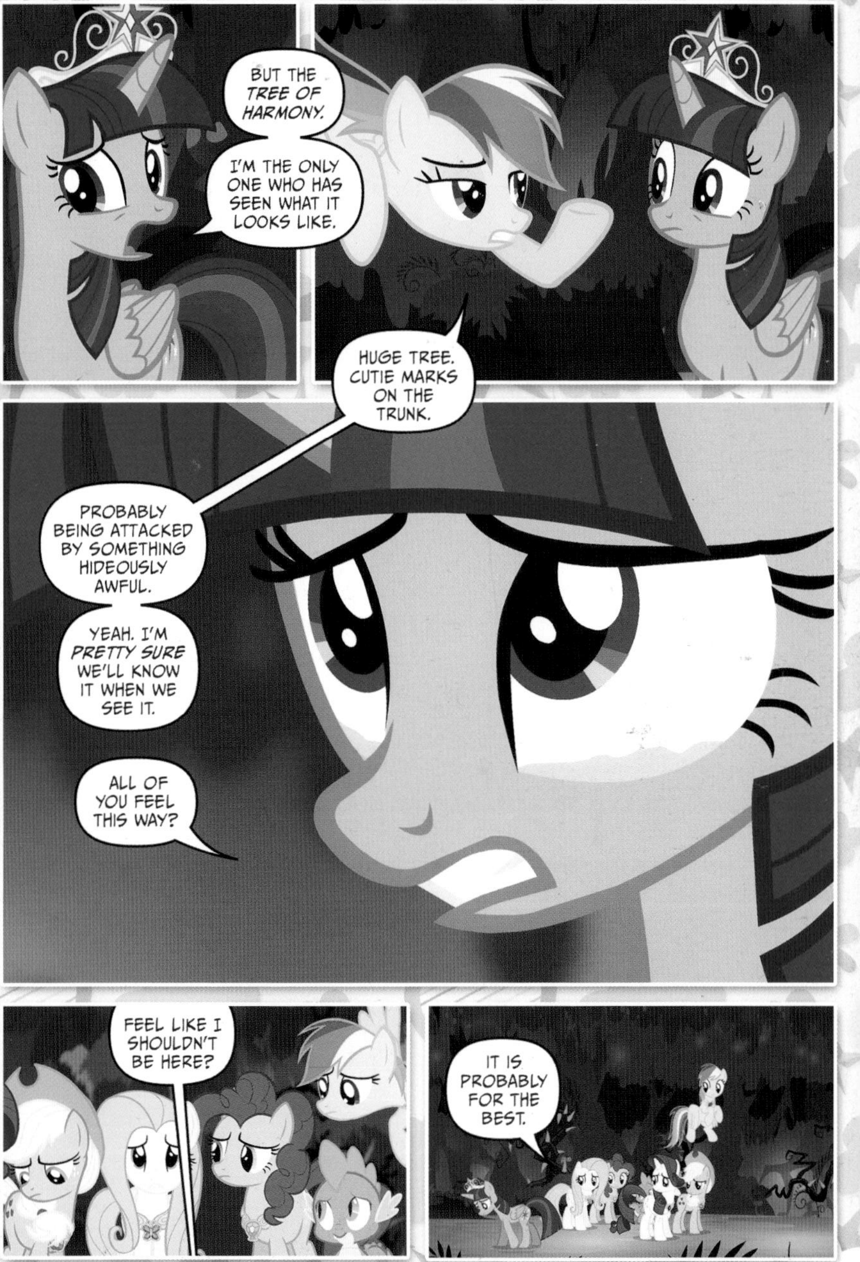

BUT THE *TREE OF HARMONY.*
I'M THE ONLY ONE WHO HAS SEEN WHAT IT LOOKS LIKE.
HUGE TREE. CUTIE MARKS ON THE TRUNK.
PROBABLY BEING ATTACKED BY SOMETHING HIDEOUSLY AWFUL.
YEAH. I'M *PRETTY SURE* WE'LL KNOW IT WHEN WE SEE IT.
ALL OF YOU FEEL THIS WAY?
FEEL LIKE I SHOULDN'T BE HERE?
IT IS PROBABLY FOR THE BEST.

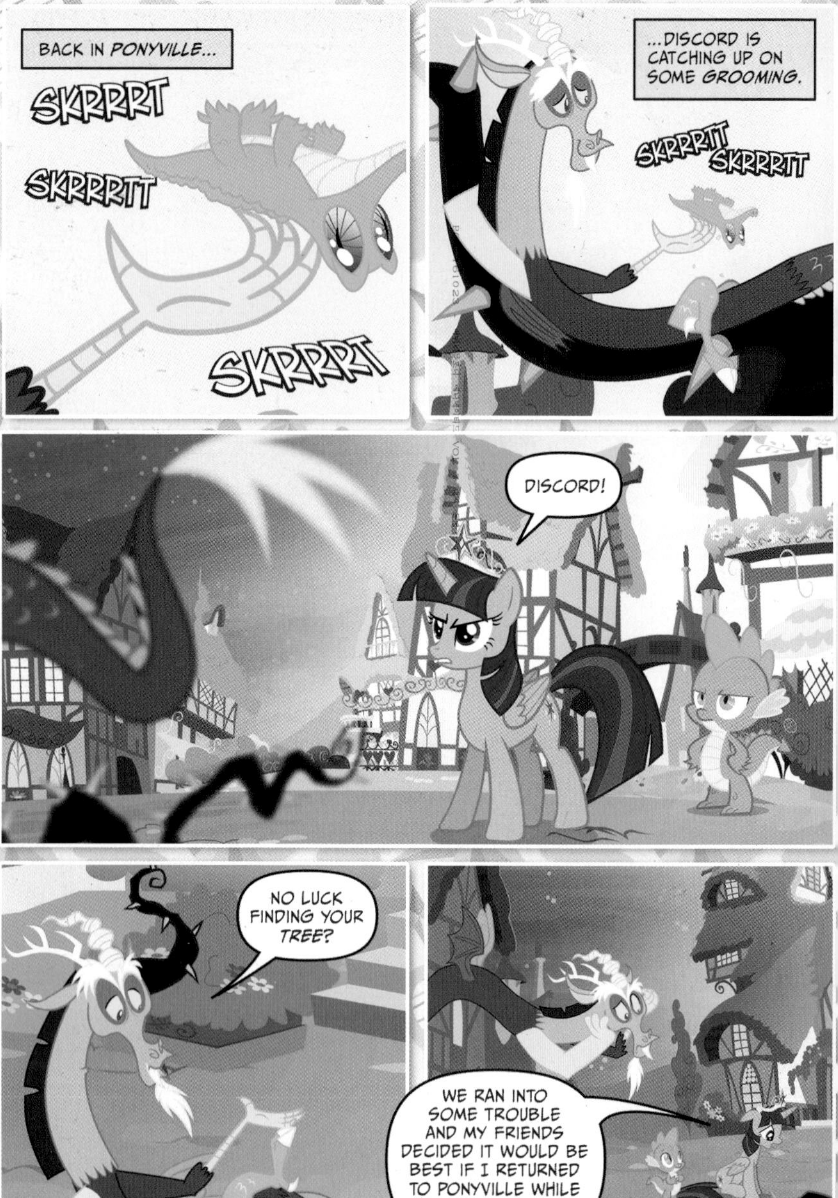
BACK IN PONYVILLE...
SKRRRT
SKRRRTT
SKRRRT
...DISCORD IS CATCHING UP ON SOME GROOMING.
SKRRRTT SKRRRTT
DISCORD!
NO LUCK FINDING YOUR TREE?
WE RAN INTO SOME TROUBLE AND MY FRIENDS DECIDED IT WOULD BE BEST IF I RETURNED TO PONYVILLE WHILE THEY CONTINUE THE SEARCH.

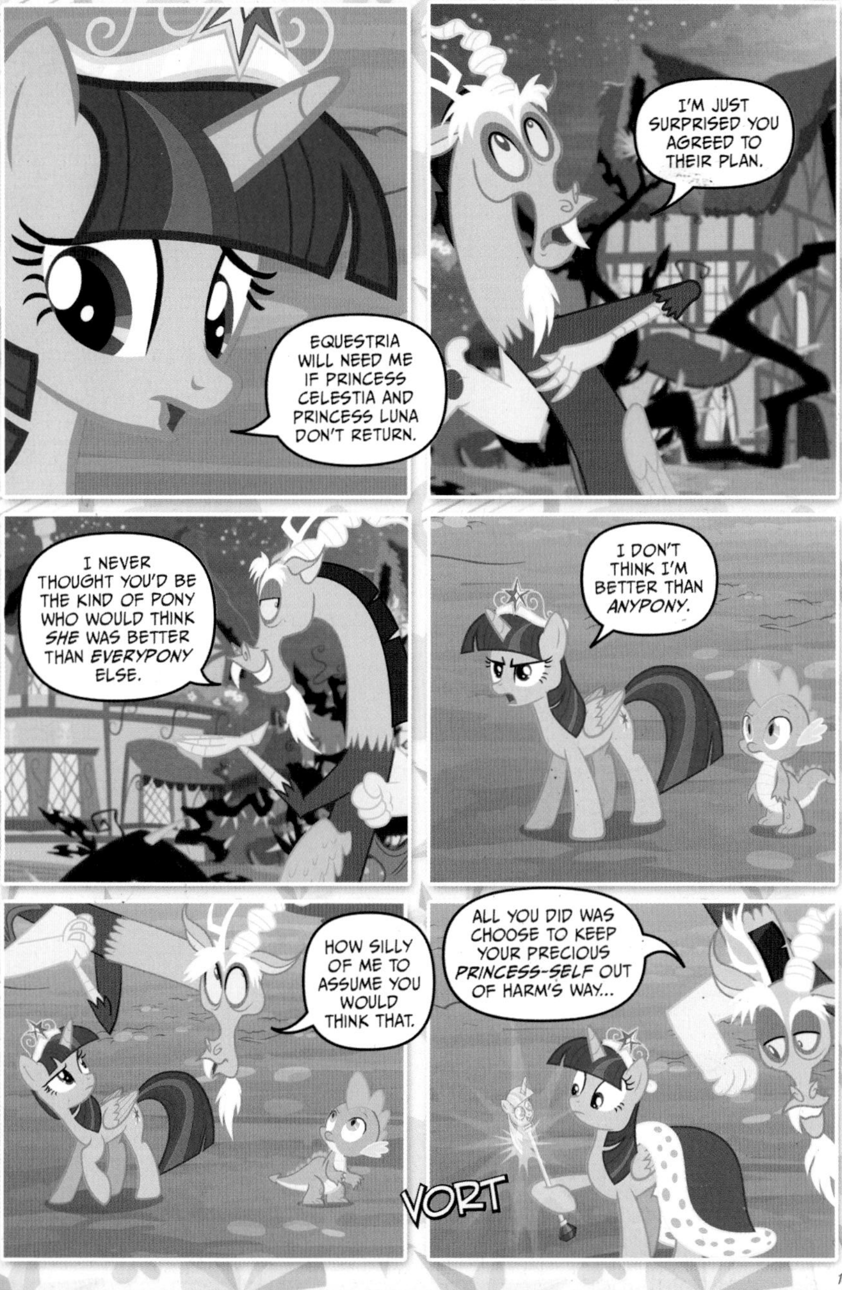
EQUESTRIA WILL NEED ME IF PRINCESS CELESTIA AND PRINCESS LUNA DON'T RETURN.
I'M JUST SURPRISED YOU AGREED TO THEIR PLAN.
I NEVER THOUGHT YOU'D BE THE KIND OF PONY WHO WOULD THINK *SHE* WAS BETTER THAN *EVERYPONY* ELSE.
I DON'T THINK I'M BETTER THAN *ANYPONY*.
HOW SILLY OF ME TO ASSUME YOU WOULD THINK THAT.
ALL YOU DID WAS CHOOSE TO KEEP YOUR PRECIOUS *PRINCESS-SELF* OUT OF HARM'S WAY...
VORT

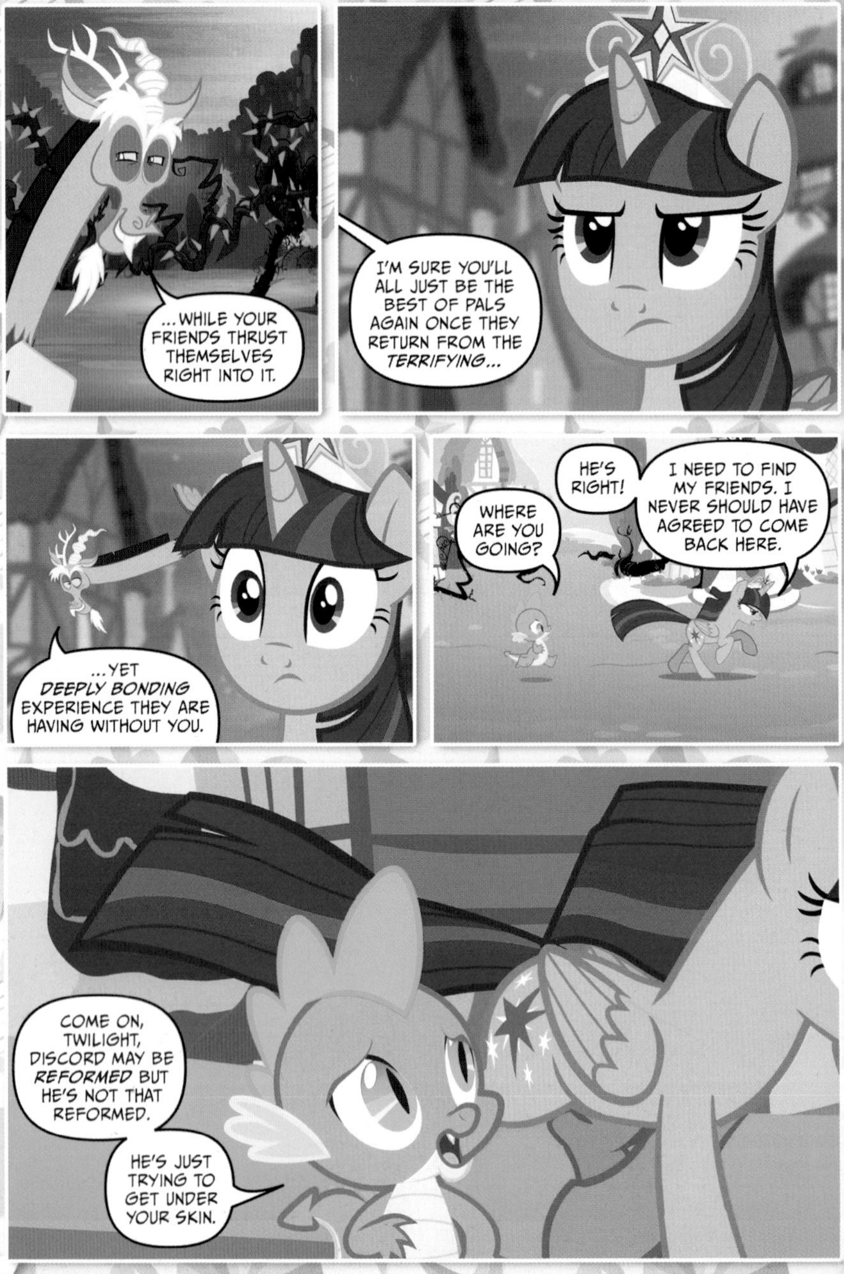
...WHILE YOUR FRIENDS THRUST THEMSELVES RIGHT INTO IT.
I'M SURE YOU'LL ALL JUST BE THE BEST OF PALS AGAIN ONCE THEY RETURN FROM THE *TERRIFYING*...
...YET *DEEPLY BONDING* EXPERIENCE THEY ARE HAVING WITHOUT YOU.
HE'S RIGHT!
I NEED TO FIND MY FRIENDS. I NEVER SHOULD HAVE AGREED TO COME BACK HERE.
WHERE ARE YOU GOING?
COME ON, TWILIGHT, DISCORD MAY BE *REFORMED* BUT HE'S NOT THAT REFORMED.
HE'S JUST TRYING TO GET UNDER YOUR SKIN.

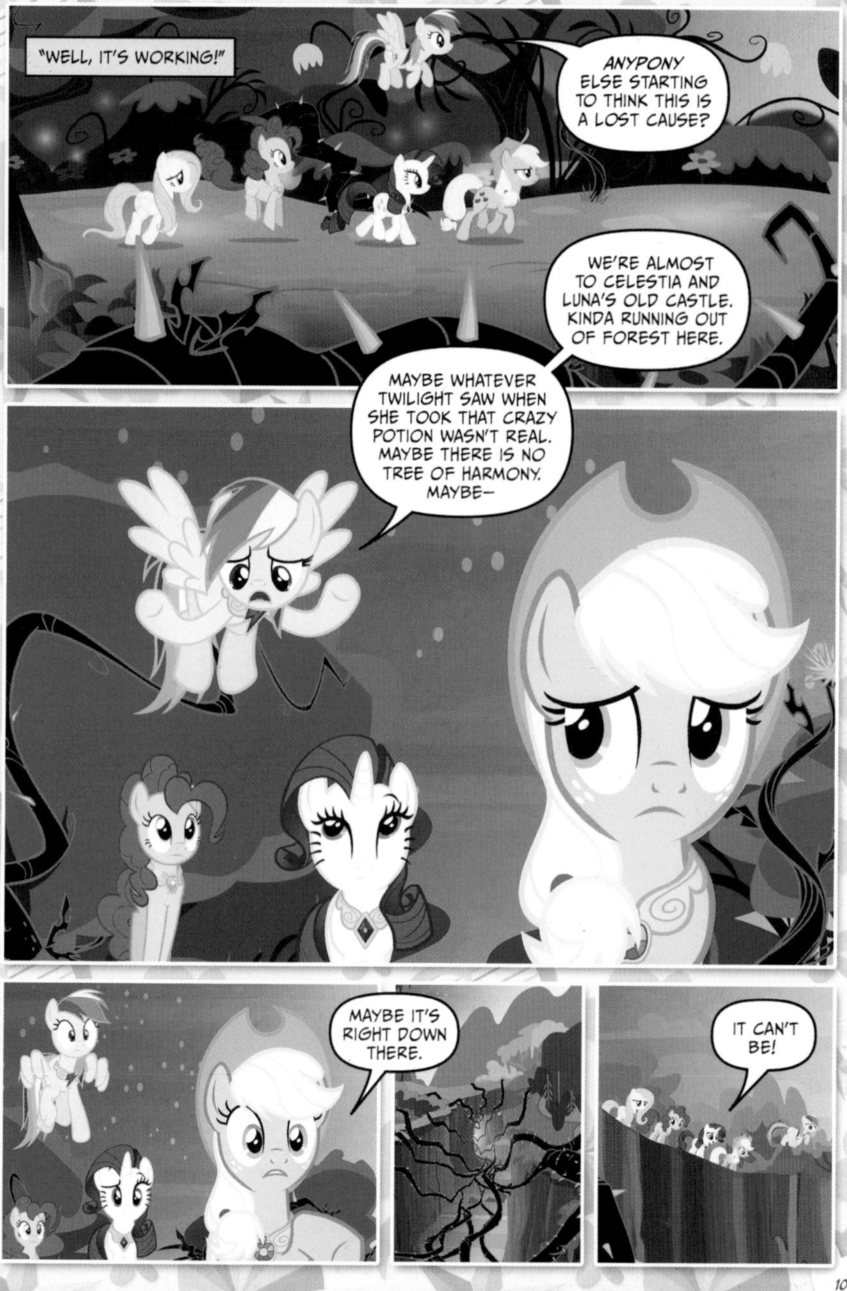
"WELL, IT'S WORKING!"
ANYPONY ELSE STARTING TO THINK THIS IS A LOST CAUSE?
WE'RE ALMOST TO CELESTIA AND LUNA'S OLD CASTLE. KINDA RUNNING OUT OF FOREST HERE.
MAYBE WHATEVER TWILIGHT SAW WHEN SHE TOOK THAT CRAZY POTION WASN'T REAL. MAYBE THERE IS NO TREE OF HARMONY. MAYBE–
MAYBE IT'S RIGHT DOWN THERE.
IT CAN'T BE!

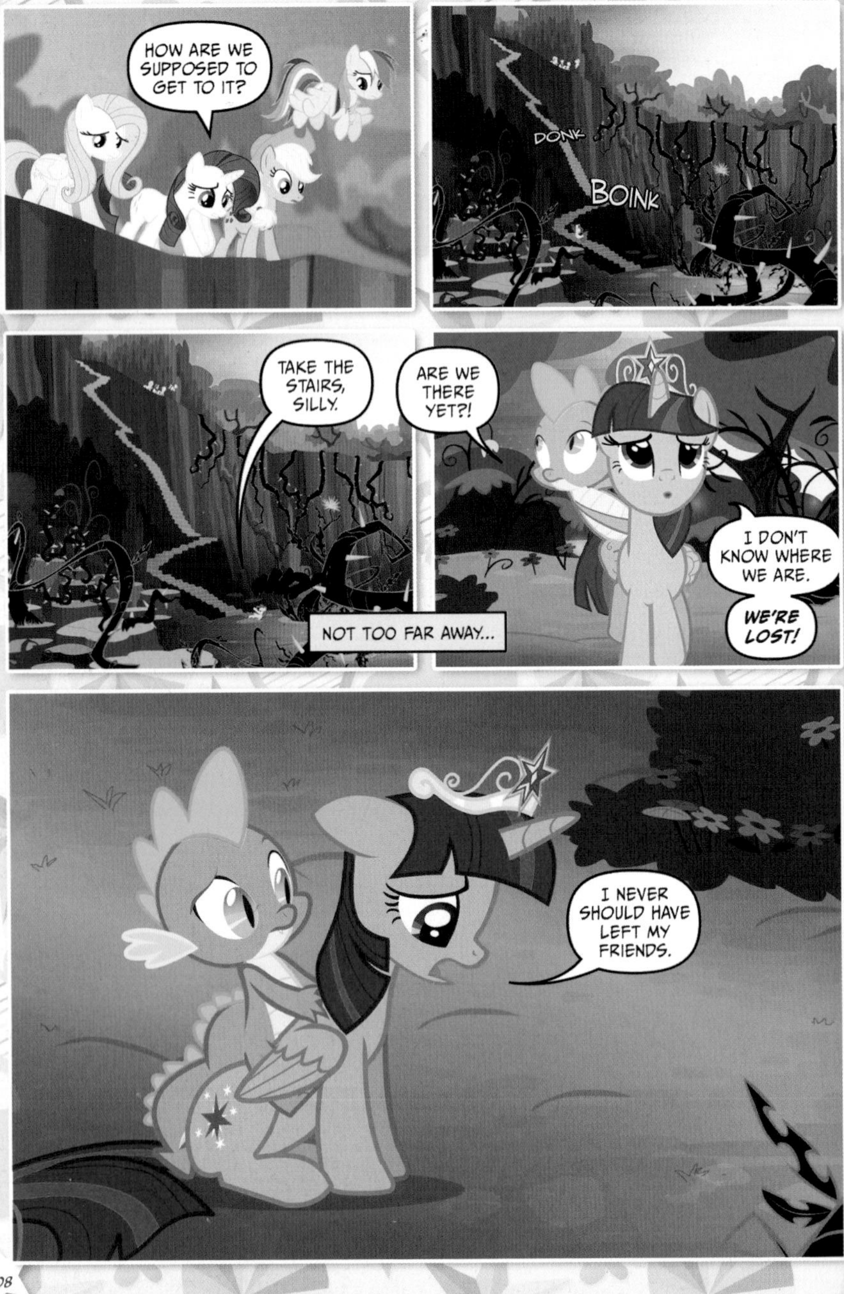
HOW ARE WE SUPPOSED TO GET TO IT?
DONK
BOINK
TAKE THE STAIRS, SILLY.
NOT TOO FAR AWAY...
ARE WE THERE YET?!
I DON'T KNOW WHERE WE ARE.
WE'RE LOST!
I NEVER SHOULD HAVE LEFT MY FRIENDS.

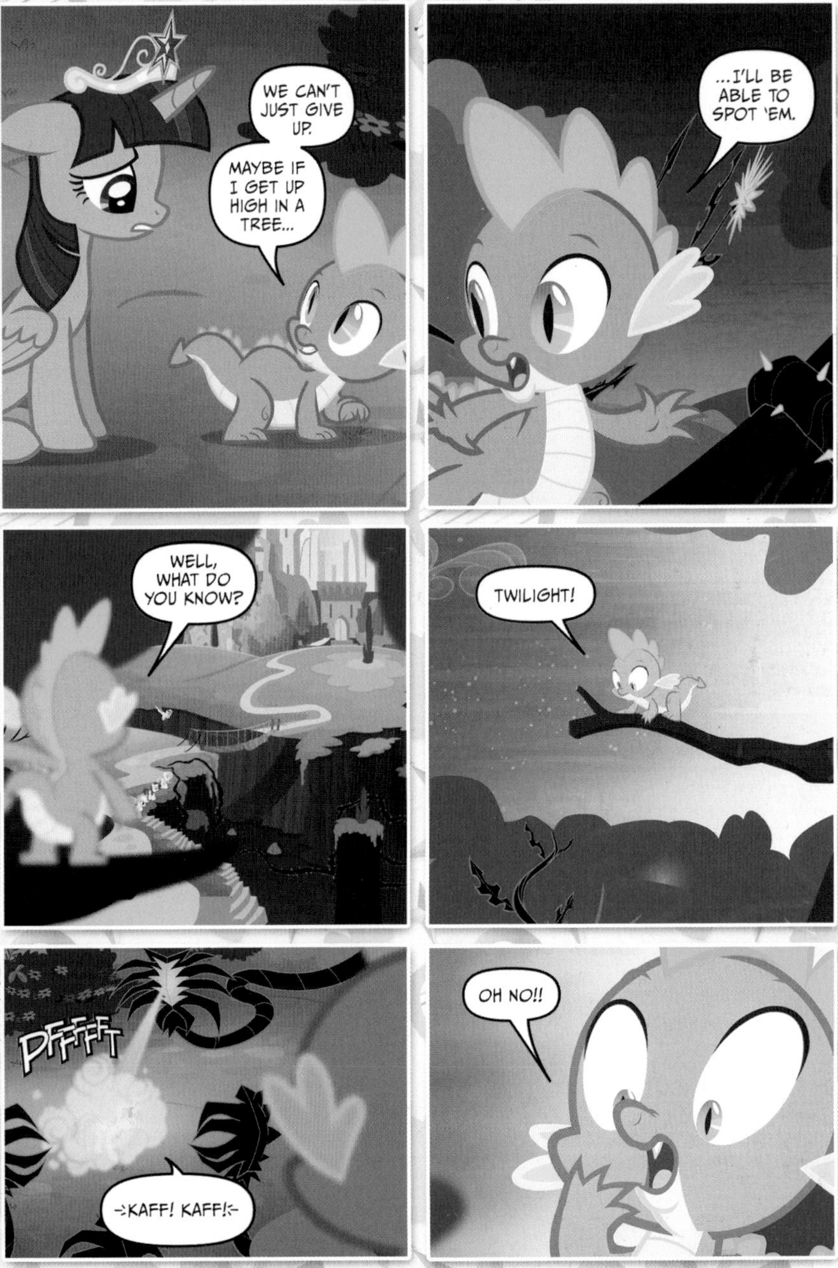
WE CAN'T JUST GIVE UP.
MAYBE IF I GET UP HIGH IN A TREE...
...I'LL BE ABLE TO SPOT 'EM.
WELL, WHAT DO YOU KNOW?
TWILIGHT!
PFFFFFT
-KAFF! KAFF!-
OH NO!!

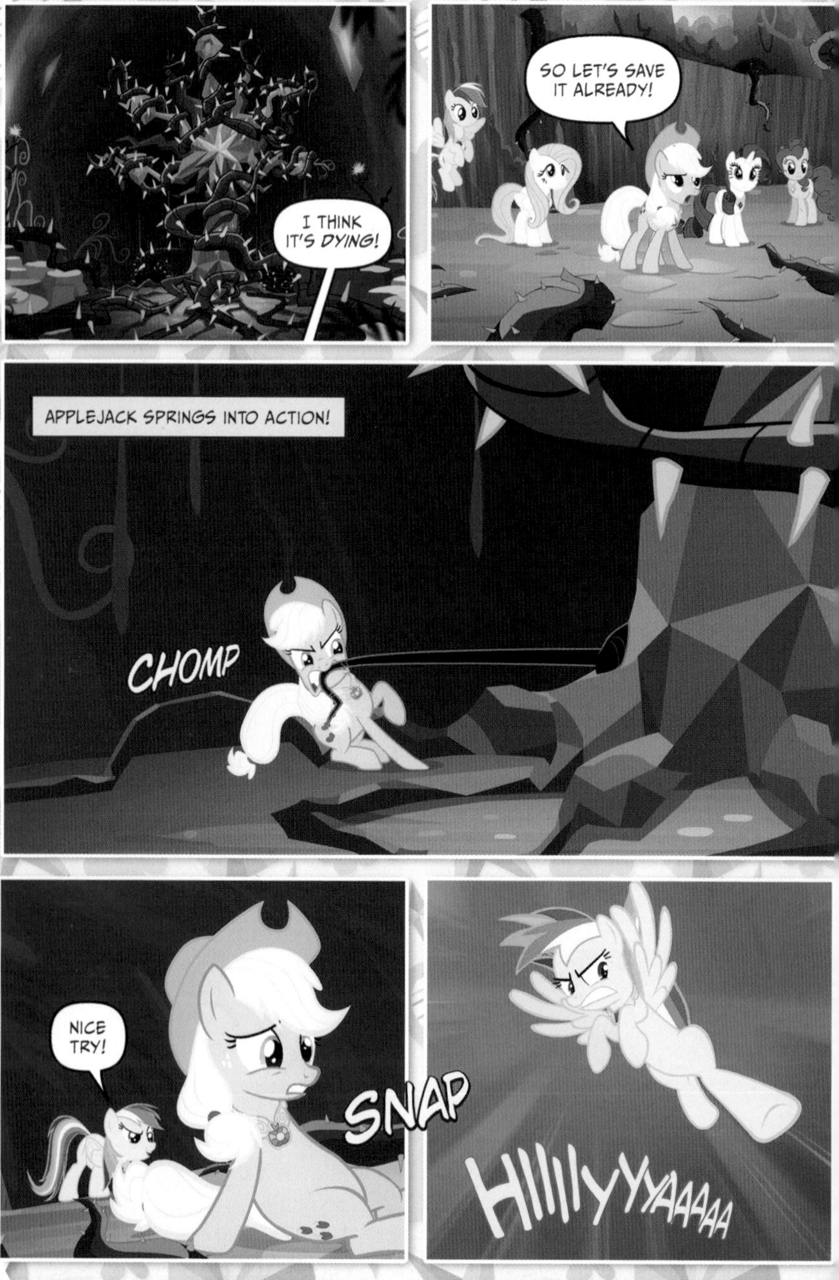
I THINK IT'S DYING!
SO LET'S SAVE IT ALREADY!
APPLEJACK SPRINGS INTO ACTION!
CHOMP
NICE TRY!
SNAP
HIIIIYYYAAAAA

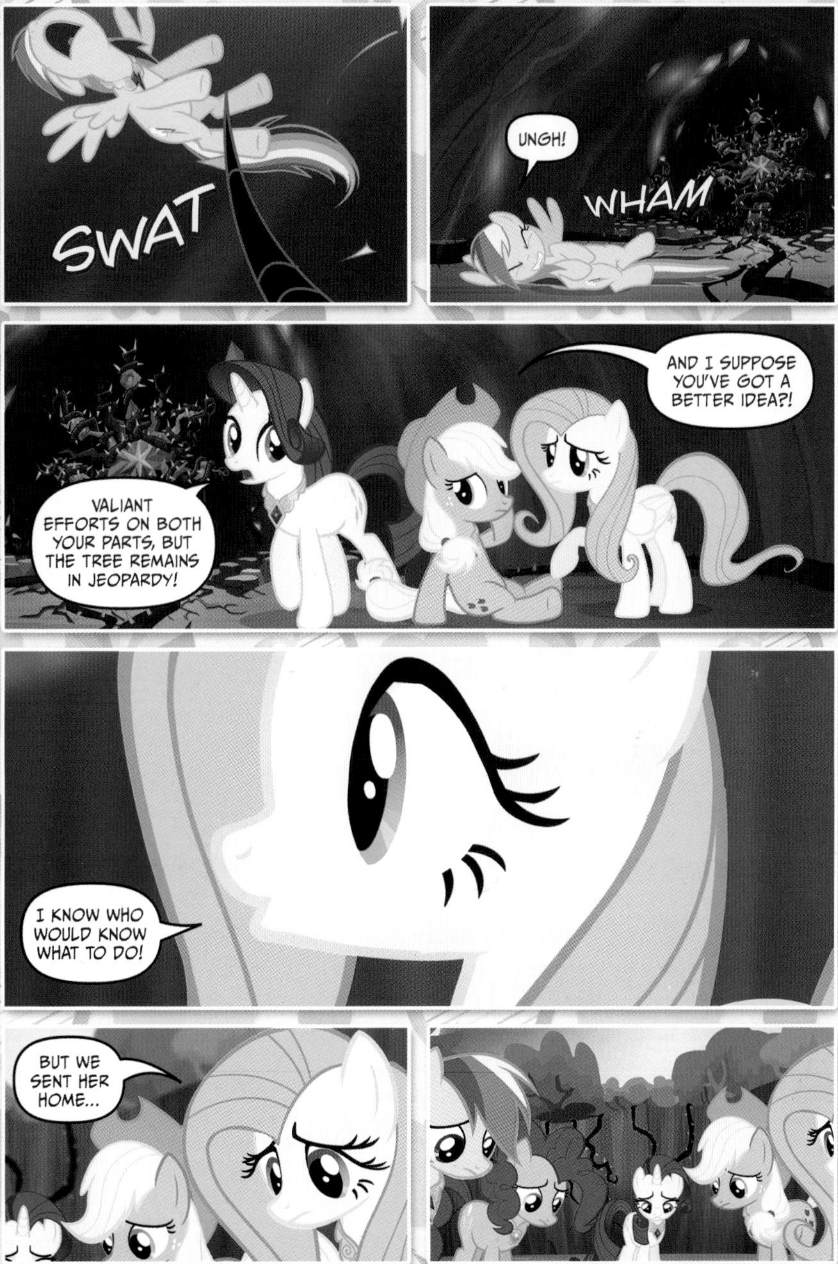
SWAT
UNGH!
WHAM
AND I SUPPOSE YOU'VE GOT A BETTER IDEA?!
VALIANT EFFORTS ON BOTH YOUR PARTS, BUT THE TREE REMAINS IN JEOPARDY!
I KNOW WHO WOULD KNOW WHAT TO DO!
BUT WE SENT HER HOME...

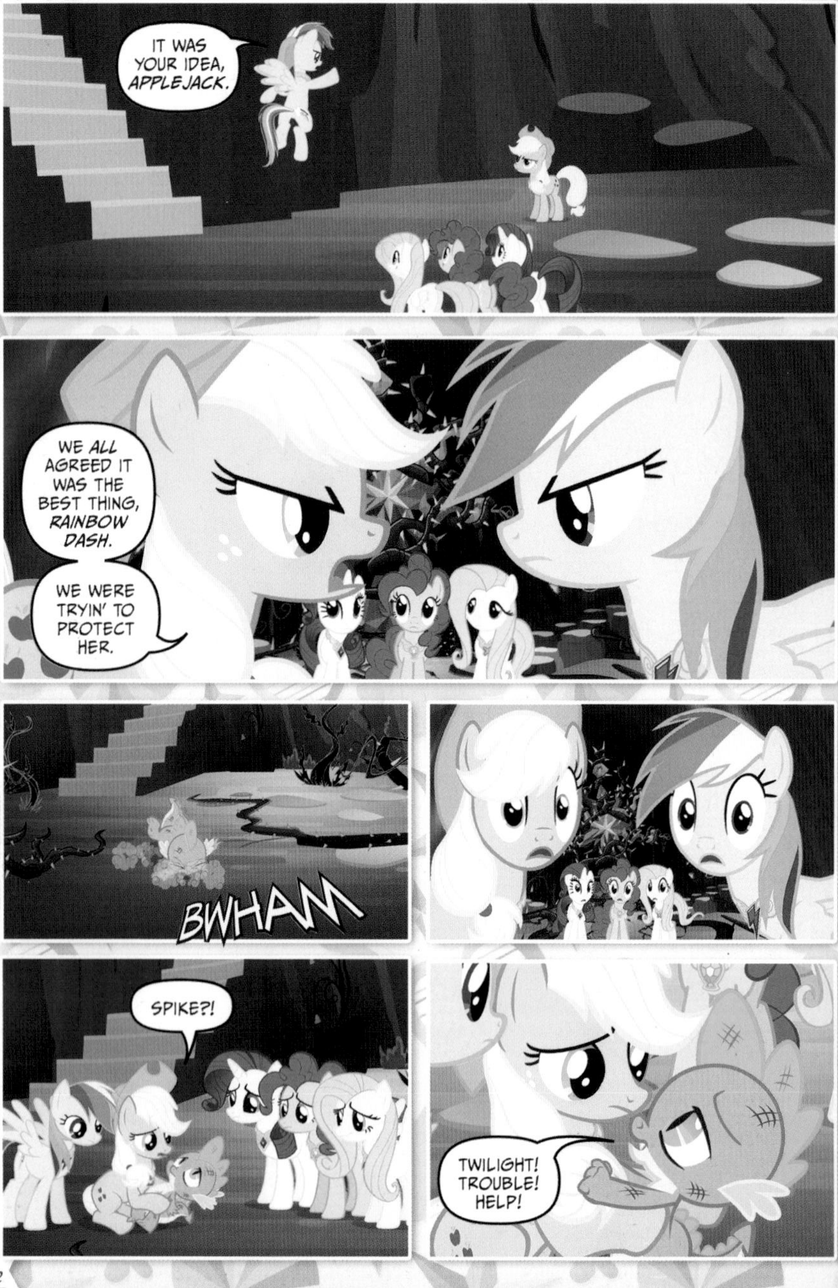
IT WAS YOUR IDEA, APPLEJACK.
WE ALL AGREED IT WAS THE BEST THING, RAINBOW DASH.
WE WERE TRYIN' TO PROTECT HER.
BWHAM
SPIKE?!
TWILIGHT! TROUBLE! HELP!

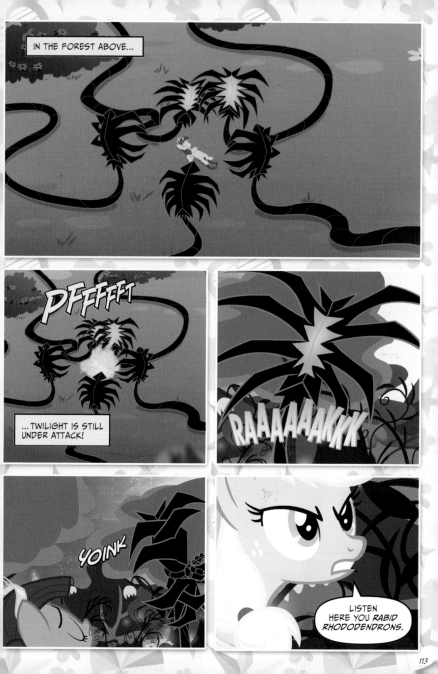

IN THE FOREST ABOVE...

PFFFFFT

...TWILIGHT IS STILL UNDER ATTACK!

RAAAAAAKKK

YOINK

LISTEN HERE YOU *RABID RHODODENDRONS.*

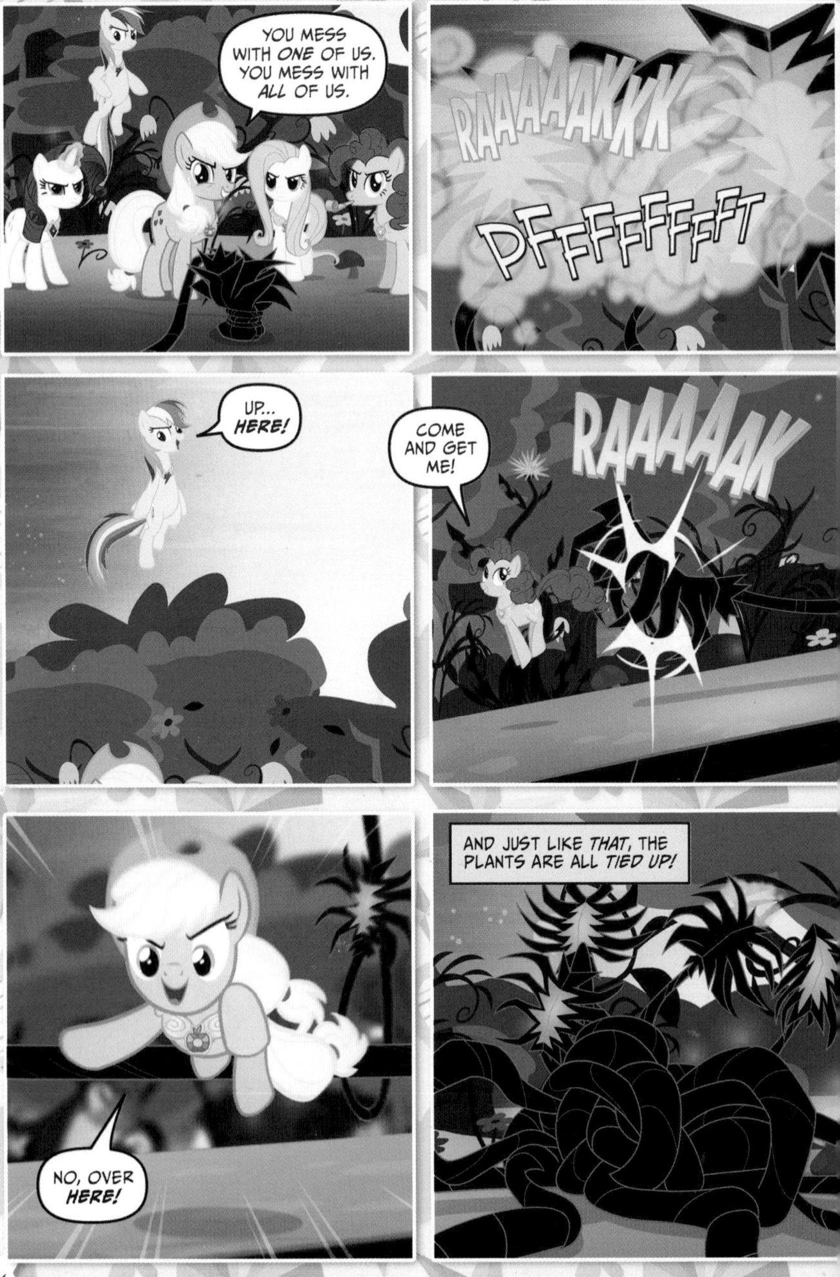
YOU MESS WITH ONE OF US. YOU MESS WITH ALL OF US.
RAAAAAKKKX
PFFFFFFFFFT
UP... HERE!
COME AND GET ME!
RAAAAAK
NO, OVER HERE!
AND JUST LIKE THAT, THE PLANTS ARE ALL TIED UP!

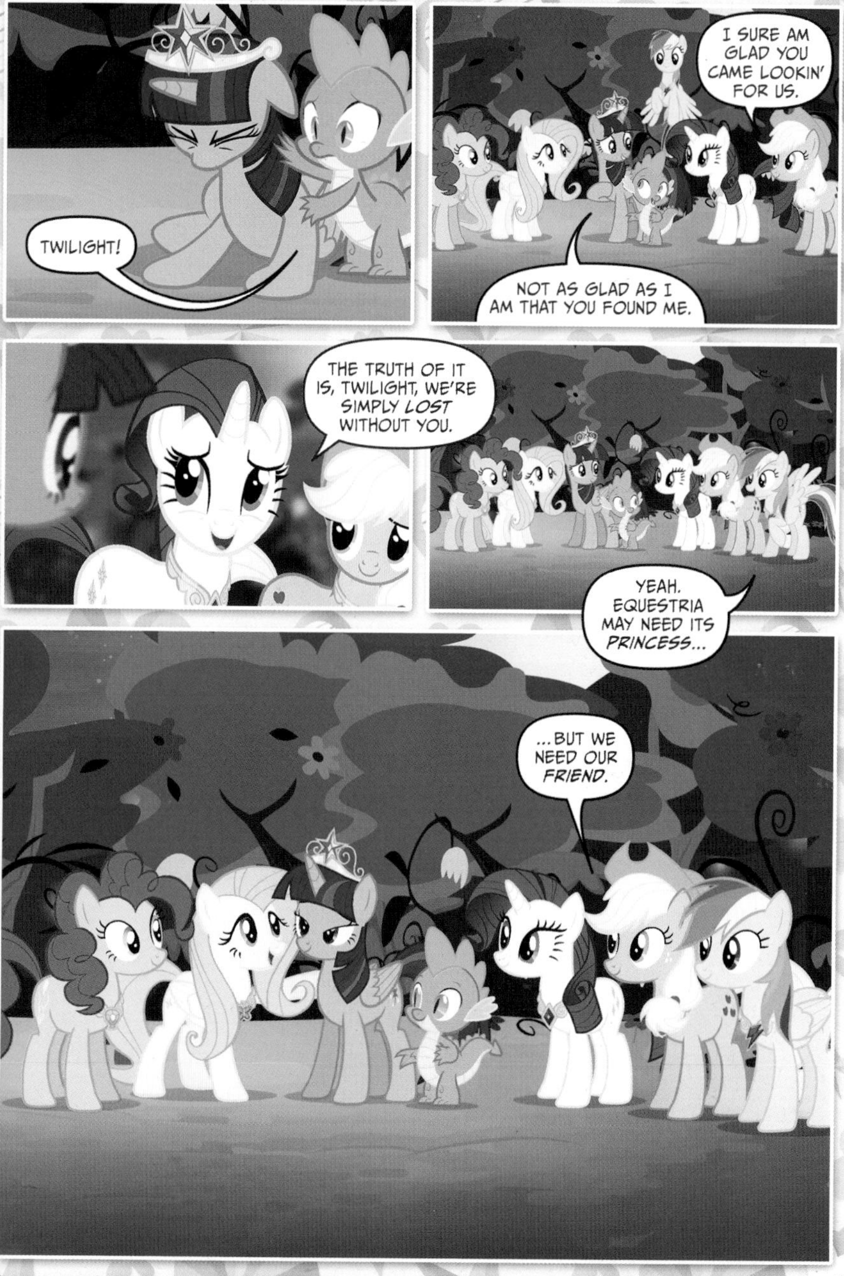
TWILIGHT!
I SURE AM GLAD YOU CAME LOOKIN' FOR US.
NOT AS GLAD AS I AM THAT YOU FOUND ME.
THE TRUTH OF IT IS, TWILIGHT, WE'RE SIMPLY *LOST* WITHOUT YOU.
YEAH. EQUESTRIA MAY NEED ITS *PRINCESS*...
...BUT WE NEED OUR *FRIEND*.

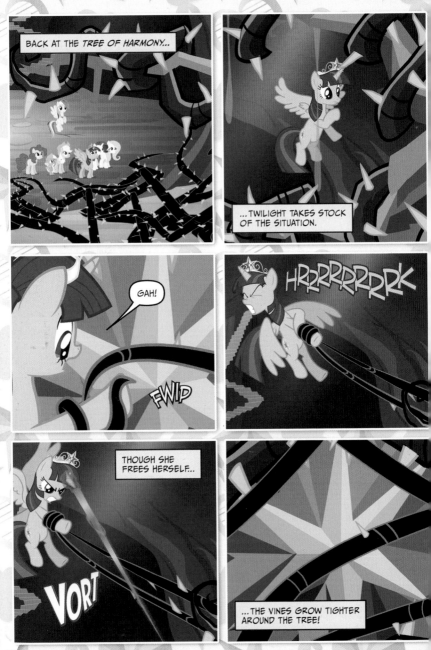

BACK AT THE *TREE OF HARMONY*...

...TWILIGHT TAKES STOCK OF THE SITUATION.

GAH!

FWIP

HRRRRRRRK

THOUGH SHE FREES HERSELF...

VORT

...THE VINES GROW TIGHTER AROUND THE TREE!

116

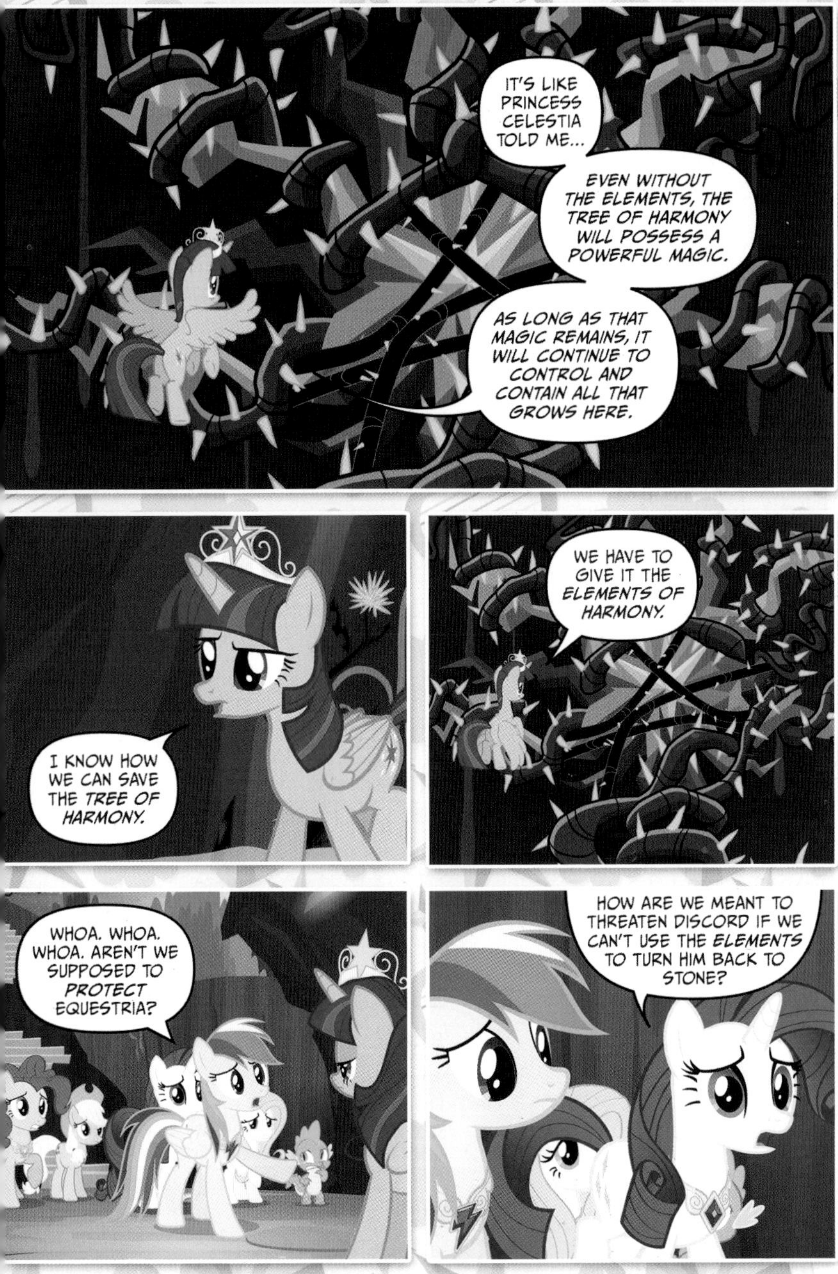
IT'S LIKE PRINCESS CELESTIA TOLD ME...
EVEN WITHOUT THE ELEMENTS, THE TREE OF HARMONY WILL POSSESS A POWERFUL MAGIC.
AS LONG AS THAT MAGIC REMAINS, IT WILL CONTINUE TO CONTROL AND CONTAIN ALL THAT GROWS HERE.
I KNOW HOW WE CAN SAVE THE *TREE OF HARMONY.*
WE HAVE TO GIVE IT THE *ELEMENTS OF HARMONY.*
WHOA. WHOA. WHOA. AREN'T WE SUPPOSED TO *PROTECT* EQUESTRIA?
HOW ARE WE MEANT TO THREATEN DISCORD IF WE CAN'T USE THE *ELEMENTS* TO TURN HIM BACK TO STONE?

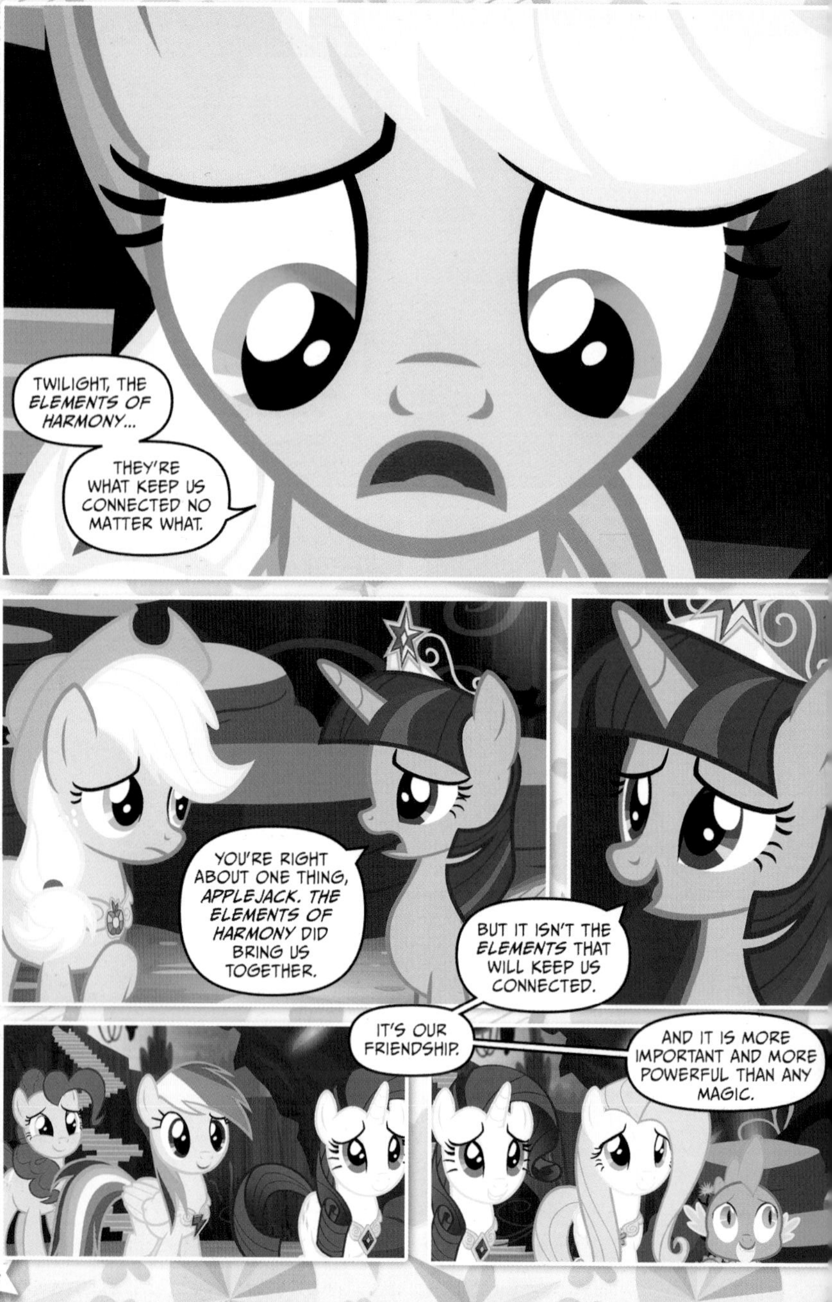

TWILIGHT, THE *ELEMENTS OF HARMONY*...
THEY'RE WHAT KEEP US CONNECTED NO MATTER WHAT.
YOU'RE RIGHT ABOUT ONE THING, *APPLEJACK.* THE *ELEMENTS OF HARMONY* DID BRING US TOGETHER.
BUT IT ISN'T THE *ELEMENTS* THAT WILL KEEP US CONNECTED.
IT'S OUR FRIENDSHIP.
AND IT IS MORE IMPORTANT AND MORE POWERFUL THAN ANY MAGIC.

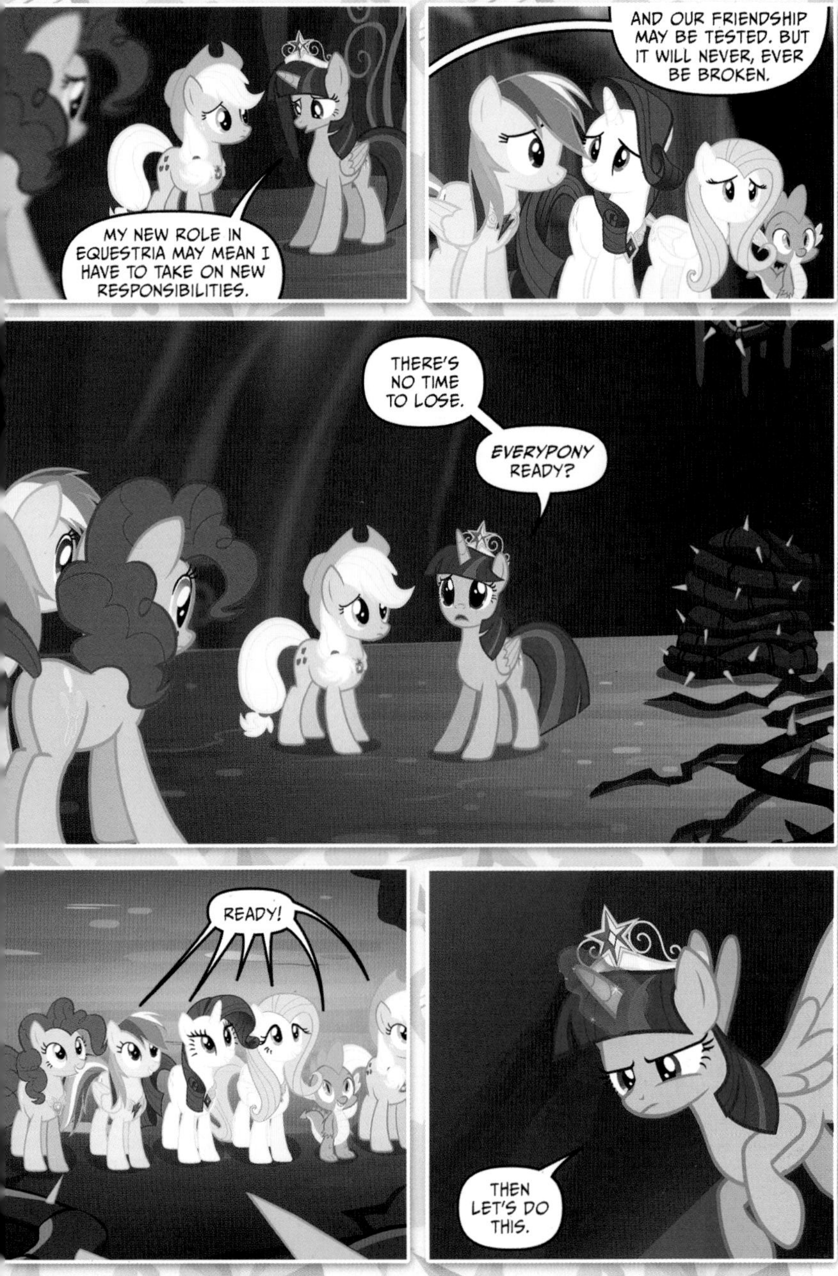
MY NEW ROLE IN EQUESTRIA MAY MEAN I HAVE TO TAKE ON NEW RESPONSIBILITIES.
AND OUR FRIENDSHIP MAY BE TESTED. BUT IT WILL NEVER, EVER BE BROKEN.
THERE'S NO TIME TO LOSE.
EVERYPONY READY?
READY!
THEN LET'S DO THIS.

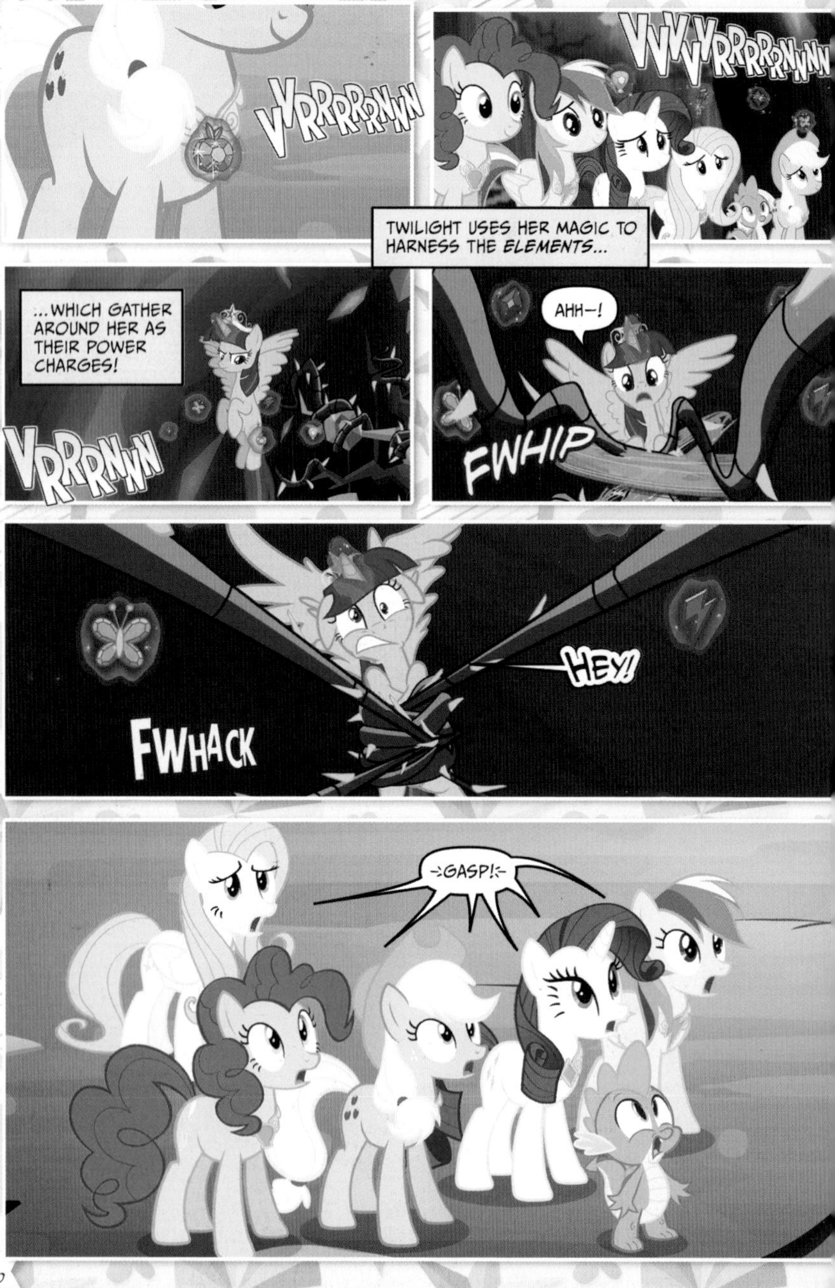

VYRRRRRNNN
VVVVVRRRRRRNNNN
TWILIGHT USES HER MAGIC TO HARNESS THE *ELEMENTS*...
...WHICH GATHER AROUND HER AS THEIR POWER CHARGES!
VRRRNNN
AHH—!
FWHIP
HEY!
FWHACK
-GASP!-

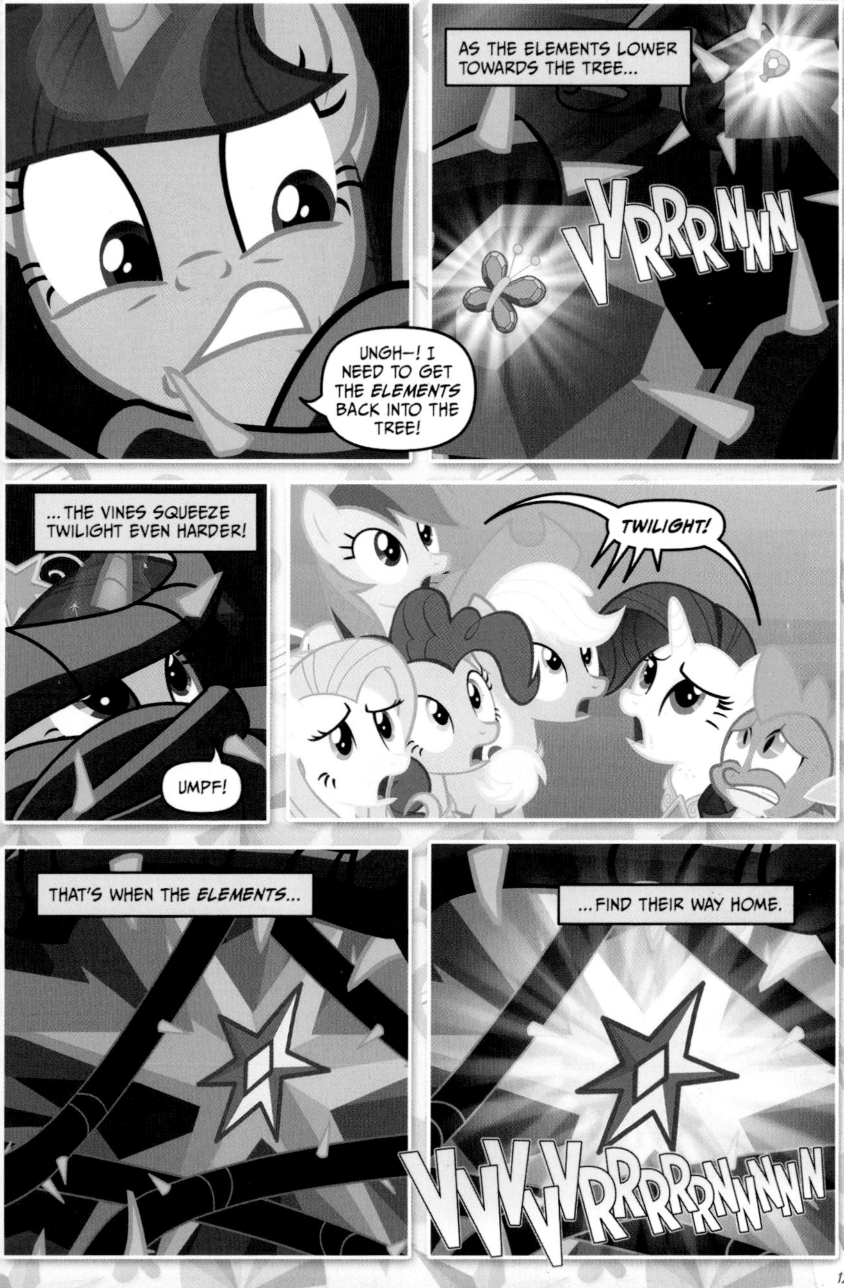
UNGH—! I NEED TO GET THE *ELEMENTS* BACK INTO THE TREE!
AS THE ELEMENTS LOWER TOWARDS THE TREE...
VVRRRNNN
...THE VINES SQUEEZE TWILIGHT EVEN HARDER!
UMPF!
TWILIGHT!
THAT'S WHEN THE *ELEMENTS*...
...FIND THEIR WAY HOME.
VVVVVRRRRRNNNNN

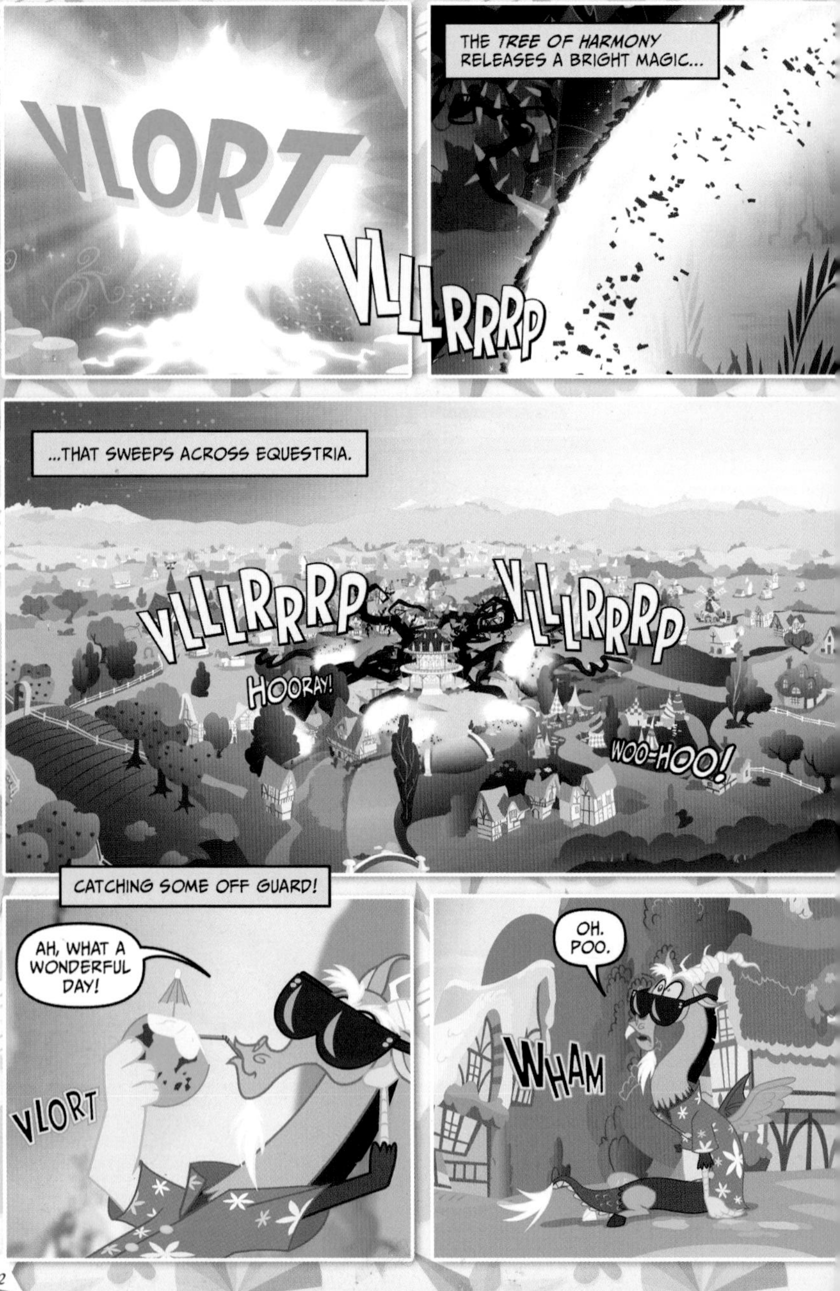
VLORT
THE *TREE OF HARMONY* RELEASES A BRIGHT MAGIC...
VLLLRRRP
...THAT SWEEPS ACROSS EQUESTRIA.
VLLLRRRP
VLLLRRRP
HOORAY!
WOO-HOO!
CATCHING SOME OFF GUARD!
AH, WHAT A WONDERFUL DAY!
VLORT
OH. POO.
WHAM

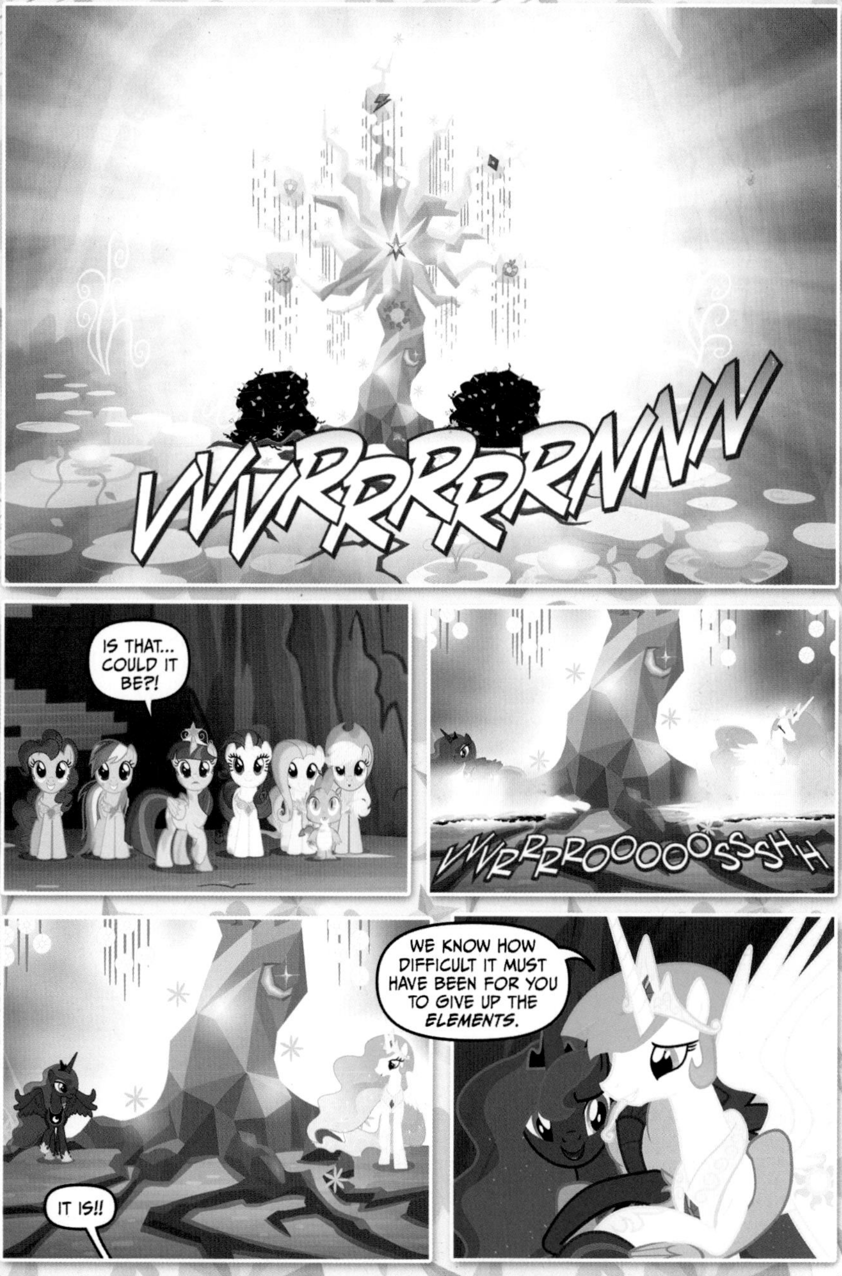
VVVRRRRRNNN
IS THAT... COULD IT BE?!
VVVRRRROOOOOOSSSHH
WE KNOW HOW DIFFICULT IT MUST HAVE BEEN FOR YOU TO GIVE UP THE *ELEMENTS*.
IT IS!!

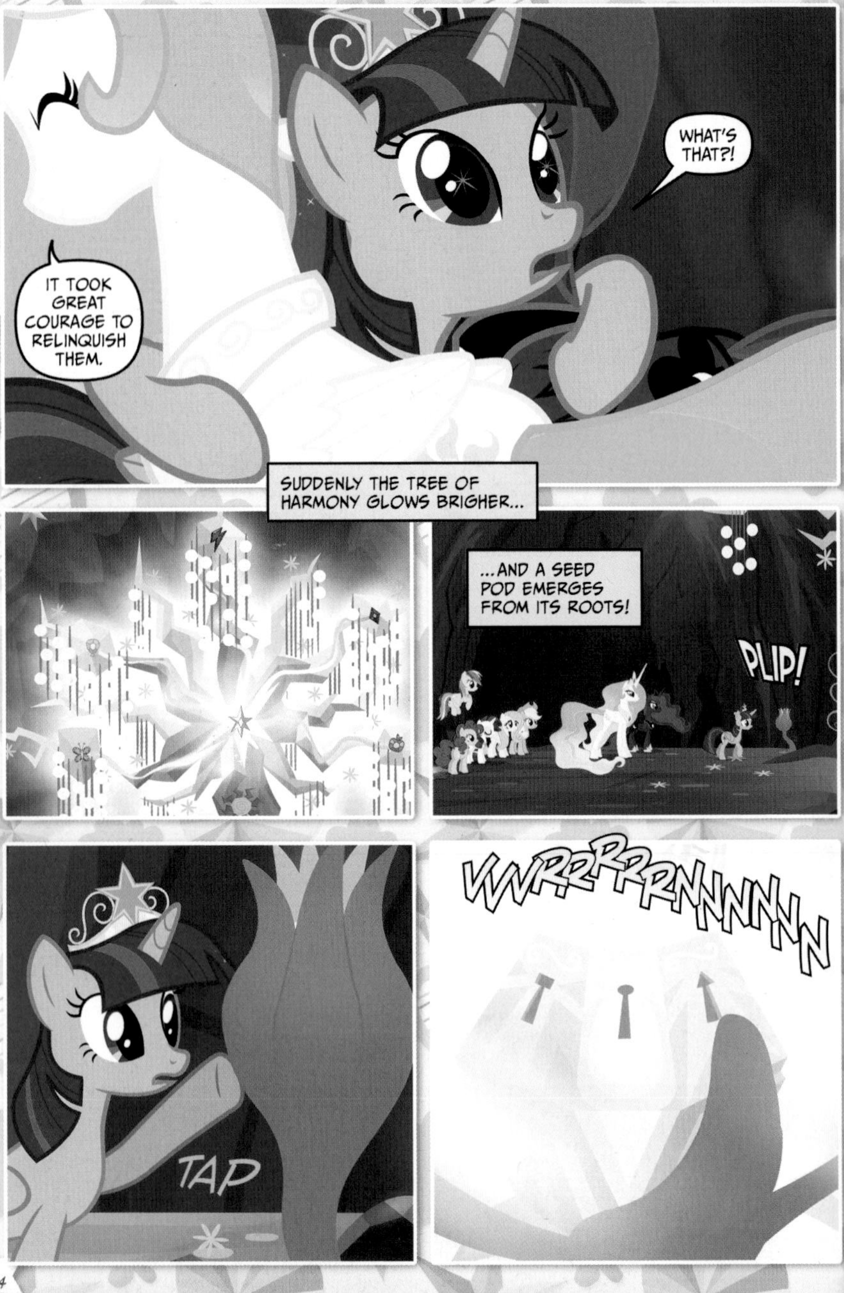
WHAT'S THAT?!
IT TOOK GREAT COURAGE TO RELINQUISH THEM.
SUDDENLY THE TREE OF HARMONY GLOWS BRIGHER...
...AND A SEED POD EMERGES FROM ITS ROOTS!
PLIP!
TAP
VVVRRRRRNNNNNNN

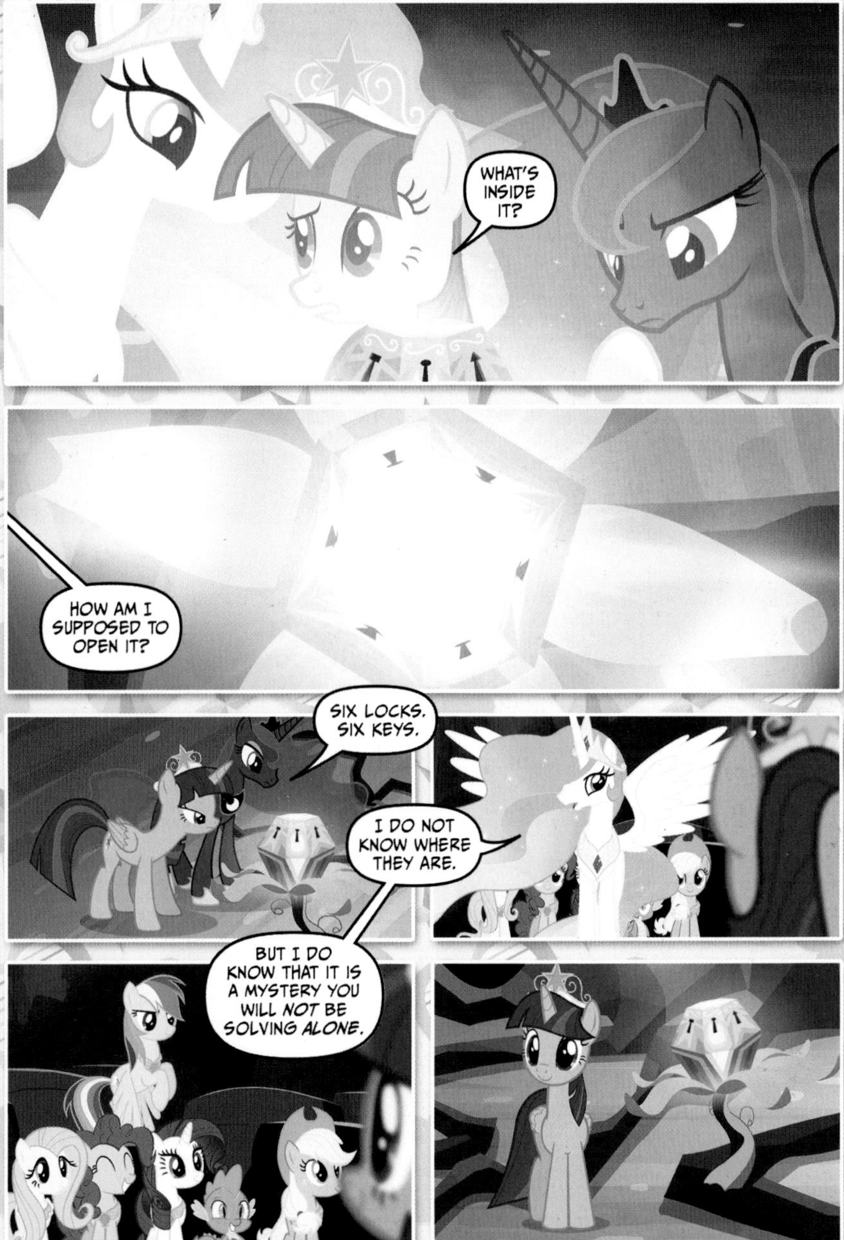
WHAT'S INSIDE IT?
HOW AM I SUPPOSED TO OPEN IT?
SIX LOCKS. SIX KEYS.
I DO NOT KNOW WHERE THEY ARE.
BUT I DO KNOW THAT IT IS A MYSTERY YOU WILL *NOT* BE SOLVING *ALONE*.

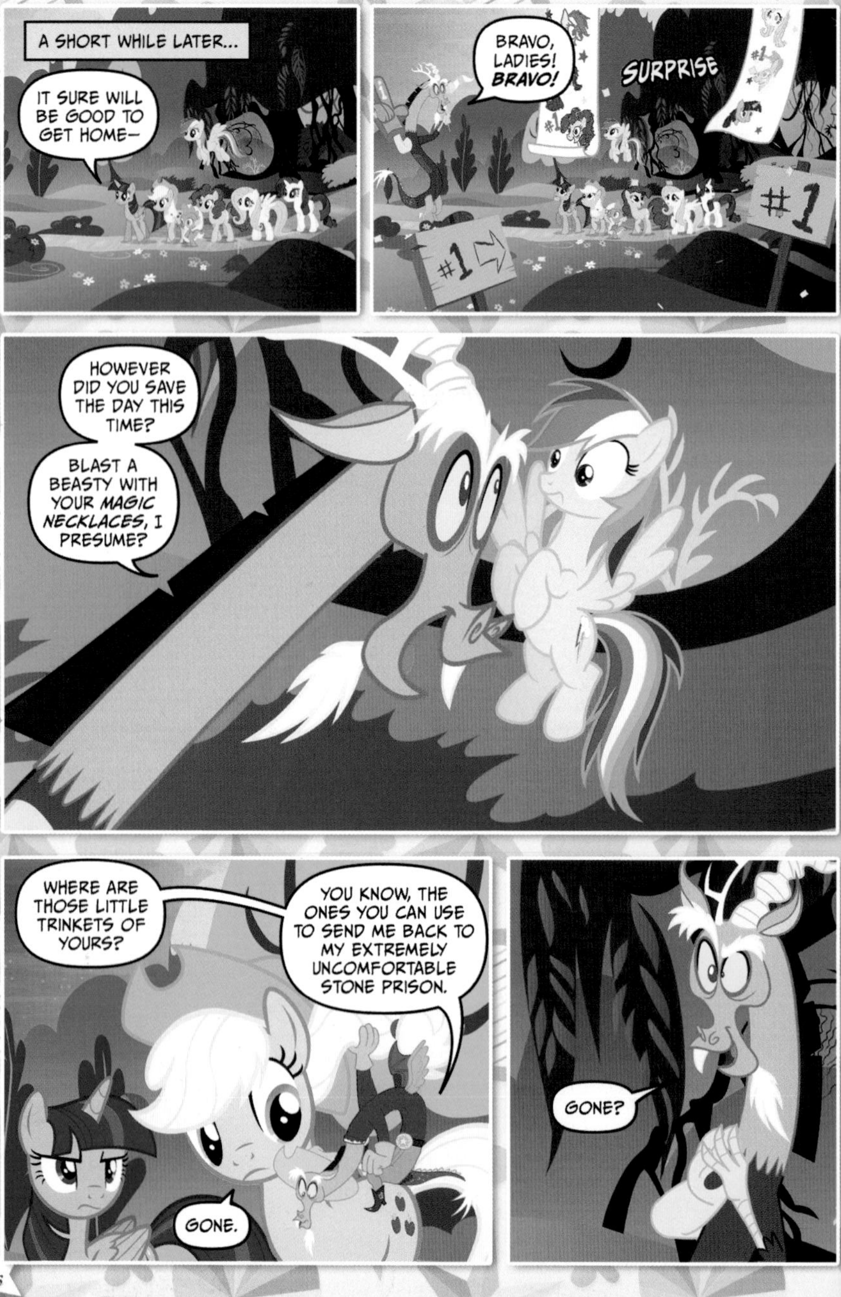

A SHORT WHILE LATER...
IT SURE WILL BE GOOD TO GET HOME—
BRAVO, LADIES! *BRAVO!*
SURPRISE
#1
#1
HOWEVER DID YOU SAVE THE DAY THIS TIME?
BLAST A BEASTY WITH YOUR *MAGIC NECKLACES*, I PRESUME?
WHERE ARE THOSE LITTLE TRINKETS OF YOURS?
YOU KNOW, THE ONES YOU CAN USE TO SEND ME BACK TO MY EXTREMELY UNCOMFORTABLE STONE PRISON.
GONE.
GONE?

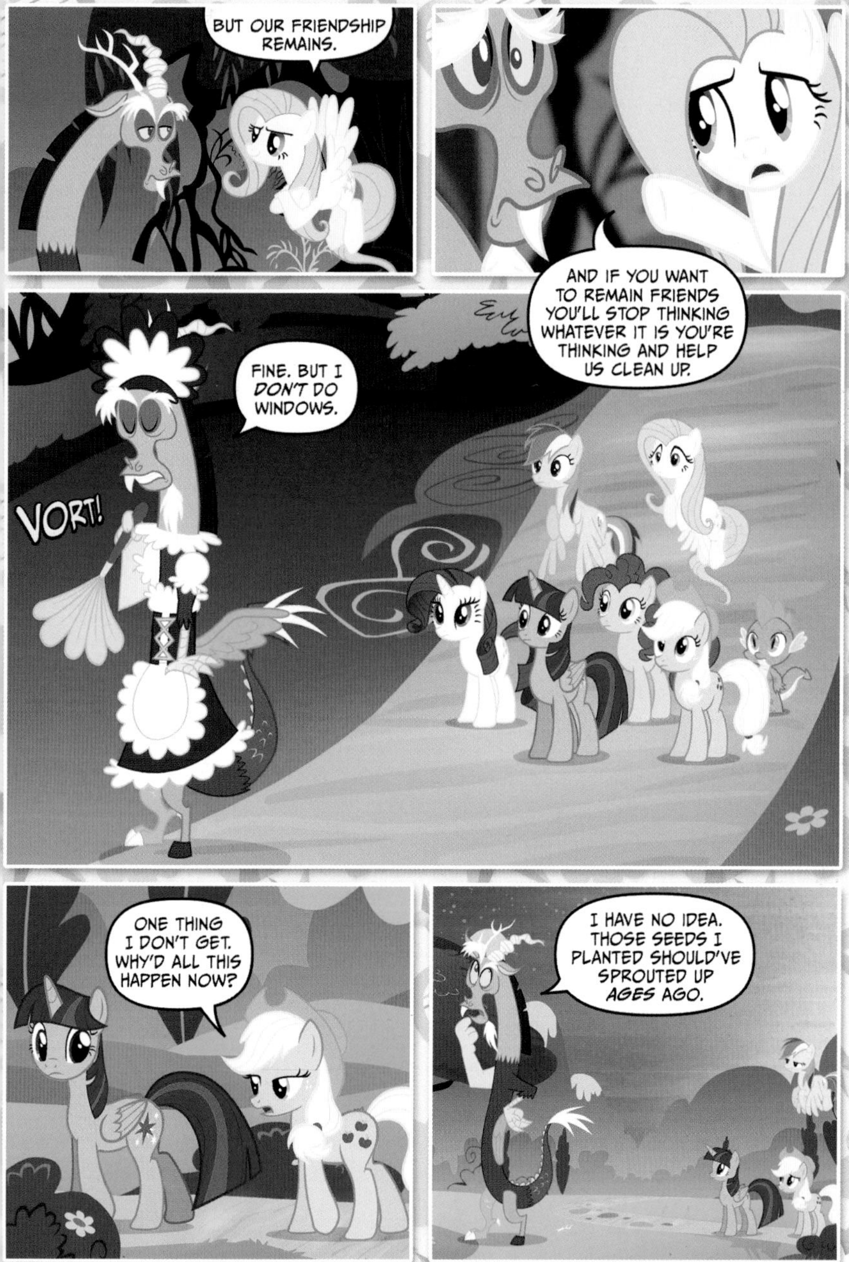
BUT OUR FRIENDSHIP REMAINS.
AND IF YOU WANT TO REMAIN FRIENDS YOU'LL STOP THINKING WHATEVER IT IS YOU'RE THINKING AND HELP US CLEAN UP.
FINE. BUT I DON'T DO WINDOWS.
VORT!
ONE THING I DON'T GET. WHY'D ALL THIS HAPPEN NOW?
I HAVE NO IDEA. THOSE SEEDS I PLANTED SHOULD'VE SPROUTED UP AGES AGO.

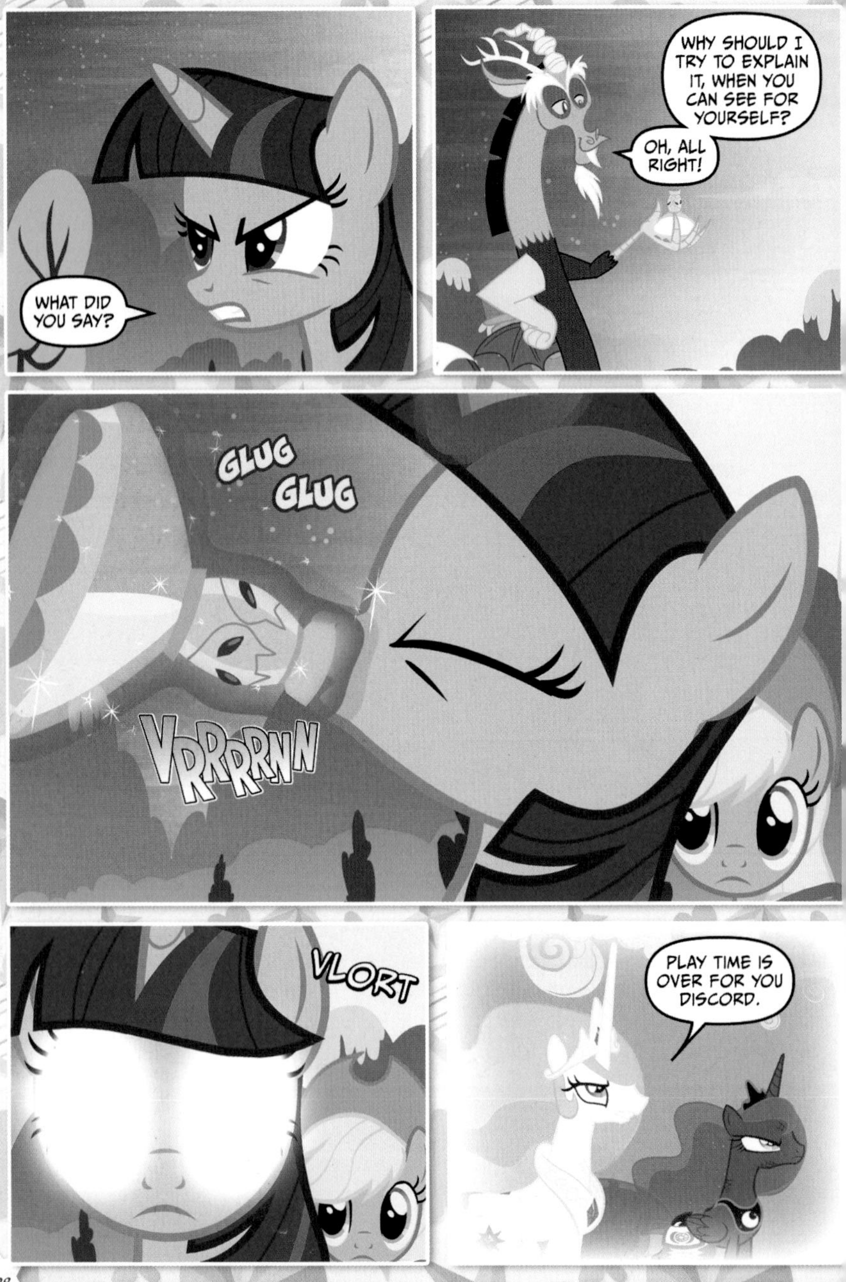
WHAT DID YOU SAY?
WHY SHOULD I TRY TO EXPLAIN IT, WHEN YOU CAN SEE FOR YOURSELF?
OH, ALL RIGHT!
GLUG GLUG
VRRRRNN
VLORT
PLAY TIME IS OVER FOR YOU DISCORD.

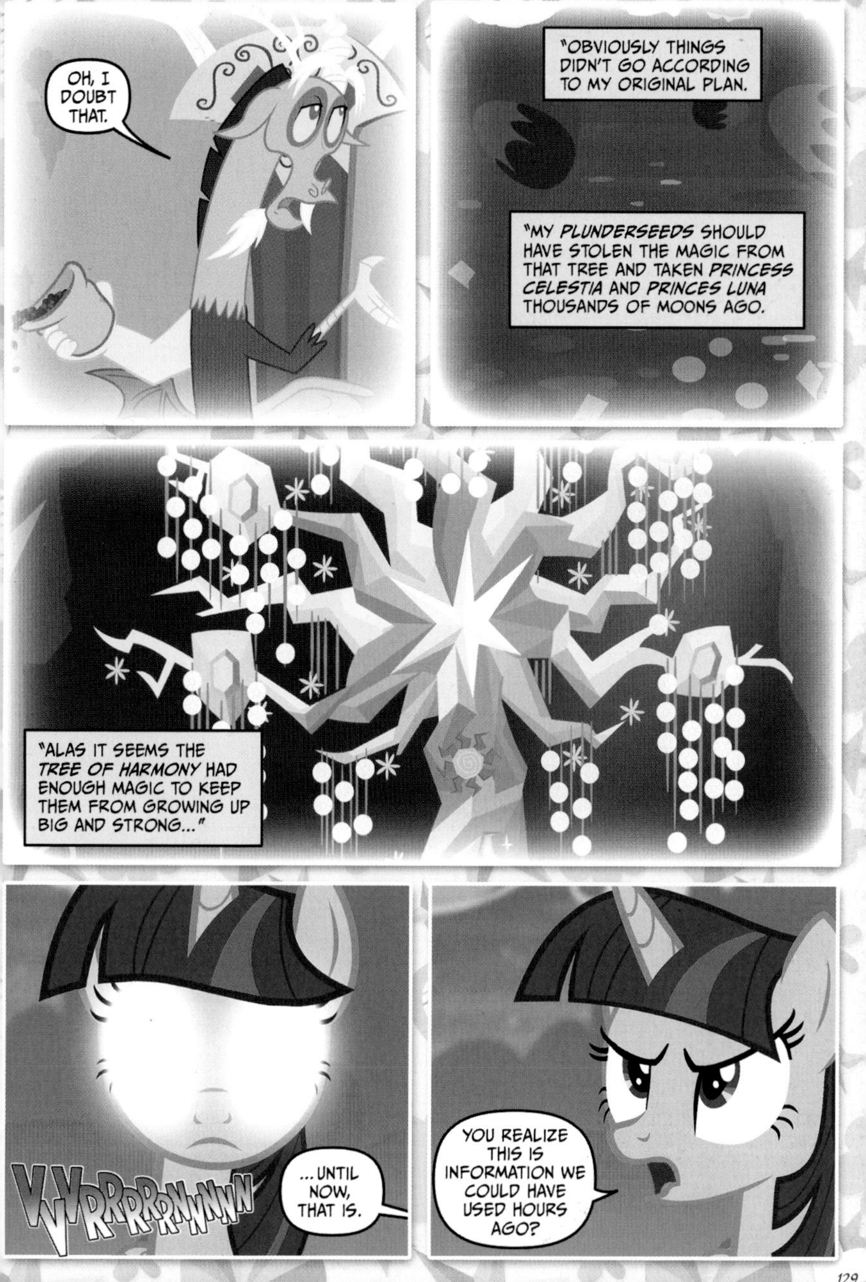
OH, I DOUBT THAT.
"OBVIOUSLY THINGS DIDN'T GO ACCORDING TO MY ORIGINAL PLAN.
"MY *PLUNDERSEEDS* SHOULD HAVE STOLEN THE MAGIC FROM THAT TREE AND TAKEN *PRINCESS CELESTIA* AND *PRINCES LUNA* THOUSANDS OF MOONS AGO.
"ALAS IT SEEMS THE *TREE OF HARMONY* HAD ENOUGH MAGIC TO KEEP THEM FROM GROWING UP BIG AND STRONG..."
VVVRRRRRNNNNN
...UNTIL NOW, THAT IS.
YOU REALIZE THIS IS INFORMATION WE COULD HAVE USED HOURS AGO?

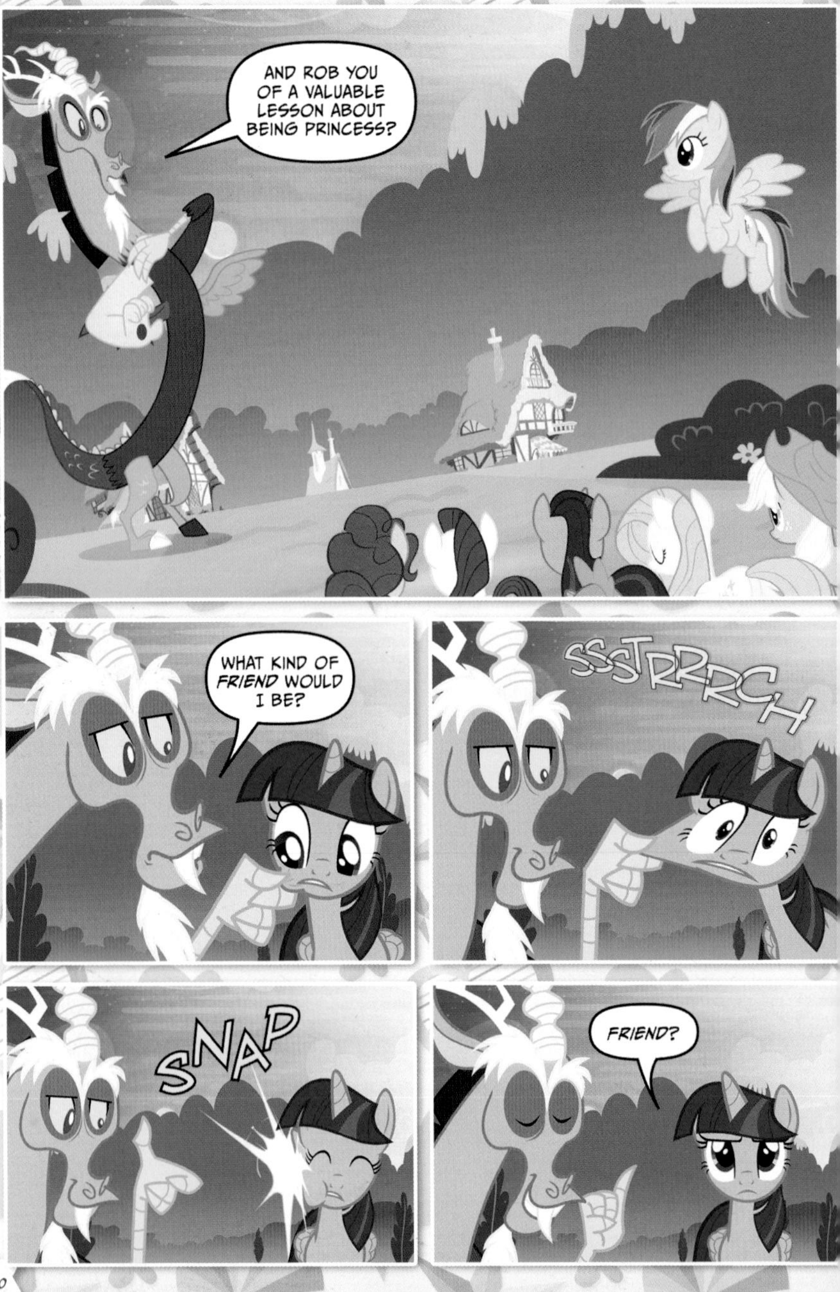
AND ROB YOU OF A VALUABLE LESSON ABOUT BEING PRINCESS?
WHAT KIND OF FRIEND WOULD I BE?
SSSTRRRCH
SNAP
FRIEND?

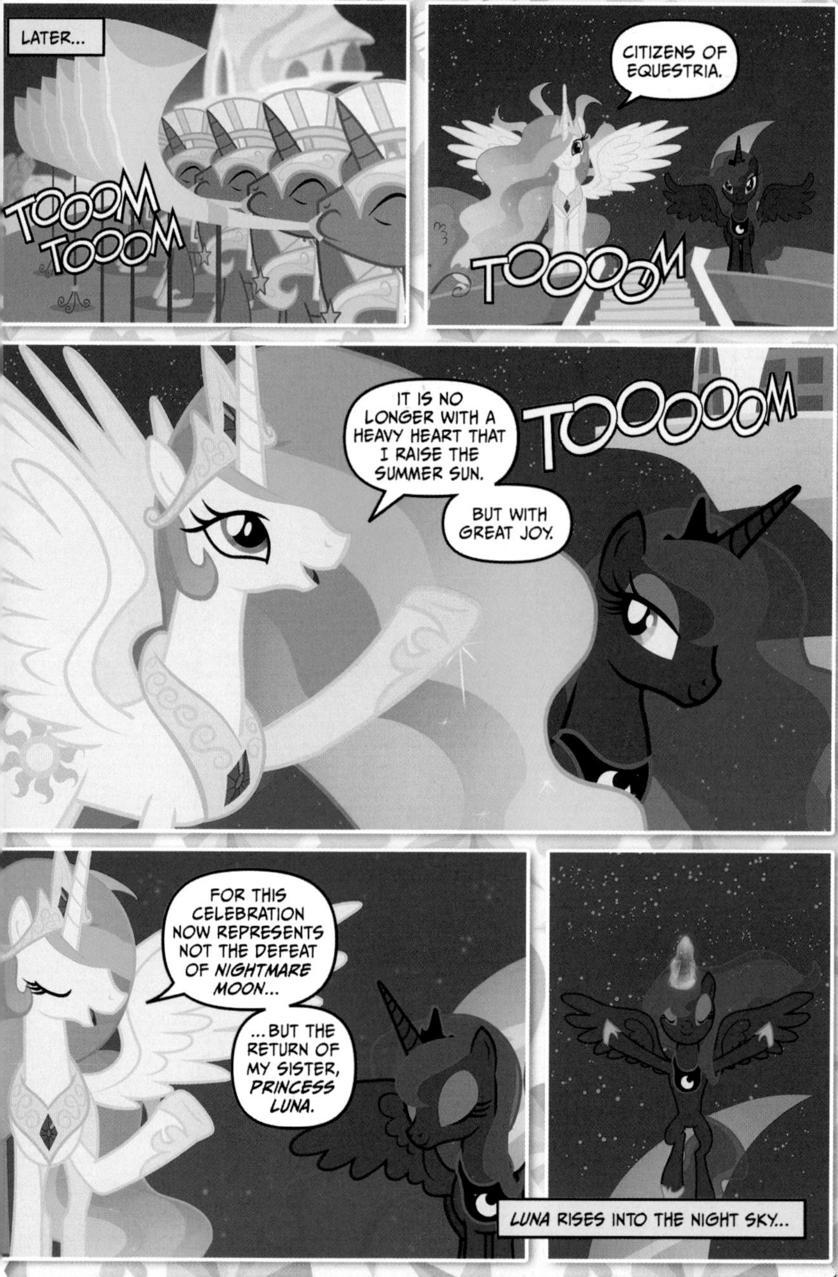
LATER...
TOOOM TOOOM
CITIZENS OF EQUESTRIA.
TOOOOOM
IT IS NO LONGER WITH A HEAVY HEART THAT I RAISE THE SUMMER SUN.
BUT WITH GREAT JOY.
TOOOOOOM
FOR THIS CELEBRATION NOW REPRESENTS NOT THE DEFEAT OF *NIGHTMARE MOON*...
...BUT THE RETURN OF MY SISTER, *PRINCESS LUNA*.
LUNA RISES INTO THE NIGHT SKY...

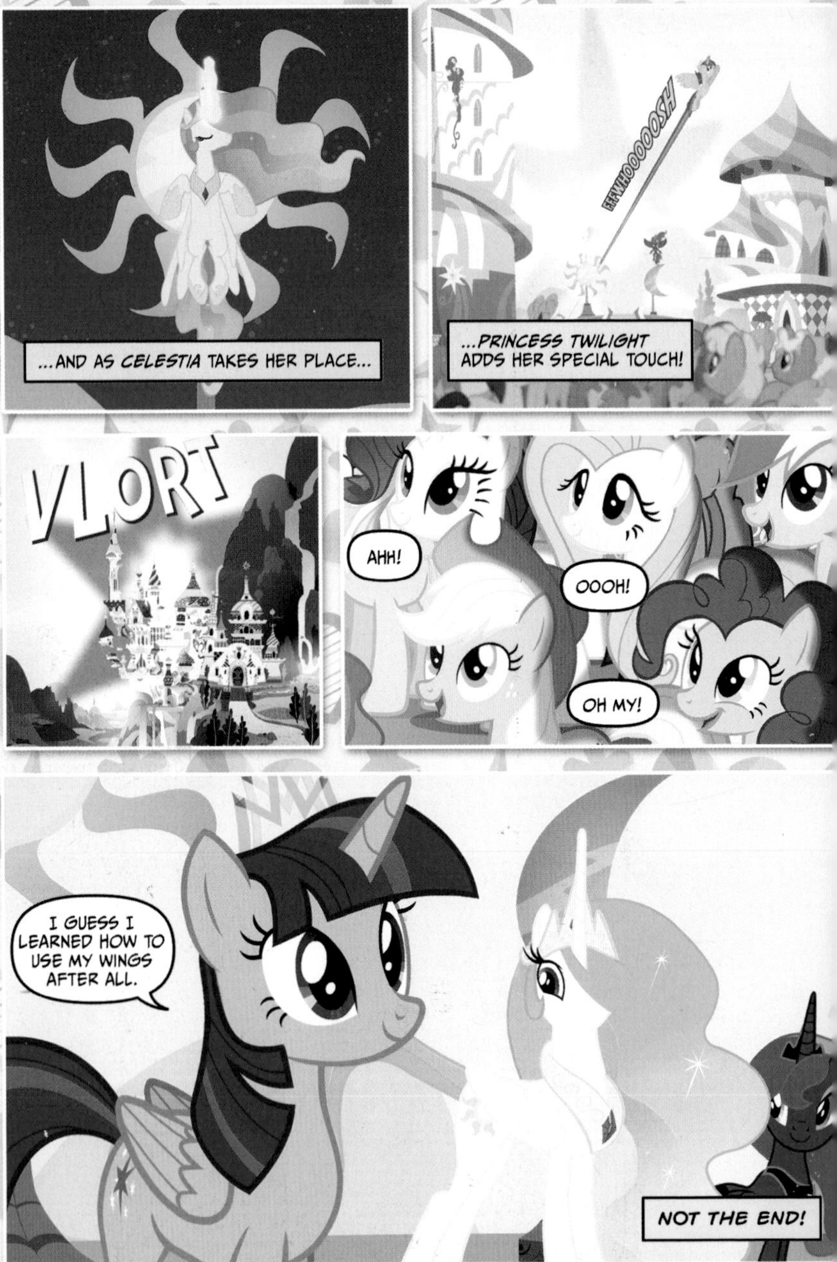
...AND AS CELESTIA TAKES HER PLACE...
...PRINCESS TWILIGHT ADDS HER SPECIAL TOUCH!
FFFWHOOOOOOSH
VLORT
AHH!
OOOH!
OH MY!
I GUESS I LEARNED HOW TO USE MY WINGS AFTER ALL.
NOT THE END!